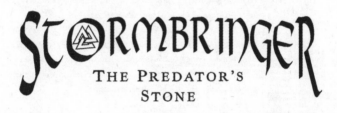

STORMBRINGER

THE PREDATOR'S STONE

To my wife, my Valhalla.

—G. R. B.

**MILK &
COOKIES**

Published by Milk + Cookies, an imprint of Bushel & Peck Books. Bushel & Peck Books is
a family-run publishing house in Fresno, California, that believes in uplifting children with
the highest standards of art, music, literature, and ideas. Find beautiful books for gifted
young minds at www.bushelandpeckbooks.com.

This is a work of fiction. The story, all names, characters, and incidents portrayed in this
production are fictitious. No identification with actual persons (living or deceased), places,
buildings, and products is intended or should be inferred.

Type set in LTC Kennerley Pro and Viking.
Cover illustration by Polina Graf.
Graphic elements licensed from Shutterstock.com.

Bushel & Peck Books is dedicated to fighting illiteracy all over the world.
For every book we sell, we donate one to a grandchild in need—book for book.
To nominate a school or organization to receive free books,
please visit www.bushelandpeckbooks.com.

ISBN: 978-1-63819-160-5
LCCN: 2023932122

First Edition

Printed in the United States

1 3 5 7 9 10 8 6 4 2

STORMBRINGER

THE PREDATOR'S STONE

G. R. BODEN

CONTENTS

CHAPTER 1

DEATH OF A HOAGIE SANDWICH

I should've seen it coming. The make-your-own-sandwich line in the cafeteria was moving *way* too smoothly. The condiment tubs were practically bursting at the seams, and there was even a container of super-rare wax peppers. Something had to give—which was exactly when two eighth-grade girls walked up and ruined everything.

"Grab us some sandwiches," said the taller of the two. She was what I call an LW—a label worshiper. You know, the people who pray to the gods of Fashion and Style. Not a blond-streaked hair was out of place, and her lips were so glossy, it looked like she'd smeared them with petroleum jelly.

I knew she had no intention of forking over money for the sandwiches, but I couldn't resist. "Who's going to pay for them?"

"Nobody, if you do it right," snapped the shorter girl. She was an up-and-coming LW, her labels not quite as prestigious as her friend's, but still light years beyond anything I could put together. She had managed to match the color of the rubber bands in her braces with the rest of her outfit. I have trouble matching a pair of socks.

"Sorry," I said, jerking my thumb over my shoulder, "the line starts back there." I turned away, trying hard to ignore the pre-fight tingling sensation that is all too familiar. Trust me, it's not a pleasant feeling. It's like someone's plucking the strings on a badly out-of-tune guitar. Apparently turning away was the wrong thing to do, because the taller one stepped so close to me, I could smell the peppermint in her chewing gum.

"You're really stupid for a seventh grader, you know that?"

I stopped constructing my sandwich (which I take very seriously) and looked at her. "Do you *really* want to fight over a hoagie?"

The wannabe LW glanced at her friend, no doubt wondering if it was worth it to press the issue. Full disclosure: from time to time, I've been known to trigger people. Especially females who have a hard time forming a sentence and chewing gum at the same time. Could be a scent I give off, like I roll on layers of come-kick-my-butt deodorant every morning.

I've gotten to know Vice Principal Billivick very well.

The girl gestured at the table. "Just get us the sandwiches and we'll walk away, loser." This creative jab seemed to bolster her friend's courage. I almost laughed when the shorter girl narrowed her eyes and flicked them at the sandwiches, like a crime boss eyeing a suitcase full of cash.

The tiny voice in my head that sometimes warns me about doing something stupid was trying to get my attention, but as usual, I wasn't listening. I held up my sandwich. "I make it a habit to never fight anyone dumber than my lunch."

Both girls stared at me wide-eyed for a fraction of a second, then the taller girl shoved me. Instinctively, I shoved her back. She stumbled over her friend's foot and crashed into the condiments table. Shredded lettuce, tomatoes, pickles—and I noted sadly—wax peppers, crashed to the floor, making everyone turn and stare at us.

Here we go, I thought, shrugging out of my backpack and pulling the imitation silver studs out of my earlobes.

I knew the drill well.

♠

The name on my birth certificate reads *Cindrheim Vustora Moss.* Before you start laughing—and I wouldn't blame you if you did—it roughly translates to *She Who Wanders, Then Conquers.*

Has a nice ring to it in English, doesn't it?

Except that until this past September, the only wandering I'd ever done was a few inner-city neighborhoods in Richmond, Virginia. And my conquering? Even less impressive, unless you count beating every level of *Galaxy Rangers* down at the Lend-N-Spend on Fifth and Bermer.

Not exactly the stuff you'd chisel into a tombstone, and definitely not what my mom had in mind when she named me.

In my defense, I'm only twelve years old. Realistically, how much real wandering and conquering can I do?

About the name. I know what you're thinking—there *must* be an intriguing story behind it. I'm sure the doctors and nurses of Our Lady of Compassion Hospital were certainly curious, but my mom just said my name belonged to one of our ancestors from Iceland.

I guess I should tell you, my mom tends to shade the truth. Need further proof? How about when she handed me over to one of the nurses a day after I was born and then told her she was going out for fresh air? She got the fresh air, but she never came back.

As for my dad, he ghosted before I was born. The jury's still out on that mystery. But with both my parents missing from the picture, this meant I was a ward of the state before my third diaper had been changed. Welcome to the world.

Carl, my foster parent, tells me my mom got the translation for my name all wrong. It's actually: *She Who Wanders, Then Finds Herself in Deep Doggy Doo.* He's right, you know. I've managed to live up to *this* name more times than I can count. And every time I step in it, Carl tries to correct my behavior with an old-timey phrase. My favorite? "Let's not be dotty, Cinder." Maybe my knack for finding trouble is the reason no one is knocking down my door to adopt me. Getting passed over like the funny-looking, older dog in the pet store can really mess with your head.

Don't get me wrong—Nancy and Carl are great. But they refuse to make it official. What are they waiting for? I found the courage to ask them once, and Nancy just said something really weird about the sun shining bright after a long dark winter. Carl's response was a dusty star chart he pulled from the attic and a few awkward jokes that had me wishing I'd never asked in the first place.

The one thing I have that links me to family (and never leaves my back pocket) is a battered pic of my dad's brother, Uncle Robert, holding me the day I turned one. When I asked my foster parents why Uncle Robert couldn't take care of me, they said he's a big shot in the Navy and his responsibilities keep him traveling all over the world. On the back of the picture, in handwriting even messier than mine, it says: *We love you, C. Stay frosty! —Uncle Robert.* Where is he now? Who is "we"? And how exactly does one *stay frosty*?

There was no doubt about it—Nancy and Carl were holding something back. But there was no time to puzzle over it. Things were about to get . . . dotty.

ॐ

The girl climbed to her feet, peeled a tomato slice from her backside and threw it to the floor. Snarling, she moved towards me, her hands outstretched, her painted fingernails extended.

That's when Vice Principal Billivick stepped in front of me, blocking the girl's attack. I watched as campus security moved in to help, herding the fashion twins in the opposite direction. I offered my arm to Mr. Billivick, who took it firmly and began to steer me towards the exit.

"Not again, Cinder," he said.

I slumped, ready for another Billivick lecture about life's choices—when the bomb exploded.

At least, I thought it was a bomb. Directly in front of me, maybe fifty feet away, graffiti-covered tables and plastic purple chairs began to fly in every direction.

Everyone started screaming. Even the boys. People stampeded to the back of the cafeteria, where they ignored the bewildered campus security and barreled into the crash bars of the exit doors.

It looked like whatever was scattering the tables and chairs was headed straight for me. I shook loose of Mr. Billivick's grasp. He stared at me for a fraction of a second, his eyes round with fear, then he bolted into the kitchen.

No, don't worry about me, I thought, glancing over my shoulder. I saw there was no escape out the north exit; a thick knot of middle schoolers had bottlenecked the back doors. The kitchen was clogged with frantic ladies wearing hairnets, and administrators in pantsuits and rumpled dress shirts were running every which way, shouting into radios.

I turned back around, ducking as a chair flew my way. Whatever the force was, it was nearly upon me.

So this is how it ends, I thought. *In a school cafeteria. Before I even get to eat.* I closed my eyes.

A moment later I heard a sickening thud right in front of me. I opened my eyes and saw a young girl with gleaming white hair sliding across the floor, twisting and rolling as if she were grappling with the world's greatest invisible wrestler. She reared up on her knees, swiped through the air twice with her arm, then leaped backward. Backpedaling, she shouted a series of rapid-fire commands in a language I didn't understand.

The girl looked at me over her shoulder. With a voice beyond her years, she ordered, "Through the kitchen is a door that leads outside. Run, Cindrheim!"

Her authoritative command jolted me out of my stupor. My brain told me to turn and flee, but I was rooted to the floor. Seemingly from thin air, three more girls flowed around me and joined the white-haired girl. Together, the four of them danced around the invisible force, thrusting their hands at it, twirling away, then rushing back in to slash and hack with make-believe swords.

Their movements were breathtaking. They complemented each other so well, I had to wonder if it wasn't a preplanned skit. Every once in a while their attacks would elicit an animal-like grunt from their enemy, quickly followed by a counterattack that would send one of the girls sliding backward.

I cringed as the white-haired girl suddenly cried out in pain. She doubled over, clutching her rib cage, then was knocked into a rolling cash register. "Run, Cindrheim!" she bellowed again, straightening up and issuing a string of new commands. The fact that she had used my true name was lost on me. You tend to miss things like that when four teenage girls are fighting an invisible monster in the middle of your school cafeteria.

Whatever they were battling was now scrabbling towards me. I could hear claws clicking and scratching across the slippery tiles. Chairs were knocked aside, a table thrust hard against the wall. The quarterback for our football team was sitting on the floor, crying for his mother. I threw my arms up at the last moment, heard several objects whistling through the air—then abrupt silence. Something grunted a few feet from me and crashed heavily to the floor. A searing hot pain exploded high in my left arm.

I looked down. I wasn't surprised to see that I was still gripping my sandwich.

⁂

The overturned tables and the scattered chairs were real. The chunks of meatloaf, the crushed milk cartons, and the smashed Cool and Classy ice pops were real. The awful smell that had me wishing I didn't have a nose was real.

The pain was *very* real.

Everything else . . . well, it never really happened. At least that's what I kept telling myself.

But the pain was getting more intense. I tried gripping my bicep to see if I could stem the throbbing sensation, but that only made it hurt worse. Wincing, I pulled my hand away and found it slick with blood. I was beginning to feel faint. Not a good sign. Objects in my line of sight were losing their shape and color. And was my blood beginning to boil? It felt like someone had laid down a line of gunpowder through my arteries and then ignited the end with a match. I could almost see the fire in my veins flickering beneath the skin of my wrists.

For a brief moment, my vision cleared enough that I could see a girl standing in front of me. It was her, the one with hair so white it almost hurt to look at it. She wore it long and tightly braided with bits of dull metal. She was dressed in a form-fitting forest green top with lots of straps and pockets and badly scuffed gray leather pants and boots.

There had been others with her as well. Girls that looked and moved like she had. I searched for them but they were gone now, making me wonder if they'd ever really been there.

You've got some heavy-duty explaining to do, I thought, turning back to the girl. Now that she was standing still, I could see that she was very pretty. She had an exotic, foreign-exchange look, though which country she might've come from I couldn't tell. Her large eyes were almond-shaped, the color a deep blue-green, like the water I'd seen in a postcard from the Fiji Islands. I was surprised at how calm she looked after what I'd just seen her do. Not a bead of sweat on her flawless skin. Despite her beauty and cool demeanor, she appeared ready to launch into lethal motion like a coiled snake. I was beginning to suspect she wasn't a student at Copperpenny Middle.

She pointed at my arm and said, "You are bleeding." Her voice held no concern or pity or even curiosity. She could have been telling me the weather. "You need to come with us."

"Us?" I said, looking around the destroyed cafeteria. Every last seventh and eighth grader, and all the custodians and kitchen workers, had fled. Mr. Billivick was nowhere to be seen. Far away, I could hear the rising wail of sirens. Someone had called the cops. "There's no one—"

"Look again," she said.

I nearly jumped and slipped in a puddle of gravy that was near my foot. Standing around me were three girls, two of them with white skin, the other black. They, too, were pretty, with long, tightly braided hair and clothes that screamed medieval role-playing games.

"Who are you?" I managed to say. The tables and the chairs and the spilled food weren't sliding to one side of the room, even though the floor was suddenly starting to tilt. Wasn't that breaking one of the laws of physics?

The girl with the white hair stepped forward. "I am Freya," she said impatiently.

I gestured at the other three. "And who—"

"We do not have time for this," Freya snapped. "Droma, bind her arm. Tori, sweep the perimeter."

In a flurry of motion, the one named Droma wrapped my wound with a bandage she pulled from a pouch at her waist, then peered into my eyes. "She's going into traumatic shock. Eyes are dilated, breathing is erratic."

I was about to tell her she was dead wrong, but I felt myself tipping over.

"Edda, pick her up and carry her out," Freya ordered.

Pick me up? Not happening. Especially by someone only slightly bigger than me. I took a step backward but stopped when I felt the ground try to swallow me.

"I want to kill more grints," growled Edda, her shoulders

bunched, her hands balled into fists, her eyes scanning the cafeteria.

Grints? The world had stopped making sense. "Would someone please tell me—"

"Stop talking," said Freya, cutting me off. She snapped her fingers and said, "Ranged weapons from here on out." The girl named Tori raced off towards the kitchen, pulling something invisible from her back.

Clearly frustrated with the idea of having no grints to slay, Edda growled again and scooped me up like she would a kitten.

I tried to protest, but I found that I couldn't talk; my throat had closed and my lips felt like fully loaded water balloons.

Freya started moving quickly towards the north exit, stepping nimbly over the clutter. "Droma," she called out over her shoulder, "we do not have time to properly erase our presence, but you must dissolve the creature."

Droma dipped her hand into a breast pocket, then made a flinging motion with her hand. I could hear a faint sizzling, like frying bacon, then a sharp odor caused me to turn my face into Edda's shoulder.

When I looked back, Droma was flinging her hand again, as if she were tossing invisible feed to invisible chickens. More sizzling.

I made a brief attempt to break free of Edda's embrace, but it was like she had wrapped me up in a Texas Cloverleaf, which would make perfect sense if you watched as much professional wrestling as I do.

What had I done to deserve this? I wondered. *Had my free and reduced lunch card expired? And why was I unable to fight back?* It was the one thing I was good at.

We exited the cafeteria with Freya taking the lead. Tori and Droma swooped in from either side to flank us. My eyes were dazzled by the bright sun, but I caught a glimpse of a beautiful silver sword hanging from Freya's hip. A moment later, it flickered and vanished.

Then I did what anyone would have done that had just lost a quart of blood and watched their cafeteria get destroyed by an invisible monster.

I fainted.

ЩORSƮ. CAMPOUƮ. EVER

I awoke to stars. Lots of stars, scattered and framed by dark, swaying branches. The girl with the magical pockets and the impressive medical vocabulary leaned over me, blocking out the silver pinpricks of light.

"She's awake," she said, using her fingers to pry my eyelids open. "Her vision has stabilized." She pressed her hand against the side of my neck. "Heart rate has returned to normal."

I struggled into a sitting position, wondering if there was anything these girls *couldn't* do. That's when I felt the dull throbbing in my left arm. I reached up and was reminded that she had wrapped my bicep with a bandage, which reminded me of the invisible creature that had nearly had me for lunch, which reminded me nothing made sense anymore. I waited for my head to clear, then climbed to my feet.

"Thank you, Droma," said a commanding voice. The girl named Freya stepped away from a little fire that was flickering inside a ring of stones. "Resume your surveillance of the perimeter."

Droma rose to her feet but hesitated. "Are we sure it's her, Freya? Now that she's awake, we can be certain."

"How many Cindrheims living in Richmond do you know?" Freya asked.

"The enemy can be clever," replied Droma.

"She fits the description," said Freya. "Almost identical to the sketch."

"What sketch?" I asked. "You have a sketch of me? That's *super* creepy."

Freya stepped closer to me and looked me up and down as if she were assessing a mannequin in a department store. "Hair like Asgardian red gold, tall for her age, a bit on the lanky side."

"Hello," I said. "Standing right here . . . "

Freya ignored me. "Turn your face towards the light of the fire, Cindrheim." When I didn't do as she asked, she took my chin in her hand and forced me to turn. She peered into my eyes. "Eyes spaced a little too far apart, color like faded heather."

"Eyes a little too far apart?" I said, pulling myself away from Freya's grasp. "What's next, my blotchy skin?"

Freya nodded. "Yes, that too."

"Wow. Nothing worse than rude kidnappers."

Droma leaned in. "She certainly has the attitude."

"Yes," said Freya. "Her reputation precedes her."

"Can we please move on to the part where we discuss a ransom?"

Freya ignored me again. "I am certain she is the one, Droma. Join the others on the perimeter."

Droma nodded and padded away into the night. I tried to get my bearings, but all I could see in every direction were line upon line of dark trees.

"So far this is the worst campout ever," I said. "Where am I?"

It was obvious Freya was still smarting from the blow she took to the ribs in the cafeteria, because she touched her hand to her side and grimaced as she moved towards me. "You are in the state of Virginia, in a small grove of trees outside the city of Richmond. Am I right in assuming you have questions?"

Her voice somehow carried a 1700s quality, stiff and way too formal. "Like a thousand," I said, flattening my Asgardian red gold hair down with both hands. There was nothing I could do about the lanky build and the freakishly spaced eyes, but I at least wanted to appear presentable. "I was literally carried out of my school and brought to this forest . . . Am I going back any time soon?"

"No," said Freya.

"No?"

"No."

"Keeping me here against my will is against the law."

"I am not keeping you *here*. We are leaving soon."

"And I'm going with you?"

"Yes."

"What if I refuse?"

In the soft glow of the moonlight, Freya almost looked angelic. Except that angels didn't usually wear fierce scowls and dress like a mercenary from a Renaissance fair. She returned to the fire and took a seat on one of the rocks that encircled the pit. "One way or another, you are coming with us. I hope—for your sake—you decide on your own not to resist."

"Excuse me?" I said. "I know my rights."

Freya stared into the fire.

"And you said *for your sake*. Sounds like a threat to me."

Freya remained silent.

I glanced around me and noticed that Tori, Droma, and Edda were pacing the perimeter of the small encampment, like cats stalking an unseen prey. "What are they watching for?"

Freya picked up a stick and used it to stir the glowing embers of the fire. "The things that hunt you."

I stared at Freya for several seconds. "There are things . . . *hunting* me?"

She nodded. "Grints. Horrible, insect-like creatures that can kill a full-grown man with a single scratch. We defeated a particularly large, vicious one back at the learning facility, but—"

"The learning facility?"

"At the school. But we believe there are several more of its kind still on your trail. Normally grints are no match for us, but someone has dispatched a more lethal breed. Faster, stronger, smarter. We must be very cautious."

I glanced at my bandaged arm. "And was it this grint that gave me this wound?"

Freya nodded.

"So if a single scratch can kill a full-grown man, how come I'm not dead?"

"Droma gave you an elixir."

"Elixir? What is she, a wizard?"

Freya glanced at me. She looked really confused.

"Never mind," I said. "What's the elixir for?"

"To slow the poison."

My breath caught in my throat. "I've . . . been poisoned?"

Freya nodded.

"Shouldn't we call poison control . . . or a doctor?"

"Your world's medical facilities would not know how to counteract grint venom."

"My *world's* medical facilities?" When Freya didn't respond, I said, "Okay, we're circling back to that later. Just tell me what happened at my school."

"We received word that the grint was sent to kill you. We were then dispatched to hunt and destroy the creature before it could get to you."

"That was very to the point," I said. My thousand questions instantly doubled. I gestured at our makeshift campsite. "And what are we going to do now?"

"My orders are to take you to Iceland."

"Iceland? As in Iceland the *country*?"

"Yes."

I hesitated. "Wait. Does this have something to do with my Icelandic ancestors?"

Freya looked away.

"Because I'm not even totally positive my ancestors really *are* from Iceland."

"Regardless, our destination lies there."

"You're totally serious, aren't you?"

"Very serious," replied Freya.

I suddenly laughed and formed a T with my hands. "Okay, time out. Who set you up to this?"

Freya tilted her head to the side. "Set you up? What does this mean?"

"You know, who told you to pull this prank?"

"Prank," said Freya, testing the word on the tip of her tongue. "I do not know the meaning of this word."

I walked around the fire as if that would put everything into perspective, then stared down at Freya. "This is crazy. I'm going home."

"I would not do that if I were you," warned Freya.

"Why not?"

Freya pointed at my arm. "Your injury, for one thing. We merely stalled the grint's poison, but it is not altogether extracted. In your condition, you would not make it out of this forest. And even if you were fully healed, you would have to walk at least two miles before locating a long-distance speaking device."

"You mean a phone."

"Yes," she replied, slightly annoyed. "A *phone*. Those that hunt you would find you long before that."

I looked at Freya, wondering which of us was insane. The grint poison was a hard sell, but I definitely did not want to wander around in the dark for two or three hours. I started patting down the pockets of my jeans. "I don't have to go anywhere. I have a cell phone."

Freya stood. "You *did* have a cell phone."

I stopped searching. "What happened to it?"

"We had to leave it behind."

I was speechless. Abduction is one thing. Messing with a person's cell phone is next-level stuff.

"Those that hunt you are sensitive to the signals given off by your world's electronic equipment," Freya said.

"You mean they're using GPS to track me."

"No, that would be inconceivable. Grints do not carry cell phones."

"But everyone else does."

"But not everyone is hiding in the forest. The creatures will investigate isolated signals." Freya looked into the trees. "Grints do not discriminate. I feel pity for anyone that crosses paths with the creatures."

I was livid. "Do you have any idea how long it took me to save—"

"Your phone is safe," said Freya, holding up a slender hand. "We left it with Nancy and Carl Barlowe, along with a note."

"You know my foster parents?" I could feel the ground beginning to tilt again.

Freya nodded. "A bit simple, but good people."

"But the note came from *you*. They'll recognize it's not from me and they'll call the police."

"No, they will not."

"How could you possibly know that?" I demanded, then my heart suddenly performed a backflip. "Did you hurt them?"

"I would never harm Carl or Nancy," said Freya.

"Who *are* you?"

Freya studied the glowing tip of her stick but said nothing.

I moved around the fire so that I was directly across from her. "Tell me."

"The four of us are members of the Valhuri."

"In English, please."

"We are Predators."

I was *really* trying to be patient. I shook my head. "I got nothing."

"Predators are ancient warriors with abnormally heightened skills, handpicked by the Allfather and blessed by Ullr, God of the Wild Hunt. We specialize in search and retrieval, silent infiltration, and lethal force. Our sole purpose is to await orders for the next quest. Once given, we will choose death before failure."

It took me a moment to gather my wits. "Do you hear yourself?"

Freya looked confused again. "Yes . . . Do you not hear *yourself?*"

I rubbed my face, hoping when I took my hands away I would be in my bathroom, brushing my teeth. Unfortunately, Freya was still there, prodding the fire. "Look, something weird *definitely* happened today in the cafeteria, but weird things sometimes happen. But it's over now. I'm tired, hungry, and for the first time in a very long time, I want to go home. I figure if I start walking now, I'll eventually find civilization. You and your Dungeons and Dragons crew can come if you want." I turned and started walking towards the ring of trees that encircled the camp. Before I'd taken ten steps, all three Predators rushed from the shadows and blocked my way.

"Move it or lose it," I said irritably, knowing I didn't stand a chance against even one of them, but angry enough not to care.

"Stand down," ordered Freya, coming up behind me. They visibly relaxed but didn't move away. I turned to yell at Freya, but she held up her hand. "Cindrheim, I want you to do something for me."

I gritted my teeth, shook my head.

"Hold out your hands."

"Not happening."

"I promise you will feel differently if you do," she said.

Reluctantly, I did as she asked. "Do I have to close my eyes too?" I said sarcastically.

"Your eyes are already closed, Cindrheim," said Freya. "I want you to open them."

Sighing, I held out my hands. I watched Freya reach down to her hip, then draw her hand upwards. Next, she held both hands out over mine.

"Careful," she said, "it is very sharp."

A moment later I felt something metallic settling down across my palms. I blinked my eyes rapidly. It was dark, and we had only the flickering light of the small fire, but I could plainly see, or *not* see, that there was something invisible in my hands. Trembling, I curled my fingers around the object.

"Careful," warned Freya again.

My breath caught in my throat. It felt like the blade of a sword. I let my fingers fall open again. I stared, concentrating on the spot. It *was* the blade of a sword. I could see it now, the firelight glinting on its cold steel. I ran my finger along the intricate scrollwork etched into the curving blade.

Tori had come up behind Freya. "Incredible, for someone to see so quickly," she breathed, almost to herself. Freya gave her a dark look and she quickly retreated.

"What is she talking about?" I asked.

"Your eyes are opening," said Freya, but she wasn't displeased. "Quickly, too, for a Midgardian." She nodded at Tori, Droma, and Edda. Each of them drew out their own weapons and laid them on my hands. I could see them all. In the glow of the firelight, Freya suddenly looked even more fierce and proud than usual. "We were instructed to find and protect you from a darkness that will not stop until you are destroyed. We have done so. The four blades you hold in your hands saved your life today. Until we are released from our vow, we will continue to protect you, Cindrheim."

So yeah, *that* happened.

ᛟ

There was no way I'd fall asleep that night, so I didn't even bother trying. I thought about counting the stars, but I was too frightened to focus.

But the tiny voice—the one that tried to stop my more stupid decisions—was competing with a new voice I'd never heard before. It was just a murmur at first, whispers of faint names and places that were strange . . . yet familiar.

Louder it grew, echoing as if speaking across the centuries, of storms and ships and songs of the sea of victory and defeat. I remembered the weight of the invisible swords. I felt their heft and their thirst for renown. I imagined a blade of my own, raised high in my hand, its blade flashing fiercely, like a spike of pure sunlight. And at last I recog-nized the voice—it was my own.

I shivered and sat bolt upright. *What was I thinking?!* I looked around. Freya watched me impassively, but her eyes seemed to be weighing me—and I wasn't sure I measured up.

"So . . . let's say I agree to go with you to Iceland," I said carefully. "How will we get there?" Tori had offered me a blanket, so I wrapped it around my shoulders to ward off the cold wind that was threatening to snuff out our little fire.

"Leave that to me," said Freya.

I swallowed and pulled the blanket tighter about my shoulders. It helped against the wind, but nothing could melt the ice that had settled in the pit of my stomach. *Storms. Ships. Victory.*

Defeat.

Instinctively, my eyes scanned the perimeter of dark trees, but aside from the flitting silhouettes of Tori, Droma, and Edda, there was no movement. "Of all the students at Copperpenny, why did you choose me?"

"I did not choose you."

"Well, somebody must've chosen me."

"Someone did."

"Who?"

"It is not for me to say."

"You mentioned a sketch of me. Can I see it?"

"I do not have it."

I frowned. "Of course you don't. When will I get to return?"

"It is not for me to say."

I felt a spike of frustration. "Not much is for *you to say*, is there?"

"For now, what I can say is restricted," said Freya.

"I'm just feeling really confused and really scared. Try to put yourself in my shoes."

For a very brief moment, it looked like Freya actually felt sorry for me. "Are you familiar with Nordic history?"

"Like Norse mythology?" The voice inside me was back, buzzing and crackling.

"We do not care for the word *mythology*. It implies our history is myth. But yes, Norse mythology will suffice for now."

"You're talking about Odin and Thor and that trickster dude, what's his name . . . ?"

Freya's expression hardened. "Loki, God of Mischief."

"That's him," I said, pointing at Freya.

"This is the world that *I* belong to." Freya gestured at the Predators that were still pacing the perimeter of our camp. "The same world that Tori, Edda, and Droma belong to."

I grinned. "You're joking."

"I do not joke."

"No, you don't." I walked a few steps away from the fire, then turned around and came back. "Okay, I'll play along. What world do *I* belong to?"

"Presently, you belong to Midgard."

"Midgard?"

"The earthly realm."

"Got it. And you belong to . . . Olympus?"

Freya frowned. "Wrong history. When not on mission, the four of us reside in Vanaheim."

"Vanaheim," I echoed conversationally. "Sounds far away." I was probably pushing my luck. "And what will I be doing in Iceland?"

"That is not for me to say," replied Freya with a perfectly straight face. "I can tell you, however, that your initial destination will be a place in which you should be relatively free from danger."

I sat very still for several seconds. No wonder I'd be free from danger. In Iceland, wouldn't I be free from everything but frostbite?

"Mind if I step away for a moment?" I asked. I needed to clear my head, but I definitely had an ulterior motive.

"Do not go far," said Freya.

I spotted Tori learning against a tree near the edge of the clearing. I walked towards her and noticed she was bobbing her head. She instantly noticed me approaching her. Stepping away from the tree, she turned to face me and removed what looked like an earbud from her ear.

"Hello, Cinder," she said.

"Hey," I said, glancing over my shoulder. Freya had her

back to me, now poking at the fire with the toe of her boot. I turned back to Tori. "So what's up with Iceland?"

With an expression much softer than Freya's, she said, "My role regarding you is very specific, Cinder. I am to protect you, even if it means losing my life. But I cannot be the one to share information with you. That role is the burden of others."

"That's cool," I said, my legs suddenly feeling weak under the weight of what she'd just said. I hardly knew her, but the thought of her dying to keep me alive was too much. "Thanks for . . . um . . . looking out for me."

I walked back to Freya. "So let me see if I have this right. You were assigned to protect me by someone whose name you can't share."

"That is correct."

"And now you're taking me to Iceland for reasons you *also* can't share . . . "

"Also correct."

"And you don't know when I'll return . . . "

"Or *if* you will return," said Freya.

"So I might die?"

"Death is always a possibility."

"You would make a terrible motivational speaker."

"You are not the first person to tell me this."

"Do I have to pay for this trip?" I asked.

"Not with money."

"Wow, that's deep." I pulled up a rock next to Freya and stared into the fire. So I would be going to Iceland whether I wanted to or not and death was on the table. It was a far cry from the neighborhoods of Richmond and Copperpenny Middle. A fierce mixture of fear and curiosity suddenly made me dizzy. *She Who Wanders, Then Conquers.* Was this what I had been looking for? Or was I about to step into the biggest pile of doggy doo ever? Before I could pull the words back, I said, "So how's Iceland this time of year?"

Freya's smile was just like her: brief and to the point.

the binding power of the icy beverage

I slept fitfully for what felt like only minutes. When Droma woke me, the stars were gone and the trees were gray in the weak light of morning.

"I forget how soundly Midgardians sleep," she said, handing me a thin, floury pastry.

I was too famished to feel insulted, so I grabbed the pastry from her and took several large bites. "Wow," I breathed, wiping my mouth with the sleeve of my hoodie. I jumped to my feet and began bouncing on my toes. The sudden desire to bolt through the forest for no reason at all was overwhelming. "What's *in* these things?"

"It draws upon the strength of the poison in your blood," said Freya, "giving your body a quick boost of energy. It is temporary and will not last long."

"Why do your answers always remind me of my impending death?" I said, popping the last piece into my mouth.

"That is not my intention," replied Freya. She glanced at me, her brows crinkling in confusion. "Or was that another attempt at humor?"

I straightened my shoulders and gave her my best Freya impersonation. *"That was not my intention."*

"You are a strange young girl," said Freya, striding from the clearing and gesturing for me to follow.

For nearly three hours we traveled through the forests that bordered Interstate five without a single break. The supercharged energy-drink-in-a-wafer had kept me running parallel to the road at an incredibly fast clip, but it was finally beginning to lose its potency. My feet had transformed into lead blocks and I was fairly certain my growling stomach could be heard even over the passing traffic.

I was irritated that Freya and her companions didn't seem the least bit tired or hungry. I convinced Freya to stop at a convenience store called the Lil' Brown Jug, which also doubled as a gas station. I knew about the frozen treasure inside because Carl had stopped there a few times on our way out to Fort Boykin Beach.

Out front was a bench chained to the wall, a stack of tires for sale, and two rusty gas pumps with cracked rubber hoses. At the top of a towering pole sat a large sign with a huge neon-lit brown jug tipping to one side and dripping neon-yellow liquid. It was amazing what some people thought was a good idea to attract customers.

I entered the Jug, flanked on either side by Tori and Droma. Freya and Edda, I noticed, remained outside, pacing back and forth, their eyes scanning the little parking lot like FBI agents on a stakeout. An electronic bell announced our arrival. A tired-looking man with his whiskery chin in his hand looked up from his magazine, gave us the once-over, then went back to his *Field & Stream*.

"You guys can take it easy," I said. Tori and Droma looked at one another, clearly uneasy with my request. "Look, unless the corn dogs are possessed with evil spirits, I'll be fine. Just look around."

"So we should be . . . chilly," said Droma.

For a moment, I was confused, then I grinned. "You mean chill. Yeah, you guys just chill."

The two girls nodded reluctantly and stepped back. I needed a lot of sugar and a lot less of the babysitting, so I quickly made for the Slurpee machine and grabbed a Styrofoam cup the size of a bucket. Licking my lips, I began to alternate the cup between the Cherry Lime Surprise and the Tangy Tangerine.

"Hello, child."

I jumped, nearly dropping my Slurpee. Standing beside me was a man holding a Styrofoam cup as large as mine. He was so old and bent with age, I wondered where he'd found the strength to lift it.

"Hi," I said, backing up a step. I knew his kind immediately. He was homeless, probably just recuperating from a long night of drinking something fiery from a paper bag. I held my breath, but it was too late. The sour odor coming off him in waves had already ruined my appetite for the Slurpee.

"Freya's a difficult one to shake, isn't she?" said the vagabond. "And so *serious*, am I right?"

I stared at the old man, my thoughts spinning too fast to form anything coherent.

"Let's see," he said, studying me closely. "Hair the color

of Asgardian red gold, check. Oddly-spaced eyes, check. Rather tall and lanky, check. Skin—"

"I'm leaving," I snapped, but I couldn't, which made my threat really unimpressive.

He placed his cup under the Tangy Tangerine spigot. "Strange flavors in Midgard, but they're growing on me." His clothes reminded me of something an actor would have worn in one of the old black-and-white vaudeville plays my foster mom sometimes watched, only filthy and riddled with holes. A glossy brown insect skittered from under the torn collar of his coat and disappeared over his shoulder.

I swallowed and looked around. I could see the tops of Tori's and Droma's heads in the other aisle. *Get over here,* I thought, as urgently as I could. Couldn't they sense my fear? Weren't they supposed to be protecting me? Sure, I outweighed the guy by twenty pounds, but after what happened the day before, I wasn't about to underestimate the creatures that were following me.

The homeless dude chuckled softly, but it turned into a fit of wet hacking. "Tori and Droma," he wheezed, "fine Predators, though they both have much to learn."

I took another step backwards. "What do you want with me?"

"The same thing I want from all would-be heroes. Or should I say *heroines.*"

"I'm no hero," I said, holding up my Slurpee. "Just thirsty."

He chuckled again, but quickly shoved a veined fist in his mouth in time to stifle any further unpleasant sounds. "No, you're not. Not *yet,* anyway."

I checked for Tori and Droma again. Now I couldn't see them at all. *Some Predators they are*, I thought.

"The Valhuri are not aware of what is happening," said the man. "I have made sure of that. When I am through with you, I will lift the *galdr* from your protectors."

It made me more than a little nervous that this guy knew about Freya and the other Predators, not to mention he claimed to have the power to stop them. I held my Slurpee out in front of me like a pathetic shield. "Look, I don't have to talk to you."

The toothless smile vanished and in its place there was a cold, hard stare. "You will not leave until you have satisfied my curiosity."

I struggled to move, but it was no use.

"At this point in time, your mind and your vision are tiny, Cindrheim. So small, in fact, I wonder why I bother. But there are things revolving around you . . . things that even *I* cannot deny."

"Droma! Tori!" I shouted, but my voice sounded tiny and hollow. My Slurpee slipped from my hand and hit the floor, sending a spray of greenish-orange liquid splattering over both our legs. The eerie homeless guy seemed not to notice.

"Before you leave the Lil' Brown Jug today, you will state your pledge—one way or the other. Will you accept and shoulder the burdens the fates have placed before you, or will you shun them and remain in the world you have grown accustomed to?"

He was right. It didn't matter if Freya and the others

found me. I wasn't leaving until I gave him what he wanted. "I . . . I, um . . . "

"Wait," whispered the old man, leaning close to me and opening his moist eyes so wide I thought they were going to pop. I tried to back away, but it was useless; I was rooted to the spot, unable to move a muscle. He brought his face to within inches of my own, forcing me to stare into his eyes.

All at once his pupils and irises vanished, replaced with an image that flickered into focus like an old television warming up. The picture was of a young girl, soaring high over the world, the wind whipping her hair. Then, like someone switched the channel, the image changed. I cried out. Dozens of slimy, green hands twisted and writhed over the screen. The image changed again. A twisting tunnel. Then again. A mouth in a silent scream. Faster and faster the images blurred. A tiny house. A snarling wolf. A tree. A rat. The images changed so fast now, a whirling blur of color and fear that threatened to engulf me. And always there was the same girl—a girl in danger, a girl alone.

"Stop!" I screamed.

The homeless man suddenly blinked and the images were gone. His pale blue irises suddenly appeared, and there was a satisfied smile on his face.

I was breathless and sweating. I didn't have to ask him. I knew the girl was me.

"Now choose," he said firmly. "State your pledge."

"Freya said I didn't have a choice . . . "

"Freya does not have the authority to offer choices. I do."

"Help me choose," I begged. Just deciding to go with

Freya had been hard enough. Now choosing to be a . . . a *hero*? Heroes died. Heroes got turned into statues because they didn't live long enough to be remembered any other way. I wiped my brow with the back of my hand. The paralysis had gone.

"I frankly don't care if you accept or not," he said, shrugging his bony shoulders. "The gods have demanded a hero's vow, so I carry out my responsibility. I can envision the excitement—and the potential for violent death—with either choice, so my opinion should not be considered."

"If you're not trying to convince me one way or the other," I said, "why did you show me those images?"

The bum rolled his eyes. "The gods, in all their great mercy, forced me to let you have a glimpse of what's in store for you if you so choose to accept, blah, blah, blah." He suddenly giggled maniacally. "But even if it weren't required of me, I'd probably show you just because I get a kick out of seeing your terrified expressions."

"You're sick."

"Not for long," said the man, holding up a bottle of cough syrup. "Aisle two, half off." He stuffed the medicine back into a coat pocket. "Now choose, Cindrheim Vustora, before I grow bored of this quest and frame you for shoplifting."

Cindrheim Vustora. She Who Wanders, Then Conquers. For some strange reason, the name finally meant something to me. Someone before might have once had this name, and I knew exactly what she would have done if she were in my place.

"I accept what the fates have placed before me," I whispered. I tried to smile. "Do I have to seal it with blood now?"

"How'd you know?" said the old man. Before I could object, he grabbed an empty cup from beside the Slurpee machine and swiped his other gnarled hand across my fingers. I saw a flash of bright silver, then felt a sudden, brief stab of pain. Faster than my eye could follow, he moved the empty cup beneath my hand and caught a few drops of blood. "Thank you, my dear," he said cheerfully. "This will do nicely." He tucked the cup inside his coat, turned to leave, then looked back at me. "You'll find first aid kits on aisle three." Then he winked one bloodshot eye. "Let the scar be a reminder."

I nodded, too shocked to say anything at all. What had I just done? As the homeless man shuffled away, he dragged his hand across the Slurpee machine. A moment later, the plastic lid at the top flew off and multi-colored ice began to spurt from the large bin like an erupting volcano.

The owner of the Lil' Brown Jug came barreling around the Moon Pie rack, his eyes wide, his face beet red. The spell having been lifted, Droma and Tori appeared from out of nowhere, Droma clotheslining the store owner with her forearm. The man landed on his back and groaned feebly.

Droma stared down at him, her hands resting casually on her hips. "Just chill," she said.

CHAPTER 4

ss ANALiseL

The owner of the Lil' Brown Jug spluttered several colorful words and jabbed his finger at the dripping Slurpee machine as if we'd pulverized his mint-condition Ferrari. He stopped immediately, however, when Tori produced a handful of crisp bills.

"I think this will cover any inconveniences you have endured today," said Freya, entering the store, taking the wad of cash from Tori and counting out nearly fifteen thousand dollars. She handed it to the store owner, whose eyes had gone wide with greed. I think I was gawking as much as he was. I had never seen that much money in person.

As soon as I was able to refill my cup with the cherry-lime-tangerine combo, we left the Lil' Brown Jug. Outside the store, Droma inspected and cleaned my wound, then patched me up. While she worked, I used the delicious Slurpee to distract me from the pain. I realized that it hadn't even been twenty-four hours yet, and already I had been slashed twice. At this rate, I was going to arrive in Iceland a dry husk. Droma also gave me another shot of the wafer, which sent my energy level through the roof again. We set off as soon as she was done.

Even though I knew questions were discouraged, I said, "So, anyone wanna tell me what just happened back there?"

"You purchased a cold beverage in the hopes that your blood-sugar level would increase," Freya said.

"Yes, that happened," I replied, "and then there was the *other* thing with the homeless man who showed me a horror movie through his eyes, then took a sample of my blood."

Freya kept walking. Almost to herself, she said, "So he appeared as a vagrant. Interesting."

She was walking so briskly, I had to jog to keep up. "How could you miss him? Didn't you see him leave?"

"You spoke to Skuld. He is a norn. I had heard that he would approach you; I just did not know when it would happen."

I was trying very hard to remain patient, but with Freya, it was never easy. "Oh, a norn. Well, that's all you had to say."

Freya continued to walk in silence.

Either Freya didn't get sarcasm, or she just wasn't a fan of mine. "Who is Skull and what exactly is a norn?"

"*Skuld* is his name, and a norn is a spirit that can take any shape it chooses. Today, with you, he chose to appear as a vagrant. Tomorrow he may be a tomcat with a missing leg, or a child's voice through your microwave." She looked over at Droma and Tori with a skeptical eye. "I am assuming he did something to avoid detection."

"He cast some sort of magic," I said. "A gopher, I think."

"A *galdr*," said Freya. "A spell that momentarily suspends time. Skuld is very good at what he does, but he is extremely mischievous. In fact, I have always suspected Skuld was a direct descendent of Loki. The exploding beverage machine is no longer a mystery. We should thank the gods he did not do something more . . . *lasting*. When norns fulfill their duties correctly, they can help determine someone's fate."

"That doesn't seem fair," I said, realizing quickly how childish I sounded. "I mean, why would they do that?"

"As powerful as norns are, they are still at the bidding of the gods. The gods would like to see things go their way, so they use the norns to help . . . *persuade* a potential hero in the direction that serves them most. There are very strict rules, however, that govern how much influence a norn can have upon a person, but they are allowed to impart a small degree of persuasion. Even gods have to follow laws."

Two days ago, I would have laughed. But things had changed in the last twenty-four hours. A *lot*. I had seen things, and *not* seen things. And suddenly, gods and their magic homeless bums were no laughing matter. I tried to ignore the throbbing in my hand by concentrating hard on what had happened in the Lil' Brown Jug. The norn *did* seem neutral, as far as good and evil went, but why frighten me so much if he wanted me to accept? Or was it all some sort of bizarre reverse psychology? I'd had social workers try that sort of thing. "So you're saying this homeless guy was sent from a god?"

"Skuld is far from homeless," said Freya. "He resides in Asgard with the Twelve. And yes, his presence here confirms his involvement with one of the major gods.

Which one, I do not know. It also confirms that we have the correct target."

"And I would be the target, right?"

Freya looked at me. "Did Skuld demand a pledge statement?"

I was feeling dizzy with everything that was happening. "A what?" I asked absently.

"A pledge statement, a hero's vow . . . did Skuld demand this of you?" Before I could answer, she stopped, grabbed my hand, and flipped it over. "Yes, that is his work." She released my hand and resumed walking, her voice betraying a hint of relief. "A portion of our mission is finished, then."

"Don't you want to know which way I pledged?"

"You would not be beside me if you had denied what the fates have placed before you."

I shook my head. I suddenly wanted nothing more than to sit down and work everything out. "I guess all of this is normal stuff for you, but I'm feeling a little overwhelmed here."

"This particular event is a first for me as well," admitted Freya. "I have heard of norns delivering messages to poten-tial heroes before, but this is the first time I have ever been so closely associated with the receiver."

I thought about my vow to Skuld. Thinking about it made my hand throb even more. It wasn't like I'd just committed to a six-month cell phone deal. "So what exactly did I just agree to?"

"You accepted to face your fate instead of running from it."

My heart started to tap-dance against my ribs. "And what is my fate?"

"That is yet to be decided. Not even Skuld knows."

I frowned. "So if he doesn't know, what is the point of all this?"

"Someone must know," replied Freya thoughtfully. "Or at least have an idea . . . "

I was getting frustrated. "So what would happen if I went back on my promise?"

Without looking at me, Freya said, "To my knowledge, only one has before. Things did not go well."

&

After a few more miles, Freya abandoned U.S. One and picked up her pace as she led us through the residential section of Smithfield. I tried my best to keep pace with Tori, her powerful legs propelling her through the neighborhood like pumping pistons. I was still feeling the energy boost from the wafer, but my liquid sugar high from the giant Slurpee had peaked, and now it was sending me into a tailspin. "So I noticed you girls don't seem to be short on cash," I said conversationally. "Why not Uber?"

Tori shook her head. "We cannot put your life into someone else's hands."

There it was again. Another reminder that their lives weren't important—only mine. If the grints didn't kill me, the guilt certainly would.

We continued our hurried pace till sundown, then turned down Pillagree Street. Pockets of gray were suddenly glimmering between houses and shops, and the smell of salt and suntan lotion and fish and chips washed over me. I breathed in deeply. The sea had always had a calming effect on me.

Within minutes, we found ourselves on the sun-washed shores of Tyler's Beach. Large seagulls wheeled overhead, and a few ancient sun worshipers were baking their leathery skin in the heat. Several families with children too small to be in school sat on blankets eating sandwiches out of coolers or stood knee-deep in the curling waves.

I felt a brief stab of jealousy. I couldn't dwell forever on my lack of an official family, though. I had just pledged my soul to a homeless man from another world.

Freya led us along the shoreline at a fast clip, her eyes always scanning the distant horizon. We skirted a rocky outcropping and entered a narrow bay that looked as if a giant hand had scooped it out with a hooked finger. The bay was empty of beachgoers, probably because the sharp rocks extended all the way to the water, and the waves were choppy and choked with driftwood and mounds of floating seaweed.

"Are we waiting for our ship to sail in?" I asked, standing precariously on the tip of a rock that jutted out over the water.

"Actually, we are," said Freya. She looked at Tori and nodded. Without hesitation, Tori pulled off her boots, removed her earbuds, then dove headlong into the rolling surf.

I gasped, then relaxed when I remembered these weren't your average teenage girls. Three minutes passed, however, and Tori still hadn't surfaced.

"Is she—"

"She is fine," assured Freya. "Tori can stay submerged for over ten minutes."

I found that I was still worried. I had grown to really like Tori and the other girls, even though we'd only been together for less than two days. Three more minutes passed. Just as I was about to demand an answer, Tori's brown-braided head popped out of the water. Apparently the thumbs-up signal spanned the Nine Realms.

"She is rising," said Freya. For the first time since meeting the Predator, she looked happy.

Tori climbed out of the water, shook her hair, and took a seat. Freya patted her shoulder and sat beside her. "You should rest, Cinder," said Tori. "Our transportation will be here shortly."

I sat down beside Droma. She offered me a tube of Ritz crackers from one of her many pouches. "You don't keep these crackers in the same pocket as that powder that dissolves magical creatures, do you?" I asked.

Droma grinned. "Chill, Cinder."

I smiled back and began to cram the buttery crackers into my mouth. "What was that stuff, anyway?"

Droma reached into her breast pocket. "You mean this?" she said.

I peered into the cup she'd formed with her fingers and saw that it was filled with a silvery gray powder. "I can see it now," I said excitedly. "You threw it on that thing in the cafeteria, right?"

Droma nodded, dumping the powder back into her pocket. "It's actually soil from the garden of Joro. She is the Goddess of Plants, Trees, and Flowers. The soil is so pure that when it comes in contact with something evil, it dissolves it like salt on a snail."

"That's one way to clean up," I said, reminding myself never to turn evil.

"Those who do not have their eyes open would probably never see the grint sitting in the middle of the cafeteria," explained Droma, "but the blind can still trip over something they cannot see. We dissolve what we kill so that your world does not raise a fuss."

My world. I turned the words over in my mind. It frightened me to think I was getting closer and closer to something that wasn't my world. I turned and watched the water crash against the craggy wall for a while.

It suddenly occurred to me that the Predators had given up their world—at least for a time—to keep me from becoming grint gruel. "Freya says you're all from Vanaheim . . ."

"Yes," said Droma.

"So you're all out-of-towners."

"If by out-of-towner you mean out of this world, then, yes. Vanaheim is one of the Nine Realms and home to the Vanir—a group of gods associated with fertility, wisdom, and the ability to see the future."

"What's it like?"

"It's a beautiful place," said Droma. "Too beautiful to put into Midgardian speech." Droma looked quickly at me. "Sorry, no offense."

"None taken. I'm still trying to figure out what Midgardian even *means*."

Droma laughed—a sound I hadn't heard from her up until now. I turned and looked at her. "Do you miss Vanaheim?"

Droma stared out at the water for several seconds before answering. "With every second that passes."

And she's here, I thought, *a million-trillion light-years from home . . . because of me.* I was on the verge of saying something really lame about how grateful I was, but she suddenly turned and dumped what was left of the Ritz crackers into my hands. "You Midgardians do make a good flaky, buttery snack, though."

Freya finally stood and stepped nimbly over the rocks till she was standing alone at the point. I looked back at Droma. "How was Freya chosen to lead the Predators?"

"As Valhuri, each of us has our strengths. Freya's talents lie in combat and the ability to decide a course of action under extreme pressure. She is a natural-born leader."

I looked over at Freya again. She was staring out to sea. I felt a surge of newfound respect for her.

A moment later I heard a sound like thunder. It was coming from the waves below us. I felt a trembling in the rocks that made my heart leap into my throat. Leaning forward, a Ritz cracker dangling from my mouth, I watched as the water began to churn and bubble. It was like a giant leviathan was rising from the depths. A moment later, I spotted a dark shape, deep in the water, steadily growing in size. Was it a whale? A submarine?

"Stand clear," warned Droma, easing me back with a firm but gentle nudge. My jaw dropping, I scrambled backward as fast as I could.

A moment later, the tip of a wooden pole broke the surface, followed by a thick canvas mast. Wet ropes whipped around and lashed at a sail decorated with red and white diamonds.

It was a ship.

A cold spray of seawater hit me like tiny pellets of ice, but I ignored it. A fine mist now hung in the air, but through it all I could see the gunwales, the gleaming deck studded with heavy-looking chests, and the curving body of the hull. My eyes flew to the prow. A beautiful replica of a fierce falcon had been carved from the wood. Brightly painted shields with carven images of attacking beasts lined the entire length of the ship, and long oars sprouted from the ship's sides like the legs of a caterpillar. I had never been a straight-A student, but I had listened enough to know I was looking at a Viking longboat. It was weathered, maybe a little battle-worn, but it looked perfectly seaworthy.

I noticed immediately, however, that there seemed to be no one on board.

Speechless, I turned and found Freya standing next to me. She was smiling from ear to ear. "Cindrheim," she said, her voice bubbling with pride, "I would like to introduce you to *Analisel*, my closest and dearest friend."

☙

The Predators leaped aboard, and I gingerly stepped on deck. As the other girls got busy setting the rigging, I stood beside Freya at the gunwale. "So this ship is your best friend . . . "

Freya pointed at the main sail and shouted a command to Edda in what must have been ancient Nordic. "Yes."

"Is there a story behind that?" I asked.

"We have work to do."

"Tell her, Freya," said Tori.

"Any opportunity to get out of work," said Freya, shaking her head.

"If you don't, I will," replied Tori.

Freya looked at me. I gave her my best puppy-dog eyes. "Please?"

Freya sighed. "When I had only six months as a Predator, I was paired with a girl my age named Analisel. I hated her, she hated me. She was stubborn, arrogant, and snored like a mountain shearing in half. She was also my equal in every way, which made me despise her even more."

"Why did she hate you?" I asked.

"That is not important," said Freya. Tori grinned at me. The boat suddenly leaned to the left, and the three of us had to grip the gunwale tightly to avoid pitching into the water. When the boat finally righted itself, Freya continued. "Anyway, we were forced to track together, and we nearly killed each other out of frustration. One day, our captain put us on the trail of a creature who had been terrorizing a small village on the south side of the island. The beast fled, and of course we gave chase. We tracked it for nearly two days, and we found ourselves miles away from camp. We knew our enemy was a formidable one, so we began to discuss our options. Our discussions turned to heated arguments, mostly due to Analisel's hardheadedness."

The boat lurched again. I bumped my hip hard against a brightly painted shield that was fixed to the railing. "So what happened?" I said, rubbing the sore spot.

Freya's turquoise eyes clouded over. She stared down into the water. "While we argued, the creature attacked us. It had purposely drawn us out into the wild where we would be far from the other Predators. We were foolishly unprepared, and I was wounded in the attack. Analisel fought the creature by herself and defeated it. When she returned to me, she found that I had lost so much blood, I was close to death." Freya gripped the gunwale tightly. "She gave me her life gift to keep me alive."

I shook my head. "What is a life gift?"

"All Predators are issued a life gift from Eir, the Goddess of Healing. When given freely to another person, it can mend almost any wound."

"How many times can you give this gift?"

"Only once," said Freya softly.

"So she saved your life."

"Twice, in my book."

I nodded and stared down at the water lapping against the side of the boat. "And what happened to Analisel?"

Several moments passed before Freya spoke. "After she gave me her life gift, I recovered quickly. When I tried to embrace her, she fell against me and died in my arms."

"Whoa. I, um—" Suddenly I wished I hadn't asked. "Sorry," I finally mumbled.

"She suffered a wound that might've been healed with my own life gift . . . had I been aware of her need."

Tori and I glanced at each other. "You don't blame yourself, do you?" I said.

Freya looked away. I didn't press her.

"I could not bring her back, but the gods allowed me to place her spirit in an inanimate object that was dear to me."

Before I could stop myself, I said, "Did Analisel have a choice?"

"It was her idea," said Freya. She cleared her throat and raised her head, a small smile lifting the corners of her mouth.

I nodded and looked down at the rail we were gripping. "So her spirit . . . is in this longboat."

"That is correct."

"Will she ever be released?"

"When I die, her spirit will rise with mine to be judged by the gods. Until that day comes, we will travel together as we once did."

"What if the ship sinks?"

"That will never happen."

"But what if it did?"

With a pained expression, Freya said, "I do not know, but I fear she would go with it."

I shook my head. "I can't believe it. Her spirit's in this boat . . . " Then it hit me. "Is that why the boat rocked when you said she was stubborn and arrogant?"

Freya patted the railing. "You see what I have to put up with?"

This time I was prepared. When the boat rocked to the side, I braced myself. From somewhere far off, I heard a young girl laughing softly.

TROUBLE ON THE STARBOARD, PORT, STERN, AND BOW

We waited until nightfall to leave the little bay. I was amazed at how frightening the ocean appeared after the sun had gone down, especially when you were sailing across it and not standing safely on the shore. Edda decided it was time to give me a crash-course lesson on trimming the sails.

I handed Edda my end of the thick rope (she informed me it was made from walrus hide) and watched her skillfully lash it to an iron ring pin. The sail instantly billowed with the captured wind, and I felt us surge forward. "Shouldn't we have left during the day?" I said, staring into the fathomless water around us.

"And how would we explain the invisible boat?" she replied.

For the tenth time that day, my jaw dropped. "This boat is . . . *invisible?*"

Edda nodded. "To anyone who has not been trained to see what is hidden, it's not there. If you're able to see something as large as this ship," said Edda, reaching out to pat my shoulder, "then your eyes are fully open."

I was too stunned to speak. My legs felt a little wobbly, so I sat down on a nearby chest.

"You should be proud of yourself, Cinder," she added. "Most do not see so early. You are an exceptionally quick learner."

"Thanks," I mumbled, staring intently now at the worn wood of the chest I was sitting on. Was it real, or was I imagining it? Was any of this real?

I wasn't able to sit for very long. Until we made it out into the open sea, it would take all of us working together to safely guide the longboat over the curling waves. Freya stood at the prow, her hand gripping the graceful wood carving of the falcon, her other hand shielding her face from the cold spray of the Atlantic.

"Can't we just give *Analisel* directions and she can take us there?" I shouted to Freya.

"It does not work like that."

"Of course it doesn't. That would be too easy."

At times I was directed to grab an oar and pull steadily through the water, and at other times I was instructed to release tension on the sail by loosening the mast ropes. The work was difficult but surprisingly satisfying. Two hours passed. My hands were becoming raw to the point that I couldn't touch a single thing without wincing.

"Freya says we can relax," said Edda, gesturing at a chest near the gunwale.

I practically collapsed, then felt an irresistible urge to pull out my picture of Uncle Robert holding me as a baby. I stared at it a moment, then turned it over and silently read his message to me.

"What's that?" Edda asked, pulling up a chest next to me.

I showed her the picture. "It's me and my uncle Robert. Kind of lame, but looking at it gives me courage."

"Nothing lame about that," said Edda. She stared at the picture a moment, then tapped Robert's image. "Your uncle . . . that's . . . "

"You know him?" I asked.

"What? No. Looks like someone I know."

I frowned and was about to press her, but she suddenly grabbed my free hand and turned it over. "Your hands are close to bleeding, and yet not a single complaint."

I smiled, grateful for the compliment, but even more grateful for the chance to rest. "That's because I haven't had *time* to complain."

Edda smiled back. "Sometimes staying busy is the best medicine."

I tucked my picture away, still puzzled over Edda's reaction but too exhausted to give it much thought.

⚭

For the next three hours, as the waves slapped against the curved hull, Edda shared everything she knew about life at sea. I was fascinated. She explained that the prows of most Viking longboats were carved in the likeness of a dragon in order to instill fear into the hearts of their enemies.

"So why is the prow of Freya's ship carved to look like a falcon?" I asked.

"The falcon has always been the symbol of the Valhuri," said Edda proudly. "The ultimate hunter. As soon as you are rested, we will remove the prow and store it safely on deck. Before we reach our destination, though, Freya will have us put it back in place."

I crinkled my brow in confusion.

"It is a bad omen to leave the Viking prow standing while at sea."

I pointed at the brightly painted shields attached to both sides of the ship. "And these?"

"Warriors traveling across the sea affix their shields to the boat whenever they are being attacked. When they reach the shore, they remove them and carry them into battle."

I looked up at the sail, its red diamonds now brown in the darkness. "Let me guess. There's a reason for that too."

Edda grinned. "When it comes to Viking warships, everything is intentional. The red symbolizes blood, anger, and aggression. Three components that strike fear into the hearts of our enemies."

I swallowed. "Just like a cruise ship."

Edda tilted her head, obviously confused.

"Sorry. I say stupid things when I get anxious."

Edda leaned back, stretching her muscled arms languidly across the gunwale. She closed her eyes. "Well, you do not have to be either while you are out at sea with us, Cinder. You are perfectly—"

"*Valhuri!*" shouted Freya, her voice shrill in the misty gloom. "*Cindarus hablitock! Rin curri, rin curri!*"

"Cinder!" whispered Edda. "Lie down flat on your stomach and do not get up!" I watched Edda scurry away, pulling her bow from her back and knocking an arrow. What had she asked me to do? I couldn't remember. All I could do was stand and watch the Predators tiptoeing across the deck, drawing back their bowstrings, staring into the dark water.

Freya leaned over the gunwale. "Tori, Droma," she whispered. "*Naheim il bestock.*"

Tori and Droma immediately began to raise the sail.

"*Kry il savaheim vesti,*" said Freya quietly.

The two Predators kept the sail closely furled around the center mast.

The sea had gone deathly silent. My heart was pounding so hard against my rib cage, I wrapped my arms around my chest to stifle the noise.

I couldn't help it. I leaned over the edge and stared into the water.

"Cindrheim!" hissed Freya. "Get down at once!"

What I saw caused my heart to stop beating altogether. The water beneath the longboat was softly glowing a greenish blue color. Millions of bubbles were rising through the murky glow like a giant carbonated soda. Something was moving through the glow, something huge and shaped like a snake. It passed under the hull. I counted off six seconds before the end of it disappeared.

"Lie down or I will stick one of my arrows in your ankle," whispered Freya, turning her bow in my direction.

"Lying down," I said quickly, dropping to the deck like a sack of bricks. I watched Freya shift her bow so that it was pointed into the water. Several tense minutes passed. It felt like the familiar sounds of the sea had been silenced with the flick of a giant switch. Aside from *Analisel* rising and falling with the swell of the ocean, nothing moved at all. Even the wind had died down. I waited for what felt like an eternity, but I couldn't stand it. "Will it attack?" I whispered.

All four Predators looked at me like I'd screamed. Freya, her face crinkled in anger, put her finger to her lips, then drew it menacingly across her throat. The universal threat for *shut up or you're dead* was well received. I didn't say another word.

A moment later, I heard something big and powerful breach the surface on the starboard side of the longboat. Droma pointed. The other three nodded. Edda drew back her bowstring. Tori fingered the mast ropes. Freya drew her sword, pointed it at the sail, and whispered, "*Oni, triem—*"

Her countdown was cut short by a watery explosion on the opposite side of the boat.

I curled into a tight ball as a shower of icy cold seawater struck me from above. I looked up, but I shouldn't have. Something towered over us, much taller than our mast, hissing and swaying back and forth like an enormous cobra. A bank of tattered clouds that was blocking the moon was suddenly shredded by the wind, and moonlight illuminated greenish-blue scales and a mouthful of razor-sharp fangs.

Now I knew where the strange glow had come from; the sea snake's entire body was haloed with a sickly fluorescent light.

Despite all that I'd seen in the last twenty-four hours, I decided immediately that I was dreaming. And as long as I was dreaming, I was determined to enjoy the idea of a giant sea-dwelling serpent pretending to rip us into tiny little pieces, then drag our remains down to the bottom of the ocean. I had to admire my ability to dream up such detail too. Squinting through the gloom, I could now see a long, forked tongue flicking between its teeth and a thick mane of green fur rippling down its spine.

Freya began shouting commands. The Predators fanned out, releasing arrows as they moved. Two of the arrows bounced harmlessly off the creature's thick hide, but one buried itself deep in its open mouth. The snake-thing hissed and reared back, smacking the surface of the ocean so hard it sent a plume of water high into the air.

A wave washed over the gunwale, drenching me from head to foot. I was shocked at how cold the water was. But that wasn't the worst of it. One of the chests from the starboard side slid towards me, my legs taking the brunt of the impact. Groaning and hoping nothing had broken, I shoved it away. The intense pain in my right shin made it official: I wasn't dreaming.

The ocean had gone deathly still again. One of the Predators had struck a solid hit, but somehow I knew it wasn't over. Feeling suddenly embarrassed to be cowering down amid the scattered chests, I rose up onto my knees and said, "Freya, give me a weapon. I can help you fight."

Freya pointed her sword at me. "You can be swallowed whole, you silly girl; now get back down."

Silly girl? You're lucky my leg's hurt, I thought. *And that you're ten times stronger than me.*

Cindrheim Vustora. I tried to picture her, whoever she was, here on the *Analisel.* What would *she* do? I grabbed one of the fallen shields, surprised at how heavy it was. I climbed to my feet, wincing as a sliver of pain shot up my left leg. "No," I said, "I'm not going to lie down."

Freya stared at me. It wasn't hard to see she was thinking of the quickest, most painful way to punish me. But then she nodded. "Very well," she said, sliding her sword across the deck. I stopped it with my foot, bent, and snatched it up. "Keep it in front of you at all times," she said firmly. "Keep your grip tight around the hilt. Aim for the eyes or mouth."

Tori shook her head. "*Freya, valtanheim il quafta.*"

Perhaps for my benefit, Freya responded in English. "I know. But her stubbornness may save her life."

Tori looked at me, her face lined with concern. "If it strikes, Cinder, let the weight of its own body do the work for you. Use both hands and lock your arms. Do not let them bend."

"Sound advice," said Freya, turning to scan the still surface of the ocean.

Now that I was holding the sword, I had to heft the shield with only one arm. I knew I must've looked terribly pathetic; the shield was sagging against my hip, and the sword felt unwieldy in my hand.

"Open up," said Tori. She stuffed a large section of the Valhuri bread into my mouth. I gobbled it down and imme-diately felt a wave of energy surge through me so that I was able to lift the shield a little higher and grip the slippery hilt of the sword a little tighter.

The five of us waited, but we didn't have long. The sea snake erupted near the prow, its black eyes rimmed in red and blazing now like smoldering coals.

"*Hile!*" shouted Freya, and all four of the Predators let fly a second wave of arrows. Two of them stuck quivering in the prow, one whistled into the darkness, and one glanced off the side of the creature's snout. A moment later, their bows were loaded with fresh arrows, but the sea snake darted forward, sweeping Droma and Edda off their feet.

I shouted in alarm, but my voice was drowned out as the serpent hissed and reared back for another strike. The two fallen Predators leaped to their feet, Droma clutching her arm to her side, her bow hanging useless from her other hand. Freya and Tori backpedaled, releasing their arrows as they moved. They missed, and the serpent swiped its diamond-shaped head horizontally across the deck. Freya, Edda, and Tori ducked, but Droma, still favoring her injured arm, failed to crouch in time.

The blow sent her flying from the deck. Nothing I had seen so far since meeting the Predators was anywhere near as horrible as watching Droma sail through the darkness and hit the water at least fifty yards from the boat. Freya screamed and let fly another arrow that found its mark. The serpent screamed much louder, Freya's arrow sticking from its ruined eye. In its agony, it thrashed back and forth in the water, emitting a sound so horrible I instinctively turned away and lowered my head.

I watched Tori fling her bow down, toss her sword to Freya, then leap over the gunwale. Freya caught the sword, dropped her bow, and instructed Edda to do the same. The serpent sank back into the water.

Freya and Edda both raced to the gunwale, frantically searching the dark water for any signs of Tori or Droma. Before I could join them, I felt the ocean swell as if a tsunami was gathering beneath us. A moment later, the serpent erupted directly beneath the prow. *Analisel* was lifted like a toy boat, catapulting Freya and Edda into the ocean. A heavy chest smashed me into the stern gunwale, pinning me in place.

The longboat splashed back down into the water, and all was silent again. I was alone. How far had Freya and Edda been tossed? Was Droma halfway down to the bottom of the ocean? Where was Tori? I couldn't lose Tori. I couldn't lose any of them.

Growling in anger, I pushed the chest away and readied myself for the next attack. A moment later, the serpent rose out of the water to my left. I spun around and shook my sword at it. "Come and get me, you stupid worm!" The insult must've worked, or maybe it was still sore about the arrow sticking out of its eye, because the creature shrieked in rage, then thrust its head at me. I brought my shield up just in time, but the force of the impact knocked the wind from my lungs and sent me skidding across the deck. My shield spun away and agony flooded my body as I slammed up against the gunwale. For a moment, my eyes swam with glittering points of light. Panicking, I started gulping air.

The serpent, surely sensing victory, reared back, then struck again. Remembering Tori's advice, I braced myself against the gunwale, and stuck Freya's sword straight out. The serpent threw its full weight against the sword, impaling itself through the throat. I turned my head, instantly sick from the thing's fetid breath. Wishing I had an awesome Viking war cry ready, I screamed something unintelligible and pushed forward, sinking the blade even deeper. The serpent's hiss turned to a gurgle, then the fire in its eyes went out. With a wet wheezing sound, it fell heavily to the side, its thick body smashing into the main mast. The wood gave an ear-splitting crack, split in half, then slowly toppled over.

Wincing, I scrambled out from beneath the weight of the creature's head, withdrawing Freya's sword from its throat as I moved. I watched the mast tumble over the side of the longboat and into the ocean.

That can't be a good thing, I thought. I looked back at the serpent. It flopped a few times, curled reflexively around the base of the broken mast, then went still.

I stared down at the sword in my hand, unable to believe I had killed a living creature. Something black and sticky was sliding down the blade, covering my fingers. I dropped the sword and sank to my knees. I wanted to get up. I wanted to run to the gunwale and see if anyone had survived. But I couldn't move. It felt good to let my eyes close.

"Cinder!" The shout had come from the prow of the ship. Or was it the starboard side? It was difficult to tell. Every bone in my body felt bruised, and my senses were fuzzy, like someone had stuffed my skull with gobs of cotton.

"Freya . . . is that you?" I managed to say.

"Cinder, are you there?"

It was Tori. Tori was alive! I breathed a huge sigh of relief. All wasn't lost. "I'm here, Tori!" I called back. "I'm okay! Do you have Droma?"

"I do, but she's badly injured. Can you lower a rope?"

Knowing Droma was alive gave me the willpower to struggle to my feet. As quickly as I could, I crossed the deck, scooping up a rope as I went. There was Tori, bobbing in the dark ocean, one arm treading water, the other grasping an unconscious Droma. I tied off my end of the rope, then tossed what was left into the water. Tori quickly secured her end around Droma. With my help, Tori scrambled up the rope, then together we leveraged Droma into the longboat.

We lowered her to the deck as gently as we could. Tori began to breathe air into her mouth, and that's when I remembered. "Freya and Edda!" I cried. "They were thrown from the—"

"We are here, Cindrheim."

Spinning around, I saw the two Predators climbing over the gunwale near the stern. They looked like drowned rats, but neither of them appeared seriously injured. I was so happy, I found it difficult to speak.

Freya looked at the dead serpent, the weight of its body

causing the longboat to list precariously in the water. She shook her head. "Is it possible? Did . . . *you* kill it?"

"I think so," I said. "It all happened so fast."

She saw her own sword lying on the deck. She bent to pick it up, stared at the black goo that was dripping down its gleaming edge. She looked at Edda, who was shaking her head in disbelief. Both of them turned to stare at me.

"Midgard has its share of mysteries," said Freya in obvious wonderment, "but an untrained mortal slaying the offspring of Iormungand defies all logic."

"Maybe it's written in the stars," said Edda, eyeing me skeptically.

"Maybe," said Freya.

I shrugged my shoulders and offered the only explanation I could. "That thing was really ticking me off."

CHAPTER 6

ROMANCING THE WYRM

Freya was not a happy Predator. Granted, none of us had been chewed to pieces by the giant sea snake, but that didn't seem to matter at the moment. She stared at the shattered remains of her mast as it floated away from us. I could see the tendons in her neck standing out. I moved close beside her at the gunwale.

"Will we have to row all the way to Iceland now?" I asked.

"No."

"That's good," I said, though I had no idea what she had planned. "So . . . I guess when we get there, you can always get another—"

"You do not understand, Cindrheim," said Freya, cutting me off. "I have fought in over a dozen open-sea battles, and *Analisel*'s mast has never been severed before."

"Well, over a dozen battles . . . it was bound to happen sooner or later."

"I am finding that you have many hidden talents, but consoling a person is not one of them." Freya turned and strode away.

I could've punched myself (and would have if I weren't so sore). "Freya, wait. I actually was trying to make you feel better. Freya?"

"Let her go," said Tori. She grinned, and whispered, "I think she cares for this boat as much as she does any of us."

"We don't come close," said Edda, who was near enough to hear the comment.

"She'll be fine," added Tori. "Holding grudges is not productive, and Freya does nothing that isn't productive."

"I hope not," I said, kicking myself. "I never say the right thing."

Tori pretended to lunge forward with an imaginary sword. "You fought and killed a wyrm, Cinder! A creature that has taken the lives of thousands. After a feat like that, you're entitled to a few tiny mistakes."

Tori had a wonderful way of making me feel better. "So what exactly was that thing? Freya said something about the offspring of Ignoramus . . ."

Tori laughed. "The offspring of *Iormungand*—the world-encircling sea serpent, also called the Great Wyrm—the same creature that battled Thor and lost."

My jaw dropped. "World *encircling*?"

"That's right. Her body wrapped around the Earth, lying deep in the ocean trenches. She was a symbol of pure evil, a darkness encased in hardened scales, each one the size of *Analisel*'s largest sail. She could swallow you whole like a whale swallows plankton. Thor, the God of Thunder, encountered her while on a fishing trip. She knew of his legendary power and fame and wanted to devour him." Tori grinned. "Iormungand underestimated Thor's strength and the bite of his mighty hammer."

I nodded, barely able to conceive of such a battle. "How do you kill something that can wrap around the world?"

"Not sure—she's not dead yet. Thor is fated to face her one final time."

"And she had babies?"

"Two that we know of," Tori said. "One of the wyrms was crushed by Ymir the Frost Giant and made into belts for his personal bodyguards. To our knowledge, the other one survived through the ages." Tori winked and grinned again. "Until tonight, that is."

I tried to picture a creature large enough to catch Iormungand's eye. Such a romance was something I didn't want to dwell on for very long, but it *was* intriguing. "What about the father? Where is he?"

"Iormungand did not have a mate. She was impregnated through magic."

I held up my hands. "Enough said."

⚭

There's nothing more breathtaking than the sun rising over the ocean. Even the Atlantic, with its steel gray waters and its leaden skies, is something to behold at dawn. We sat motionless on water as still as glass, *Analisel* looking worse for wear with the splintered stump rising from the middle of her deck, but still floating proudly.

It took all of us all morning to cut the serpent into chunks that were small enough to lift and toss over the gunwale. It reminded me of the field trip I took in sixth grade to the slaughterhouse, where we were shown what it takes to prepare a full-grown cow for the market. Only, this was a thousand times worse. It took even longer to swab the sticky black goo from the deck. The horrid odor had me leaning over the gunwale every five minutes.

Just as I was about to toss the last chunk into the ocean, Freya stopped me. "Remove the scales from this piece before you discard it. Keep them in a safe place."

I stared at her. "Are you serious?"

"I am always serious."

"Aye-aye, Captain." I lowered the hunk of serpent meat to the deck and began the grisly job of prying each greenish-blue scale from the flesh with a tool that Tori gave me. An hour later, I handed my bucket of scales to Freya. She took them without a word.

Edda prepared a simple breakfast of dried meat (it reminded me of salted beef jerky) and Tori produced a few leather skins of fresh water. We ate quickly, then huddled around Droma, who had been stretched out on a pile of thick woolen blankets near the prow. Her arm was tightly bound in a sling, and her dark skin was mottled with purple bruises. One of her eyes was completely swollen shut. Tori propped Droma's head up and Edda poured water into her mouth. Droma mumbled something, cried out, then went quiet.

"We now have two aboard ship that require healing beyond what we can provide," said Freya. "We must hurry."

For a moment I wondered who the other person was that required this special form of medical attention, then

I remembered she was talking about me. I turned my hand over and stared at the veins in my wrist. Was the poison getting closer to my heart? I didn't feel any different, aside from the incredible soreness from the previous night's battle. But that had nothing to do with the injury I had sustained in the cafeteria. I thought it was ironic that the worst of my wounds had come while I was holding a half-constructed hoagie.

Freya interrupted my thoughts with a string of new commands in ancient Nordic. The Predators leaped into action. I was eager to see how we were going to get to Iceland without a sail or using the oars. My curiosity would have to wait, however, because our first task was to remove the prow.

The job fell to me and Tori. "Freya believes part of the reason we were attacked last night was because we failed to take the prow down while at sea."

"Oh, the bad luck thing?"

"Exactly."

"What's the other reason?"

Tori looked at me, then over at Freya, who was busy studying a compass. "You had better ask Freya, Cinder."

When we had stowed the large carving of the falcon head safely against the gunwale, I walked over to stand beside Freya. She was holding an old-fashioned spyglass up to her eye, twisting the end piece in both directions.

I fidgeted around for several agonizing minutes before finding the courage to speak. "I'm sorry about what I said about the mast, Freya," I managed. "It was insensitive."

Freya continued to stare through the spyglass. "You are forgiven. But I must apologize as well. My anger clouded my senses."

"Oh . . . well, that's okay. I had a bike once that I tried to keep in mint condition, but I realized that all of the scratches and dents just gave it more character."

"I should learn to adopt your way of thinking, though it may take some time." Freya turned her focus to the star-board side of the longboat. "Is there something else you need?"

"Yes . . . I was wondering why that monster attacked us last night."

Freya squinted into the lens, clicked her tongue in irritation at something she could see (or not see) on the horizon, then said, "The forces of evil are attuned to your whereabouts, Cindrheim. That much is clear. The spawn of Iormungand is just another in a long line of enemies that has been sent to kill you."

"And you don't know why you were sent to protect me?"

"I do not," replied Freya.

"Then why do it?"

"I am Valhuri. I follow orders without question. One thing I can tell you, though, is that there is something about you that has the gods riled up beyond comprehension."

"I knew I was unpopular, but this is ridiculous."

Before Freya turned her attention back to the sea again, a tiny smile curled the corners of her lips.

☌

While Edda and I drew in the oars, Tori leaped over the gunwale. I heard a tiny splash. "What is she doing?" I asked in alarm. I ran to the back of the longboat and stared into the choppy water.

Edda called out, "Help me with the oars, Cinder. She's fine."

I made my way reluctantly back to Edda. "Is this part of Freya's plan to get to Iceland? I hope it's a five hundred horsepower engine."

I noticed that the Predator was trying to hide a mischievous grin. "Now that wouldn't be the Viking way, would it?"

"No, it wouldn't. But if we don't have a sail, and we're not going to row, how else are we going to travel?"

"Perhaps Tori has gone to ask the dolphins and the sea turtles to push us there," said Edda. She burst out laughing.

I paused, more than a little confused. After what I'd seen in the last few days, being carried to Iceland on the backs of dolphins and turtles didn't seem that far-fetched. At that moment, Tori hopped over the gunwale. She was soaking wet but looked extremely happy. "Come see!" she said excitedly.

I ran to the stern and looked overboard. I couldn't have been more shocked at what I saw than if a crew of blue-skinned mermaids had been lined up in the water, ready to propel us across the Atlantic. Sticking out of the back end of the longboat was a glossy black motor the size of a baby elephant. Someone had taken the time to adorn the impressive machine with green and yellow flames.

I was totally speechless. That's when a low thrumming sound started emanating from deep in the water. I felt *Analisel* begin to tremble, the shields on the gunwale rattled and the chests began to vibrate around the deck. All at once, a flurry of tiny bubbles blossomed just below the surface of the gray water, followed by bubbles the size of basketballs.

I spun around. "You have an *engine* down there?"

"And top of the line too," said Tori proudly. "One thousand pounds of raw horsepower."

The large propellers began chopping up the water, obviously eager to show us what they could do. It sounded like the *Columbia* was preparing to launch from Cape Canaveral.

Edda reached over, gripped the throttle, and gave it a hard yank. *Analisel* surged forward. "A thousand pounds of horsepower," she shouted over the roar of the engine. "Now *that's* the Viking way!"

For three straight hours we traveled at over twenty-five knots, which Edda explained was about fifty miles per hour. I guess for a ship the size of *Analisel*, such speed was no joke. Edda pointed out that the North Atlantic Drift, a strong wind that blew in from the southwest, aided us on our journey, even though our sail was somewhere at the bottom of the Atlantic, probably draped over a few good-sized chunks of wyrm flesh.

It felt good to sit near the prow of the longboat and let the salty wind whip through my hair. Off to our right, we saw the broad blue backs of whales breach the surface, spout jets of water high into the air, then disappear below the waves.

Edda killed the motor only to refuel, then we were off again. This routine continued through the night and into the following day, each of us helping to refill the engine with the large cans of gasoline that had been stored in the chests. Night fell again, and still we sped across the choppy water. I was a little alarmed, however, that even though we were traveling so quickly, I had yet to see any signs of dry land.

As was typical with the Predators, they had failed to answer the question that was hanging in the air. I finally approached Tori. "So tell me. If *Analisel*'s been equipped with a gigantic motor, why haven't we used it before?"

Tori looked around, then dialed down the volume of her voice. "Freya hates it. She had it mounted only for extreme emergencies."

"Have you ever had to use it before today?" I asked.

"No. Edda's the sailing specialist and she became fascinated by the modern machines mortals use to propel their ships. She—"

I stopped her. "Are you guys *not* mortal?"

Tori sighed. "Once we become full Valhuri, we are blessed with immortality."

"So you can't die?"

"Not from old age, but we can certainly be killed."

"And how does one get to be a Predator?"

Tori suddenly appeared uncomfortable. "Cinder, I don't really—"

"I think we're losing Droma!" blurted Edda, bounding across the deck. She looked terrified.

Tori and I leaped to our feet. It felt like I had swallowed a rock and it was lodged in my throat.

"Get Freya," ordered Tori, racing over to where Droma lay on her blanket. Edda scurried to the stern of the ship.

I felt useless. What could I possibly do? I quickly followed Tori, kneeling down at Droma's side, but keeping back far enough that I wouldn't be in the way.

I gasped. Droma's once beautiful face had turned to something I barely recognized. What had happened in the last six hours? Her skin was now pale and hanging like crepe paper on a Halloween skull. Her eyes were closed, but the lids were fluttering rapidly and her mouth was opening and closing like a fish sucking air. Every inch of exposed skin was beaded with sweat.

It was awful. I covered my mouth with my hand and backed away a few feet. "What's wrong with her . . . ?" I mumbled.

Freya suddenly nudged me aside and knelt beside her. She placed her ear close to Droma's mouth and listened for a while.

Droma was the healer of the group. Now that she was so close to death, who would be the one to keep *her* alive?

Freya whispered a few words to Droma that I didn't understand. Tori and Edda both nodded and murmured something similar. When Freya turned around, her eyes were brimming with tears. "She has but a few hours left."

No, it wasn't possible. She was a Predator. She was more powerful than five strong men. We were so close. Beside me, Tori buried her face in her hands. I could hear her crying softly. Edda shook her head almost defiantly, then strode away towards the prow of the longboat. She snatched up Freya's spyglass as she moved. I saw her use it to stare out across the water, but I couldn't watch anymore. It was so depressing to see her vainly looking for something that wasn't there.

Wait! I nearly fell over with a sudden jolt of excitement. She wouldn't die! Not with three Predators standing around. I grabbed Freya's arm.

"Freya," I said breathlessly, "you three have life gifts! Use one on Droma."

Freya shook her head. "When we left, each of us swore we would preserve our gifts for one person."

"What! Who?"

"You, Cindrheim. Each of our life gifts is to be saved for you, and you only."

I was too stunned to respond. Then my shock turned to anger. "Well, I'm telling you that you can use it on Droma. I officially give you permission! I don't need all three of your life gifts. Just—"

"You do not understand," said Freya, her voice unusually soft. "We made a pledge, a binding vow that cannot be undone. It does not matter what we may *wish* to do in our hearts. All four of our gifts are yours whether we like it or not."

I shook my head, unable to get any words past the lump in my throat. Rising to my feet, I started to back away. I couldn't look at Droma. I couldn't look at any of them. I wanted to leap off the longboat and sink to the bottom of the ocean. Why had I agreed to something like this? My chest felt like it was caving in. *I'm done*, I thought. *I can't do this anymore.*

That's when Edda shouted, "Land! Thank the mighty Norse gods! I see land!"

CHAPTER 7

OEAT1) FROM BELOW, LIGHT FROM ABOVE

I couldn't remember ever feeling so happy. Edda's words hung in the air, each of us trying to digest what she'd said. Then all at once we bolted to the prow of the longboat and leaned far out over the gunwale, our hands shielding the sun's glare. Freya took the spyglass.

At first, my heart sank. "I don't see anything but more water."

"No," said Freya, her voice gruff with emotion, "Edda is right. At our current speed, we can be ashore in half an hour." Tori squealed with delight. Edda did a little jig.

A few days ago, I was in Richmond, excited for Hoagie Thursdays at school. Now I was approaching Iceland in a boat that encased the spirit of a dead girl. Not too far away sat a bucket full of sea-serpent scales. Times had changed.

Edda checked our distance with the spyglass. She called me over. "Cinder, help me with the prow." In less than ten minutes, the two of us had the falcon head reattached to the front of the longboat.

We passed a tiny island called Surtsey, then a larger one called Heimaey. A heavy layer of fog kept me from making out any distinct features on either island, though. Twenty minutes later, Edda called out, "Iceland, straight ahead!"

My breath caught in my throat. We were finally here. I stared through the thick screen of cold mist that blanketed most of the rocky beach, but poking through the fog were tall spears of black volcanic rock. I half expected to see a waiting party lined up along the shore, but we seemed to be the only living things for miles around. Tori explained that our destination was purposely placed on the northern side of the giant island because there were very few settlements anywhere near. Isolation, according to Tori, was crucial.

What am I getting myself into? I wondered as I unwrapped my sweatshirt from around my waist and quickly put it on. Shivering, I drew the hood up over my head. Edda moved to the stern and throttled back on the engine. The powerful roar died down to a steady purr.

It wasn't until I felt the hull of the longboat scrape against the sandy shore that I accepted the fact that we were in another country. I supposed passports weren't needed since we were working for a group of Norse gods.

Before the longboat came to a complete stop, Freya began shouting commands. We scurried around like ants to comply. We cut one of *Analisel*'s oars into two pieces, then used them to transform Droma's blanket into a makeshift stretcher.

Freya was first to walk up onto the shore. "We make directly for the Proving Grounds," she said, pointing towards a large gap in the rocks. "Edda and Tori, head for the border. I will catch up."

The Proving Grounds? That sounded ominous.

Nodding, the Predators quickly obeyed. Droma groaned weakly as she passed me on the stretcher. "Stay close to us, Cinder," said Tori. Before I turned to follow them, I watched Freya tie *Analisel* to a sturdy piling, then pat the side of her hull. I couldn't help but smile. I turned and made my way up the gravelly incline after Tori and Edda.

When I reached them, I said, "Is it always this cold in September?" I pulled the drawstrings on my hood as tightly as I could.

"This is high summer," said Edda.

And me without my swimsuit, I thought gloomily. Freya soon joined us. Her eyes seemed a little red, but I didn't know if that was over her concern for Droma, or because she had left *Analisel*.

We trudged through a narrow gully, lined on either side with thick stands of scrub brush and rocks covered in moss and lichen. I was a little disappointed that there were so few trees. When I asked about it, Tori said, "The island was covered with trees at one time, but human settlement has taken its toll."

I never considered myself a tree hugger, but the lack of foliage made the land seem so harsh and barren. "Don't fret, Cinder," she added. "Where we're going, you'll get your fill of trees."

We crossed a broad expanse of grassland, the thick tufts of vegetation rolling like waves on a pale green ocean. The gentle swaying of the grasses was almost hypnotic; I could feel myself growing tired, but one look at Droma kept me going. I distracted myself by counting the number

of black-furred foxes that darted across our path and disappeared down dark holes.

Freya stopped and pulled what looked like a silver
whistle from a pouch at her waist. She blew into it, but I
heard nothing.

"Is that like a dog whistle?" I asked, but Tori shushed me.

"We've reached the point of our journey where the
Valkyries can hear her call," whispered Tori. She glanced
apprehensively at Droma. "Without their help it would take
us days to reach the Proving Grounds."

"Valkyries?" I asked.

With a nervous grin, Tori said, "You'll see."

Freya tucked the whistle back into her pouch, stared at
the sky for a moment, then rejoined us. "Let us hope they
heard my call," she said, glancing at Droma. "Keep moving."

That was when the grints attacked. And this time, I
could see them.

Several black shapes burst out of a shadowy cleft to our
left. Each one was roughly the size of a large sea turtle, the
bulk of their bodies covered in a glossy shell. Their long,
hooked legs moved so quickly, I couldn't get an accurate
count. All of this was disturbing enough, but it was nothing
compared to the faces that protruded from each carapace.
They were soot-colored and smashed flat, like a pug-nosed
dog, but otherwise so close to human faces that my skin
crawled in disgust. Some chittered in rage. Some gnashed
their teeth. Some grinned with wicked malevolence. But all
of their eyes blazed with a sickly green light as they swept
towards us.

I suddenly wished I had never learned to truly see.

"Do not allow Cindrheim to perish in your attempt to protect Droma!" shouted Freya as she slapped a long dagger into my hand.

Edda and Tori quickly lowered Droma's stretcher to the ground, then whipped their bows from their backs. In an instant, all three Predators had nocked a gray feathered arrow. Their bowstrings twanged simultaneously, and three grints dropped like lead weights.

Problem was, three more took their place.

Their bows sang again, and three more creatures died instantly.

"Swords!" yelled Freya, dropping her bow and unsheathing her silver blade. Tori and Edda followed suit. "Surround Cindrheim! Fight till your last breath!" The Predators crowded around me, their blades whirling as more grints scuttled and leaped. I couldn't bear to see Droma left to be swarmed by the creatures, so I backed up till I was standing in front of her, my dagger held out in front of me.

It was horrible. Whichever way I turned, I saw black appendages with shiny hooks at the end, and sharp teeth, and glowing eyes. I also saw the Predators' swords moving like the blades of a high-powered fan; the result was a noxious-smelling spray of black goo.

It seemed like we were winning. Dead grints were piling up around the Predators, and their glittering swords continued to twirl and dip and thrust without slowing. At one point, Freya snatched her bow up off the ground, shouted something in Nordic, and three arrows appeared on her bowstring. A second later, three grints dropped to their bellies, their hides pierced with silver arrows.

Tori suddenly cried out and fell to one knee, dropping one of her twin blades and clutching her stomach. Screaming in anger, I lashed out at the grint that moved in to sink its teeth into the back of her exposed neck.

The creature shrieked and skittered backwards, the front ends of both legs now missing.

"Excellent work, Cindrheim!" shouted Freya, parrying a grint's attack and then skewering it with her sword. "But do it again, and I will feed you to them myself!"

"But it was—"

"No!" said Freya, ducking beneath a grint as it lunged at her. She shoved her blade up into its underbelly, then dumped it to the side of her. "I did not give you the dagger to protect one of us. It is to protect *you*! Now follow my orders!"

You're not my boss! I thought, instantly glad I hadn't said it out loud. I crouched and gripped the dagger tight in my hand.

Edda cried out and went down. But before I could react, another long black appendage reached through our defenses and struck Droma. I kicked at it, which made it flinch back, but nothing more.

"They are breaking through!" hollered Freya. "Fight to your last breath, Predators!" Tori tried to wave her sword in front of her, but she was too weak to do any real damage. A ring of dead grints surrounded us now, but more were coming.

At that moment, a shiny black hook slashed through the air. Freya flinched and spun around. She was holding her hand across her eyes. "Last breath!" she shouted again. One of the grints had its hook in Droma's stretcher, dragging it away from us.

Growling, I lunged forward and sank my dagger into the space between the thing's hard shell and its head. The grint collapsed, its legs splayed out like a smashed spider. I snatched up the corner of the blanket and heaved it back to where it was.

If Droma was to die, she would die with us.

Just as Freya began to berate me for risking my life, a piercing note tore through the clearing. The sound was coming from above us, like a referee had blown a whistle. All of us stopped fighting and looked up. Even the grints.

Whatever was up there, it wasn't just one, but three. And I could tell they were angry.

With a sound like a hundred trumpets, they left the sky and arrowed toward us.

CHAPTER 8

UNDER THE WEATHER AT TEN THOUSAND FEET

The grint directly in front of me looked terrified, and I was willing to bet it wasn't because of me. Squealing hysterically, it tried to turn on its hooked legs, but a golden shaft of light pinned it to the ground. I ignored the grotesque twitching legs and focused on the weapon. It wasn't a shaft of light after all. It was a spear. A moment later, the spear wriggled out of the dead creature and whipped back into the air.

Before I could exhale, two more golden spears struck down a pair of chittering grints. The monsters that hadn't been skewered were bolting in terror now, most of them scrabbling over the rocky ground and disappearing into the surrounding shrubs.

I looked up. Whatever had thrown the spears was a lot closer now. I blinked. Then I tried to speak, but nothing came out. Three sleek white horses with wingspans as wide as a school bus were descending from out of the sky. Steam billowed from flaring nostrils and powerful legs pawed at the air. Each horse bore a woman dressed in silver armor and red capes that danced in the wind. All of them had golden spears, round white shields with a raven in the center, and bright white hair that flowed from beneath gold conical-shaped helms.

And one of them was wearing sunglasses. Mirrored aviator sunglasses.

Do men ever do any of the fighting? I wondered, gaping at the women's fierce expressions. They were beautiful, but it was a terrible beauty. I couldn't picture them ever smiling.

"Valkyries," breathed Tori, trying hard to climb to her feet. She said the word as if they were royalty. And maybe they were—Tori had already pointed out my knowledge of Norse history was lacking to say the least. "They heard Freya's call."

The horses landed with a thud (one of them squashing a grint in the process), and the women dismounted in one fluid motion. Throwing their shields over their shoulders, they approached us. Each of them had to be at least seven feet tall, but they moved quickly and decisively.

Freya stepped over a dead grint and presented herself to the lead Valkyrie. She had dropped her hand away from her face. I saw that there was an ugly cut that angled across her left eye. It was swollen shut.

"My lady," said Freya as firmly as she could. Her head was slightly bowed. "My companions and I thank you for your timely intervention. We would have perished without you."

"You do not have to tell me what would have happened," said the Valkyrie, towering over the Predator. "We could see from on high that your chances were fast dwindling."

"Yes, my lady," said Freya.

Then the Valkyrie turned her icy blue eyes on me. It felt like someone had ignited a spotlight and trained it on me so that it bore into my head, revealing my most secret thoughts. I took an involuntary step backward. "Is this she?" said the woman curiously.

"It is Cindrheim Vustora Moss, my lady . . . the young Midgardian we were ordered to retrieve."

The Valkyrie nodded. "I am Brunhild. First Chooser of the Slain, Last to Leave the Field of Battle, Shield Maiden to Odin the Allfather. Welcome to Isilhiem."

"Thank you, but I thought this was Iceland," I said nervously.

I could hear Tori sigh behind me. Brunhild nearly smiled. Or maybe it was a smirk. "Isilheim *is* Iceland, but the mortal word for this country has never set well on my lips."

Before I could further embarrass myself and say *I know what you mean*, I just pursed my own lips and smiled back.

"You will travel to the border with us," said Brunhild, "but first we will cleanse the area." She nodded at one of her Valkyrie companions, who loosened a leather bag at her hip and began to walk about the clearing, sprinkling the same powder that Droma had used in the cafeteria. There were so many dead grints to dissolve, the sizzling sounded like someone had set off a string of fireworks. I watched the grint closest to me begin to shrivel and collapse into the trampled grass. I'm not embarrassed to say I turned away.

The other Valkyrie began to load Droma onto one of the winged horses. Brunhild was a ways off, conversing with Freya in quiet tones. I stepped close to Tori and Edda.

"What exactly are Valkyries?"

"They are Odin's personal guards," said Tori, wincing as she spoke, "but their primary duty is to gather the souls of the slain after a battle and present them to Odin so they can celebrate with him in the Great Hall. After the celebration, the dead warriors are awarded eternal glory in Valhalla."

"Valhalla?" I asked.

"Viking afterlife."

Edda was looking at me as if she'd never seen me before.

"Mount up!" ordered Brunhild, striding away from Freya.

Terrified of our transportation, but even more so to disobey Brunhild, I scurried over to the closest horse. Before I could figure out a way to climb the massive creature, the Valkyrie with the aviator shades grabbed me around my waist and hoisted me up onto the horse's back. Tori was quickly plunked down behind me.

"My name is Trigga," said the Valkyrie, gripping the area of the horse where its snowy white wing attached to its flank. She pulled herself up better than any actor I'd seen in any cowboy movie. Adjusting her stylish eyewear, she said, "Risen will bear the three of us easily and quite comfortably, but he will not tolerate your heels in his sides or your nails in his back. Use the muscles in your thighs to grip him."

Hoping she didn't throw me down onto the ground or shoot laser beams at me from her silvery glasses, I said, "What do I do with my hands?"

"You will hold onto me," said Trigga, "and the young Predator will hold onto you."

"Got it," I said, grateful I was still alive after questioning her. The horse began to prance excitedly. I could feel the muscles in its back rippling beneath me. My heart started to hammer in my chest, and I instinctively threw my arms around the Valkyrie's waist. It felt like I was hugging a tree.

I looked over and saw that Freya was atop Brunhild's horse, holding onto a semi-conscious Droma so that she wouldn't fall. Edda, being the largest of the four Predators, was with the last Valkyrie. I could see that she, too, was in pain from her recent injury. Three of the Predators had been wounded in the fight against the grints. *Were they now poisoned like me?*

Brunhild raised her spear in the air. Her mount unfolded its wings, gave them a few flaps, then pushed off the ground with a loud snort. My jaw dropped as I watched Freya, Droma, and Brunhild soar into the air. Then my jaw snapped shut as our horse did the same. I had never flown on an airplane, but I imagined that this had to be worse. Much worse.

Confession time: I started screaming. Not the "Oh look, there's a mouse!" type of scream. It was a bloodcurdling, "Someone save me!" scream.

Shouting into the rush of wind, Trigga said, "Please refrain from ruining this flight! I haven't dropped anyone in months."

I decided that if I survived this harrowing ordeal, Trigga and I might become good friends. How often do you come across a seven-foot woman who rides a flying horse and has a sense of humor?

Unless she wasn't trying to be funny. Not willing to take any chances, I clenched my legs around the horse's flanks and gripped Trigga as tightly as I could. Fortunately, she didn't seem to notice.

We climbed high into the dark sky, the air growing colder as we gained altitude. My hair was soon wet with condensation, but I was far too scared to really worry about it. In fact, I realized that I hadn't once opened my eyes since leaving the ground. Tori was ooohing and aaahhing behind me, prodding me in the back to look to the left and to the right. After several vigorous shakes of my head, she finally gave up.

After a half hour or so of flying, Trigga said, "You are still alive, child. Open your eyes and look about you."

"I can't," I said, pressing my face against the back of her hard leather corselet. Why was this more frightening than facing the wyrm or a horde of grints?

"You may not get this chance again," the Valkyrie added.

She's right, I thought. Even if I found myself in an airplane someday, it wouldn't be the same. I allowed my eyes to crack open. At first all I saw were gray, tattered clouds as we shot through them. I opened my eyes fully, and my breath caught in my throat. Bright moonlight illuminated black volcanic rock, punctuated by silver patches of ice, spread out as far as I could see. Carved into the rock, like private hot tubs, were pools of steaming water, probably caused by some underground phenomenon. There were trees, but they looked more like gray-green needles, clumped together as if warding off the harsh elements. A few tiny farmhouses, like a child's toys, dotted the rolling grass plains. Looking over to the left side, I spotted a drop of water that must've been a lake, and a miniature truck rambling down a narrow dirt road. Flying level with us was Brunhild and the others. I whooped in delight, and stuck both hands in the air.

"It is wise to have a *little* fear, child!" warned the Valkyrie.

Nodding and laughing uncontrollably, I wrapped my arms around her waist again. "Sorry!" I yelled back. A little more confident and relaxed, I asked Trigga about the grints.

"Grints are a hybrid of insect and human," answered the Valkyrie.

I nodded, remembering the monsters' revolting glossy shells and expressive faces. "Were they formed by accident?"

"Nothing is formed by accident in our world. Grints start out as humans, then are changed into insects when they fail to appease the gods of darkness."

"How awful," I said.

"Do not feel sorry for them. These humans are the lowest of your species, bent on thievery and violence. They seek rewards to quench their greed and risk the consequences."

"Talk about doing hard time," I muttered.

The Valkyrie shifted in her saddle and said, "We are approaching our destination. A powerful ward has been placed around the perimeter to keep those who are unin-vited away from us. It causes extreme physical discomfort to those not accustomed to our world."

By physical discomfort, she meant I would yak up my breakfast. And I did. Over and over until I had nothing left but fumes. *So this was one of the images I saw in Skuld's bloodshot eyes—me, soaring over the world. But it didn't include me tossing my breakfast into Risen's slipstream!*

"Are you okay?" shouted Tori, scraping something off her sleeve with a handkerchief.

"Never felt better!" I bellowed, clutching my stomach. "Now can we please turn around!"

"It will pass!" shouted Tori, crushing me tighter against the rigid Valkyrie.

But that's the thing: it wasn't passing. I considered struggling free of Tori's embrace and plummeting to the ground, but the Predator just held me tighter. Just when I thought I couldn't bear it any longer, I saw Brunhild hold up her golden spear, then point it downwards.

"We are about to cross over!" exclaimed Trigga. "Hold on, Cinder!"

For a moment I forgot my misery as I felt Risen angle his body so that I was smashed up against the Valkyrie. Then we were shredding clouds as we plunged towards the earth. *I'm not tall enough for this ride!* my mind screamed. Through slitted eyes I could see Trigga's gold-white hair and Risen's wing feathers aflame with sunlight. A few dizzying minutes later, we landed with a jolting thud. Trigga hurriedly dismounted so she could catch me as I fell.

CHAPTER 9

ASGARD'S FINEST

I was only vaguely aware of what was going on around me. Here's what I *did* know: I was fairly positive that I was still alive. My stomach, throat, and jawbone hurt too much to be dead. Secondly, I knew that someone very strong was carrying me. It had to be Trigga, the Valkyrie. Cradled in her arms and looking up into her stern face, I felt like a newborn baby waiting for her pacifier. It was embarrassing, but I couldn't do anything about it.

Trigga took about a dozen paces, then set me down as gently as she could, which for someone so big wasn't very gentle at all. On a brighter note, I no longer needed to hack up my guts. I had to admit, it was a vicious, but effective method of protection. Without the help of someone from the inside, I would've turned back long ago.

"You did better than expected, Cinder," said Trigga, patting me on the shoulder. "You come from good stock."

Good stock? Was she referring to my Nordic ancestors? I looked at Freya and saw in her eyes that she was pleased.

Droma was transferred over to Plyvis, the third Valkyrie, who tucked the dozing Predator into the crook of her arm.

"Take her to the healers," said Brunhild, patting the horse's flank. "With all speed."

Nodding, Plyvis shouted, "*Fenri!*" and the horse sprang into the air. I turned away as a cloud of dust billowed around us, then turned back to watch them fly off to the north.

"Welcome to the Proving Grounds, Cindrheim," said Brunhild.

"Thank you," I said, relieved to be on solid ground. I looked around me. We were in a little valley hemmed in on all sides by black volcanic rock that glittered with some type of mineral that I probably learned in school at one point but had forgotten the same day. The tips of each peak were capped with blinding white snow, though some of it was turning to slush in the bright sun and running in tiny rivers down the mountains' steep sides. At the bottom of the valley, on the southern side, was a crystal blue lake. I could see people gliding across the water in ancient-looking canoes, others swimming, and some running around the lake's perimeter.

On the northern side, I noticed a huge wood and metal contraption. *What in the world?* I wondered. Even from where I stood, I could see a man raising and lowering a hammer against one of the wooden posts.

"I see you've spotted the Gauntlet," said Tori, trying to hide a grin. "You'll never hate or love anything more in your life, I can assure you."

"Okay . . ." I murmured.

Next to the Gauntlet was a dense forest, perhaps small when compared to others in the world, but definitely in need of exploring. Right below me were several rows of strangely shaped tents, small at one end and large at the other. It was difficult to tell, but it looked like they were made from animal hides. Very Viking.

"The lake is called The Mirror," said Tori, her features turning serious. She pointed at the large cluster of swaying trees. "And that is the Night Forest. Don't go into either without talking to one of us first."

I nodded, wondering what each held that would prompt the Predator to give me such a stern warning.

There were several other things to look at, and people to watch, but my eyes were continually drawn to the center of the little valley, where I could see a giant log cabin with a pitched roof covered in a thick mat of grass. Large silver banners flapped at each of the four corners. Outside the cabin's opening was a massive fire that flickered inside a wide, metal dish atop a towering wooden pole.

"What building is that?" I asked.

"That is the Long Hall," said Brunhild. "A suitable substitute for the great long halls in Asgard."

"That's new," said Tori, obviously staring at the same thing I was. She looked at Brunhild, who was running her fingers through her horse's curly white mane.

"What has happened since we departed?" Freya asked.

Without looking away from her horse, Brunhild said, "The Allfather has chosen to pay a visit. The Long Hall is his." The Valkyrie tugged on her steed's reins and began to stride across the grassy plain. "Follow quickly. We are late, and Odin does not take tardiness lightly."

Freya suddenly looked sick.

The other Predators looked at each other in obvious surprise, then turned as one to stare at me.

Something strange was going on. I could feel it. I hadn't known the Predators for very long, but I felt that I knew them enough to know when they were freaked out. And if Freya and her Amazing Sisters-in-Combat were freaked out, I *definitely* had a right to be freaked out. It had something to do with what Brunhild had said.

Something about Odin.

If there was one thing I'd learned since hooking up with Freya and company, it was to keep my trap shut till someone provided an explanation. Brunhild was moving away, gesturing for us to follow. Biting my lip in anticipation, I trotted after her.

Along the way we passed people of all ages, most of them male, each of them staring first at the Valkyries, then at me. By the time we'd passed through the first row of Viking tents, I was feeling like the main attraction at a carnival.

"Why is everyone looking at me?" I mumbled. "Is my zipper down?"

"What is a zipper?" said Brunhild.

"Mortals use them to fasten their clothes together," stated Trigga, dipping her aviator glasses. "I'm thinking of acquiring an article of clothing that requires this . . . *zipper*."

I couldn't help but smile. Trigga, and possibly all the Predators (besides Freya), wanted to live in both worlds at the same time. Brunhild and Freya were obviously resisting the powerful influence. *Resist it as long as you can*, I thought.

Most of the people I saw appeared to be in their twen-
ties, though it was difficult to tell. Every once in a while,
I spotted someone who looked like they might've been my
age, or others that looked like they were a step away from
the grave. The old folk shuffled around with scrolls tucked
under their arms, shouting at anyone younger than they
were, which was pretty much everyone. No one seemed
to pay them any mind. Everyone else seemed to be in top
physical condition. Some of the boys and men wore board
shorts with tank tops or no shirts at all. Expensive-looking
running shoes completed their outfits. Their hair was
stylishly messy, like they moonlighted as members in a
grunge band, and all were tanned and corded with muscle.
Everyone was in constant motion; running, leaping,
bending, spinning, or stretching, and all the while laughing
and poking fun at one another.

But some of them obviously felt like Brunhild and the
Predators, choosing instead to stay true to their Viking
heritage. These dressed in heavy fur boots, leather pants
and shirts, studded belts and steel bracelets that covered
their entire forearms. They wore their hair long, fanned
out over their broad shoulders or tied back in ponytails.
No laughter came from this group—just grunts and growls.

Here and there, I noticed a female. They were sorely
outnumbered, though. If I had wondered before about the
absence of boys, I didn't need to wonder any longer. Boys
were everywhere.

Like the males, the girls seemed split in their choice of
attire. Some wore fancy Lycra shorts and tops, name-brand

running shoes, and colorful ribbons in their salon-styled hair. Others mirrored their male Viking counterparts, decked out in knee-high fur boots, leather pants, and shirts and shiny armbands.

It wasn't hard to see that the two groups wanted to remain separate, eyeing one another as if they were enemies. I couldn't help but feel like I was back at Copperpenny Middle.

"Who are all these people?" I asked.

"Soldiers in training," said Brunhild.

My heart skipped a beat. Soldiers meant armies and armies meant war. "Training for what?"

"For the Great Battle at the end of the long, dark winter," replied the Valkyrie. I was reminded of what Nancy, my foster parent, said when I asked her why they couldn't adopt me.

"Ragnarök," added Trigga.

I promised myself I would do some serious research on this winter-ending great battle.

"Everyone you see," said Brunhild, "is part of Odin's Army, or *will* be when they have proved their worth. Not all make the cut."

"What happens if they don't make the cut?" I asked. *Please don't say they lose their head,* I thought.

"They are sent home. Shame is then their lifelong companion."

"Ouch," I said softly.

"There is no greater honor than to be part of Odin's Army," said Trigga. "And no greater sorrow than to be kept from it."

And here I was worried about not graduating from middle school.

As we walked, I scanned the valley. To the east of the lake I could see row upon row of soldiers in formation, lunging with spears, twirling quarter staffs, chopping with axes or swords, all the while chanting Nordic war cries in perfect unison. With a start, I realized that some of them were as young as eight years old. It was all very impressive, but it sent icy fingers up my spine.

"Some of them are just children," I said.

Brunhild nodded. "Like the Spartans in Midgard, select candidates are chosen at a very young age. It is their destiny to fight the final enemy or die in the effort. Not even Odin knows when Ragnarök will commence, but he senses it is close." The Valkyrie used her spear to point. "Those children you see might be in their forties when the Great Battle begins."

Or they might be eight, I thought, cringing at the thought of a child running into battle for a being he or she will more than likely never meet.

"How are they chosen?" I asked.

"Most have at least one parent that is a god," said Brunhild, "which means they are born with superior strength or speed or intelligence—sometimes all three. Those that have no godly parentage come from magical races, like elves or dwarves. This heritage typically results in heightened attributes and talents that Allfather can use on the battlefield."

Is this what gods do? I wondered. *Use everyone around them to fight their battles? How many families had lost a son or daughter to Odin's Army?*

What in the world am I doing here? I suddenly felt like hijacking one of the Valkryies' winged horses and flying back to America. Even if it meant I had to turn my stomach inside out ten times over.

I fell back so that I was walking with Tori. "Seriously, why am I here?"

The Predator was staring apprehensively at the Long Hall. It was drawing closer and closer. "I doubt even Brunhild knows, Cinder. But whatever it is, you've managed to stir up quite a fuss."

Staring at my sneakers as I walked, I said, "Yeah, I'm good at that."

The Ultimate Man Cave

The Long Hall had to be some sort of magic cabin. From where I was standing, it looked fairly spacious, but when I walked in, I saw that it was at least three times as big as it looked from the outside. You could hold an NFL football game inside here, the crowd included.

The first thing I noticed was the large flat squares of polished marble that had been laid down over the grass. My worn sneakers squeaked loudly as I walked across the floor, but luckily there seemed to be no one in the Long Hall but our small party.

Hanging from the walls were large animal skins—some of them I recognized, but others had me wondering. One was covered in dark red fur and had six legs, and another had a scaly green tail with blood-covered spikes on the end. Huge iron cauldrons spaced every twenty feet or so crackled with a bluish-white fire. The reflections of the flames danced across a vaulted ceiling that dripped with silver streamers and sparkling white lights. We made our way between rows of heavy wooden tables, each set with silver plates and unlit candles.

"You could throw one heck of a wedding reception here," I said in awe, trying desperately to quiet my squeaking feet. "Minus the freaky-looking animal pelts."

I looked over at Freya. I had never seen her look so terrified. In fact, I had *never* seen her look terrified. Not even when she was facing the wyrm or fighting the horde of grints. What had gotten into her? Her turquoise eyes were darting around the Long Hall as if something were about to leap out at her.

Was it our meeting with Odin that was causing this?

Brunhild led us across the wide space, the *click-tap*, *click-tap* of her boots sounding a lot more dignified than my Chuck Taylors. When we reached the back wall, we found two more Valkyries standing guard, their hands gripping golden spears, their expressions grim. They nodded at Brunhild and stepped to the side. As they did so, a doorway opened up in the wall.

"Tori, Edda, wait here," said Brunhild. "Freya, you will accompany us."

I heard Freya swallow.

My heart started to somersault inside my chest. If Freya had a right to be scared, I should've fainted long ago.

"Enter," said Brunhild.

We quickly filed into the adjoining room, and I gasped. The first thing that hit me was the music. Elvis Presley was belting out "Blue Suede Shoes," his smooth velvety voice echoing from a brightly lit jukebox in the far corner of a room that was much smaller than the room we'd just left.

My fear turned to confusion. The walls were covered with posters of famous athletes. Thanks to Carl, I was a self-proclaimed expert on sports figures way before my time. I saw Wayne Gretzky, Michael Jordan, Babe Ruth,

Joe Montana, and a hundred others whose talents had immortalized them forever. Female athletes seemed to be conspicuously missing from the collection.

I shook my head in disbelief. Why would a god care about mortal sports? I looked down. My sneakers were lost in lime green shag carpet. Off to my right was a glossy oak pool table with thick gold tassels hanging from each pocket. There was also Ping-Pong, air hockey, and foosball, all of them separated by overstuffed La-Z-Boys. Next to one of the recliners was a soda dispenser that looked like it had thirty different flavors, and next to that was a huge popcorn machine. I could hear the kernels popping in time to the beat of "Blue Suede Shoes." The buttery smell had my stomach growling.

This is a guy's dream, I thought. Odin's a guy, but this *couldn't* be for him. I looked at Freya. Was she actually sweating?

Directly in front of us was a raised platform with a worn leather recliner.

"Allfather?" said Brunhild, gesturing for us to fan out in front of the platform.

"Be right with you." The deep voice seemed to be coming from somewhere near the back of the platform.

A moment later a bearded man wearing baggy cargo pants and an oversized Los Angeles Chargers jersey popped up from behind the recliner. He had a ratchet in one hand and a screwdriver in the other. Long gray hair streamed from under a faded Dodgers cap, and a battered patch covered his left eye.

My jaw dropped. No way.

Freya dropped to one knee, her head bowed. She yanked on the hem of my sweatshirt, pulling me down with her.

He smiled warmly at Brunhild, and said, "Hello, my flower." Frowning, he jerked a thumb at me. "Is this she?"

"Allfather, I present to you Cindrheim Vustora Moss. Accompanying her is Freya, the Valhuri that led the protection and retrieval mission."

Freya's skin flushed pink, but the man ignored her. Instead, he turned to look at me, his one frigid blue eye far more piercing than anything I'd experienced so far. I wanted to shrink away from his gaze, curl up into a little ball, but I knew that wouldn't do any good. He seemed as old as the stars and as young as me, all at the same time.

"You decided to show up, huh?" he said, plopping down in the recliner. He rubbed his hands on his pants, staining them with black grease. "Both of you stand up."

Freya and I jumped to our feet. It felt like I'd stuffed a spoonful of peanut butter in my mouth. "I . . . uh . . . came as quickly as I could, sir," I said.

Brunhild looked at me, frowning. "Cindrheim, I would like you to meet the Allfather, or Odin, if you follow the Eddas of Norse history."

Odin. The Norse god of all gods. The Big Kahuna, the Top Dog. Dressed in a football jersey and a Dodgers cap and his hands filthy from working on his La-Z-Boy. Why not?

What do you say to a god? I wondered. "Nice to meet you, sir," I said. And what was with the eye patch? Was the most powerful god in the universe unable to magic up a proper eye?

Odin pulled down on the wooden arm on the side of the recliner and the footrest popped out. "Are you surprised?" he asked, propping up his dusty boots.

Then I did what any mortal would do when confronted with an all-knowing god. I tried to hide what he already knew. "Surprised? Surprised at what?"

Odin tugged at the brim of his baseball cap. "Surprised that I'm dressed like your next-door neighbor."

It was time to drop the act. "Yeah, you're not . . . what I expected."

Brunhild drew in her breath, and I could hear Freya slowly dying inside.

"And what did you expect?" said Odin.

I looked around, hoping someone else would chime in. When no one offered anything, I said, "Well, I don't know . . . someone less . . ."

Odin leaned forward in his recliner. His eye glittered. "Less *what?*"

"Less . . . casual?" I braced.

Odin stood up. He was right. He *did* look like my neighbor. "A little too casual, huh?"

My heart froze in my chest. "No, I didn't mean that you *shouldn't* be casual, only that I hadn't *expected* you to be so casual. You don't have—"

"You're extremely particular," Odin said, sweeping his arm in front of him. A very bright light flashed in front of my eyes, momentarily blinding me. When my vision cleared,

I saw that Odin had changed. Now he was decked out in an expensive looking navy blue suit with stylish pin-striping, complete with a baby blue flower in the lapel. The Dodgers cap was gone, his silver hair now gathered into a topknot. His ruddy face was cleanly shaven. He still wore the eye patch, but it was a navy blue fabric that matched his suit.

Odin buttoned his jacket. "You prefer a god who is formal, I see."

"Wow," I breathed. I noticed that the music had changed as well. Elvis had left the building, and something from Mozart was now filling the air. The La-Z-Boys, popcorn machine, foosball table, shag carpet, and sports posters were gone, replaced by sleek-looking steel and black leather furniture, a cappuccino machine, chess boards, and fine works of art.

Odin adjusted the knot of his silver tie. "How's this?"

"Uh . . . definitely formal. If you—"

Freya kicked me. "It's perfect, sir," I said, throwing the Predator a dark look.

Odin pointed a mocking finger at me. "I can see you're still not satisfied. We can't have our potential *hero* not satisfied, can we?"

He's playing with me, I thought. *I leave my home, risk my life facing horrible monsters, travel halfway around the world, and he wants to be a jerk?* I felt humiliated. "I didn't come here to be—"

Freya kicked me again.

Odin flicked his hand and the light flashed in front of my face for a second time. What I saw made me stagger backwards. He now stood over nine feet tall, and he was as thick as a redwood tree. He was so heavily muscled it looked like someone had draped skin over a bunch of boulders. A raven sat on each shoulder, their beady black eyes scanning the room. The Wall Street look had vanished, replaced by a blue robe flecked with white. When he moved, it looked like actual clouds were drifting across the shimmering material. On his feet were the largest pair of sandals I'd ever seen, and each of his massive forearms was wrapped in steel. A shiny silver helmet with gold eagle wings, swept back as if in flight, sat on his head. His silver hair was fanned out across his broad shoulders, and his full beard was tucked into a wide leather belt. In the crook of his arm was a huge spear. The eye patch was missing, which was really unfortunate, because now I could see an empty eye socket. I was grossed out and impressed all at once.

Now *here* was a Viking god.

"It is not always easy to maintain the image your world expects," said Odin. His voice now matched his physique, powerful and commanding. It shook me to my core. "Mortals are allowed to change, yet we cannot. Doesn't seem fair, does it?" The god smiled through his bushy beard. "Where was foosball and popcorn six thousand years ago, huh? You don't fault a god for a few simple Midgardian pleasures, do you, girl?"

My intimidation evaporated. "I have a name."

Freya's head drooped. Brunhild cursed under her breath.

I could see that the old recliner was gone. A huge wooden throne, adorned with rubies and sapphires, now stood in its place. Odin eased his massive frame into the chair and laughed. "You do indeed, and yet you haven't earned the right to be called by that name." He whistled and two monstrous hunting dogs, their shaggy gray fur brushed to a fine sheen, padded slowly around the raised platform. They took their place at the god's feet, staring at me with large yellow eyes.

Odin gestured at the dogs. "This is Geri and Freki. They were three hundred years old before they earned the right to have names." Odin then pointed at the birds sitting on his shoulders. "Same with Hugin and Munin." The ravens cawed.

"What do you mean I have to earn my name?"

Brunhild's grip on my arm tightened, but I didn't want her to know it hurt so I held my tongue. "Do not assume the Allfather will answer your petty questions, child," she said.

Odin nodded. "If she has the courage to ask, I will answer her. Your grandmother bore the name Cindrheim Vustora, a name we hold in reverence."

So, it was true. Someone in my past meant something to someone. To a god no less.

I felt a sudden all-consuming need to tie myself to my ancestor. "I want to live up to my name—not for your sake, or anyone else's in here, but for my grandmother's sake."

The Valkyrie still hadn't released my arm. Her grip tightened so that I had to bite my lip to keep from crying out. "Please," I said, forcing myself to be polite. "Tell me why I'm here."

Odin reached down with both hands and rubbed his hounds between their ears. He smiled, but it wasn't too friendly. "I can move mountains with a wave of my hand, or divide the seas with a thought, and yet I find myself bound by an ancient prophecy that will determine my very existence. Regrettably, girl, you are part of that prophecy, and now that I've met you, I wonder if I should start making my own funeral arrangements."

So much for first impressions.

CHAPTER 11

Big-Time Oracle, Small-Time Digs

So Odin and I didn't get off to a great start. Big surprise. I mean, I'm used to it, though this *was* the first time it had happened with someone who ruled the universe. Before I could ask about the prophecy, Odin made a shooing motion with his hand. Apparently, he was done with me.

I stepped forward and said, "You can't just bring me in here and—"

Brunhild clapped a hand over my mouth, then turned me around and frog-hopped me from her father's private quarters. Before the magical door closed behind me, I heard the melancholy lyrics of "Love Me Tender" suddenly kick in.

When we were clear of the Long Hall, Brunhild spun me around. "You are a very impertinent young lady."

"Have you completely lost your senses?" cried Freya, bearing down on me.

How many times had I been in this situation before? Everyone around me, angrily questioning me. It only gets me more ticked off. "I'm sorry! He's a big, egotistical, rude bully."

Brunhild's jaw dropped. In the blink of an eye, her gloved hand was raised, ready to strike me. I tried not to turn away, but I knew the blow would bury me ten feet underground. "How dare you," she said, her raised hand trembling. "You obviously have no idea who the Allfather is."

"I know who he is. He's the god of all gods. The supreme ruler and all that." I looked down at my sneakers, some of my fury draining away. "It's just that . . . I thought he'd be . . ."

"Kinder?" said Brunhild, lowering her arm, but still rigid with anger.

I nodded.

"He is a god, Cindrheim. Your concept of kindness has no meaning for him." Brunhild looked away. "And you cannot possibly conceive of the things he has passed through, nor what he will be asked to endure in the coming years."

"So he's stressed out," I said. "We all are. Why does he have to take it out on me?"

Everyone stared at me. I wasn't getting a good vibe. Even Tori looked like she wanted to wring my neck, and she hadn't even witnessed my epic fail. I had had enough. "I just want to go see Droma," I said, "then take a really long nap."

"You will see Droma," assured Brunhild, "but it will be quite some time before your stubborn head hits a pillow."

&

Our visit to see Droma was brief and to the point. Brunhild led us to the Healing House, a long, flat-roofed building, complete with a waiting room and a clipboard for visitors to sign. We were allowed to visit Droma one at a time. I was the last to see her. Most of her body was still bruised and swollen, and the parts I couldn't see were wrapped in white bandages, but I knew she was recovering because she smiled when I squeezed her hand.

I sighed in relief. "We need you to get better."

"I will," she said. Then she grinned and murmured, "I heard you hit it off better with the sea serpent than you did with Odin."

I laughed, though she was closer to the truth than she realized.

We talked for a while, which was nice because she was able to explain why Odin was one eye short of a complete set. Apparently, the Supreme God of Everything had dug out his eye himself with his own dagger in exchange for vast amounts of knowledge and wisdom. His eye now belonged to a god named Mimir, who makes Albert Einstein and Stephen Hawking look like grade-school dropouts. Call me rude, but I'm thinking if all the knowledge and wisdom in the cosmos led Odin to fixing La-Z-Boy armchairs, Mimir got the better part of the deal.

"Fun fact," added Droma, her eyes half-lidded. "Mimir is actually Odin's uncle, on his mother's side."

Hearing that made me think two things. First: ew. Second, I supposedly had an uncle, and as far as I knew, he never tried to strike a deal with me that would require me to give up a body part. I thought about the crumpled photo Carl had given me and wished for a billionth time that I had at least one blood-related relative that kept in contact.

Droma looked really sleepy, so after saying goodbye, I made my way back to the waiting room. Everyone was gone. "Where'd everyone go?" I said, spinning around. Standing before me was a short, plump woman in a long green robe who looked more toad than human. Grunting something about mortals, she grabbed my hand.

"My name is Clora," she said. "Come with me."

I started to panic. "Where're we going?"

"You are heavy with grint poison," said the woman. She glanced back at me. "You want to shrivel up and die?"

"No."

"Then you come with me."

I had forgotten that I had been infected earlier that week. My head *was* starting to hurt, as if a grade A fever was coming on. Was this how it started? A headache, then I shrivel up and die?

I quickened my pace.

My stay at the Healing House was over in ten minutes. The green-robed woman made a tiny cut in the crook of my arm, then pressed a series of rough leaves against the wound. The entire time she worked on me, she sang a very bizarre song that may or may not have had anything to do with the healing. By the time her song was over, though, my headache was fading.

"Thanks," I said, jumping down from the table. "I'm not sure how I'm supposed to pay you, though."

"Your debt will be paid through your training," said Clora grimly. There was a tiny hint of a smile on her wrinkled face, like she'd just snatched a fly out of the air with her tongue.

I wasn't sure what she meant, but it definitely sounded worse than whipping out a credit card. "Okay," I said. "Do you know where my friends are?"

"Your friends?" asked Clora.

"Freya, and the other Predators. They came in with me."

"Oh, them. Each was led to a different room. Nasty wounds they had." The woman narrowed her beady eyes. "You call them friends. Very curious."

"Why is it curious?"

"The Valhuri," said the healer, "typically don't have . . . friends." Before I could respond, she grabbed my hand and turned it over. "Did you receive this from the norn when you made your vow?"

I groaned, remembering the moment Skuld had left his mark on me.

"With Eir's power, I can remove scars, you know. Even pledge scars."

"No," I said, withdrawing my hand from her grasp. "Thank you, but no."

"Very well. Till next time, then."

My heart skipped a beat. "Next time?"

The strange smile flashed across her face again. "Why yes, child. You and I are going to become very well acquainted. Healers and new recruits always do."

⚭

When I left the Healing House, I wasn't overly thrilled to see Brunhild waiting for me. "Come with me," she said.

I could tell she was still sore at me for calling her dad an egotistical, rude bully.

"I hope you're taking me to dinner. I'm starving."

"There will be time to eat, but that time is not now." Her long strides were carrying her across the grass so quickly I had to run to keep up. The Valkyrie led me through the middle of a basketball game where the happy, cool-looking Vikings were playing against the gruff, traditional-looking Vikings. A boy wearing black and silver Nikes, camouflage shorts, and a tank top executed a two-handed dunk that involved a full front flip. When he landed, he pointed a finger at the opposing team and hooted triumphantly. One of the boys, dressed not unlike Odin, grabbed the ball, whipped out a curved dagger, and slashed it open like a melon. Boos erupted.

"What happened to training for the Great Battle?" I asked.

"Even soldiers need to let off a little steam now and then," replied Brunhild. "Plus, Allfather likes them to compete so that he can make bets on who he thinks will win. A habit he picked up in Midgard."

"I see they practice good sportsmanship here at Camp Wanna-be-a-Viking," I said, craning my neck to see if the other boy would retaliate after the ball had been sliced open. I was a bit startled to see that every one of them was staring at me. I quickly turned away.

"There are passions, talents, and tempers here at the Proving Grounds that you may never comprehend."

Just when I thought my anger was buried deep, Brunhild had to go and dig it up. "I might surprise you, you know?"

Without looking back at me, the Valkyrie said, "I sincerely hope so."

At the far end of the valley, nestled between a stand of towering oak trees, was a small log cabin with a little wraparound porch and a stone chimney. The chimney was belching gray puffs of smoke. It looked like a cozy place to stay for a night or two, except for the fact that it had no windows. Standing in front of the door was a . . .

"Stop gawking, Cindrheim," said Brunhild. "It is a dwarf."

"Sorry, never seen one before."

The dwarf was shorter than I was, but what he lacked in height he made up for in muscle. What little I could see of his face was covered in Nordic runes and was mostly hidden behind a blue-dyed beard whose braided tip reached all the way to the porch. Small, dark eyes glittered like black gems, and his huge nose bore a giant silver ring with a chain that for some reason connected to his right ear. His gnarled hands, which were far too big for the rest of his body, rested on the pommel of a huge war hammer. Spraypainted on his gleaming mail shirt was a big happy face with an ax stuck in the side.

"M'lady," grunted the dwarf.

"The girl is to be allowed inside," said Brunhild. "And only her."

The dwarf nodded. "Yes, m'lady."

Brunhild looked down at me. "It is time you learn of the prophecy spoken of by the Allfather. Do your best to take it seriously." The Valkyrie suddenly looked tired.

"Cindrheim, you have a gift for provoking people. Do not provoke the seer." I nodded, wondering if my tombstone would someday read: *Here lies Cindrheim Vustora Moss. She tried not to misbehave, but greatly provoked a lot of people along the way.*

"When the seer is finished with you," said Brunhild, "knock on the door, and the dwarf will let you out."

"Okay," I said. Brunhild gave me one last warning glance, then strode away. The dwarf stepped aside, eyeing me as if he'd never seen a human before. He fumbled with a series of locks, then opened the door just wide enough for me to squeeze through.

"You really the one?" he said. His voice sounded like his throat was filled with rocks.

"I'm sorry," I said, "I don't know what you're talking about."

"Never mind," grunted the dwarf, pushing the door open.

I stepped over the threshold. As soon as I was inside, the door snapped shut and I heard at least half a dozen locks reengage.

There wasn't much to look at. The cottage was roughly the size of my living room at home. Next to the door was a plain wooden table with a single chair. An oil-burning lamp sat on the table, casting the room in a soft, buttery glow. A few soot-covered logs were smoldering in a little fireplace set in the wall. Against the opposite wall was a cot with a few blankets and a flat pillow. On the back wall was a floor-to-ceiling shelf that held at least three hundred books.

Sitting cross-legged on the bed was a small boy. He was reading a book nearly as large as he was.

"Hi," I said, startled to see someone so young. Instinctively, I said, "Is your . . . mother or father here?"

The boy cocked his head to the side, then smiled sadly. "If they are, someone has been playing a very cruel joke on me."

My jaw dropped. He *looked* like a child, *sounded* like a child, but he definitely didn't *talk* like a child. "How . . . old are you?"

The boy set the book down, then swung his legs over the edge of the cot. He was skinny and pale-skinned, with wispy blond hair, large expressive gray eyes, ruby red lips, and a pointed chin. "I stopped counting after four hundred," he said.

"Four hundred . . . *years?*"

"That is correct."

"Are *you* . . . the seer?"

"I am. My name is Saemund." He stood up to his full height, making him about level with my shoulders. "Wonderful titles they give me. Seer, prophet, visionary, oracle." There was a hint of mischief in his tone. "My favorite is prognosticator."

I worked hard to wrap my mind around this. I pointed at the door. "How often do you get out?"

"Get out?" said Saemund, smirking. "The only blue skies I ever see are when someone slips inside to have their future explained and I am able to catch a glimpse through the door."

My jaw dropped again. "You haven't been outside . . . in four hundred years?"

"No," said the seer, then he held up one tiny finger. "Unless you count the time in the spring of 1709 when my guard was passing me my food and left the door open while he stared at a flock of dragons passing overhead. I was able to stick my head out while he was distracted. Does that count?"

I felt too sorry for him to focus on the idea of dragons flying over Iceland. "No, it doesn't. How can they do this to you?"

"It is not so awful." The seer pointed at his collection of books. "Every year, I am allowed to make one request. I always ask for a book, though one year I felt a warmer blanket was in order."

"What about getting outside once a year?"

"Too dangerous. Books are safe, you see. With a story, I can travel wherever I want, see what I want, and end my adventure whenever I choose."

"Books are great," I admitted, "but they're not the same . . ."

Saemund walked to the table and took a seat. "Everyone has a calling in life. Mine is to warn the world's inhabitants—and the gods—of their impending doom."

"But they can't *force* you to do this . . . can they?"

Saemund pointed at my hand. "You made a vow, did you not?" I nodded. The seer flipped his small hand over and I saw a tiny white scar across his knuckles. "I made the very same pledge, though I was four at the time."

"I don't understand. Why can't you go outside?"

"I am the only seer alive, child. According to some, I am much too valuable."

"So this is all for your protection."

"Precisely."

"You can't even have windows?"

"A stray arrow, or even worse, a stray bolt of lightning, could end my life, right?"

"That's ridiculous."

Saemund put his chin in his hand and stared at the tiny flame flickering in the lamp's glass globe. "There are times I feel the same way." Before I could lay down any plans for escape, he said, "So . . . ready to hear how you fit into the scheme of things?"

CHAPTER 12

PROPHECIES BEFORE DINNER

Saemund insisted I take his chair at the table. Once I was seated, he moved across the room, got down on his hands and knees, and dragged a large wooden box from beneath his cot. Throwing back the lid, he began to withdraw a series of tightly rolled scrolls, each one more ancient looking than the last.

"Ah, here it is," he said at last, climbing to his feet with some difficulty. It was strange watching someone who looked like they were in kindergarten moving as if they were in their eighties. He unraveled the scroll as he approached me. My throat and chest tightened. "This one came to me just as I finished breakfast, nearly a hundred years ago."

"Does it involve Odin?" I asked.

Saemund placed the scroll down on the table beneath the lamp's glow, tucking one end under the lamp and the other beneath a heavy mug of water. "I cannot say," he said.

"You *can't* or you *won't*?"

Saemund's smile was *way* too mischievous.

Have to admit, I was more than a little frightened to read my Nordic fortune, so I went for the classic stall tactic. "So . . . you receive these prophecies often?"

"They are rarer than one would think," replied Saemund. "In fact, of the billions of humans and non-humans alike, only a small handful ever see themselves pop up in an honest-to-goodness prophecy."

I swallowed. "I feel so special."

"And so you should," said Saemund, apparently missing my sarcasm. He pointed at the scroll and said, "Now go on, child. No sense putting this off."

Nodding, I took a deep, steadying breath and stared at the scroll. The prophecy was broken up into four pairs of sentences, the top line written in ancient Nordic, the line under it written in English.

"The prophecy has been translated from the original language I uttered that morning ninety-seven years ago," said the seer.

I frowned again, more than a little skeptical. "I don't speak that language. How do I know what's written in English is actually translated correctly?"

"How do you know what was written in the ancient language was *spoken* correctly? It is all a game, child, and you have been asked to participate. Like a game of checkers, you can push the board away and tell me you do not wish to play. Or you can survey the location of each piece, plan your moves carefully, and aim to win."

Amazed at the wisdom coming from someone who looked like they still had their baby teeth, I nodded again and began to read out loud.

"Born at the crux of the world's spine,
windows of gold, daughter of nine.
Darkness falls before its climb,
winter ends before its time."

When I was finished, I looked at Saemund. "This is supposed to be about me?"

The seer nodded. "Undoubtedly."

"Well, I have doubts. *Lots* of doubts."

"I would be surprised if you did not."

I looked back at the scroll. "Mind if I break this down?"

"My afternoon is free," said Saemund.

"Right away, the last line stands out to me . . . 'winter ends before it's time.'" I looked at the seer. "The day we met, Brunhild mentioned the long, dark winter. Trigga said she was talking about Ragnarök."

"Sounds reasonable," said Saemund.

"Sounds reasonable?"

"Anything is possible."

"And even weirder, Nancy, my foster parent, once told me something about the sun coming out after a long, dark winter . . . "

"Some people cannot stand the cold."

"I guess we'll move on," I said, frowning. I looked back at the scroll. "Born at the crux of the world's spine . . . " I murmured. "Not sure where the world's spine is and I'll definitely need to google the word *crux*, but I was born in Richmond, Virginia, so . . . "

When the seer didn't respond, I looked at him. "Any thoughts?"

"On Google?"

"On the first line of the prophecy."

"My role is to deliver the divination, not interpret it."

Part of me wanted to say, *How rude!* But coming from Saemund it bordered on adorable. "I thought you agreed to break this down?"

"You asked if *you* could break it down. Had you used the pronoun *we*, I would have politely declined."

"So, this is something I have to figure out on my own . . ."

"Are you sure it *needs* to be figured out?"

I stabbed the scroll with my finger. "This is apparently talking about *me*. About *my* life. What *I'm* supposed to do. *Who I am*. Of *course* it needs to be figured out."

Saemund studied me for several seconds. "How do you know the sun will rise in the morning, Cinder?"

"What . . . ? Because it rises *every* morning."

"You know it rose today because it already happened. But how do you know it will rise tomorrow if it has not happened yet?"

"I don't think about it. It just happens."

"Allow me to rephrase the question: How do you know it will *not* rise tomorrow?"

So much for adorable. I could actually *feel* my blank stare.

"Are you a scientist?" he pressed. "Or a seer? Do you have proof that the sun will rise?"

"No . . . no, I don't," I said, my frustration growing. "What does this have to do with my prophecy?"

"It has *everything* to do with your prophecy, child," replied Saemund.

I looked back down at the scroll and silently reread the words several times. I had hoped the repetition would spark some inspiration, but no light bulbs. I closed my eyes, knowing Saemund would wait patiently while I let the words of the prophecy sink in. Then it hit me. I needed to let *his* words sink in.

I opened my eyes and looked at the seer. "Faith," I said softly.

A tiny smile curled the corners of Saemund's mouth. He nodded.

"I have *faith* the sun will rise tomorrow. Nothing else."

"And it is enough," said the seer.

"But I don't have faith in this prophecy," I said, pointing at the scroll.

"I would be surprised if you did. You read it for the first time five minutes ago. Give it time to settle."

"But what if I don't *have* time?"

"The prediction will unfold whether or not you believe in it."

I reached up and rubbed my face. "So, in the meantime, I can't hope for any clarification?"

"If it is clarification you seek, Cinder, such enlighten-ment may come in unexpected ways, at unexpected times. But do not spend too much of your time speculating on the rising of the sun."

I nodded. "Just wish I had a little more to go on."

"There is something else," said Saemund. He returned to his trunk, withdrew a second scroll, and brought it to the table. When he unrolled it, I saw that it was actually multiple scrolls rolled into one. The first one was a rough sketch of a baby's face.

"Is this supposed to be . . . me?" I asked.

"Undoubtedly," said the seer.

I flipped to the next piece of parchment and found what looked like a sketch of a one-year-old toddler. "Me again?"

Saemund nodded. "So cute," he said, smiling.

I began shuffling through the scrolls, watching as the sketches depicted me as I grew older and older. The last one was an image of me as a current twelve-year-old. A bit on the angsty side but fairly accurate. Was this the same sketch Freya had been referring to that day in the forest outside of Richmond? I looked at Saemund. "Did you draw these?"

"Valhalla no," said the seer. "That is the work of Bragi, God of Art, Media, and Entertainment. I described what I saw in my visions; he drew."

"You had *visions* of me? Why didn't you start with this!"

"The images were for *my* benefit, not yours."

I took another deep, steadying breath. "Is this another rising sun thing?"

"Perhaps. Perhaps not. I showed you the sketches not to prove the prophecy speaks of you, but rather to prove that your faith will be required to believe you are the one spoken of."

"Sorry," I said, sifting through the sketches again, "but seeing is believing. Holding proof in my hands is the evidence I needed."

Saemund shook his head. "You will see in time that such is not true."

"You're blowing my mind, Saemund," I said, rolling the scrolls up. I handed them back to the seer. "Did you receive these visions all at once?"

"No. They came to me once a year, always in April."

"My birthday is in April . . . "

"I suspected as much." He wrapped the prophecy scroll around the sketches, returned them to his trunk, then came back to stand beside me. "Most people believe to *see* or *hear* or *touch* something is the most powerful form of evidence. Not true. What you *feel inside* is more powerful than all three combined. In the end, it is the only true witness." The seer winked at me. "Never forget that, Cinder."

I sighed. "What I *feel inside* would never hold up in court."

"The evidence you seek will never be presented in court."

I stared at the small lamp on the table, watched the flame flicker and dance. "Odin mentioned my grandmother." I turned and looked at Saemund. "Did you know her?"

"And I still do," replied the seer, smiling.

My heart leapt up into my throat. I had assumed she had already passed. "She's still alive?"

"Last I checked."

I gripped his little arms, probably a bit too hard because he let out a tiny squeak. "Is she here? At the Proving Grounds?"

"She could be, I guess. Though I doubt it. Her responsibilities keep her very busy."

"Busy doing what?" I asked breathlessly.

"She is one of the Valhuri."

"My grandma's a *Predator* . . . ?"

Saemund nodded. "One of the greatest to ever hold the title, though you would never hear it from her."

"Can I meet her?"

The seer's smile faded. "I am afraid I do not have the authority to call for her, Cinder. She comes when she wants or when she has business . . . "

While I was excited to hear of her existence, I now felt like I might never meet her. Fat chance Odin would allow me to set up a meet-and-greet. I released his arms.

"You know, Cinder, when you do not have much to look at day after day, you tend to focus on the things you *do* see. I will never forget your grandmother's eyes. If I live for four hundred more years, I will not forget." Saemund pointed at me. "You have those same eyes, and judging by the rumors that have already come my way, her fiery spirit. Make no mistake, child, if you are anything like your grandmother, you possess what is required to see this through."

I rubbed the long scab across the back of my hand. The symbol of my commitment. I had been backed into a corner many times in my life, but never like this. Could you run from a prophecy? It seemed there was no escape. At least I didn't know of a way just yet.

"What do I do now?" I asked.

"You train."

"For the Great Battle?"

"You may yet play a part in the war that will end the long winter, but I think your role is unique from that of a soldier. I believe you will be given a good-fashioned quest, like the heroes of old."

"Is that a prophecy or just a guess?"

Saemund smiled at me, touched my arm with his little hand. "Just train, Cinder. Make your grandmother proud."

Standing up, I said, "I'm ready to go."

Saemund followed me to the door, his tiny body close to mine, as if he hoped we would get stuck.

♠

Brunhild was there to meet me the moment I left the seer's cottage. I was still angry over his imprisonment, but too shocked about what I'd just learned to say or do anything about it. I followed behind the Valkyrie like a lost puppy dog.

"I know you have many questions," said Brunhild. "I can feel it in your stunned silence."

"You have no idea."

"A fair observation," Brunhild admitted, her voice softening a tiny bit.

I was suddenly feeling very surly. "Let me guess, you're leading me to the edge of the world where I'll need to overcome the evils of the universe."

"You must be trained before you do such a thing."

"You sound like Saemund," I said. The sun had set below the darkening purple peaks that surrounded us, casting the valley in deep shadows. We skirted the southern half of the lake, then passed between the oddly shaped tents that were glowing from within.

"Where are we going, then?"

"You told me earlier that you hoped I was taking you to dinner. Well, now I am."

My stomach was growling too powerfully to refuse out of pure stubbornness.

Without turning, the Valkyrie said, "I think you will be pleased."

Brunhild led me towards Odin's Long Hall. Even though I was ravenous with hunger, I wasn't too thrilled to see that we would be dining with the God of Grumpiness.

"We're eating with your dad?"

"Believe me," said the Valkyrie, "you will be glad you did. There is no better spread in all of Iceland. Perhaps in all of Midgard." It looked like she winked at me. "And the entertainment is to *die* for."

"Dinner and a show, huh? Don't get *that* very often." As we got closer, I began to hear a strange mixture of stringed instruments, punctuated by laughter and loud shouting.

"Is it a party?" I asked, glancing down at my clothes.

"It is the *Plougheim il Farthen*," said Brunhild, "or the End of Battle Festival."

My heart leaped into my throat. "There was a battle?"

"Yes," the Valkyrie said, "about fifteen hundred years ago."

I relaxed a little bit. "And you're just now getting around to celebrating the end of it? Talk about anticlimatic."

"It was a great battle, one of the largest Midgard has ever known. We honor the valiant who fell during that time, one night every year. You should count yourself fortunate that you are here during such an occasion. In fact, no mortal can view the feast without express permission from the Allfather." Brunhild frowned at me. "Or *my dad* as you called him."

As we walked across the flattened grass that led to the Long Hall, the most delicious smells smacked me in the face. I felt my mouth water. "Wow, too bad those dead guys aren't here to enjoy the good times."

Even in the semi-darkness, I could see the Valkyrie turn and grin at me.

As soon as the hulking warriors guarding the Long Hall's door nodded us through, I found myself unable to move.

The huge room was filled with people, but half of them were transparent.

"Are those . . . ghosts?" I said, shivering as one of the wispy images passed right in front of me.

The Valkyrie nodded grimly. "Good evening, Brimwold."

The apparition returned the greeting by slapping a closed fist against his chest.

"*Ghosts* is an extremely Midgardian term for the soul of a fallen warrior," replied Brunhild. She gestured for me to follow her, cutting a wide swath through a cluster of partying warriors whose food and drink could be seen gurgling down their throats and pooling in their stomachs.

Everywhere I looked, the image of a dead soldier was either sitting, dancing, laughing, drinking, eating, or sleeping. They appeared to be having the time of their lives, despite the fact that none of them had physical bodies. It was far too loud to ask Brunhild any questions, so I hurried after her, trying to take in the strange sights as I ran. Off to my right, a towering ghostly warrior was tearing a chunk of meat from a turkey leg (at least I thought it was a turkey leg) with his teeth and trying to tell a joke at the same time. The warrior next to him, a smaller man with an arrow sticking from his neck, apparently understood the punch line; he burst out laughing, spraying his huge friend with chunks of food that I actually saw swirling around in his mouth moments before he blew.

I turned away, only to see two transparent warriors shoving each other, their smoky white cheeks and necks suddenly glowing red with anger.

"Viking temper!" shouted Brunhild over her shoulder. "No emotion in the mortal world compares to it!"

Nodding, I made an effort to catch up to the Valkyrie. Brunhild was careful to go around a swaying warrior. I tried to do the same, but he stumbled into me. I shuddered as I passed through the ghost, feeling like I'd been doused with ice water. Brunhild suddenly stopped and pointed at the table in front of her. My heart leaped into my throat.

"Tori!" I squealed, plunking down next to the Predator.

Tori's eyes widened. She wrapped her arms around my neck and gave me a fierce hug that nearly snapped my spine. "Cinder!" she said. "You came!"

"I never pass on a free meal," I said, grinning from ear to ear.

"Nothing here is free, Cindrheim," said Brunhild solemnly. "You will pay for it one way or another."

Talk about a mood-killer, I thought, rolling my eyes. I was too thrilled to see Tori, however, to worry about the end of the Nine Realms and my involvement in it.

"I shall return," said the Valkyrie. She looked at me, flashing a dire warning with her cobalt blue eyes. "And, Cindrheim . . . do not make trouble. This is a fifteen-hundred-year-old tradition, and my gut tells me you have the ability to disrupt it with a single fell stroke. Make the living *and* the dead proud this night, and be on your best behavior."

"Geez, Brunhild, have some faith in me," I said, and I really meant it.

"Very well," the Valkyrie said tightly. She spun on her heel and strode away. We watched her pass through the throng of partying dead guys, her red cape billowing behind her.

I looked at Tori. "Now that Mom's gone, we can have fun. So where is everyone?"

The Predator's excited expression turned grim. "Freya is meeting with Odin. I feel so bad for her. She threw up twice before she entered his throne room. Droma is still with the healers. She'll recover, but a festival of the fallen warriors is the last place she should be right now. And Edda . . . I'm not sure. I haven't seen or spoken to her since this morning."

"I wish they were all here."

Tori tried to comfort me with a pat on the back, but her strength turned it into more of a hearty slap. "Don't worry, Cinder. You'll see them soon. In the meantime, let's enjoy the party. It's not every day you get to see the souls of some of the greatest warriors Midgard has ever known."

"I wish I didn't have to see their food while it's being chewed and swallowed."

Tori laughed. "You get used to it."

"Speaking of great warriors, I just found out my grandma is a Predator! How cool is that?"

Tori nodded, her expression suddenly solemn.

"Do you know her?" I asked, desperate for any information I could get.

"We have met a few times—"

Tori fell silent as Brunhild, Trigga, Plyvis, and several other Valkyries entered the Long Hall from a door in the back. Each of them was wearing beautiful gowns of flowing white, and their feet were bare. A glittering ring of silver was woven into their hair.

Their missing armor and weapons surprised me. But the trays of food and drink they carried in their arms surprised me even more.

"They're waitresses?" I asked.

"If by that word you mean servants to the fallen heroes," said Tori, "then yes, they are waitresses. Though only for this hour. It is the only moment that a Valkyrie submits to the will of someone other than Odin."

I had been so captivated by the ghostly warriors, not to mention pumping Tori for information about my grandma,

I hadn't noticed that a set of Valkyries had been passing food out from the beginning. Before I could respond, Trigga stepped up to our table and set down a large silver platter heaping with steaming chunks of pork, beef, chicken, and fish. A ring of plump red grapes encircled the meat.

"Good evening, ladies," said Trigga. Her aviator glasses were gone, but she maintained her rebellious streak with a leather Rastafarian necklace strung with red, yellow, and green beads. It totally clashed with her elegant white gown, and I loved it.

"Cool necklace," I said.

For a brief moment, a tiny smile flickered across Trigga's face. "Thank you, Cinder."

She moved away, and within seconds, a line of Valkyries passed by our table, dropping off loaves of buttered bread, dishes of chocolate pudding, tureens of thick gravy, and plates of dripping fruit. The meal was complemented with golden goblets filled with a pinkish liquid that smelled strongly of raspberries. I didn't know where to start.

Tori placed a gold fork in my hand. "As they say in Midgard, dig in!"

Grinning, I followed her instructions. The moment the first bite of food touched my lips, I dropped my fork, gasping.

"Well?" said Tori, already on her fourth bite.

I wished I could leave the food on my tongue forever. "I've never tasted anything like it!" I gushed. My eyes got wider as six more platters of food were placed in front of us.

"It *is* prepared by Valkyries," said Tori, popping a white chocolate–dipped strawberry into her mouth. "What did you expect?"

CHAPTER 13

PARTY CRUSHERS

halfway through dinner, Freya and Edda joined us. I had to shout over the festivities. "Freya! Edda! You've got to try this stuff!"

Both of them nodded knowingly and took a seat across from us. "Have you enjoyed yourself so far, Cindrheim?" said Freya stiffly.

"It's amazing," I said. In between bites, I finally noticed her appearance. Freya looked like she just found out she had two weeks left to live. Her eyes were red, as if she'd been crying. "Are you alright, Freya?"

"I am fine," said Freya. But we all knew she wasn't. Knowing there was nothing I could do about it, I decided to drop it. Who could figure out a Predator?

"Whatever you guys don't eat, pass it over," I said. A ghostly warrior danced too close to us and fell into our table. His wispy remains spilled over me like icy smoke. Shaking off the disturbing chill, I dove back into the food.

I paused long enough to watch Odin enter the Long Hall. In honor of the fallen heroes, he was dressed as a true Viking warrior, though he was so large, his horned helmet bumped against the rafters, and his pounding footsteps caused the marble floor plates and the fire cauldrons to tremble. He was followed by his two enormous hunting hounds, Geri and Freki, and both of his ravens, Hugin and Munin, were perched on his shoulders. The fallen heroes dropped to one knee, thumped their fists against transparent chests, and then bowed their heads as Odin passed through their ranks.

Odin fell heavily into his throne, laying his spear across his knees. Within seconds, one of his daughters handed him the cooked leg of what looked like a dinosaur. He promptly began to gnaw on it, every once in a while tossing strips to his hungry pets. In between bites, I saw him look over at me.

"Odin's watching you," said Tori. Even over the noise of the party, I could hear her music blaring from her earphones.

"I know. Kinda creepy."

"Well, you *are* the one that will eventually determine his fate."

"I was hoping everyone had forgotten that."

Tori gave me a sympathetic smile. "Hard thing to forget."

I had barely returned to my food, when I heard Freya say, "Cindrheim, I would like you to meet my half-brother, Tristan."

I looked up from my plate, my mouth chock-full of mashed potatoes. The moment I saw him, I felt a bolt of electricity zip through my body. Breathless, and with gravy dribbling down my chin, I tried to smile.

Wow.

I don't usually worry too much about boys, but Tristan was hands down the cutest boy I'd ever seen. I could also see the striking resemblance to Freya, though where his sister's hair was silvery white, Tristan's was as dark as Odin's ravens. If I had to guess, I would peg him as a sophomore in high school, though it was impossible to tell, really. He had smooth olive skin, high cheekbones, and arching dark brows that gave his sea-colored eyes a stormy look. Faded jeans, boots, and a black T-shirt completed his outfit. He pushed a lock of hair away from his forehead and said, "*You* are Cindrheim Vustora?"

I definitely didn't like the way he said my name. I straightened up, tucked my hair behind my ear and said, "That's right. You got a problem?"

Tristan smiled, but it was more of a smirk. "I just expected . . . so much more."

"Really," I said, rising from my chair.

Freya put a cautioning hand on my arm. "Cindrheim, sit back down." She turned and scowled at her brother. "Tristan, put aside your petty judgments. You do not know her as I do."

Coming from Freya, it was a wonderful compliment, but I was still on edge. I glared up at Tristan, daring him to make another crack. It was difficult to be too upset, though, seeing as how just looking at him made my cheeks flush. It was just like they say: you can't have looks *and* a personality.

Tristan grabbed an apple from off the nearest platter and took a huge bite. Bowing mockingly, he sauntered away. Freya got up and followed him.

Tori leaned in close. "Tell me he's not the cutest boy you've ever seen . . . "

I shrugged.

Tori grinned and nudged me in the ribs, which caused me to nearly topple out of my chair. "Come on, Cinder. Have you *looked* at the guy?"

"He's alright. I've seen better. His personality takes away from his looks, though."

Tori looked through the partying ghosts, her eyes lingering on Tristan. "Yeah, he's an ornery one. Too bad, huh?"

"Yeah. Too bad." I had lost my appetite, though I sipped my berry-flavored drink and tried to avoid looking at Freya's brother. "So what does Tristan do when he's not offending someone?"

"His is an interesting story," said Tori, her eyes still riveted on the boy. "Freya was born first, raised by her mother and a stepfather till she was three. Tristan was born and immediately dropped off on the doorstep of the Healing House. He never cried once, but the healers came out the next morning and found him wrapped in furs. His father was one of the gods, which explains why he was left."

"What do you mean?"

"The gods often mate with mortals, then leave them to care for the child. Sometimes the mother cannot do it, so they leave them with someone who can."

"But if Freya is Tristan's sister, why was she not left on a doorstep?"

"Different mother," said Tori simply.

"Oh." Unable to look away from Tristan, I watched him

conversing with some of the warriors as if he'd known them for years.

"When the healers unwrapped him, his lips were blue with cold."

I felt a quick stab of sympathy, but I brushed it away. And then I felt something else. In so many ways, Tristan and I were as different as two people could be. But regret-tably, we shared something very similar. Quietly, I said, "His mother abandoned him."

Tori nodded, chewing on a strip of juicy meat. "Tragedy is sometimes a way of life in both our worlds."

"He's not a Predator, is he?"

"No," said Tori. "Males cannot be Predators, but Tristan's easily as talented as any of us, if not more so."

"Even Freya?"

Tori nodded. "That would be quite a contest. She may have him in experience, but Tristan is faster, stronger, more agile."

"Wow," I breathed, trying as hard as I could not to be impressed. "So is he a soldier-in-training?"

"No."

"Then he just hangs out here at the Proving Grounds all day?"

"Tristan's been allowed to stay because he's good with his hands. He built the Gauntlet by himself, you know."

I looked at Tori. "That big wood and steel eyesore behind the Long Hall?"

"That *eyesore* has turned average humans and even a few minor gods into lethal killing machines."

"Quite a legacy," I replied, suddenly dreading the day I would have to face the Gauntlet.

"Do not pay Tristan any mind, Cinder," said Freya, taking a seat across from me. "He is actually not as cold-hearted as he seems."

"We all have our issues," I said evasively.

Freya leaned across the table. "Cindrheim, most of the females, well actually *all* of the females who see Tristan, think that he is . . . how should I say it . . . ?"

"Unbelievably handsome?" said Tori. Edda nodded as she shoved a peeled shrimp into her mouth.

"Tori," said Freya reprovingly. "Remember your station."

Tori lowered her eyes. "Yes, Freya."

Freya turned back to me. "I am Tristan's sister, so I do not notice how . . ." She glanced at Tori, ". . . unbelievably handsome he is. But apparently there is something about the way he looks that causes the female species to . . ."

"Swoon?" said Tori dreamily.

"Tori!" snapped Freya, "leave us in peace for a few blessed moments!"

Tori pushed herself away from the table and stood up. "I'm sorry. I'll go mingle with the crowd for a while."

"Wonderful idea," said Freya, "but stay away from Tristan."

Tori sighed and drifted away. Freya turned back to me and found that I was giggling. "I'm sorry, Freya."

"What I am trying to say is be careful around him. Though I do not comprehend what others see in his appearance, Tristan's looks can ensnare you like a spider's web. You can see what he has already done to Tori, and she is trained in self-control. We cannot afford to have you . . ."

"Swooning?"

"Precisely."

I shook my head vigorously. "You don't have to worry about me. He's cute, but I was turned off the moment he opened his mouth."

"Good," said Freya, a smile playing at the corners of her mouth. I was glad to see that she seemed to be cheering up.

I pulled a giant bowl of peanut butter cookies off a platter and sampled one of them. Grinning, I said, "So why are you warning me about your little bro? It's not like Mr. Fix-it boy's gonna be sent off on a quest with me."

Freya had been surveying the boisterous crowd. She turned and looked at me. "Actually, Cindrheim . . ."

"You can't be serious! Is that what you were talking to Odin about? Is he sending me somewhere with that walking ego?"

Freya bit her lip and turned away, pretending to watch the partying warriors.

"Freya? When you came back, it looked like you'd been crying. Did Odin—"

"I do not cry," Freya snapped.

"Fine. You don't cry. But did Odin tell you that Tristan is somehow involved in my prophecy?"

Edda stopped eating long enough to look at Freya.

I reached out and touched the Predator's arm, but she pulled away from me. "Pay attention, Cindrheim. The fallen heroes are about to commence in battle."

Classic denial, I thought, then suddenly the idea of me and Tristan working together hit me full force. I felt like throwing up and jumping for joy, all at the same time.

Odin waved his staff and all the tables and benches in the center of the room lifted up into the air and settled down along the room's perimeter. Those who had been sitting at the tables either fell to the ground or stayed seated for the ride. Free to move around, the armored apparitions milled about the area, clanking smoky white swords and axes against their chests and shouting out threats in ancient Nordic.

"What are they doing?" I asked.

Without taking her eyes off the warriors, Freya said, "Now that supper is over, the fallen heroes reenact the battle that took their lives. Those left standing receive greater rewards in Valhalla."

"Do they feel pain?"

"Tonight they will," said Freya. "Pain is a badge of courage for them. Tonight they are also allowed to taste food again. Reigniting their mortal desires prepares them for this glorious event."

I saw Odin stand and brandish his tall spear. "Fallen heroes of ages past!" His voice boomed throughout the Long Hall. "You are all well fed—some of you more than others" (at this several Vikings laughed and slapped each other on the back) "and you are prepared for battle. Each of you fought valiantly in your mortal life, and you will do so again this night!"

The ghosts punched the air with their various weapons and hollered so loud I had to clap my hands over my ears.

"Each of your bloodied corpses was found by one of my daughters," said Odin, "the beloved Valkyries. My Shield Maidens drew out your spirits, passing over the fallen warriors whose achievements on the field of battle did not compare to yours!"

At this, the ghosts shouted so loud I thought the Long Hall was going to come crashing down.

"This night!" yelled Odin, "you shall prove to me once again that we have chosen wisely! This night, you shall honor me and the lesser gods through your renowned bravery and savagery! Tonight you shall die in Isilheim and live again in Valhalla!"

The sound of their shouting was now deafening.

"Those who stagger to the High Throne, though you may do it with only a single limb, shall remain by my side throughout the eternities!" Odin concluded his rousing speech by slamming the end of his spear against the ground. The bluish-white fire in the cauldrons along the Long Hall's walls sprang up like geysers from Yellowstone Park, forcing me to turn away.

The loud bang of the wood meeting marble had sent the warriors into a chaotic frenzy. Screaming and shaking their weapons above their heads, they rushed at each other, their pale faces masks of rage and aggression.

"This is insane," I said, wincing as each of the ghosts slammed into one another at full speed.

"Not much different than American football," said Edda.

I turned away as a transparent leg went spinning under a table. "It's a *little* different," I said, already feeling queasy. I wasn't surprised to see that their smoky white appearance had turned fiery red with the heat of battle. It was easy to see why the Viking warrior had been so feared throughout history. They were like machines built specifically for war.

At one point I covered my eyes with my hand, then heard Freya say, "Cindrheim, did you see the man off to your right, the one with the ax stuck in his back? Watch how he counters his opponents' attacks and at the same time presses his own attack with measured strikes."

"I was going to point out the exact same thing," I said, lifting my feet as a wispy head rolled under our table.

Soon, most of the warriors had fallen to the floor, defeated. Only a handful remained. I had kept my eye on one Viking in particular, a man who had chosen to attack only those who were double and triple teaming an opponent. Whenever someone would fall, whether friend or foe, he would risk being felled himself to drag them away from the chaos.

Was it possible to admire a savage killing machine? He was more honorable than *some* immortals I could mention.

All of a sudden, the Viking noticed that he was being triple teamed himself. Unable to deflect the flurry of blows, he fell to one knee, then took a hit that crippled his shield arm. His attackers hooted with excitement, sensing victory.

"Come on," I said, "get up, get up . . ." I looked around and saw that the wounded Viking was the last of his companions. Even while bent on one knee and badly hurt, he managed to defeat two of his attackers, but the third delivered a vicious blow that put an end to any further resistance. Bowing his head with exhaustion, the Viking waited for the final strike.

Don't do it, said the tiny voice in my head. *Think of the repercussions!*

You gotta do better than that, I thought back.

Ripping one of Tori's swords from the scabbard at her hip, I scrambled over the table, just barely dodging Freya's grasping fingers.

"Cindrheim!" she shouted. "Do not interfere!"

Too late, I thought, raising the sword high over my head. At the last moment, the warrior turned, his expression a mixture of surprise and confusion. I heard the Predators scream, "NO!" as I brought the sword down. The apparition easily blocked my attack but grimaced in shock as the kneeling warrior's long blade exploded through his chest with a puff of ragged smoke. Frowning, he fell into me, drenching me with his icy cold vapors.

The Viking was still on one knee, his silvery eyes filled with wonderment. He pulled his sword free of his opponent. Through his bushy beard, I detected a tiny smile.

The room had gone silent. One of Odin's hounds growled from deep in its belly. An apple fell from the tray of a stunned Valkyrie.

"Oh no," said someone behind me. It sounded like Tori.

Odin rose from his throne, his chest heaving. Tori had told me during dinner that his spear was enchanted, and it never missed its target, so I knew he could throw it over his shoulder with his eyes closed and still impale me from where he stood. I waited, hoping death by super-sharp spear point would be quick.

With an ear-shattering roar Odin hurled his spear. The Viking, still on one knee, took the spear through the chest. His eyes were still on me when he toppled over. The spear whipped back into Odin's hand. He turned and looked at me, and I thought the heat of his gaze would kill me. In the blink of one furious eye, he was standing over me. He opened his mouth to say something, then closed it. I cringed as he turned and exploded through a side door so quickly, his hounds and ravens were left blinking in his sudden absence.

I stared at the dead Viking for a moment, then walked slowly back to the table. The Valkyries were like statues, grim and unmoving. I avoided everyone's stares, though I could feel their eyes boring into me.

As quietly as I could, I took my seat, handing Tori her sword. Wordlessly, she took it and slid it into her scabbard. In the morgue-like silence, I could hear her music seeping from her earbuds.

I stared at my lap for as long as I could, then finally looked up. Smiling sheepishly, I said, "Anyone for seconds?"

CHAPTER 14

Che Boy with the Diabolical Mind

No one took me up on my offer.

"Not good," whispered Tori from the side of her mouth.

Edda had her eyes squeezed shut, like a child waiting for the sting of the doctor's needle.

I spotted Tristan near the entrance, leaning casually against a weapons rack. He was shaking his head and chuckling softly.

I glanced at Freya, suddenly realizing I had hurt her most of all. I was surprised, and saddened, to see that she wasn't glaring at me in rage. Instead, she appeared to be in a daze, her mind floating somewhere far from Odin's Long Hall.

With Odin gone, the lights and the roaring blue flames fizzled out. The only illumination came from the silvery corpses that littered the floor.

The awkward silence was broken when Tristan said, "Classic," then he, too, walked out. One by one, the images of the dead picked themselves up off the floor, glared at me with smoldering eyes, and then drifted through the wall of the Long Hall. The Viking who had been speared by Odin was the last to rise. He looked at me once, nodded, then followed his comrades. The arms, legs, and heads that were left behind quickly dissolved.

"I think we better go," said Tori uneasily. She and Edda rose from their chairs, gesturing for me to follow.

I found that I was even more worried about Freya's reaction than I was Odin's. She was still sitting there, staring off into the gloomy darkness.

"Freya . . ."

"Just go," she said softly.

"Freya, I—"

"Go."

I got up and left the Long Hall, wishing that I was one of the ghosts and that I could drift away.

♨

After such a long day, you'd think I would fall asleep the moment my head hit the pillow. But after disrupting a fifteen-hundred-year-old tradition and humiliating the most powerful Norse god in the universe, sleep was hard to come by. I tossed and turned, feeling every bump and crease of the thin mat beneath me.

When I finally did fall asleep, my dreams were racked with the worst nightmares I had ever had. They were filled with savage, half-dead Vikings, relentlessly hounding me wherever I went. And in my dreams, they would catch me and run me through with their pale cold swords or cleave me in half with glittering axes. After the unbearable pain,

I would heal and begin running again. The cycle continued till morning.

I woke up when Tori stuck her head through the small opening of my tent, and said, "Did you sleep well?"

"The few moments when I wasn't being chased by a horde of zombie Vikings were wonderful," I replied, rubbing my swollen eyes.

Tori nodded, her features lined with concern. "Yeah, that would be the *Tonlil Sur*, or the Viking Vengeance. Freya told me you might experience such a thing for interfering in their battle."

"So I've been cursed."

"Looks like it."

"Probably lasts forever."

"Probably."

"No chance of a do-over?"

"You'll have to wait a hundred years."

"Of course."

Tori grinned. "You ready to face the Gauntlet?"

"The day can only get better."

Tori's grin faltered. "Unless you *die* in the Gauntlet."

I climbed wearily to my feet. "What are we waiting for?"

After a quick breakfast of peppery eggs and toasted bread, Tori and I left the dining hall and skirted the lake. There were already dozens of soldiers-in-training canoeing or swimming with gleaming black wet suits to ward off the frigid temperatures of the snowmelt. I spotted two boys and a girl standing at the lake's edge, each of them singing at the top of their lungs and waving their arms in unison.

Before I could question Tori, though, the Predator tugged on my jacket sleeve, and said, "Come on, your date with fate was five minutes ago."

I made it to the Gauntlet without committing a single mistake. I was too distracted by the ominous vibe it gave off, though, to feel too proud of myself.

I stared in awe at the towering contraption. If it were laid out on a football field, it could've easily reached from one end zone to the fifty-yard line. And certain pieces of it looked to be at least seventy feet tall. It was all polished wood, thick rope, and glittering steel, each section more diabolical than the one before it.

"What was Tristan thinking?" I muttered.

Tori nodded, her gray eyes swimming with pure admiration. "Odin asked him to build something that would test a soldier's limits, and at the same time, train them to be lethal on the field of battle."

"Did he build this by himself?"

"Tristan drew up the plans, got them approved by the Allfather, then set to work with a crew of dwarves—"

"Dwarves?"

Tori nodded. "The Bearded Folk are great with their hands, but one of them died while building it, two were fired by Tristan for shoddy work, and the last dwarf quit before Tristan could let him go. So, essentially, he *did* build this by himself."

I swallowed. "One of them died?"

Tori pointed to a large box-like structure, not far from where we stood. I could see the silvery tips of three blades the size of snow saucers, slicing through the air in alter-nating patterns. "Right there in the scythe pit," she said. "Healers couldn't get to him in time."

"The scythe pit, huh? Nice and clean?"

"Not really," said Tori. "When he fell, he splattered—"

"Tori," I said, putting my hand up. "That was rhetorical."

"Oh."

I stepped to the side as a group of scared-looking teenage boys brushed past me, heading for the ladder at the base of the Gauntlet. A large adult Viking with a braided blond beard pointed to the platform at the top of the ladder. "Up you go, dogs!" he shouted.

One by one, they climbed to the platform, occasionally glancing back as if to say: *Tell my mother and father I loved them and I'll miss them.*

"Surely no one expects me to do this," I said.

Suddenly, Tori's voice was in my ear and considerably deeper in tone. "A hero-in-training, afraid of the Gauntlet?"

Turning, I saw that it wasn't Tori. It was Tristan. "I'm not afraid of it," I said, backing away. I could still feel his breath on my ear.

Tristan laughed. "I can see your knees shaking through your pants."

Horrified that he could actually see through pants, I moved closer to Tori. "I just don't understand the point in taking such a risk."

"All recruits run the Gauntlet," Tristan said. He turned to Tori. "Right, Tanya?"

"Right," breathed Tori, her eyes glazing over.

I frowned, realizing Operation Swoon was in effect. "Her name's Tori."

Tristan smiled with only one side of his mouth. "Tori, Tanya, what does it really matter? She's just a Predator, right?"

Tori was grinning even though Tristan had just insulted her. Twice. I could see that her powers of self-control were slipping away. I had to end our conversation before mine did the same. "Fine. When do I start?"

"Right now," answered Tristan. He pointed at the ladder. "Up you go."

Leaving Tori behind, I walked to the ladder and began to climb.

"Cinder!" called out Tristan. Without looking back, I heard him say, "I'll alert the Allfather that, without a head, you may be unable to complete any quests he gives you!"

"Jerk," I muttered. With every rung my sneaker touched, the speed of my heart rate doubled. Just before I reached the platform, I looked back down and saw several green-cloaked healers gathering close to the Gauntlet.

That can't be good, I thought.

When I made it to the top, I found the group of boys even more scared than they were before. They were leaning over the opposite side of the platform, looking down at something. Curious, I joined them—then immediately wished I hadn't. The large, blond-bearded Viking was standing on the grass below, gripping a rope in his huge hands. Foot by foot, he was using the rope to lower a boy on a stretcher-like piece of wood. The boy was groaning and clutching at his leg. Even from where I stood, I could see blood seeping through his fingers and staining the wood beneath him. The moment he reached ground level, three healers converged on him, their hands moving fast to mend his wounds.

"Gotta watch your footing," said a familiar voice in my ear.

Spinning around, I found a grinning Tristan. *How did he get up here so fast?* I wondered. He moved to the edge of the platform, facing the first obstacle, which was a log stretching out over a deep gap like a balance beam. He turned to look at the frightened boys. "Do you fellas mind if Cinder goes next?"

They all vigorously shook their heads and fell over each other to let me through.

My heartbeat tripled its rate.

"It's quite easy," said Tristan, glancing towards the injured boy who was being carried across the field. "Well, for *most* of us, that is."

"If it's so easy," I said, "why don't *you* show us how it's done?"

Tristan stepped backward onto the log, then took another step, then another. Soon, he was halfway across, his eyes never leaving mine. "My ability to run the Gauntlet does nothing to further Odin's cause." He took a few more steps. The log was perhaps three inches wide at most, and he was doing it backward as if he were walking forward on flat ground. "I'm no hero-in-training, but for you, Cinder, I will oblige."

Before I could throw an insult at him, Tristan gave me another one of his mocking bows, spun in place, then sprinted the rest of the way across the log. I watched as he approached an imposing wall, strung with a length of rope. Like a jungle cat, he leaped, and ignoring the rope, skittered up the wall, then flipped over the top.

The boys behind me were oohing and ahhing, though one of them had taken the opportunity to hightail it down the ladder and make a break for it. For a few moments, I couldn't see Tristan, then all of a sudden his tousled dark hair and tanned face popped into view long enough for me to see that he was racing through the Gauntlet as fast as a jackrabbit. A moment later, I heard a loud grunt and turned to see the blond-bearded Viking pulling himself up onto the platform.

"Mical will not be returning today," huffed the man. He emphasized his point by wiping his bloodied hands against his leather shirt. "Found out the hard way the Gauntlet is unforgivin' to those who don't respect it." The Viking's blue eyes landed hard on me. "What's this? Are you Cindrheim Vustora?"

"I am."

He looked me up and down, then used his bushy beard to hide his frown. "Well now. Here for some trainin'?"

"I guess."

We all turned as one to watch Tristan race across a swaying rope, leap over a swiping blade that was leveled at his feet, then fall into a roll as another blade tried to decapitate him.

The Viking shook his head. "I don't expect any of you to compete with Tristan, but you will learn to survive the Gauntlet." A moment later, something landed next to the Viking. It was Tristan and he had barely broken a sweat. He was holding a piece of bright red cloth in his hand.

"He got the flag," breathed a boy behind me.

"I believe it was Cinder's turn," said Tristan, waving the red cloth in my direction.

I could feel my anger rising. "So if I get my foot cut off, or I fall and break my neck, what then?"

Tristan smiled. "Do you have a sister?" One of the boys chuckled till the Viking swatted him on the back of the head.

"I'm serious," I said. "If I'm missing a limb, Odin won't be happy."

"Not to worry, dear Cinder," Tristan purred. "The healers wait at the base of the Gauntlet. They will be happy to heal any mangled body parts."

"He aint lyin'!" boomed the Viking. "Them gals can do some amazin' things. 'Course it will hurt somethin' fierce till they do it."

"Alright," I growled, "give me some room." Everyone stepped back so that I could approach the beam. Trying to calm my nerves, I stepped out onto the log. I took another step, then another. *This isn't so bad*, I thought. I locked my eyes on the wall ahead of me and increased my speed.

As I neared the halfway mark, I heard Tristan say, "Atta girl. Just don't look down."

I looked down.

The ten-foot drop was bad enough. The slithering black snakes added a twist.

"Gah!" I screamed, as my foot slipped off the edge of the log. Flailing my arms, I teetered to my right. In a desperate attempt to regain my balance, I spun in place, and tried to lunge to my left. Now both feet slipped out from under me. With a giant WHOOOSH! the air left my lungs as my chest smashed against the log. Grimacing in pain, I slipped over the edge and fell the ten feet to the ground. I shrieked as I felt my ankle turn, though the rest of my body was cushioned by the blanket of snakes.

The snakes actually waited a few seconds before attacking me.

"Get me outta here!" I shouted, trying to struggle to my feet. A sharp spike of pain shot up my left leg the moment I put weight on my injured ankle, but I quickly forgot about my twisted ankle when I felt an even sharper spike of pain from my other leg. I batted away the snake that had sunk its fangs into my calf. "Tristan! Do something!"

Tristan was shaking his head. "You may have set a new Gauntlet record, though it's not one I'd be very proud of!"

I ripped another snake from my sneaker and shook it at Tristan. "Get me out so I can strangle you with this thing!"

Sighing heavily, Tristan reached up and pulled down on a lever. A wooden panel at my right suddenly lifted, allowing me (and several snakes) to scurry out. The moment I was free of the Gauntlet, half a dozen hooded healers rushed up to me and pushed me into a sitting position. Slimy, smelly leaves as large as dinner plates were quickly slapped onto my snake bites, and before I knew it, the excruciating pain began to fade. While they worked, they sang to Eir (none of them on key), and another healer pulled my sock down and began to rub a gravelly black substance over my swollen ankle. The swelling and the pain subsided, though it was still tender.

Clora pulled back her hood and grinned her frog's grin. "Up you go," she said.

I stood, tested my weight on my ankle, then started to hobble away. "I can make it on my own."

"Where are you going?" said Clora.

"To the Healing House."

Clora shook her head. "Your training is not over, child."

I felt that familiar warmth in my cheeks and neck as my anger began to boil. "But I just fell ten feet into a pit of snakes!"

"And I would advise not to do it again," said Clora. "We are low on salve." The other healers were nodding their heads in agreement.

"This place is unbelievable!" I shouted. "Is everyone here insane?"

Clora pointed to one of the healers next to her. "Sisilee is, but we are working with her."

"Fine," I muttered, heading for the ladder. "Let Odin know he'll need to find a new hero, because I'll be dead within the hour."

"Not if we can help it, child!" sang Clora.

CHAPTER 15

SLUG REMOVAL ONE OH ONE

I fell from the log two more times before I made it to the wall. The third time in the snake pit wasn't so bad. I re-sprained my ankle, but the snake bites seemed less painful, plus half of them had slithered out the first time the side door had been opened. As soon as the healers patched me up, I scurried back up the ladder, determined to try again.

Not that I'm a glutton for punishment. I just couldn't stand to see Tristan leaning against the platform wall with his gigantic smirk. He was still smirking when I made it to the wall and scrambled up and over, but it was a much *smaller* smirk.

I slid down the opposite side of the wall, and my excitement quickly evaporated. I was forced to land on a narrow ledge that wasn't even wide enough for me to stand on without plastering myself to the wall. After a few horrifying moments where I wasn't completely balanced, I finally regained control and looked over my shoulder. It was another pit, but this one was filled with a sickly brown liquid that looked thick enough to support my weight. Right in front of me was another wooden beam, though this one protruded for six feet, then stopped. The

next beam was spaced nearly three feet away from the end
of the first beam, and to make matters worse, it was offset
by a foot or two. I saw that if I could make it to that beam,
I could run across it safely to the opposite platform.

"Don't look down," I muttered. I had to turn on the
narrow platform and step out onto the beam all at the
same time, which wasn't easy. I swayed for a second or
two, then took a few slow steps forward. I was doing a
wonderful job of not looking down into the brown sludge
beneath me, but I could hear bubbles popping and a soft
squelching that sounded like someone pulling their sneaker
out of the mud.

Don't look down.

I took two more steps and found myself teetering at the
end of the beam.

Don't look down!

"Cinder!" It was Tristan. I tried hard to ignore him.
"You don't have to worry about snakes anymore, though if
you fall, you may have to contend with the bloodsucking
slugs."

"Shut up!" I growled. For a moment, my eyes flicked
downward and I thought I saw something black and shiny
poke its head up out of the sludge. *He's not kidding,* I
thought.

"Not to worry, Cinder!" called out Tristan. "They're not
half as hungry during the day as they are at night!" After a
few moments he said, "Or is it the other way around . . . ?"

I couldn't stand on the end of the beam forever, and I
couldn't turn around without falling. I had to jump.

I looked down.

The drop was only a few feet, but now I could see at least a dozen shiny black slugs breaching the surface like miniature whales, some of them pausing to test the air blindly, then slip back under.

Holding my breath, I jumped. I landed on the opposite beam as well as any Olympic gymnast, my arms hardly flailing at all. I smiled and began to walk forward.

That's when the beam began to rotate.

"Oh, come on!" I shouted, shifting my weight and side-stepping to my right as the log rolled to the left. "This is totally unfair!"

"You think the enemies you face will treat you fairly?" Tristan asked.

"I'm in *training*!" I screamed.

"They can't stand mortal blood!" called Tristan. "No, wait . . . I'm sorry. They *love* mortal blood. It's *immortal* blood they don't care for."

"Right now, I don't much care for it either!"

I saw that I had perhaps four feet to go before I reached the platform, but the beam was picking up speed, spinning faster than my feet could move. Just as I began to fall backward, I made a desperate leap towards the platform. I grunted as I crashed against the platform's edge, felt the air explode out of my lungs for the second time that day, then cried out in alarm as I slid down the wall and into the bubbling sludge.

The mud bath wasn't as thick as I'd thought. I sank like a rock to the bottom of the pit, then pushed off from the ground as quickly as I could. Whatever I had fallen into was disturbingly warm and smelled like someone had left a dead cow rotting in a dumpster. Before I broke the surface, I felt several hot stinging sensations on my neck, back, and arms.

Slugs. Mortal-blood-loving slugs.

I spluttered to the surface, slapped my hand against something warm and slimy that was stuck to my neck, then tore it off. I frantically looked for a way out and spotted a ladder rising out of the sludge.

To get to it, I would have to swim. Naturally. I paddled through the sludge, ignoring the slugs that were attaching themselves to me faster than I could pull them off. Yelling in frustration and fear, I clambered up the ladder and found myself back on the platform from which I started.

Tristan's voice was filled with laughter. "Pinch the heads! They come off much easier—or so I'm told."

I looked down and found at least seven of the hideous things stuck to me. Each one was about six inches long and as slippery as a catfish. Shaking my head in anger, I said, "Which end is the head!"

"I don't know," said Tristan. "You'll have to experiment!"

"Disgusting!" I muttered, peeling slugs off me and wincing in pain as each one tried desperately to cling on. I purposely tossed each peeled slug over the wall so that they would fall into the snake pit. "Dinnertime," I said, grinning as I heard a loud hissing on the other side.

"Hurry, Cinder!" called Tristan. "There are soldiers-in-training dying to run the Gauntlet."

Cursing, I stepped out onto the beam, ran across it, then leaped to the adjacent beam. This time my foot caught the edge and I sprawled across it, then flipped upside down. Now I was hanging from the beam, pleading, "Please don't turn. Please don't turn . . . "

It began to turn.

Unable to hold on while the beam rotated, I fell back into the pit. I screamed in anger, which wasn't smart because I was under the surface when I opened my mouth. I can tell you, the taste was worse than the smell. I was just thrilled that I didn't slurp up a slug.

As soon as I broke the surface, I saw Tristan's arrogant face peering over the wall. Shaking his head, he said, "Cinder, you're done for the day."

"Oh no I'm not!" I shouted, peeling a slug off my cheek and flinging it in Tristan's direction. Tristan ducked.

"Slug pitching," he said, chuckling. "Could be something you're good at."

I made for the ladder. "You can't keep me from trying again."

"Yes, child, you are done." Looking up, I saw Clora standing on the platform. She flicked a spot of dirt off her emerald green robes, and said, "The healers have exhausted their power with you. It will take them the rest of the day to recuperate."

I grabbed the ladder and pulled myself out of the sludge. "Thanks, but I don't need you guys." I clambered up onto the platform and prepared myself to cross the beam for the third time.

"Cindrheim," said Clora, grabbing my arm. "Look at what the slugs are doing to you."

Huffing, I stared at my arm. "Oh no," I whispered. My entire forearm was turning a sickly green color. I looked at Clora. "But I already tried to leave and you said my training wasn't over. Now you want me to quit?"

"We have never had someone fall that many times—"

My anger surged. "Well maybe walking on a log three inches wide is not my thing! How—"

"Let me finish, Cinder," said Clora. "We have never had someone fall that many times and go back for more. We were not prepared for such . . . persistence."

I paused, wondering if she was giving me a compliment. It was difficult to focus because there was a slug that had slipped down the back of my pants. I slapped hard at the bulge, and felt it slide down my leg.

Clora sighed. "One more trip into that pit and it may be your last."

I could still see Tristan leering from over the top of the wall. "Game over," he said. His lopsided smile was far more painful than the slugs.

My picture! I quickly pulled the picture of me and Uncle Robert from my back pocket, afraid my fall into the muddy slug tank had ruined it. It was a bit damp but otherwise unharmed. Breathing a sigh of relief, I stared at my uncle's face, and felt a sudden surge of courage. "One more time," I growled, slipping my picture carefully into my back pocket. I stepped towards the beam.

Clora shook her head. "The Gauntlet only gets more

perilous, child." The healer pointed to a door on the side of the platform that was so well hidden, I would've never noticed it. She opened it and scowled up at Tristan. "Rest and heal," she said to me, "and come back another day."

Shaking the stunned slug from my pant leg, I followed Clora through the door.

ॐ

Tori didn't have to be the Goddess of Psychology to see that I was upset. She was fast becoming an expert on judging my mood and then doing what she could to make me feel better. As soon as the healers had withdrawn the slug poison with more slimy leaves and off-key singing, she helped me construct a nearly identical replica of the first two Gauntlet obstacles, minus the poisonous vipers and bloodsucking slugs. With her strength and knowledge of woodwork, we finished it by nightfall.

"You don't give up, do you?" said Tori, stepping back to admire her work.

I stepped up onto the first beam, which was only three feet off the ground, but still provided me with the challenge of walking across a piece of wood that was only three inches wide. "It's Tristan's face. I can't get it out of my mind."

"I know what you mean," said Tori wistfully.

I took a few tentative steps across the beam. "That's not what I meant, Tori. I mean his condescending expression. He's so smug, like he's Odin's gift to mankind."

"He's just confident."

"*Confident?*" My dismay caused me to pinwheel my arms. "Tori, you're so captivated by his eyes, and his hair, and his smile, and . . . and all the rest, that you look right past his glaring faults."

Tori laughed. "You sure gave me a very specific list."

I suddenly felt flush with embarrassment, which caused me to lose my balance. Falling to the grass, I got up and mounted the beam again. "I'm just assuming that's what *you're* looking at. His stormy gray eyes don't do anything for me."

Tori nodded. "Whatever you say, Cinder." She turned away from me and started to walk towards the dining hall. "I have to meet Freya before dinner. I'll see you then, okay?"

"If you haven't already died from lovesickness."

Tori smiled over her shoulder. "It's all about self-control, Cinder."

I shook my head, fell to the grass, and tried again.

CHAPTER 16

SCYTHES, SPIDERS, AND
SARCASM

The next morning, as I was eating breakfast with the Predators, an old man in a Los Angeles Chargers jersey and faded jeans passed through the dining hall. He was moving quickly, tying his silver hair into a ponytail. It took me a moment to remember that Odin often chose to walk the earth in the guise of a normal sports-loving human being. He seemed pressed for time, his features set hard in a scowl.

"Where's *he* off to?" I asked, trying to hide behind a forkful of scrambled eggs.

Tori didn't hear me; she had both earbuds in and she was bobbing her head to her music.

Edda turned and craned her neck, seemingly eager to watch Odin's every movement.

Droma, who had been given a clean bill of health from the healers, sat next to Edda. I had already filled her in on everything she had missed. She glanced at Odin, frowned, and shrugged her shoulders.

We all looked at Freya and saw that she was immediately more anxious now that Odin was in the hall. She gave us the *Just Keep Eating and Mind Your Own Business* stare.

I watched Odin stride up to a trio of Valkyries and pull one of them aside. It was Brunhild. She definitely looked alarmed as she listened to her father talk.

"Something's going down," I mumbled.

"Gods are busy people," said Freya quickly.

I watched Odin touch Brunhild's cheek, then quickly leave the hall.

I wiped my mouth with the edge of the tablecloth (which got me a withering glare from Freya) and stood up. "Well, that was delicious. I'll be right outside if anyone needs me."

Freya emptied her glass of juice and said, "Do not stray far, Cindrheim, and stay clear of Odin unless he requests your presence."

I saluted her. "Yes, ma'am."

"Tori, go with her. And keep her away from any sacred traditions."

"I see you've decided to let that go," I said frowning.

"Not yet," said Freya. She turned to look at Tori. "Keep an eye on her at all times. That is an order."

"I won't leave her side," assured Tori.

I looked at Edda and Droma. "Wanna come?"

"I've got things to do," said Edda quickly.

"I'm still feeling a little weak, Cinder," said Droma. "I'll catch up with you later."

Tori and I quickly left. When we emerged from the dining hall, we found Odin, still disguised as someone's uncle, talking with Tristan.

"My two favorite people," I said frowning, though seeing Tristan sent a bothersome thrill up my spine.

"They've become close lately, haven't they?" said Tori.

I contemplated telling Tori that the Nine Realms' best-looking jerk could be somehow involved with my future quest, but I wasn't sure I'd been cleared to share such information, so I shut my mouth.

"So what's Brunhild got you doing today?" Tori asked, trying not to look over at Tristan.

"She has me training on the Gauntlet in an hour, but I wanted to practice on the one we made first." We started to walk in the direction of my makeshift gauntlet, pausing as Tristan spun around, and shouted, "That's never going to work, Allfather! I'm sorry, I can't do it!"

There was no way I could *not* watch. I mean, it's not every day you get to see the most powerful Norse god arguing with a walking ego. We continued to walk, but we heard Tristan say, "That's fine, but you'll be disappointed." Even from our distance, I could see the deep-set scowl lining Tristan's face as he stormed away.

We reached my version of the Gauntlet and I jumped up onto the first beam. I found that I could quickly navigate the obstacle, even while talking to Tori. "What do you think?"

Tori was watching the boy walk into the dining hall. "He looks good in black."

I frowned. "No, I mean what do you think about those two arguing?"

"I don't pretend to understand the dealings of the gods, Cinder, but whatever Odin said, it sure got Tristan angry."

I moved to the second beam, fully confident about my

newfound abilities. "Odin probably told him he can't stare into any mirrors."

Tori nodded, too captivated by Tristan's rebellious saunter to notice my joke. Then I heard Odin shout, "To Odin, Sleipnir!" A moment later, a huge gray horse pranced around the corner of the dining hall and stepped up to Odin, pawing anxiously at the ground. I squinted, then rubbed my eyes.

"Tori, does that horse have more than four legs?"

"Sleipnir? Yeah, he has eight."

"And the purpose of that would be . . . ?"

Tori shrugged. "Who knows? Sleipnir was a gift from the gods of Valhalla, along with his spear and shield. No steed can move faster, he never grows tired, and his hide cannot be pierced by any known weapon."

I watched Odin rub the freakish creature's head, then try and climb up onto its back, but Sleipnir snorted and shied away.

"Dratted beast!" bellowed Odin. "It's just a football jersey!" With a wave of his hand, Odin instantly transformed into his true Viking form, dressed in his cloudy blue robes, matching hat, and iron bracers. "Better?" he growled.

Satisfied, Sleipnir stopped snorting and kneeled, allowing Odin to climb up onto his back. Odin pointed his spear to the west, and the horse bolted like an expelled cannon ball, leaving behind a cloud of swirling dirt and grass.

It felt like something I wasn't supposed to see.

&

An hour later, I found myself back on the real Gauntlet. I skipped across the first two sections so quickly I didn't hear the oohhs and aahhs till I was safely on the platform on the opposite side of Slug Alley. Tristan was there waiting, perched on the wall like a bird of prey.

"Impressive," he said. "The Allfather would be *so* proud of you."

If there was a gold medal for sarcasm, Tristan would be an Olympic phenomenon. I shook my head and started up the ladder that would lead me to my next obstacle. "Isn't there anyone else in Iceland you could torment?"

Tristan tried to look offended. "Cinder, I take time out of my busy day to watch you train, and this is how you treat me?"

I laughed. "Your busy day? Batting your eyes at the girls and insulting the rest? Wow, how do you find the time to eat and sleep?"

Tristan stood and walked easily along the top of the wall. If my insults bothered him, he didn't show it. "You should count your blessings, Cinder. You won't see a single slug or viper from here on out."

I reached the top of the ladder, lifted myself over the wall, and peered down. Jutting from the next platform was a wooden walkway, much wider than the narrow beams I had crossed earlier, but a dozen large crescent-shaped blades were slicing horizontally across the path at alternating levels.

"Nice," I said dismally. I looked over at Tristan. "What goes on inside your mind?"

For a brief moment, Tristan's bravado faltered, but he quickly recovered. With his lopsided smile, he said, "Scythes . . . Try and keep your head."

Sighing, I slid down the wall and landed on the platform. I remembered Tori saying this was where one of the Gauntlet's builders had died. A horrible, messy image suddenly filled my mind. I contemplated turning back.

"Study the movement of the blades," he said.

I waited for the insult.

"If you can figure out the pattern of their rotation, the scythes can be one of the easiest obstacles in the Gauntlet."

No sarcastic comment? No insult? I looked up at Tristan, wondering who had possessed his body. I didn't want to ruin it by saying something lame, so I nodded and turned my attention back to the glittering blades. The first scythe was slicing horizontally at neck level, which would require me to duck to avoid losing my head. The second scythe was a bit lower, but the third would give me a deadly haircut if I didn't crouch in time. The fourth blade would make wearing shoes pointless, and the fifth would hit me just above my belt. The pattern started over after the fifth scythe and repeated three times. There was just enough room between each slicing blade to stand and prepare for the next but cutting through that space was a huge scythe swinging like a pendulum, making it a really bad idea to stand and ponder the next rotation for too long.

I saw that the scythes were actually not moving as fast as I thought they were. I realized then that the real challenge of this section was not being sliced to ribbons but overcoming my *fear* of being sliced to ribbons. Freya had once said that fear can be one's greatest enemy, and so I took a deep steadying breath, stepped forward, ducked the swinging blade, then crouched even lower to avoid the second. I paused to measure the speed of the oncoming scythe, stepping into its path in order to miss being impaled on the pendulum. I ducked again, missed the scalping path of the third blade, paused, then leaped over the fourth blade. After a final pause, I rolled beneath the final scythe that would have divided me in two.

From the corner of my eye, I could see Tristan perched on the wall like a handsome gargoyle. He remained perfectly silent. I took his silence as a compliment, even if it wasn't meant to be one. I didn't have time to bask in my success, though; the scythes weren't through with me, and the pendulum was on its way back. Quickly, I stepped forward and repeated the process, popping up out of my roll and clearing the second set of scythes in half the time.

Before the pendulum could urge me forward, Tristan said, "Time the blades and make your path even easier."

Easier? How could it be easier? And then I saw it, as clear as day. The scythes hadn't changed their speed at all, but now I was seeing them as if they were moving in slow motion. I began to walk, just missing the pendulum so narrowly, I felt the back of my shirt flutter from the passing of the blade. Holding my breath, I continued to walk, speeding up and slowing my pace whenever I needed to. I finally stepped onto the platform, releasing my breath as the last scythe barely missed drawing a deep groove across the base of my spine.

Not once did I have to duck or jump or roll. "Yes!" I shouted excitedly.

"You do not have the flag in your hand, *yet*," said Tristan. "It's just like you to celebrate before it's time."

"Good to have you back," I muttered, pulling myself up the rope that was dangling down the next wall. Once on the other side, I found myself staring at a series of tiny platforms spaced about three feet apart, each one positioned diagonally from the last. The drop was about ten feet, and instead of vipers or oozing mud filled with slugs, a carpet of furry orange spiders rippled across the ground.

I looked up at Tristan in disbelief.

He shrugged. "Hey, I said there wouldn't be any more snakes or slugs." He pointed down at the ugly rust-colored spiders. "Those are *definitely* not snakes or slugs."

"Let me guess. Extremely hungry."

"Haven't eaten since yesterday."

"Painful bite?"

"A single bite is not bad. Several can have you wishing you'd never stepped off my sister's boat."

"Poisonous?"

"Only if bitten."

"I hope you haven't named any of them, because if I fall, I'm taking out at least five."

"I'll mourn in silence." Then Tristan smiled and said, "For you *and* the spiders."

Knowing it was doing me no good standing still, I leaped to the first platform, swayed for a moment, then jumped to the next. I glanced behind me and saw two healers were already standing on the platform I'd just left, each one gripping a fistful of slimy leaves.

I made two more successful jumps, then felt my sneakers slide across the next platform. I slipped over the edge, twisted around, then tried to grab onto the wooden pole that was holding up the platform. Unfortunately, Tristan, or someone else just as diabolical as he is, had lathered the pole with grease.

Despite the thick coat of bacon fat, my fireman act slowed my descent so my ankles didn't crumble beneath me when I hit the ground. Just as I had promised, I squashed several spiders, then yelped as several more scurried up my legs. I ran to the ladder, swatting the hand-sized creatures as I went. I scrambled up, but not before several painful sets of fangs went through my jeans.

When I got to the top, the healers moved towards me, but I pushed the leaves away and jumped back out onto the first platform, trying hard to ignore the fiery pain from the spider bites. I moved quicker this time, deciding not to use the platforms as two-footed stopping points to judge the next jump, but instead as a place to land with a single foot before leaping to the next. Before the healers could shout for me to stop, I was standing on the large platform on the other side.

The red flag was dangling at the end of a rope just above me. Seeing it so close made my heart seize up in my chest. I jerked on it, but when it came free, the platform beneath me fell away. Just as it began to fall, I stuck the flag in my mouth and leaped up, grasping the rope with one hand, then two. It was just like Tristan to place one final trick at the end.

I could hear him say, "Can't have a spider pit without the web."

Grunting around the flag in my mouth, I pulled myself up the rope till I was able to clamber onto the beam from which it was tied. Feeling at home on the beam, I ran across it till I was safely perched inside a large basket, kind of like a crow's nest on a pirate ship. The healers were cheering and clapping and one of them said, "Very good, child, but you will want to hurry down that ladder because within the hour, your flesh will fall off your bones."

The pain from the spider bites was making me dizzy, but I had never felt better in my life. I looked for Tristan, but he was gone.

CHAPTER 17

WEST COAST HALF-ELF

I slept great that night. Well, not great, but better than I had in quite a while. And that's saying a lot, considering the fact that my bed was a wool blanket laid over a reed mat. Hadn't the Vikings heard about memory foam mattresses?

I was lying there awake, savoring my victory over the Gauntlet, when Tori, who doubled as my alarm clock, stuck her head through the opening in my tent. Only it wasn't Tori.

"Oh, hi, Edda. Where's Tori?"

"She's meeting with Freya this morning." She heaved a huge dramatic sigh. "Looks like I get to babysit today."

I threw my pillow at her, but being inhumanly fast, she was able to snatch it out of the air and wing it back at me. The force of the blow left my head ringing. "Come on," she said, laughing. "Brunhild wants you to eat a quick breakfast, then get in some running before you do any Gauntlet training." Edda tossed my hoodie to me. "Congratulations, by the way."

"Thanks," I said, climbing to my feet. "I hate to say it, but the best part about it is knowing how much it must be killing Tristan that I beat his precious Gauntlet."

"You're evil," said Edda, though she couldn't help grinning.

We made it to the dining hall moments before they closed down for breakfast and joined Droma and a few non-traditional soldiers-in-training who were stuffing their faces with scones and biscuits smothered in thick, white gravy.

I took a seat next to the Predator. "You look better than ever, Droma," I told her.

"Thanks, but I'm still not a hundred percent."

"Want to run today with me and Edda?"

Droma shook her head. "I'm afraid I wouldn't be able to keep up with you two."

"Wow," I breathed, "I can actually outrun a Predator?"

"Enjoy it while you can," said Droma as she playfully pushed me away.

Our conversation was put on hold while I devoured everything on my plate. Scraping up the last bite with my fork, I was suddenly distracted by a flash of color. I looked up. A boy with shocking red hair and freckles was staring at me from across the table. He was wearing a green T-shirt that said "My Chemical Romance," which clashed horribly with his red hair, but stretched nicely over his lean muscles. He was certainly no Tristan, but he was cute in a goofy sort of way. I swallowed a mouthful of biscuits. Why did I always have food in my mouth every time a boy came around?

"Hey, aren't you Cindrheim Moss?" he said.

I glanced over at Edda and Droma. I was hoping they would come to my rescue, but they only bounced their eyebrows up and down and grinned. It was the universal code for: *He's kinda cute. Make a move while you have a chance.* They both turned away, leaving me to fend for myself. Did I have to have a grint after me to get their help?

"You can call me Cinder," I said finally.

He leaned forward eagerly. "Cinder. Cool. Are you the one that interrupted the end of the battle feast?"

I shook my head. "That was someone else."

The boy seemed disappointed. "No, it was you. It has to be. You ran out there with someone else's sword and tried to—"

"What's your name?" I said, eager to change the subject.

"I'm Brandon. I'm from Pismo. It's a small beach town in California." Brandon pulled back his hair to reveal pointed ears. "Got these from my mom. She's an elf. Dad's as human as they get."

Two weeks ago, if someone had shown me a set of pointed ears and stated they were half-elf, I would've run screaming, but now it takes a lot to surprise me. I found it more strange that a half-elf would be into My Chemical Romance. "Cool," I said, pulling back my own hair to reveal my boring rounded ears. "As human as they get."

"Nothing wrong with that," said Brandon. "At least you know exactly what you are."

I nodded. "So your mom's a full-blooded elf, living in California."

Brandon laughed. "She won six surfing competitions before my dad convinced her it wasn't fair." When he saw that I was confused, he said, "Full-blooded elves are three times as agile as a human."

"I see. Does anyone other than you and your dad know she's an elf?"

"She lives among people who don't have their eyes open; know what I mean?"

I nodded. It made me wonder how many elves I'd encountered in my life and not known it. I had a teacher in fourth grade that *had* to be half troll. "I guess if anyone found out, she could ask them to keep it a secret," I said.

"Hard to keep something like that on the down-low."

"How long have you been at the Proving Grounds?" I asked.

"Oh, about three years. Why?"

I smiled. "No one says 'on the down-low' anymore."

Brandon smiled back. "Thanks for the tip." We sat there listening to the noise around us, then Brandon said, "So you're from Virginia?"

"How'd you know? Is it my accent?"

"No. Most everyone knows about you. You're sort of the hot topic around here."

Droma and Edda both turned and grinned. Edda mouthed the words *hot topic*, and the two Predators broke into giggles.

I stared, my juice cup halfway to my mouth.

Brandon looked around, then lowered his voice. "It's not every day we get a new recruit who's here on account of one of the Twelve."

"You mean Odin?" I said, purposely letting my voice be heard over the breakfast commotion.

Edda and Droma both spun around and glared at me.

"Keep it down, will you?" said Brandon. "You wanna get us fed to Tristan's slugs?"

I laughed. "Those things are tired of me."

"So do you miss it?" said Brandon. "Virginia, I mean."

That was a great question. For a moment I just sat there. "Part of me misses it, I guess. Things move too quickly here to think about home."

"Yeah," sighed Brandon.

He looked away. I could see that he didn't completely agree with me. Time to change the subject again. "So are you part of a prophecy?"

Now it was Brandon's turn to laugh. "Me? No way. I'm your run-of-the-mill soldier-in-training."

"So if you're not part of a prophecy, how did you know you needed to come to the Proving Grounds?"

"Mostly it's my half-elf blood. But I also scored high on some aptitude tests that somehow are related to the skills needed on the battlefield."

I tried not to look at his hand. "Have you made a . . . pledge?"

"A hero's vow?" said Brandon. "I wish. Those are for potential heroes."

"So you're training for the Great Battle."

Brandon suddenly looked very nervous. "I just hope I make the cut."

I took a long swig of my orange juice. "Must be hard . . . waiting for a war to start."

I saw him staring enviously at my hand, so I tucked it under my other arm.

"I heard Skuld gave you that," he said, whistling in awe. "He's the most famous norn in the Nine Realms, you know."

I thought of the strange vagabond who had a penchant for Slurpees. "You'd think the most famous norn in the Nine Realms would dress a little better."

Brandon appeared confused.

"It's a long story."

Brandon looked around again. I thought he was going to bring up Odin, but instead he said, "Hey, there's going to be a *darfinhael* tonight in the Long Hall. It's the Viking version of a dance. Do you want to . . . go with me?"

Was he asking me out? It all seemed so strange. Here I was training to help the greatest Norse god in the universe and a boy from California was asking me to a dance. And me without a dress. "I don't know," I said, feeling my face flush. "It's just that—"

I felt Droma kick me under the table. "Ouch! Sounds fun." I tried to smile. "What time will you pick me up at my tent?"

Brandon's cheeks were suddenly the color of his hair. "How's seven?"

"Oh, seven's fine. I'll tell my daddy to put away the shotgun."

For a moment, Brandon thought I was serious. "Put away the shotgun. That's a good one."

Just then, I saw Tristan two tables over, walking by with a tray full of food. The dark glitter in his eyes made me suddenly want to cancel with Brandon. But he passed without even glancing at me. The feeling quickly faded. I used the tablecloth to wipe my mouth (which made Brandon raise his eyebrows), then I stood up. "See you at seven, then."

I looked over at Tristan again, but he had eyes only for his scones and biscuits.

✤

Running with a Predator (without first inhaling one of their enchanted wafers) is like running with someone who's driving alongside you in a car; Edda showed no signs of tiring, and at any moment, she could leave me in the dust by stepping on the pedal. But she kept pace with me, humoring me the entire time.

"It must be torture to run with me," I panted, eyeing the cool waters of The Mirror off to our left.

"You've gotten stronger, Cinder," replied Edda. "Remember your first days with us, how you weren't able to run half a mile without stopping to take a nap?"

I would've laughed, but laughing required oxygen, which I had none of, so I nodded and said, "Ready for the Boston Marathon."

Edda veered away from The Mirror's edge and I followed. Soon we were running alongside the Night Forest. The trees were now whipping by in a blur of green and brown. Edda teased me about my date with Brandon while we jogged, but thinking about it only made me anxious, which depleted my oxygen even faster.

Edda noticed me falter. "Let's break for a rest," she said.

I slowed to a stop and put my hands on my knees. Panting,

I looked up and saw that her breathing hadn't changed at all. In between ragged breaths, I said, "Can't hack it, huh?" I felt a painful stitch in my side, so I pressed my fist against my rib cage. "I'll slow down for you on the way back."

Edda was staring into the forest. I followed her gaze. Large, majestic oaks and towering firs stood in tightly packed clusters, their branches swaying gently in the morning breeze. Even with my blood pounding in my ears, I could still hear birds chirping as they hopped about the dark canopy. A black-coated fox darted from behind the wide bole of a tree directly in front of me and disappeared down a hole in the ground.

"Want to see the Night Forest?"

I couldn't say yes fast enough.

The Predator glanced at her wristwatch. "It's nine fifteen. I promised Brunhild I'd have you over to the Gauntlet by ten."

"Then we have forty-five minutes," I said excitedly. "Come on, Edda. I'll tell the Valkyrie you ran me into the ground."

"She *would* like to hear that. Fine. Twenty minutes, no more."

Just as we were about to enter the first ring of trees, someone called out, "Cinder, wait up!"

I turned and saw Brandon hurtling towards us. While I was impressed with his elf-infused super speed, I wasn't sure I wanted him stuck to me everywhere I went.

"Now's not a good time, Cinder," said Edda. "Try and get rid of him."

"Maybe he's coming to tell me he can't make it to the dance tonight."

Brandon skidded to a halt. "What're you guys up to?"

"Nothing," I said. "Just jogging."

"Me too."

Several seconds of awkward silence passed. "So did you come to let me know you found a better date?"

Brandon laughed. "No. Why, did you?"

"The day's still early," I said.

Brandon stopped laughing.

"She's joking, Brandon," said Edda with obvious impatience. "She does that a lot."

A tentative smile crept back onto Brandon's face. "Right. The day's still early. That's a good one."

More uncomfortable silence.

Edda stepped forward. "Brandon, don't you have some training to do?"

"I have combat practice at eleven thirty, so I'm free till then."

Brandon was starting to remind me of one of Tristan's slugs—definitely not as slimy, but a bit too clingy. "Listen, Brandon," I said, "Edda and I were going to check out the forest and we—"

The boy's eyes lit up. "Mind if I tag along?"

"Yes," said Edda quickly.

Brandon frowned. With his red hair and sad brown eyes, he looked like an Irish setter who'd been left out in the cold. I turned to Edda. "Please, Mommy? Can we keep him?"

Edda shook her head. "Fine." Under her breath, I heard her mutter, "I really *am* babysitting."

Brandon looked like he'd won the Icelandic lottery. Pumping his fist, he said, "This way, ladies. Allow me to be your guide through the Night Forest."

"Allow me to be sick," muttered Edda.

"Heard that," said Brandon, pointing to his ears. "Half-elf and everything."

CHAPTER 18

PLEASE DON'T FEED THE ANIMALS . . . OR FREE THEM FROM PRISON

Like Odin's Long Hall, the Night Forest had to be magical, or I was a full-blooded Valkyrie. Unless I was mistaken, trees didn't grow like this anywhere in the world. They were straight out of a fantasy painter's dream, times ten. The deeper we got, the more unreal the forest became. Trunks as thick as houses, with branches that soared like the arches of a cathedral, made me feel the size of an ant.

Some of the trees were brown or grayish white, of course, but some were phosphorescent blue or pale purple, wrapped in thick carpets of glowing green moss with huge floppy leaves the color of ripe tangerines. I walked beneath an arching root as thick as my waist, wishing I had a camera.

"Just when you thought Iceland was nothing but ice and scrub brush," said Edda, plodding a few paces behind me.

I was so entranced by my surroundings, I didn't answer for several seconds. "Botanists all over the world would give their right arms to see these trees."

Brandon, eager to be part of the conversation, said, "Takes special soil to grow these babies." He looked over at Edda. "Didn't Joro, Goddess of the Earth, plant these herself?"

Edda nodded. "Sounds like you know your Norse history."

Brandon beamed. "You have to if you're going to fight for Odin."

I ran up a sloping root that spiraled around the massive trunk of the nearest tree.

"Careful, Cinder," warned Edda. "All I need is for you to fall and break your neck, then have to explain to Brunhild that you died jogging around the lake."

I hardly heard a word she said. Before I knew it, I was several stories high, skipping along the curling root.

"Come back, Cinder," called Brandon. "Do you have any fear at all?"

I looked down. The Predator and half-elf looked small now. "Come down, Cinder," yelled Edda, "and I'll show you something much more interesting than a silly tree!"

"Deal," I called back. Spotting a dangling vine as thick as my wrist, I leaped out and grabbed hold of it. Brandon yelped in surprise, and Edda began to curse in ancient Nordic as I shimmied down. When I was safely on the ground, the Predator whacked me on the back of the head.

"You live your life as if you can't die, Cinder," she said.

"Let's go," I said. "Clock's ticking."

Shaking her head, Edda led us deeper into the woods. Before long, I began to hear a distant rumbling, like building thunder. "What is that?" I asked.

Brandon stopped and cupped his hand to one of his pointed ears. He mumbled something about *second year of study*, then said, "Please tell me that's not what I think it is." His face had gone a shade paler. "Because if it is, we should stop and turn around."

"We're safe," assured Edda, "as long as we keep our distance."

My heart rate jumped from first to fourth gear in seconds. I grabbed Edda's arm and pushed her forward. "Lead on, girl!"

But Brandon was shaking his head. "There's other things in the forest to see!" he called out.

"Then go find them!" shot Edda right back.

Despite Brandon's reluctance, we made good time as we passed beneath the towering trees. I noticed that the upper branches were so thick now that they formed a virtual roof that blocked out all but tiny shafts of pale sunlight. Melon-sized insects fluttered past my face, and I had to bat one away when it landed on my shoulder.

"I hope you didn't bring me this deep into the woods to show me overgrown bugs," I complained.

"What we're about to see is certainly overgrown," Edda said with a laugh, "but it's definitely not a bug."

Brandon had caught up with us. I could tell he had had a recent run-in with one of the giant insects, because one long crooked leg was draped over his shoulder. Grimacing, I flicked it off.

"Thanks," he said. "Nothin' like that in Pismo."

"Or Richmond," I replied. I wrinkled my nose. "What's that horrible odor?" Whatever it was, it smelled like a football stadium full of wet dogs.

"Well, you would stink, too, if you—" began Brandon, but Edda cut him off.

"Let her see for herself. Just a little further."

"I think I better wait here," said Brandon. "Just in case, you know . . . you ladies get lost or something."

"Come with us," I urged. "You made it this far, right?"

Edda slapped Brandon on the shoulder, which sent him stumbling to the side. "I think it's a great idea. I knew there was something I liked about you."

Brandon gave her a half smile, then pleaded with me with his eyes to stop and reconsider.

But Edda grabbed my arm and pulled me away. "Like you said, Cinder, clock's ticking." I trusted the Predator with my life, but there was something about the way Brandon had suddenly stopped that had me doubting my decision to follow Edda. But a moment later, the half-elf was lost in the shadows, and my mind was now filled only with the anticipation of what lay ahead of us.

The awful smell and the rumbling were getting stronger. We labored up a steep incline and dropped down through a narrow gulch that left me bruised and scraped by the time I reached flat ground.

"This is it," whispered Edda. "I just hope he comes out of his cave so you can get a good look at him."

"*Him?*" I said. My heart was now flip-flopping inside my chest.

"Come on." Edda ran quietly around an outcropping of granite, motioning for me to follow. Once on the other side, I immediately spotted the cave. How could I miss it? Its yawning mouth was large enough to admit a 747 jet.

Following the Predator's lead, we crept forward till we

were positioned behind the bole of a giant moss-encrusted tree. The smell was so bad now, I had to keep my hand over my nose and mouth. The rumbling suddenly stopped, and I heard a loud snuffling.

"He knows we're here," whispered Edda. She turned and grinned. "He's caught our scent."

I peered into the thick gloom of the cave. My hands were slick with sweat. "If something in there has *caught our scent*, shouldn't we be running for our lives?"

"I think it's time for a history lesson," said Edda. She gestured at the cave. "The creature's name is Fenrir. He's the eldest son of Loki, God of Mischief. His mother was a giantess named Angerboda. Fenrir can appear as a man, but he prefers the shape of a giant wolf. Most prophecies claim that his father, Loki, will someday be responsible for the destruction of the Nine Realms, and so the gods, in all their great wisdom, tried to capture Loki. They caught Angerboda and Fenrir, but Loki, being much more cunning, managed to escape. Angerboda was killed as she struggled to get free, and Fenrir was imprisoned."

"In this cave," I said, peering around Edda, but still unable to see anything at all in the darkness.

Edda nodded. "At first, the gods kept him in a cage, but no cage could hold him. So they ordered the dwarves to construct a chain strong enough to keep him bound for eternity. The dwarves crafted a thin ribbon called *Gleipnir*, fashioned from the footstep of a cat, the roots of a mountain, the breath of fishes, a woman's beard, a bird's spittle, and the sinew of a bear." Edda must've seen the look on my face because she said, "I know. Difficult to swallow, but we're talking high-end Bearded Folk magic here. And speaking of difficult to swallow, if Fenrir comes out of his doghouse, you'll see that he has a golden sword between his jaws, put there by the gods to ensure he doesn't bite anyone."

I took my hand away from my mouth long enough to say, "Why don't the gods just kill this thing?"

"No one knows," said Edda, "though my guess is they want to use Fenrir as a bargaining chip if they ever capture his father. He used to be imprisoned on the island of Lyngvi in the realm of the dwarves, but a little over a hundred years ago, enemies of Fenrir came looking to kill him. Odin thought it wise to move him here to Iceland in Midgard."

"How does he eat?"

"That's part of the punishment. Fenrir constantly feels the ravenous hunger of a wolf, yet can never eat. The magic of the gods can't prevent Fenrir from being murdered, but it keeps him from starving."

"That's awful. Is he really as bad as his father?"

Edda shrugged. "That's debatable and depends on the person you ask. But according to the gods, if your father's an enemy to Odin, everyone in the family must be as well."

"Bum deal," I whispered, straining to see any movement at all.

I nearly jumped out of my skin when a loud growl erupted from the mouth of the cave. Edda surprised me by striding out from behind the tree.

"What're you doing!" I hissed.

"It's perfectly safe," said Edda. "*Gleipnir* holds Fenrir in place like a chain on a rabid dog."

"But we don't know how long that chain is," I squeaked.

"*I* know," said the Predator. "I've been here before."

Shaking my head, I moved away from the tree and joined Edda. We took a few tentative steps forward. We stopped, however, when a pair of bright yellow eyes the size of trash can lids suddenly blinked in the darkness.

"We should get back to Brandon," I whispered.

"Brandon can take care of himself," said Edda. She startled me by shouting, "Fenrir! Come out and play, why don't you?"

More growling, only louder. Before, the creature's noises sounded curious. Now they sounded downright angry.

Edda shielded me with her arm. I gaped, unable to move a single muscle. My blood seemed to freeze in my veins. A wolf the size of a semitruck emerged from the cave. Bluish-black matted fur covered his sinewy body and grew in spiky clumps on his shoulders. His teeth and claws were like polished black spears, and his yellow eyes narrowed as they focused on us. Just as Edda had said, the golden blade of a sword gleamed in the creature's open mouth, propping open Fenrir's massive jaws.

I wanted to back up a step, but I couldn't move.

"Incredible, isn't it?" said Edda breathlessly.

Before I could respond, Fenrir moved forward, his huge claws shredding the ground. Now I could see the glittering silver ribbon that trailed from the wolf's neck and disappeared inside the gloom of his prison.

Edda pointed. "That would be *Gleipnir*, the enchanted tether made by the dwarves."

"And I would be Cinder, scared out of my mind."

"Fenrir's been imprisoned for nearly a thousand years, Cinder. You think he's going to suddenly break his magical chain the moment you and I show up?"

As if on cue, the giant wolf lurched forward with an ear-splitting growl, but the silvery rope jerked Fenrir violently back. Fenrir tried again and again, then threw back his head and howled so loudly I had to cover my ears.

Maybe it's not rage, I thought. *Maybe it's sorrow*. I suddenly thought of Saemund, locked up in his little cottage, unable to take more than ten paces in any direction, unable to see the sun or starlight.

"You said he can change into a human," I said out of the side of my mouth. "Can't he change shape and then slip out of the rope?"

"Fenrir hasn't been able to change into a man ever since he became a prisoner."

Fenrir finally stopped howling and looked at us. His exertions had caused him to pant, and now his large black tongue was hanging from his mouth, pushed to one side by the sharp sword.

Edda shook her head. "Seems a shame that he has to have that sword stuck in his mouth."

"Can't he just knock it out himself?"

"The punishment is an enchanted one. Someone else has to do it."

The tiny voice in my head started to warn me, but I smothered it by saying, "Let's remove it, then."

Edda stared at me.

"Come on," I said. "It's not like we're going to set the thing free. Just ease its pain a little. Imagine having your mouth propped open by a toothpick for a thousand years."

Edda studied the wolf for several moments. "It's probably the stupidest thing you've ever suggested . . . but a thousand years of confinement, made worse by Odin's cruelty . . . "

I nodded. I was already cooking up a plan. "Will he understand if we talk to him? If he knows we're trying to help him, maybe he won't snap us up like doggie snacks."

Edda shrugged. "Can't hurt to ask." The Predator strode forward, then stopped when she was a stone's throw away. Switching to ancient Nordic, she began to explain our offer. Completely in the dark now, I just watched the two of them. At first, Fenrir seemed to hate the idea, his huge, shaggy head shaking so that big glops of spittle flew in every direction. But the more Edda talked, the more he appeared to relax. *It's working*, I thought, watching as the wolf grew steadily calmer, then finally nodded his great head up and down in a gesture of apparent agreement.

Edda returned and said, "Fenrir has agreed to our offer, but on one condition."

"What's that?"

"He wants *you* to do it."

"What?" I blurted. "How can he talk with a sword in his mouth!"

"He pointed at you."

"But why me?"

"Because he doesn't trust immortals."

"Got all that from a few paw gestures, huh?" I could think of at least twenty reasons why this wasn't a good idea, but Fenrir looked absolutely pathetic. "Fine," I said, straightening my shoulders. "If I don't come back, you'll have to go with Brandon to the dance."

Edda laughed. "You'll be fine. Fenrir will lower his head to the ground. All you have to do is pull the sword out."

What could possibly go wrong? I wondered as I approached the giant wolf. *A lot, apparently.*

CHAPTER 19

A WOLF IN WOLF'S CLOTHING

The closer I got to Fenrir, the more I wanted to hurl from the smell. It was worse than a football stadium full of wet dogs. It was like a football stadium full of wet, *dead* dogs. The wolf's huge yellow eyes watched me intently as I walked towards him.

"Go on," urged Edda. "Look! He's lowering his head."

It was true. A wet-sounding whimper echoed from deep in Fenrir's open mouth as he flopped his massive head onto the ground. The impact nearly knocked me off my feet. Seeing my entire body mirrored in the creature's eyes made me want to turn and run.

I paused, second-guessing my decision big-time. But Edda badgered me till I continued on. Holding my breath, I walked up and placed my hands carefully around the blade. I won't lie—my whole body was trembling with fear.

"Do it, Cinder!" hissed Edda. "Do it now, before Fenrir changes his mind."

Gripping the blade, I pulled back, knowing it would probably be painful as it tore through the roof of the wolf's mouth. Fenrir squirmed as I wrenched it back and forth and a glop of wolf spit the size of a cantaloupe splashed against the side of my face. Wasn't I enjoying a nice, leisurely jog less than twenty minutes ago? Ignoring the hot spittle that was running down my neck, I gave the sword a final tug and out it came.

Edda shouted excitedly.

I turned and flung the sword as far as I could. But before I could spin around, I felt the air suddenly explode from my lungs as Fenrir clamped me between his huge front paws.

"Let her go!" Edda screamed. She ran towards us, then thought better of it and slid to a stop, her face a mask of fear and anger. "I am one of the Valhuri, and I *demand* that you release her."

"And why should I?" Fenrir asked. The wolf was speaking in perfect English, though every word was heavily accented with a throaty growl.

Now seemed like a good time to share my own opinion. Something like, *You should let the really dumb human you're holding go because she really, really does not want to be eaten! Duh!* But Fenrir was squeezing me so tightly I couldn't get a single word out.

"You have no idea who you're about to eat," said Edda. She was obviously stalling for time. Great tactic, but I needed an Asgard-class miracle, not more time.

"Why don't you enlighten me," growled Fenrir.

The wolf and I both stared at the Predator. *This better be good, Edda,* I thought. *I have a dance to get ready for.*

"Her name is Cindrheim Moss . . . she's a mortal . . . of course you know that already . . . she was brought to the Proving Grounds, per Odin's request. If you eat her, Allfather will be *very* upset."

"Odin!" roared Fenrir. His grip on me tightened, causing me to gasp for breath. "That one-eyed, raven-loving excuse for a god is the one responsible for my imprisonment!"

Edda cringed. "Did I say Odin? I meant Thor. *Thor* would be very upset if he knew—"

"Thor!" bellowed Fenrir. "That fork-tongued, thunder-spewing spawn of *No* Father is no less guilty for what has been done to me!"

Wow. Edda, you are the absolute worst *at hostage negotiation.* Luckily, Fenrir's grip on me relaxed just a tad. "If I may," I squeaked, cutting Edda off before she could do more damage. I turned to look the wolf in the eye. "If Odin is your enemy, you and I actually have something in common. The guy *hates* me. Seriously. If there's anyone he would like to imprison in a cave for a thousand—"

"I would ask you to stop talking," said Fenrir. His huge yellow eyes swiveled back to glare at Edda. "If Odin dislikes this mortal, tell him I have solved his problem for him."

Edda cursed and jabbed her sword menacingly. "How dare you—"

"Edda, no!" I shouted. "He'll just kill you too."

The Predator shook her head in frustration, then she seemed to make a decision. "I'll come back with Freya and Tristan. He won't hurt you, not if he's still chained where we can find him," she said. "Because if you *do* kill her—" Now she looked the wolf in the eyes. "—we will avenge her death in the most unpleasant manner imaginable."

"Great," I muttered. Not that I doubted Freya or Tristan's abilities, but this *was* Fenrir we were talking

about. Wouldn't Odin or Brunhild have been better? *Yep.*
You'll have *to avenge me,* I thought, *because I'll be swim-*
ming in this monster's stomach juices long before anyone gets
back. I watched Edda bolt through the trees.

"Well, that was unpleasant," said Fenrir, his gaze
returning to me.

I closed my eyes. "Just get it over with!" I shouted. "Eat
me, you flea-bitten doormat!"

"Do the insults take away a measure of the fear?"

I opened my eyes and swiveled my head. I tried to ignore
the wolf's breath, but it had to be melting my eyebrows.
"No . . . I . . . If you're going to eat me, I want you to do it
now."

"It is strange, but I sense more anger than fear in you."

"Yeah, well, I feel really stupid for trying to help you.
Shoulda known a god would never appreciate anyone doing
them a solid."

"A solid what?"

I sighed. "A favor."

Fenrir nodded his huge head. "I am not surprised.
Mortals can be so gullible."

"Seriously, though," I said, my anger blooming. "Having
a conversation with someone who's only going to tear me
to pieces is really disturbing. Let's cut the chitchat, please."

I don't know if you've ever seen a wolf smile, but Fenrir
did at that moment. "I am not going to eat you, mortal."

"Oh no," I breathed, my heart sinking. "You're going to
bat me around like a ball of string till I die of head trauma,
aren't you?"

Fenrir set me down. "I have to admit, I have done that before and it *is* quite liberating, but no."

I had been so filled with fear, my legs were useless. I immediately crumpled to the ground. "What . . . what are you doing?"

"I am setting you free," Fenrir said.

"But why?"

"Do you know how long I have had that infernal thorn in my mouth? Three hundred of your lifetimes, mortal. That is a very long time. Even for someone like me."

"So, you're . . . you're going to let me live?"

"They say the prisoner, if left long enough in shackles, comes to a realization. A reckoning of what they have done wrong, coupled with a sorrow that only the prisoner can ever understand. I believe I have passed through this. Perhaps twice."

I was speechless with relief. Finding my voice, I said, "So what now?"

"Well, I suspect you have a sizable choice to make," said the wolf. "Whether or not you should set me free . . . "

"I can do that?"

Fenrir pointed into the trees with one of his giant paws. "Only the sword that was placed in my mouth can sever the *Gleipnir* around my neck."

Seriously? I thought. *The gods would be dumb enough to make the sword the one thing that could also break the chain?* Then I remembered Odin's Chargers sweatshirt. *Yeah, maybe they would.*

"You may not eat *me*," I said, "but if I set you free, how

do I know you won't eat everyone in the Proving Grounds?"

The wolfish smile again. "You cannot be sure, can you?"

"Not the answer I was hoping for."

"Sever *Gleipnir*," said Fenrir, "and I give you my word I will not harm anyone in the Proving Grounds."

"Including Odin?" I asked carefully. "I'm not a big fan, but I *am* here on account of him and so it probably wouldn't be good for him to become your next meal."

Fenrir growled from deep in his belly, then nodded his head. "I imagine No Father would not taste very good. You have my word I will not eat him."

I climbed to my feet, retrieved the sword I had flung into the nearby trees, and returned to Fenrir. "I've done a lot of stupid things in my life, Fenrir, and this may very well be the granddaddy of them all." Without another thought I raised the sword, then brought it down hard on the glittering ribbon that hung from the wolf's neck.

A bright flash exploded in front of my face, forcing me to shield my eyes. I staggered back, watching as Fenrir stood and arched his back. He shook his thick mane of spiky black fur.

Fenrir chuckled, and his laughter was like an avalanche. "The mouse sets the lion free!" he roared. I waited for him to strike me down, because if he was going to do it, now would be the time.

But the strike never came. "Now tell me, little mouse," he growled, "what can I do for *you*?"

I asked to keep the sword. Wouldn't you?

CHAPTER 20

ΠΕVΕR ΤΙCK OFF A PREDATOR

"So what's your plan for the day?" I asked, slicing the magnificent sword through the air.

"The first thing I am going to do is fill my stomach," answered Fenrir.

I held the sword out in front of me. "Changed your mind, huh?"

"Not with you, Mouse. You are much too bony." Fenrir startled me by suddenly leaping into the air and snapping his jaws on a large bird that was winging over his cave.

"I have more meat than *that*," I said, slightly stung by the bony comment, and slightly nauseated by the puff of feathers that signaled the bird's last flight.

Fenrir licked his muzzle and eyed me intently. "You are a very peculiar mortal."

"This coming from a talking wolf the size of a school bus." Fenrir surprised me by laughing, though it was layered with throaty growls. "Well, I guess I should be getting back," I said. "If I know Edda, she'll be on her way with half of Asgard with her."

The wolf nodded. "Shall I carry you to the border of the forest?"

I thought of Fenrir's pungent odor and wondered if I could sit in his fur without yacking. "Sure . . . but are you going to stay in the woods?"

"I *am* part wolf," replied Fenrir, squatting down so I could clamber aboard. "That is what wolves do, you know. Besides, I need to stay hidden for a time. Decide my next move. I have been here for six hundred years. A few more weeks will not kill me. Although when No Father discovers I've been released . . . "

"Odin's the one who put you here, huh?" Fenrir nodded and there was a deep rumble in the back of his throat, like a Rottweiler preparing to attack.

"Odin's good at the imprisonment thing," I said, thinking of poor Saemund. "I can't promise he and the Valkyries don't already know, but as soon as I can talk to Edda, I will make sure word doesn't get out." I slid the sword down the back of my sweatshirt, then held my breath as I climbed up behind Fenrir's ears. Once in place, I dug my sneakers into his thick coat and grabbed a few handfuls of spiky fur. "Though once everyone sees I'm alive, they'll wonder how I escaped."

"Tell them you removed the sword from my mouth, then I turned on you and attacked. I was wounded; your skills with the blade were too much. You had mercy on me and left me to die."

"Aren't *we* the storyteller?"

"My father *is* Loki, father of lies. A boy learns by example."

It was difficult for me to picture Fenrir as a boy, or even a man for that matter. I didn't have much time to think about it, though, because Fenrir suddenly crouched, then leaped up and over the ridge in a single bound. It reminded me of the heart-dropping sensation of exploding off the ground with Trigga and her winged horse. We landed with a colossal thud, then Fenrir immediately began to race through the forest, dodging trees and leaping over boulders the size of small apartment buildings.

"Still there, Mouse?" growled Fenrir.

"Barely!" I shouted. I was hanging down the left side of his head, bouncing against him like a leaf caught in his coat.

"I apologize, but you cannot imagine the feeling of stretching your legs after six hundred years of confinement!"

I couldn't help but think of the little seer again.

It took us about sixty seconds to reach the forest's border. "This is fine, Fenrir, thank you."

The huge wolf skidded to a halt. The momentum caused me to somersault over his forehead and land on his muzzle. It hurt, but I was just grateful I didn't skewer myself on the sword that was still stuck down the back of my hoodie. I grabbed a few whiskers to keep from toppling to the ground.

"Ouch!" growled Fenrir. "My fault, I suppose." He quickly lowered his head and I dropped to the ground.

"I'll let you know how it all plays out," I said, pulling the sword out.

"Please do," said Fenrir. "Even a wolf enjoys drama. Goodbye, Mouse."

I smiled, patted his huge wet nose, and walked out of the forest. I instantly spotted Edda racing across the field with Freya and Tristan just a few steps behind her. All three of them had their weapons drawn. I waved, excited to tell them my story.

"Cinder!" Edda called out as she approached. "You escaped!"

Freya looked extremely pleased. Tristan did a masterful job of hiding anything he might've been feeling. Edda sheathed her sword and stared into the forest behind me.

"I have a really big favor to ask of you three," I said.

"Does this have to do with your escape from the wolf?" Freya asked.

I nodded, suddenly out of breath. "That's the thing—I didn't have to escape. Fenrir decided not to kill me. I guess because he appreciated me pulling the sword from his mouth. I—"

"Wait, back up," said Tristan, his mouth gaping. "Did you just say you pulled the sword from Fenrir's mouth?"

"Yep. Wanna see it?" I said, pulling out the storied weapon.

All three stared, slack-jawed at the golden blade in my hands.

"Is this a joke, Cindrheim?" said Freya, her tone deadly serious. "Because if it is, it is in poor taste."

"Very poor," echoed Tristan.

"No, it's not a joke," I said, handing Freya the sword.

Freya turned the blade over in her hands for nearly a minute, Edda and Tristan crowding close to see. Freya finally looked up. "This is indeed the blade that was placed in Fenrir's mouth." She handed the sword to Tristan, then started to rub the bridge of her nose. With her eyes closed, she said, "Please tell me you did not sever the cord that held him in place . . . "

"When you say 'sever,' do you mean cut or—"

"Odin save us all," said Freya, spinning around. She dug her fingers into her hair and walked away a few paces. She was muttering *foolish mortal* over and over, which I assumed meant me.

Tristan was swishing the blade through the air, chuckling softly.

Edda was still staring into the forest, her face stricken.

"Speaking of Odin," I said, "Fenrir asked that we not say anything while he figures out his next move."

"*His next move?*" Edda said incredulously. "I can tell you his next move, Cinder. He's going to eat every soldier-in-training in the Proving Grounds."

"Listen," I said. "Fenrir's changed. He's not the same wolf—person—god that he was when he was first imprisoned."

Freya spun around. "The great wolf was imprisoned for a *reason*, Cindrheim!"

"And he did his time!" I fired back. I was feeling a little defensive now.

"Who are you to decide when a fallen god has paid the price for his sins?"

"I was trying to show compassion. I guess it's a weakness us *Midgardians* have."

"Did you stop to think that maybe Fenrir was using you?"

"I did think of that. But if he was using me, why didn't he eat me after I released him?"

"Good point," muttered Tristan.

Freya glared at her brother.

"Sorry, just saying . . . "

"I cannot say why the wolf would spare your life, but your compassion may be the death of us."

I stared at Freya. Tristan and Edda were suddenly looking anywhere but at the two of us. "I did it. It's over," I said, as confidently as I could.

The Predator returned my stare, her eyes suddenly sad. "That is the thing, Cindrheim. It is *not* over." She spun on her heel and walked away.

Edda approached me, her eyes red and filled with tears. She gave me a quick, hard hug, then pulled back. "I am *so* sorry, Cinder. It's my fault you almost died. I—"

"Stop it, Edda," I said, squeezing her arms. "The trouble I find myself in is always on me. Please don't feel guilty for the stupid things I do."

"*So* stupid," muttered Tristan.

She embraced me again and whispered, "I'm just so happy to see you safe," then turned away and followed Freya.

When it was just the two of us, Tristan shrugged. "Once Freya knows you haven't kick-started Ragnarök, I'm sure she'll forgive you."

Was Freya right? Had Fenrir been kind, only so that he could use me to his own advantage later on?

He was Loki's son, after all.

☖

I made it all the way to the dining hall without a single person pointing at me and screaming, "Ghost!" Apparently Edda hadn't told anyone besides Tristan and Freya. My suspicions were confirmed a moment later when I heard a scream from across the room. Before I could step back, Tori had leaped across six tables and was crushing me in her arms.

"You're alive!" she shouted, holding me at arm's length. "What happened?" I tried to shush her, just in case Odin was anywhere close, but it was no use. Her words tumbled out in one long unbroken stream and not very quietly. "DromaandIwereoutonahuntwhenEddacamelookingforus-sowedidn'tfindouttilljustnowand—"

Droma was just a step behind Tori. She gripped my hand with both of hers. "We just heard," said Droma, cutting Tori off. She kept her words to a low whisper and her eyes flitted above her, probably scanning for Odin's nosy ravens. "An explanation is in order, Cinder."

I shared my story, leaving out the part of Edda encouraging me to see Fenrir; I didn't want Droma and Tori to think I blamed her. When I finished, Droma shook her head. "I'm afraid I'm not surprised you released a god from prison. It's a typical Tuesday for you."

Tori was staring at the sword strapped to my back. "Is that the sword . . . from the wolf's mouth . . . ?"

I pulled the sword out. "Pretty gross, huh?"

I could see both Predators were having a difficult time digesting this. "Fenrir let you keep it?"

I nodded. "Cool souvenir, right?"

"What will you do with it?" Droma asked.

"Not sure, though I know Freya wants to run me through with it."

"You know Freya," said Droma, touching my arm. "She'll stew for a few days, but then she'll let it go."

"I'm not so sure," I said. "You should've seen how upset she was. Her eyes were *literally* glowing red."

"I wouldn't worry," Tori said. "She's been angry at me before. Though I've never released a fallen god from a prison created by Allfather . . ."

"Thanks, Tori. I think."

At that moment, Brandon came up behind the Predators. He pointed at me, his eyes flitting between my face and the sword. His mouth was opening and shutting like a landed fish.

"Hey, Brandon. I see you survived. We still on for tonight?"

i WAS NEVER MEANT TO WEAR A DRESS

I would never describe myself as the "run-out-and-buy-the-prom-dress-type," so wearing jeans, a sweatshirt, and my Chuck Taylors to the dance that night was not going to ruin my evening. Unfortunately, they were covered in wolf spit. Even more unfortunate, Tori borrowed a dress for me from one of the soldiers-in-training from New York, whose mother was a fashion designer. It was a pale yellow number, which I didn't mind, but it was covered in bling, which I *did* mind.

"You look very pretty," said Tori, forcing me to spin around in front of a mirror she'd erected in her tent. "Brandon's going to be drooling."

"I look like a plaque-covered tooth."

"Stop it. Just seeing you like this makes me want to go."

I turned from the mirror and looked at her. "Then why don't you?"

Tori sighed. "It's frowned upon for the Valhuri to attend dances."

"Frowned upon?"

"When we make our vow, we promise not to . . . "

"Not to what?" I prodded.

"Not to attend any events that might lead to romantic possibilities," finished Tori. She mustered a valiant smile. "But that's fine, right? I'll live through you."

I stared at Tori. "I didn't know that about Predators. That's ridiculous. Who came up with that?"

Tori's smile slipped. "Allfather."

"Big surprise," I said, frowning. "*He* gets to *mingle* with whomever he wants."

"It keeps us focused," said Tori, though I could tell she didn't really believe it. She spun me around so that I was facing the mirror. "This is your night, Cinder. Enjoy it."

I frowned at my reflection and tried to pull the hem down. "If I'm the only one in a dress, Tori, I'm feeding you to Fenrir."

Brandon appeared at the mouth of my tent three minutes early. He was wearing a white tuxedo with a turquoise cummerbund and matching bow tie. It wasn't all that bad, except it clashed badly with his red hair.

I stepped out of the tent, totally embarrassed and ready to duck back inside. It didn't help that the spikes on my high heels quickly sank into the soft earth, pinning me to the ground.

"Wow," said Brandon. "You look . . . "

"Like a banana?"

Brandon was visibly nervous. "Bananas aren't bad. I prefer pears, but bananas are always in season. Okay, I need to stop talking."

"Let's go," I said, grabbing him by the arm. We hurried down the row of tents, but I veered off to my left before we reached the path that led to Odin's Long Hall. "Tori wanted me to stop by," I lied. "She hasn't seen my dress." Brandon frowned. "You know," I said, "girl stuff."

I ducked into Tori's tent, leaving Brandon outside.

"What are you doing here?" she said, startled to see me, but smiling despite herself. "Is the freckled stallion out there?"

"Listen, I'm not going unless you come with me."

"Maybe you haven't noticed, Cinder—I don't have a date *or* a dress."

"You don't need a date. You go as my protector—part of your duties as a Valhuri." When Tori began to shake her head, I said, "People around here are used to seeing someone babysitting me."

Tori grinned. "You need protection from Brandon?"

"Of course not. I'm just out of my element and I need someone like you to keep me from losing my nerve."

"Losing your nerve? You've run a sword through the mouth of a sea serpent and spent the morning between the paws of a giant wolf. You don't lose your nerve, Cinder."

"This is different."

"I don't know," sighed Tori. "I'll be a third tire."

"That's third *wheel*, and no you won't. You said there'd be food, and you love music. If you don't go, I'm telling Brandon that I don't want to go."

"I can live with that."

"Then I'll tell Freya you tried to ask Tristan to the dance, but I stopped you just in time."

Tori's eyes grew wide. "You wouldn't."

"I would, and I wouldn't regret it."

Tori shook her head and grabbed her jacket. "If the music's ancient, I'm history."

ॐ

Someone had lined the path to the Long Hall with shoulder-height torches. The flames alternated from cobalt blue to dusty rose, then finally to a glittery gold that sparked and had me skittering away before my dress went up in smoke, which wouldn't have been such a bad thing, except the dress wasn't mine and I had to return it the next day.

"Looks like they went all out," I said. The closer we got to the Long Hall, the more I was dreading stepping through the door.

"I feel so stupid," whispered Tori beside me.

"You shouldn't feel stupid," said Brandon, picking up on the Predator's soft words with his highly sensitive elven ears. "Every guy there tonight is going to have his date, plus an assistant whose duties are completely inexplicable."

I patted Brandon on the shoulder. "Finally, someone in this world who knows how to use sarcasm."

"I'm from Pismo, Cinder," said Brandon. "Not Valhalla."

"Coulda' fooled me," I said, smiling up at him. "You look like a true hero in that tux." Brandon puffed out his chest, and I said, "By the way, do they have a tuxedo shop here at the Proving Grounds?"

"No," said Brandon laughing. "We were told to pack for all occasions."

"I was never told how to pack," I said grumpily.

We finally reached the Long Hall, which was a quest in itself with me wobbling about on my matching yellow heels. The two beefy guards admitted us, snickering quietly at my inability to walk without my Chuck Taylors, and Brandon's attempt to paste a fiery red cowlick down with his own saliva.

The three of us walked in and were immediately met with a mixture of sound, color, light, and delicious smells. The walls of the Long Hall had magically been transformed to resemble a picturesque forest glade, with lifelike deer and an occasional fox. The animals actually moved, looking over at us as we entered, then darted away. I flinched as a lifelike dragon passed overhead.

"Don't worry, Cinder, I'll protect you," said Brandon.

"From a hologram?" Tori asked.

Brandon frowned.

The roof of the Long Hall was now a sunny sky that actually radiated real warmth. Fluffy white clouds drifted slowly over the ceiling before disappearing behind the towering trees on the walls. At the back end of the Long Hall, a huge Viking dressed in a baby blue gym suit stood atop a large platform, his bulky body flanked by towering speakers. He was currently firing up a song and encouraging everyone gathered in front of his stage to find a dance partner. In a semi-circle behind the DJ were twelve massive ice sculptures representing the twelve major Norse gods. Odin's icy likeness was the tallest of all (of course), the tip of his spear nearly touching the Long Hall's roof.

"This is crazy!" I shouted over the pounding music. "How often do you guys do this?"

"Three or four times a year!" yelled Brandon, bobbing his shoulders to the beat. "Keeps our morale up!"

"Do you usually have the dance in the Long Hall?"

"Heck no!" hollered Brandon. "We usually have it outside! This is a first!"

Even in the glare of the multi-colored strobe lights flashing around the Long Hall, I could see that the recruits had divided themselves into the usual groups: the traditional Vikings on one side and the modern up-and-coming soldiers on the other.

I pointed and shouted, "They need to mingle with each other!"

"Valhalla no!" Brandon called back. "They've never liked each other!"

The DJ turned the music up even louder. "Aren't they on the same side!"

"No, I don't care for any pie!"

I leaned closer to Brandon. "No, I said aren't they on the same side!"

"Oh, right! Well, they do have a common enemy, but they don't see eye to eye on anything really!"

I looked at Brandon. "What about you! Do you hate the traditional Vikings!"

Brandon was silent for a moment, then he shouted, "I've never gotten to know one to really hate them, but I do keep my distance!"

I shook my head. "You guys need to grow up!"

"You need to throw up?"

"What happened to your elf ears!"

"They're right here!" he shouted, pulling his hair to the side.

"Never mind!" I hollered. I looked over at Tori. I hadn't known the Predator for very long, but I did know that I had never seen her look frightened. Until now. I put my arm around her. "See anyone you like!"

Tori's eyes went wide and she shook her head vigorously. I leaned in close. "Thanks for coming."

She tried to smile but failed.

"Come on!" I said, grabbing both their arms. "I can smell Valkyrie-prepared food!" We headed for a long table draped in white linen and weighed down with heaping mounds of appetizers, entrées, and desserts. A tiered crystal fountain spouting a sparkling pink liquid sat at the far end of the table. We found paper cups and sampled the fruity beverage, then loaded our plates with more food than we would ever be able to eat.

The three of us grabbed fold-out chairs and took a seat. We balanced the plates on our knees and watched the recruits gyrating on the dance floor while we unwrapped our utensils. "You know how to show a girl a good time!" I shouted, popping a bacon-wrapped shrimp into my mouth. Brandon was too busy gnawing on a large chicken leg to respond. Tori just sat there, wringing her hands and staring straight ahead.

I was biting into a dumpling the size of my fist when I spotted Tristan. He was talking and laughing with a Viking who had wrapped his muscled body in a velvety red robe. Tristan, decked out in black dress pants and a tight white T-shirt that had the stylized image of a silver cummerbund and matching bow tie, slapped the Viking amicably on the shoulder, then moved on. *Rebel without a quest,* I thought to myself, though I felt a tingling sensation tap-dance up my spine. Unless his date was off getting him a drink, which wouldn't be beneath him, it appeared he was flying solo. Anyone else would've looked like such a loser, but Tristan somehow managed to pull it off.

Brandon followed my line of sight and said, "I see you've spotted Tristan. Have you met him yet?"

It was a few moments before I answered. "Uh . . . what . . . oh, yeah, we've met."

"The girls seem to really like him, but doesn't personality count anymore?"

"I know, right?" I said distantly. I saw that many of the girls were trying to focus on their dates but failing miserably. A fire-breathing dragon in the center of the room wouldn't have drawn as many stares as Tristan was getting.

"I suppose it's only a matter of time before you fall for him," said Brandon. He sounded really bummed.

"Probably," I said.

Both Tori and Brandon turned and stared at me. "Wait, what?" said Brandon. "Did you say *probably?*"

My thoughts screeched to a grinding halt. "What . . . oh no, I mean probably not in a million years. The guy's a jerk."

"You got that right," said Brandon, studying my face for any hint of deceit.

Cringing, I glanced over at Tori. She, too, was eyeing me curiously. She smiled, though it was a strange smile, as if there was a part of her that was itching to do anything but smile. Before I could stop myself, I said, "Go ask Tristan to dance, Tori."

Brandon seemed to think it was the best idea in the Nine Realms. "Yeah, Tori! Go dance with him, then ask him to marry you."

Tori slapped me on the shoulder, which stung quite a bit since she's as strong as three men. "Valhalla no, Cinder! What's wrong with you?"

"Who's gonna know?"

"Freya has a way of finding things out."

"Who cares!" I blurted. "She'll get over it. It's a harmless little dance!"

"Which could hopefully turn into something more lasting," replied Brandon.

I frowned at my date, then turned back to Tori.

For a brief moment, it looked like the Predator was going to take me up on my suggestion, then she sighed and said, "I took an oath, Cinder. It's hard to explain."

I nodded, a little grateful she had refused my suggestion.

What was wrong with me?

CHAPTER 22

CUT A RUG, SABOTAGE A DANCE

I was never going to win any dance contests, and Brandon was not much better. Put us together and you had something that resembled two people being attacked by hornets while falling down a flight of stairs. At one point, I thought the Viking DJ in the gym suit was going to stop the song and have us escorted out of the Long Hall by a pair of chaperoning dwarves.

"You would think dancing would come naturally for someone who's half-elf," said Brandon miserably as we made our way off the dance floor. "I hope if I'm ever given a quest, it doesn't require me to show my moves."

"Like an epic dance-off to the death?"

Brandon shook his head. "Please don't let me on the dance floor ever again."

"Don't feel so bad," I said. "I think I put my heel through at least five people's toes." I plopped down next to Tori and took off one of my shoes. "Who needs a sword when you have these things?" I looked at the Predator. She was busy shredding a napkin. "You look like you're having a great time."

"I shouldn't be here, Cinder," said Tori, her eyes darting

nervously around the room. She lowered her voice. "A boy came up and asked me to dance . . . I nearly said yes."

"No!" I gasped, pretending to be horrified. "It's a good thing you didn't, Tori. With a single dance, you could've jeopardized the gods' chances of saving the Nine Realms."

Tori nodded, then realized I was making fun of her. "You joke, but if Freya finds out, I'm finished."

"Finds out what? That you considered dancing with a boy, then spent the evening mutilating a dozen napkins?" I looked away for a moment, then said, "It's alright, Tori. You probably don't know how to dance, and the thought of embarrassing yourself out there terrifies you."

"I know what you're trying to do, Cinder," said Tori. "And it's not going to work. A team of Valkyries couldn't get me to—"

"Wanna dance?"

Both Tori and I looked up. There was Tristan, holding his hand out towards Tori. "Well?" he said. "Predators need a chance to relax every once in a while, don't they?"

"Okay," said Tori, rising shakily to her feet.

"You go, girl!" urged Brandon, holding his hand up so that Tori could high-five him. But Tori walked past him as if in a trance. "Maybe later," said Brandon, lowering his hand quickly.

I watched Tristan and Tori walk out onto the dance floor. I hadn't noticed that the loud pounding music had stopped, and now a sappy slow song was filling the Long Hall. Someone had dimmed the strobe lights and only a few glittering stars were spinning lazily across the marble floor. Very romantic, if you were looking for that sort of thing.

"Wow," said Brandon, "I've never seen Tristan dance with anyone before. He usually just comes to hang out. Guess it took a Predator to light his fire."

"Yeah, I guess it did," I said. I saw that Tristan and Tori were causing quite a stir (though neither seemed to notice). The crowd parted for the couple, as if they were royalty. Nearly everyone had stopped dancing to stare. In no time at all, people were whispering and pointing.

Yeah, you go, girl, I thought.

But somewhere—somewhere very, very deep—I wasn't as happy for Tori as I should've been.

"Let's dance, Brandon," I said, pulling the half-elf up off his chair so suddenly, he dropped his plate of powdered bonbons.

I dragged Brandon through the crowd, shouldering my way past startled couples. I found Tristan and Tori swaying gently back and forth. Her head was resting on his shoulder.

Don't let this get to you, Cinder, I thought. *He's a jerk, remember? You can't stand him. And more importantly, Tori likes him, and she's having a good time.*

I wasn't much better at slow dancing than I was at fast dancing, but at least neither of us were in jeopardy of knocking anyone's teeth out. Brandon and I began to move back and forth with as much rhythm and flexibility as two stone gargoyles.

"This is nice," said Brandon, tightening his grip around my waist.

I deliberately put a few more inches between us and looked over Brandon's shoulder at Tristan and Tori. They were talking about something. Then they started laughing. *What do they have to talk about?* I wondered. *And since when does Tristan laugh with someone?*

"Cinder?" said Bandon. "Cinder!"

"What . . . ? Oh, how can I help you?"

"How can I help you?" said Brandon, completely puzzled. "Cinder, you totally blanked out for the entire song."

I looked around. Most of the couples had left the dance floor. Tristan and Tori were still swaying back and forth even though the sappy music had ended and a new ground-pounding song was shaking the walls of the Long Hall.

And they were still *giggling.*

Brandon and I walked off the dance floor and took a seat. "I'm sorry," I said. "I'm ruining this night for both of us."

"Is everything okay?" said Brandon.

"Yeah, it's just that . . . well, my head's all messed up after that thing with Fenrir today."

"Kinda stinks that you had to get half mauled by a giant wolf on the same day as our dance."

"Yeah, rotten luck, huh?"

Brandon didn't say anything. He just stared across the dance floor, his chin resting in his hands. I felt terrible. "Brandon, listen. I'm not being honest with you." Brandon turned and looked at me. I seriously considered going with the wolf thing again. "You know, Tristan's been working with me, trying to train me for my quest, and he's been such a jerk. But I don't know . . . "

"I know," said Brandon heavily. "He still manages to get under your skin, right?"

"Let's forget about Tristan," I said suddenly, grabbing Brandon's hand and pulling him up. "I'm having fun with you and I don't want to waste any more time."

Brandon's green eyes lit up. "Really? Cool." We returned to the dance floor and quickly established a wide circle around us, as couples backed away from our flailing arms and legs.

After we obliterated four songs, we laughed our way back to the food table arm in arm and totally breathless. I filled a paper cup with the fizzy pink stuff from the fountain and took a long drink. Over the edge of my cup, I spotted a traditional Viking girl sitting by herself at the end of a long row of chairs. She was pretty by anyone's standards, but her loneliness made her look miserable. An idea popped into my head, and that voice that warned against doing something stupid started positively screaming. Naturally, I ignored it. I scanned the crowded room for several minutes and finally found a boy who was leaning against the wall, almost completely hidden by one of Odin's giant cauldrons. He was obviously a recruit from somewhere in America.

"I'll be right back," I said to Brandon. I hurried over to the girl and sat down next to her. "Hi, I'm Cinder."

The girl was chewing her fingernails. Cute, but no confidence. I see it all the time. She glanced at me, then looked away. "Hello."

"What's your name?"

"Sedya."

"Sedya. That's pretty. So did you come with anyone tonight?"

She shook her head.

"Really? That surprises me." We watched the people in front of us for a while, then I said, "I probably shouldn't be doing this, but I have to tell you. There's a boy here who also came alone and he thinks you're cute."

Sedya looked at me like I had just questioned her Viking heritage. "What? Who?"

I pointed. "See that boy . . . behind the cauldron? It was him."

The girl was immediately glaring at me. "Him? Never."

"You don't believe me?"

"No, he's a modern-day mess. Look at him. He doesn't even care about his culture."

"You mean because of the way he's dressed?"

"That's right. Our ancestors would be ashamed."

"Hmm. Well, if he really did think you were cute, and he wanted to dance with you, would you accept?"

Sedya chewed on her fingernail furiously as she thought about it. Finally she said, "Maybe, but only out of sympathy."

I smiled. "Okay, well, if he comes over . . . be nice."

"I won't hold my breath," said Sedya.

I hurried through the crowd, skirted the fire-breathing cauldron, and said, "Hi, I'm Cinder. What's your name?"

The boy was nibbling on a huge chocolate chip cookie. "Chad," he said, returning quickly to his cookie.

"Chad, do you see that girl over there, the one with the

brown hair? She's the one sitting down, chewing on her fingernails." Chad peered through the crowd, then nodded.

"Yeah, what about her?"

"Do you think she's pretty?"

Chad shrugged. "Sure, whatever."

"Well, she wants to dance with you," I said, cringing as I stretched the truth to the breaking point.

Chad considered the proposition, nibbled on his cookie for a few seconds, then said, "She's a true Viking. Why would she want to dance with me?"

"Who knows? I guess she can look past your horrible sins."

Chad arched his eyebrows in confusion, and I said, "Never mind. Go ask her to dance. It's better than standing around holding up the wall."

"No promises," said Chad, his eyes darting back to Sedya.

"Understood." I walked back to the food table and found Brandon trying to balance a stack of chocolate eclairs in his open palm. "Hey," I said, pulling up a chair.

"I would never call myself an expert in love," he said, adding another pastry to his leaning tower, "but it looked like you were trying to play cupid."

"Me? I was just mingling."

"You lie as well as you dance."

"Fine. I was conducting an experiment *and* at the same time trying to make two unhappy people happier."

Brandon stared at me incredulously. "How do you know they were unhappy? Maybe they *like* being by themselves."

"At a dance?"

"Who knows. You can't just assume—"

I cut Brandon off. "Look." We watched as Chad walked up to Sedya. He said something, then pointed to the dance floor. Sedya looked around as if waiting for her long-dead ancestors to materialize and strike her down for fraternizing with the enemy. Finally, she stood up and allowed Chad to lead her into the crowd of dancing recruits.

I spun around excitedly. "See! It worked! A traditional Viking and a modern Viking! Dancing together!"

Brandon sighed. "Something could still go wrong."

I pulled Brandon up. "Let's go out there so we can eavesdrop."

"Yes, let's get ourselves even deeper into this." He sighed, but he let me lead him through the crowd, spinning him around as soon as we got close to Chad and Sedya. If I thought it was hard to dance, it was nothing compared to dancing and eavesdropping at the same time.

"So you think I'm cute?" said Sedya, a nervous smile playing across her face.

"Oh no," I muttered.

"Well, I never really said that," replied Chad.

Sedya stopped dancing. "Cinder told me you thought I was cute."

"Did she?" said Chad, backing up a step. "She told me *you* really wanted to dance with *me*."

"Not good," I said, burying my face in Brandon's shoulder.

"*Really?*" said Sedya. Her hands were now on her hips. "I only wanted to dance with you because *she* said *you* said I was cute."

Chad's voice was getting louder. "And I only came over to ask you because Cinder said you *wanted* me to." At that moment, a large Viking teenager, dressed in his best animal skins, approached the couple and poked Chad hard in the chest. "You bothering Sedya, you Americanized pig?"

A small group of recruits, dressed in tuxedos, stepped up to the angry Viking. Chests started to puff and words began to fly.

When I heard someone say, "Cinder started this? Where is she?" I decided it was time to leave. "Abort, abort," I said, spinning around. I dragged Brandon through the milling crowd, my eyes searching for a place to lay low. By the time we made it to the food table, a small fight had broken out.

"Nice work, Cinder," said Brandon, his face turning a shade paler.

"Maybe this is needed," I argued. "Get the words flowing."

"And the blood."

At that moment, someone shouted, then a boy in a gray tux went sliding across the marble floor.

We watched as the dance floor turned quickly into a war zone. Those who weren't interested in fighting ran in different directions, scattering chairs and upending plates of food.

When one particularly large Viking shoved several opponents into the ice sculpture of Thor, I grabbed Brandon and said, "Experiment's over." We located a stunned Tori, then raced for the entrance, cringing as Thor toppled into Ullr, and Ullr toppled into Tyr, creating an ice statue domino effect that ended with Odin's icy spear slicing a long gouge in a painting of Allfather himself.

"If you're looking for a date to the next dance," said Brandon as he puffed along beside me, "I'm busy."

CHAPTER 23

A HARD-EARNED COMPLIMENT

Like clockwork, Tori poked her braided head through the opening of my tent just as the sun was rising. She pulled an earbud out, and said, "Brunhild wants to talk to you in the Long Hall, Cinder. Hurry, you're late."

I sat up. "Late? How can I be late if I didn't even know I was supposed to be somewhere?" My eyes were blurry and rubbing them only made them worse.

Tori shrugged. "I don't pretend to understand the—"

"Yeah, yeah," I said, holding my hand up. "You say that a lot, you know."

"Come on," she urged, gripping my hand and practically yanking me out of my tent. "If this is about last night's disaster, you really don't want to keep her waiting."

"Disaster? Wow, harsh."

"Love you, Cinder, but sometimes you don't know when to stop."

I felt my heart drop. During the night, I had completely forgotten about the failed Viking love experiment. I didn't know which was worse: that the two groups of recruits had turned the dance into a battle zone or that a dozen fifteen-foot ice sculptures had been smashed. Tori was right: it *was* a disaster, and I *didn't* know when to stop.

I shrugged into my hoodie as I trotted behind Tori, shivering in the cold morning air. A blanket of silver mist was rolling over the lake and the jagged black peaks were capped with new snow too bright to stare at for longer than a few seconds.

"Can we stop for breakfast first?" I said as we hurried past the dining hall. The aromas wafting through the open doors nearly stopped me in my tracks.

"Great Valhalla, no!" said Tori over her shoulder. "Three different people would have my head. Make that four."

We arrived at the Long Hall, nodding as we passed between the two towering Valkyries who stood sentry on either side of the door. Once inside, Brunhild stepped in front of me, grabbed my arm, and began to drag me across the polished floor. If I had to be accosted by a Valkyrie, why couldn't it be Trigga, or even Plyvis?

"Were you going to sleep away the whole day, child?" Brunhild growled.

I tried to run to keep up, but it was like an adult pulling a small child along so fast, all they can do is dangle their feet. "The sun's barely up! You haven't *seen* me sleep in yet."

The Valkyrie entered Odin's private lodgings at the back of the Long Hall, her fingers still tightly gripped around my upper arm. Odin was there, sitting on his throne, his cloudy blue robes still on, though his wide-brimmed hat was in his lap. I couldn't tell if he was angry or worried, but he was definitely not pleased. His animals were nowhere to be found.

"Bring her to me, Brunhild," he said, his voice quiet, but still terribly ominous.

The Valkyrie prodded me forward.

Odin pointed at Tori, who was standing with her head bowed. "Have the Predator wait outside."

Tori didn't have to be told twice. She turned and walked out, glancing at me as if she'd never see me again.

"You should wait outside as well, Brunhild. What I have to say is for the human's ears only."

The Valkyrie nodded once, then spun on her heel and departed. I felt my knees begin to knock against each other.

"Come forward, girl."

I was glad he called me "girl" because it made me angry and being angry had a way of taking away some of my fear. I approached his dais and looked up at him.

Odin stared down at me for what felt like an eternity, then he finally said, "You have only been here for a very short while, and already you have the residents of Iceland whispering your name as if you were a . . . what do you Midgardians call them . . . a celebrity."

I had to laugh. "You're kidding, right? A celebrity?"

Odin snapped his fingers. A bright light flashed, forcing me to look away. When I turned back there was a teenage boy with long reddish-brown hair standing next to me. He did not look happy.

"Grandfather, I simply *refuse* to be summoned without—"

"Quiet, Borghild," said Odin. "Recognize the girl?"

Borghild huffed and turned to look at me. His green eyes went wide. "This *cannot* be happening," he gushed, grabbing my hands. "Please tell me we can sit together for sketches later!"

"Sketches . . . ?" I stammered.

Borghild stepped back and excitedly pointed at himself. There on the front of his neon green T-shirt was my twelve-year-old face—the same sketch from the seer's scrolls.

"You've *got* to be kidding me," I said.

"Brilliant, right?" said Borghild. "Bragi insisted we keep his sketches private to protect the subject of the prophecy, blah blah blah, but I thought *get the word out, right?* Let the Nine Realms know Ragnarök might be the problem, but Cinder Moss is the answer!"

I vigorously shook my head and looked to Odin for help, but he'd closed his eyes and was rubbing the bridge of his nose.

Borghild pointed at his shirt. "Got a line of Cinder merch going—" Here, he frowned at Odin. "With no help from Grandpa, I might add, and I'm getting your face out to the farthest reaches of the realms. The Underworld is of course pushing back but as president of the CVM fan club, I have some pull."

"CVM . . . ?"

"Your initials, silly," he said, laughing. He looked at Odin. "See, Grandpa? Humble to a fault."

"Listen, I don't think this is a good idea. Maybe—"

Borghild reached out and covered my mouth with his

hand. "All I hear right now from you is, *Please run with this, Borghild.*"

I removed his hand. "That's not at all what I was saying. I think—"

Borghild wasn't done. "It would mean so much to me if you would—"

But Odin *was* done.

He snapped his fingers and the boy disappeared in another flash of bright light. "See what I mean?" said Odin, still rubbing the bridge of his nose.

"You let him walk around with my *picture* on his shirt?"

"Borghild is the God of Obstinance," growled Odin, propping his bearded chin in his hand. "Basically does whatever he wants. I'd have his head mounted on my wall if he wasn't my wife's favorite grandson."

"This is ridiculous," I muttered.

"You're telling me," Odin said. He gestured at me. "All this fuss and for what?"

Good. Bring on the insults, I thought. Any fear I might've had evaporated. "Listen, I didn't wake up at the crack of dawn to—"

"I will speak and you will listen." I shut my mouth. "The Twelve have officially penned your quest orders," said Odin. His icy blue eye narrowed. "Twenty-four hours ago, your role was uncertain. But no more. It seems you are to play a bigger part in our fate than I had anticipated."

"I'm sorry. I'm feeling really confused here." And I was. What happened to the tongue-lashing I was supposed to get for single-handedly ruining the Viking ball?

Odin huffed and his huge gray beard fluttered. "It would seem your involvement cannot be . . . avoided." Odin almost looked sad. "I know many things in this wide universe, but I do not understand how the life of a mortal girl, still years away from womanhood, can determine the fate of the immortals."

"You and me both." I took a step closer to the High Throne. "So what exactly *is* the quest?"

Odin huffed again. "You will be given the details of your mission when your training is complete."

I stared at Odin. "If you aren't going to tell me what the quest *is*, why pull me out of bed?"

"Because now that I know what you will be asked to do, I feel your training has not been sufficiently demanding."

"Not sufficiently demanding? Have *you* run the Gauntlet?"

"In my sleep," said Odin.

"Literally?"

"Literally."

I had forgotten I was talking to a god. I wanted to say: *Then why don't you take on this quest?* But I knew it had to do with end-of-the-universe prophecies, so I held my tongue.

"It's my quest," I said, sounding like Midgard's biggest baby. "I have a right to—"

"You have fewer rights here than you think," snapped Odin.

The two of us took deep, steadying breaths. "Don't forget, you *need* me."

Odin brushed his hand through the air. "Bah! It might be worth it to end this silly hope."

That stung. How often had I felt like the world would be better off without me?

"And speaking of the Gauntlet," said Odin, "I have heard Tristan's hero-maker no longer holds any challenge for you." I kept my expression as unreadable as I could, but inside I was screaming, *That's right! In your face, Tristan!* Odin grinned, almost maliciously. "But do not consider taking the High Throne just yet. You will need to do more than peel slugs and spiders off your scrawny hide."

Knowing I might not get the chance again, I said, "How exactly will my training become *sufficiently demanding?*"

Odin sighed. "I cannot say your new trainer is exactly thrilled to take you on as his apprentice, but since when does anyone really have a choice when it comes to my existence, right? I will let *him* give you the details."

Him? I thought. Oh no. No, not *him.* I shook my head. "Allfather, Tristan and I . . . we really . . . I just think that we—"

His whiskery cheeks were turning red again. "Most soldiers-in-training would die to be trained by Tristan, even for a single day."

"They can have it," I said, frowning. I crossed my arms over my chest. "We'll kill each other before he's taught me a single thing."

"The two of you will have to hold off any murderous plots until *after* you have completed your quest."

I threw my arms up. "But I don't even know what my quest is!"

"And you won't until the Twelve and I have finalized the particulars. Quests are never fully explained until the eve of departure. Surely someone in this frozen valley has told you this."

Now I was feeling downright surly. "And what if I decide not to go on this . . . *quest* of yours? What if I don't *want* to go? It *is* to save *you*, isn't it? Where I come from, you try to be nice to the people you need. But I guess when you're *immortal*, you don't play by the same rules." I looked away, as my eyes were suddenly stinging. "What if I change my mind about this whole thing?"

Odin turned the volume of his voice down a notch and said, "You made a vow, did you not?"

I looked down at the scar on the back of my hand and nodded.

"Vows are powerful things."

"But what if . . . what if I can't do it? What if I can't complete this quest of yours? I passed at least six people on the way over here who are much stronger, faster, and a heck of a lot smarter than me." I swiped at my eyes with the cuff of my hoodie. "Whether I back out of my vow or not, what chance do I really have?"

"Show me the flag," said Odin.

I paused, more than a little confused. "The flag?"

Odin pointed at me. "The one in your back pocket. The one you haven't let out of your sight since you first laid hold on it."

It suddenly dawned on me: the flag from the Gauntlet. It was true. The farthest it had been from me was my back pocket and I checked it more frequently than I cared to admit. I pulled it out, stared at it for a moment, then looked up at Odin.

"You are not the first to run the Gauntlet successfully," said Odin, "nor will you be the last."

I used to think it was quite an accomplishment . . . "Not that big of a deal, huh?"

"You are not the first human to do it, or even the first female."

"I get the point."

"But you *are* the youngest," said Odin. "And the first mortal to take the flag in the first week of training."

I looked up at Odin, totally speechless.

"That's right. You are the youngest to ever run Tristan's Gauntlet and take the flag, and only immortals have ever done it faster. Did you not notice that the boy was gone after you reached the end?"

I nodded, remembering how I had looked up and found that Tristan had practically vanished.

"Tristan knew what you had accomplished, and it injured his pride. He was so shocked," Odin paused to chuckle into his beard, "and a bit angry, that he fled to avoid your celebration."

"How do you know this? Did Tristan tell you?"

"Valhalla no, girl. I have eyes and ears all over this valley. I also have four different doctorates in psychology." Odin laughed again, then grew serious. "Have you ever wondered why people pick fights with you? Especially girls?"

"Yeah," I said. "Once or twice." What a lie. I had wondered this a thousand times at least.

"You have something in you, child. A hidden power, quite similar to your grandmother. People sense this in you, and they are threatened by it. Males tend to shy away, knowing it goes against society's rules to confront a female. But the girls . . . " Here Odin had to chuckle again. "The girls, they want to tear you down, even though they do not understand what it is that makes you different from them."

"And I just thought it was my clothes."

"A wardrobe change wouldn't hurt," admitted Odin. His smile faded. "I also know that you refused to let Clora heal that wound of yours. It is a reminder of your vow." Odin gestured at the flag in my hand. "Hold on to that bit of red cloth as well. It may be the only thing that reminds you that you are stronger, faster, and more intelligent than you think."

Had Odin just given me a compliment? Before I could thank him, he said, "Now quit sniveling and get out. Your training for the day began halfway through our conversation."

CHAPTER 24

DEATH BY SUPER-CUTE TRAINER

Odin wasn't kidding. My new training schedule had me starting at dawn. And there would be no more eating breakfast in the dining hall with Tori and the other Predators, where the huge fire that burned in the hearth warmed my numb fingers and the food was five-star-restaurant quality. Apparently, I could make do every morning with a slice of melon and a cup of chilled water.

"You should consider cutting back on my rations," I said irritably, taking a small nibble of the fruit. "A girl could get spoiled real fast on this stuff."

"You're lucky to get that," said Tristan. His tone was even more irritable than mine. He was leading me away from Odin's Long Hall at a brisk pace, as if he was hoping to lose me. It was obvious now why he had been so angry the other day; he had just learned that I was to be his pupil. I couldn't blame him, really. I wouldn't want me as a student either.

And he hadn't mentioned a thing about me taking the flag from his Gauntlet, which didn't surprise me one bit. I pulled the red flag out of my back pocket and made a show of tying my hair back with it.

We soon arrived at a spot near the lake where the grass had been scraped away in the shape of a large circle. Tristan walked up to a rack of weapons and started sorting through them as if he were picking out a shirt at the mall.

"Weapons training?" I said. I guess I should've expected this. He wasn't going to teach me how to cook or play chess. I sighed in relief when he passed on a wicked looking spear with a serrated bloodstained blade.

Tristan remained silent as he perused the weapons. It was difficult to even look at him because I pictured him dancing with Tori. I forced the image out of my mind. *He's a jerk*, I thought to myself. *A big, insensitive jerk. Who cares if he was dancing with Tori?*

Finally, he said, "This will have to do." He pulled out a thin sword whose blade was about three feet long and covered in rust. "Here, swing this around and try not to hurt yourself doing it." When he handed it to me, his eye caught the flash of red in my hair, and for a brief moment I could see the muscles in his jaw tighten.

Mission accomplished.

I took the sword and noticed the tip was bent. I used my thumbnail to scratch at the thick rust coating the blade. I thought of the magnificent sword that I had wrenched out of Fenrir's mouth. "I'm no sword expert, but these weapons seem a little . . . old."

"They're for practicing, you dope. Hopefully when it comes time for you to save the Nine Realms, you'll be given a blade worthy of your high station."

That does it. "Hey, look, I didn't ask for this, okay? You're not the only one who's unhappy around here."

Tristan suddenly looked really angry. "Who said I was unhappy?"

"No one," I replied quickly, remembering what Tori had told me in confidence. "It's just so . . . obvious."

Tristan spun away and started clanking loudly through the weapons, probably so he could use one of them to run me through. Before I could say anything else, he jerked out a sword that was similar to mine. He turned to face me and without hesitation, knocked the sword out of my hand.

"First lesson: never daydream while holding your weapon."

I picked the sword up off the ground, gripping the hilt as tightly as I could. "I tend to sign off whenever I'm around people that annoy me."

Before I could bring my sword up in front of me, Tristan whacked my leg with the flat of his blade. "Ow!" I shouted incredulously. "What was that for?"

Tristan should've been grinning, but he wasn't. "I tend to *hit* people that annoy me."

"Look, neither of us needs any practice at sparring with words. When it comes to swordplay, I obviously have no idea what I'm doing, and I hear you are very good, so let's get this over with so we can go our separate ways."

Tristan seemed to agree wholeheartedly: I was incredibly bad, he was amazingly good, and he wanted nothing more than to be done with me. Was there a tiny part of me, though, that hoped he *didn't* want to be done with me?

I didn't have much time to think about it. Tristan knocked the sword out of my hand again and said, "Allow me to do that a third time, and you'll be running laps around The Mirror till sundown."

I glanced at the lake and laughed. "You and what army?"

"Brunhild."

I stopped laughing.

And so my weapons training began. It was more grueling than I thought it would be. It started with learning a variety of stances, each one designed to inflict the most damage to my opponent. When he felt comfortable that I had mastered this, I was drilled on defensive stances, though he spent little time in teaching me how to protect myself.

When I questioned him about this, he said, "If you become half as good as you should be, you will not have need to defend yourself. You will be the first to strike and your opponent will not be able to retaliate because he or she or *it* will be dead."

"That's comforting," I said.

Tristan tossed me a cloth and told me to wrap my blade. "We spar until lunch. Unless I deem that you don't deserve to eat."

I smiled. "You can *deem* all you want. I'm eating lunch whether you like it or not."

"Eager to gnaw on that slice of bread, are we?" And for the next two hours, Tristan slapped, whacked, and bludgeoned me till I was covered in bruises. He paused after a particularly nasty strike that had me doubling over and clutching my stomach. "Do you need to see the healers?" There was more satisfaction in his voice than there was concern.

"As much as I need that sword of yours shoved through my rib cage."

Tristan grinned. "That can be arranged." With a flurry of movement that was too fast for me to follow, he rushed towards me, knocked my sword arm up, and stuck the tip of his blade hard against my ribs. His face was barely an inch from mine. For a moment, my mind clouded and a tremor rocketed up my spine. "The healers would have a difficult time patching *that* one up," he said. He leaned in closer. "I told you to spin to the side when you see your opponent rushing you."

"Which side?" I breathed, wincing from the pain in my ribs.

"I think it's obvious. You go to the side you feel most comfortable with."

Before he could pull away, I spun to my left, brought my sword arm down in an arc, and caught Tristan hard in the ankle so that the blow swept him off his feet. He landed hard on his back. He was so surprised, he failed to bring his sword around to block any further attacks. I quickly flicked my own sword to his exposed throat, and said, "The healers would have a difficult time patching *this* one up."

We returned to the combat circle by the lake after a very restful seven-minute break. By now, some of the soldiers-in-training were out on The Mirror in rowboats made for racing or swimming with wet suits. Tristan got my attention by whacking me on the back of the head with his sword.

"You can waste time when you're not on my clock," he said, flicking his sword at me. "Let's go. Initial stance."

Growling, I thrust my right foot forward, lowered my backside, kept my left heel raised off the ground, and pointed my sword at Tristan. I twirled the tip in tiny circles.

"Attack!" ordered Tristan, dancing backward as I moved in. "Parry!" he said, easily blocking my thrust.

This routine went on all afternoon, although it wasn't just attacking and parrying. I don't have the time or space to list all of the combat commands he bellowed at me for hours on end or the insults he hurled my way. Soon, the sun's reflection on the lake faded and night fell with an almost audible whisper, and still we fought. I could tell Tristan was holding back, but every once in a while, whether it was intentional or not, he gave me a tiny glimpse of what he could really do. I made a mental note to never push him too far.

Dinner consisted of a piece of dried meat that I'm almost positive was a strip of leather from someone's saddle. I gulped it down, though, and looked around for more.

"Anything else to eat?" I asked.

"Just the bite of my sword," replied Tristan, gesturing for me to swallow what I had in my mouth and prepare for battle. I reentered the combat circle, pausing as several young recruits came over to watch.

"Wonderful," I said, trying hard to ignore their curious stares. "All I need is for *everyone* to see me goof up."

"You're better than many who have been training for three months," said Tristan, then his face blanched as if he couldn't believe he'd paid me a compliment.

"Accidental?"

"Of course."

"Thank you anyway."

"It's true, but forget I said it. Basking in any emotion will get you killed."

I tried to forget it, but I was having a hard time doing it. We continued sparring, Tristan dancing about me so effortlessly, it made me feel as if I had huge concrete blocks tied to my feet. At one point, I stopped to lean on my sword, breathless from learning a move that had me circling Tristan while he sat cross-legged on the ground.

"It's dark, Tristan. I can barely see you anymore."

Tristan measured the moon's glow on The Mirror, then said, "Ideal for stealth training."

I could only shake my head. "Don't you ever get tired?"

"You said it yourself, Cinder. Let's get this over with so we can go our separate ways."

"Yeah," I said half-heartedly. "I guess I did say that." I suddenly thought of Tori. Where was she when I needed her? I found it odd that she hadn't been out to see me all day. One by one our audience was drifting away, obviously eager to find something more entertaining elsewhere. Don't *they* have training to do? I wondered. And what time was it, anyway?

"I require two more hours," said Tristan, "and then you can return to your tent."

I was so exhausted, I wasn't sure I could go on, but seeing Tristan's smirk by the light of the moon was enough to keep me going. I was feeling especially rebellious now, so when I spotted lights twinkling in Saemund's cottage, I grinned.

The young seer would get a visit from me soon, and it would be a visit he would not soon forget.

CHAPTER 25

A Night on the Lake

After two hours of stealth training, Tristan escorted me to my tent as if he were my big brother and he had just caught me sneaking out. It looked like he was going to say something, then he just nodded and disappeared into the night.

"Good night to you too," I mumbled softly. When I was sure he was gone, I crept out of my tent and cut a length of rope from my makeshift gauntlet. Knowing the burly dwarf would be standing guard outside of Saemund's door, I quickly ran around the lake so that I could approach the seer's little cottage from the back side.

Suppressing my fear, I looped the rope over my head, then quietly climbed to the roof. I tiptoed over to the chimney, tied one end of my rope around the brick base, then dropped the other end down into the dark flue. As I climbed down from the cottage, I couldn't help but wonder what Tristan would have to say about me using the stealth skills he had just taught me an hour ago. Laughing quietly, I circled the lake once again, then approached the dwarf with a big smile.

"Good evening, sir," I said, suddenly nervous he was going to say something about me being out of breath. Luckily, the dwarf didn't seem to notice.

"Cindrheim," he growled, visibly tightening his grip on his war hammer. "Yer here at a strange hour."

"I know. Odin's got me on this *really* tough training program, and I don't have any time during the day to do anything but swing a sword or walk over pits of snakes."

The dwarf nodded. "Nothin' wrong with swingin' a sword, and there be honor to be found in bravin' a pit o' vipers."

"I guess. But what I really need to do is talk to the seer."

The dwarf's dark eyes narrowed. "No one told me you'd be comin'. There be strict rules about visitors comin' to see the seer."

"What's your name?" I asked, flashing my coyest smile.

"Gollmaevill-Grimr-Gustr. Me lads call me Kevin."

I didn't so much as crack a smile, though it was almost painful not to. "Kevin, Odin just received a new prophecy that concerns me, and I heard it from him, but I don't believe it. He said, 'Go to the seer yourself, you flighty little human.' So that's why I'm here."

"Flighty little human," echoed the dwarf. "Sounds like Odin all right." He tugged on his beard with one hand. "I don't know . . . "

I hated to do it, but I said, "Brunhild even said I should come see the seer."

Kevin's tattoo-covered cheek twitched. "The Valkyrie said that, did she?"

The guilt was turning sour in my stomach, but there was no turning back. "Just this morning."

"Go on, then," said Kevin reluctantly. "But make it quick." With a finger like a fat sausage, he pointed at me, then gestured at the disturbing image spray-painted on his armor.

The last thing I needed was an ax in my head. "In and out," I promised, patting him on his beefy arm as I passed through the door. Kevin really was a likable guy, but if everything went as planned, no one would be the wiser.

As soon as the door closed behind me, I surveyed the small room. Saemund was sound asleep, but fortunately for me, the light was on (I didn't want to creep around in the dark and risk striking my shin on something or scare him out of his mind). I walked over to his cot, touched him gently on the arm, and said, "Saemund. Wake up."

The tiny seer stirred. He took his time opening his eyes. "Who is it?" he said sleepily.

"It's just me, Cinder. Don't be afraid."

Softly, and totally *un*afraid, Saemund said, "Ah, the hero of our age. Come to draw portents of the future out of me?"

"No," I said, shaking my head. "I came to see if you want to play."

Saemund stared at me for what felt like an eternity. His large blue eyes finally blinked, and he said, "I may be the most intelligent life-form on Midgard, but you have stumped me. What are you getting at?"

I smiled. "You know. Play. Have fun. Get out, feel the wind on your face, look at the stars. I don't know."

Another long pause. "Are you . . . insane?"

"Probably. And you better take advantage of my insanity before it's too late."

The seer sat up. "And how would you propose I get out? Did you strike down the dwarf?"

"I didn't have to. Look." I pointed at his fireplace.

Tentatively, Saemund climbed from his bed and walked over to the small brick hearth. He knelt and peered into the fireplace, then grasped the rope. Turning, he said, "Seriously, child. Have you lost your mind?"

"Yes, yes, I'm crazy already! We've established that. Grab hold of the rope and climb up the chimney."

For a moment, I thought Saemund was going to yell for Kevin, but he suddenly grinned and said, "I barely remember the wind and the stars. I think I should like to experience them again."

"Good," I said, clapping him on the back. "I'll meet you on the other side of the cottage." I opened the door, shut it behind me, and said, "Well, just as I thought. After breakfast, I'm supposed to cut off the head of Medusa."

Kevin stared at me. "Wrong mythology, ya flighty little human."

"Right. But it did have something to do with decapitating a creature, and it was definitely supposed to happen right after breakfast."

I thought for one terrifying moment the dwarf was going to seize me by the neck and call for Brunhild, but he only shrugged his huge shoulders and said, "Prophecies. Who really understands them?"

"Not me," I said, totally relieved. "Well, goodnight!" I

waved and left as quickly as I could. To be safe, I ran back around the lake. When I finally reached the back side of the cottage, Saemund was there, kneeling in the wet grass, his face and arms so covered in soot I nearly missed him in the shadows.

"This is grass," whispered Saemund. "*Real* grass."

Watching him was bittersweet.

The seer stood. "The dwarf told me that the valley now holds a lake. Is it true?"

My jaw dropped. "You didn't know about The Mirror?"

Saemund's face brightened. "So it is true, then!" He wrapped his little fingers around my hand and began to pull me away from the cottage. "Let's go see it!"

Trying to hold back our laughter, we scurried away from the cottage and headed for the lake. We were there in minutes. The Mirror's water was glassy and black, accented with the milky reflection of the moon. Saemund was silent for a long time.

I spotted a small boat not far from where we stood. It was tied to a stake that had been driven into the pebbly shore.

The tiny voice in my head said, *Cinder, put it out of your mind*, but I quickly pushed the voice away. "Want to go for a boat ride?" I asked.

The seer looked at me as if I'd woken him from a dream. He nodded, smiling.

Grabbing his hand, I led him to the boat, then held it steady while he clambered in. "Okay, sit in the back there, and I'll shove us out."

Saemund was so light, he barely shook the boat at all. He took his seat, staring excitedly all around him. Ignoring the bone-chilling temperature of the water, I stepped out into the lake, pushing the boat ahead of me. When we were far enough out, I jumped in, and we both squealed with laughter when I nearly capsized the boat.

"I could fall in and die an icy death, Cinder, and it would be worth it!"

"We'll save the swimming for another time," I said, laughing. There were two sets of oars stored in the bottom of the boat, but they were far too heavy for Saemund, so the little seer gripped the edges while I paddled us out towards the middle of the lake.

"The stars are even more exquisite than I remember them, Cinder. Billions of them, so far away . . . "

"I'm glad you're having a good time," I said. "No one should be cooped up in a tiny cottage their whole life. I don't care *who* they are."

The seer took his eyes off the stars for a moment to stare at me. "You know, you are no different than your grand-mother. And that is a good thing."

I smiled again, feeling closer than ever to my namesake. We finally reached the middle of the lake. We talked about the black mountains that hemmed the little valley, how the wind made a laughing sound as it swept across the fields, and how black-feathered cranes fished for minnows in the shallows.

Just as Saemund began to tell me what he knew about the Night Forest, our boat suddenly tilted in the water.

The seer yelped in surprise. I snatched up one of the oars and held it aloft, wishing I had my training sword, even though it was covered in rust and bent at the tip.

I thought Saemund would whimper with fear, but instead, he started giggling. It sounded very eerie in the gloomy silence. He began to peer into the water on either side of the boat.

"Why are you laughing?" I whispered.

"This is exciting!" he whispered back. "Who knows what dark thing lurks directly beneath us, just waiting to tip us into its watery realm?"

I gaped at him. "You *want* to be attacked?"

"I definitely do not wish any harm to befall *you*, child, but I am prepared for the end. Just think, Cinder, it would happen in a lake that was not even here when I entered that cottage."

"You can't be serious."

Saemund stopped giggling. "Cinder, I am over four hundred years old. I have lived out my life five or six times over. There comes a time when a person is . . . ready for the next chapter in their story."

It was breaking my heart to see someone so small and so young-looking discussing the end of his life. "But you haven't been out of your cottage for more than an hour. Don't you want to see more?"

The seer smiled. "Cinder, what you did is the greatest gift someone can give me, but we both know that all good things come to an end. As daring and as devilishly insane as you obviously are, you cannot spring me from my prison every night."

"Maybe not *every* night . . . "

The water off to my right rippled. Out of the corner of my eye, I saw something thin and pale, like a hand, break the surface of the water. I gripped the oar more tightly.

"Something is taunting us," whispered the seer. "Deal with it first, then we can discuss the terms of my imprisonment."

A moment later, I spotted a head with hair like tendrils of wet vines draped across bare shoulders. Whatever it was, it was rising up over the stern, just inches behind Saemund. Two large eyes, liquid green in the darkness, blinked rapidly, then a pair of green lips grinned at me.

I got ready to bring the oar down on the creature's head, when it giggled.

Saemund spun around, completely unafraid. "Hello!" he said cheerfully, reaching out his tiny hand. The water creature, obviously a female, disappeared into the water before the seer could touch her.

"Water nymphs," breathed Saemund, excitedly.

Before I could say that *I* was not ready to die, five or six water nymphs popped up on all sides of the boat. They were all giggling and pointing at us with slender green arms and impossibly thin fingers—fingers that ended in sharp, translucent nails. Their long green hair floated in the water around them like drifts of seaweed.

"The would-be heroine and the boy-man who brought her to life," squealed one of the nymphs in a singsong voice. "Ours for the taking, so far from home, so far from father . . . " She laughed and the other nymphs laughed with her. They glided through the water towards us.

Ours for the taking. I didn't like the sound of that at all. I raised the oar even higher. "Put one hand on this boat, and you're gonna get the business end of this paddle," I said, gritting my teeth.

The nymphs looked at each other in complete silence, then burst out laughing. "So brave," purred another, cutting around behind me. I spun around, trying to follow her movements. It was hard, though, because I was trying to keep the rest of them in sight at the same time.

The nymph who had spoken first wagged one long finger back and forth. "You did not follow protocol, Cinder-rule-bender. Such a disobedient mortal you are."

"Protocol?" I asked, glancing at Saemund. "What is she talking about?"

The little seer was staring at his feet. It looked like he was trying to recall a very difficult question on a test. Suddenly, he looked up and said, "Yes! I have it. Anyone seeking to enter the domain of a water nymph must first ask permission. Permission is almost always granted, but anyone who fails to do this beforehand faces dire consequences. Dire meaning death by drowning, or the pulling off of all four limbs, which also usually results in death." The seer smiled, obviously pleased with himself. "I *knew* I would remember." I watched his excitement fade as the truth of our situation set in.

Now that I thought about it, it made sense that I saw those recruits singing at the water's edge. They were asking for permission to use the lake.

I looked sheepishly down at the nymph, then started to sing. "Ohhhh, great water nyyyymph . . . Can we pleasssssssse enter your watery realmmmmmmm. Can weeeeeeee please?"

The nymph's mouth was hanging open in astonishment. Once she recovered, she grinned. "I have heard of your rebellious nature, *heroine*, and you obviously believe that you can tread uncaringly upon our waters and mock our laws." Her green eyes glittered with malice. "Because of this, you and your little friend will not step foot upon the shore ever again."

Fear and anger bloomed inside of me. "Wait!" I blurted, pointing at Saemund. "This isn't just my friend. He's the seer, the one Odin uses to provide prophecies for the future. You can't kill Odin's seer!"

The nymph's grin widened. "A trophy whose bones I will treasure until the dark water consumes them."

That's it, sister, I thought. *You've gone and done it now.* "If you do this, Odin will empty this lake and lay every one of you out to dry!" I yelled.

"The Allfather cannot stop us," the nymph shot back, "nor undo anything once it has been done. Haven't you been taught that even gods have rules they must live by? Odin would be bound to this ancient law even if you had the mighty Thor in your boat. Silly mortal. How sad you will learn the hard way." Giggling, the nymph glided towards me. I raised the oar up, but just as I was about to bring it down, someone grabbed the boat from the other side and gave it a vicious tug. I staggered and fell backward. When

I looked up, I saw a pair of green hands reach over the stern and pluck Saemund from where he was sitting. His expression told me that he expected such a horrible ending.

There was a tiny splash, then the seer was gone.

I screamed his name, then screamed for anyone who would listen.

When Saemund didn't surface, I kicked off my shoes and dove into the cold water.

CHAPTER 26

BRINGER OF STORMS

Diving into an ice-cold lake was like being punched in the stomach really hard. (Believe me, I know.) Once the initial blow faded, my heart seized up in my chest, and my arms and legs felt totally numb. I opened my eyes, but immediately closed them because, for one thing, I saw nothing but inky blackness, and for another, the intense cold burned my eyes like fire.

I actually screamed Saemund's name several times before I realized my voice wasn't carrying through the murky water at all. I tried to feel around with my hands, hoping I would get lucky and find the little seer, but there was nothing to latch onto besides strands of slippery weeds. Despair and guilt suddenly struck me, much harder than the cold impact of hitting the water. If Saemund died, it would be my fault. Period. I convinced him to leave the safety of his cottage, and now he was dead.

No! I thought. *I'll die trying to find him!* I pushed myself deeper, then opened my eyes again. To my surprise, I saw blurry images all around me. It had to be the water nymphs. They were pointing at me and laughing, then darting in to poke me or pull at my hair. I tried to fight back. I managed to punch one of them in the face, though the water slowed my fist down so much, the nymph shook it off and laughed at me some more.

I realized my supply of oxygen was nearly gone. Several hands suddenly gripped my ankles and wrists, and I felt myself being pulled deeper, deeper, until it felt like our descent would never end. I exhaled in a silent scream, then felt something grip my upper arm much tighter than anything I'd felt before.

I cried out in pain but felt myself rising through the water at an incredible rate. My eyes were open, but there was a torrent of tiny bubbles flowing down over my face, obscuring my vision. A moment later, I broke the surface. I gulped a huge mouthful of air, but it felt like my lungs had already burst. Before I could look around to see what had happened, a pair of strong hands grabbed me and threw me through the air so that I landed with a wet thud in the boat. I smacked my head and elbow hard on the stern, but I didn't care. Something, or someone, had saved me. Next, Saemund fell into my lap. He was shivering and giggling at the same time.

"Th-th-th-that was in-in-incredible!" laughed the seer, his teeth chattering so hard I could barely understand his words. "Do the night's adventures never end?"

I could only shake my head. An angry female face suddenly appeared over the boat's edge. My heart sank. It was Brunhild, and she looked furious enough to eat nails. Something snorted above me. Looking up, I spotted the Valkyrie's white horse hovering above us, looking just as furious as she was, his snowy white wings stirring the water like the propeller of a large helicopter. I looked back at the Valkyrie.

"Brunhild," I said, shivering uncontrollably, "it's so good to see you."

"It is best you not say a word, Cindrheim," said Brunhild through tightly clenched teeth. She swam around to the stern, then gripped the boat and began to pull us through the water. "Who knows what further catastrophe you could bring upon the world just by opening your mouth."

I was too cold and miserable to respond. Water nymphs were suddenly dotting the surface all around us. One of them said, "Shield Maiden, you know our laws. They cannot be broken, even by the gods themselves."

"I know the laws better than you do," growled Brunhild. "Now go deep, nymphs, before I tie you all together and stick you on a fishhook."

All the nymphs gasped as one. "Dump the seer and the mortal girl into the water, Brunhild. Even the Allfather cannot save you in this."

I contemplated throwing myself to the nymphs as a sacrifice, but my legs were so cold they had locked at the knees and I couldn't stand up. And I also wasn't quite ready to die.

Brunhild continued to pull us through the water at a steady pace.

"Foolish Valkyrie," said the nymph behind us. She glided through the water and floated next to Brunhild. "Your fate is now worse off than theirs would have been."

"Seek me out, water maiden," said Brunhild, gripping

the creature by the neck. "I will be waiting for you." With a grunt, the Valkyrie tossed the nymph through the air. The creature squealed and landed with a tiny splash nearly fifty yards away.

The other nymphs quickly disappeared beneath the surface.

Once we reached dry land, we were ordered to get out of the boat. As soon as we were out, Brunhild grabbed the boat and, in her anger, flung it down shore where it smashed against an outcropping of stone.

Saemund stared sadly at the splintered mess. "That will make it difficult to use again."

"Shh," I whispered.

Brunhild stamped her foot. Her white steed touched down beside her with a loud snort. She hefted the little seer onto the horse's back. "Carry Saemund to his cottage," she commanded. "Do not leave until he is safely inside." I watched Saemund grip the creature's wing joints excitedly, cheering madly as he was lifted up into the sky.

"Goodbye, Cinder!" he shouted, thoroughly enjoying the ride. "Whatever happens, I do not regret your actions!"

I didn't have the heart to respond. I couldn't even wave back.

Turning towards me, Brunhild said, "I will deal with the dwarf when I get a chance."

I cringed. I had totally forgotten about Kevin. What would happen to him?

"Brunhild," I said, pleading, "please, it wasn't his fault. I—"

"Stop talking," said the Valkyrie. "Bad things happen when you talk." As if to prove her point, the sky lit up with a brilliant sheet of lightning, followed closely by an earsplitting crack of thunder. "You see?" she said, "the gods are displeased. I may have snatched you from the water nymphs, only to have you struck down by a bolt of lightning."

I had angered a lot of people in my life, but I couldn't recall a time when I had actually affected the weather.

&

I stood before Odin, but I couldn't look at him. I was actually surprised he hadn't already skewered me with his spear. His pet ravens took wing and both of his huge hunting hounds wandered off as if they could feel the heat of his anger. Brunhild gave me one last withering glare, then left the Long Hall. *Is he waiting for me to speak?* I wondered. *Or is he deciding my punishment? And would there be consequences for Saemund and Kevin the dwarf as well?*

Outside, the thunder was still booming and a terrible storm was now beating down on the Long Hall's roof. I couldn't take it. "Allfather, say something, please."

"You are going home, Cinder."

It was a long time before I could get my mouth to work. "Wait, what?"

"It is over. Your time here is finished."

"For taking Saemund out of his *prison*?" It terrified me to think what he would say or do if he knew I released *Fenrir* from prison.

Odin shook his head. He looked very tired (if gods can look tired). "I take offense to your assumptions, girl. You do not, nor will you ever, fully understand the ways of our world. You are part of something so grand and complex, it would crush your mind into powder if I but told you a fraction of the truth."

I had a lot of different emotions fighting to get out, but as usual, my anger bullied its way to the top. "Try me."

Odin stared at me. "I will not lower myself to satisfy your curiosity."

Really, what did I have to lose, right? "How would *you* like to spend your days inside a tiny cottage? With all due respect, sir, you order people around because no one can refuse you, but you don't take the time to wonder how your plans to stay in power might be affecting everyone around you." My chest was heaving, and I was on a roll, but seeing his narrowed blue eye riveted on me like a bird of prey made me falter.

"Gather whatever possessions you brought with you, Cinder. Brunhild will fly you home at dawn."

I stood, frozen in place, trying hard to decide how I felt. Was this a good thing? Had I just dodged a bullet, or was I about to miss out on the best thing that had ever happened to me?

"Brunhild just saved my life," I said. "If you're sending me home, why didn't she just let me drown?"

"Like the Predators, her duty is to keep you alive at all costs. In the process, she broke an ancient law, a transgression for which I have not yet forgiven her. The law requires a life, but I will appease the nymph's demands through banishment."

I laughed darkly. "So someone had to die or get kicked out."

"Correct."

"I thought you needed me," I said, choking on the words.

I could tell it was taking everything in Odin to respond. "We will take our chances. You were never meant to save us from destruction . . . only to slow it down."

I could only stare in shock. Finally, I said, "You mean my part in this prophecy . . . was not to save anyone . . . ?"

A satisfied smirk ruffled Odin's great beard. "Your human ego would like that, would it not?"

Now I was really ticked. "My *ego*? You think I'm here because I signed up for this? I was taken out of my school and—"

"You showed promise, but in the end, you are too much of a liability."

"A liability, huh? Well, before I leave, explain to me why I was here if not to save someone from something."

For a brief moment, Odin looked sad, almost fearful, but it passed quickly. "Ragnarök swiftly approaches. It signifies the end of our world and the beginning of a new one. We cannot stop it. Following the long, dark winter, the gods will be thrown down in the Great War, defeated for all time. It is already written in the stars and upon the sacred tablets of the Nine Realms. Our only hope lies not in turning back the darkness but fighting to the very end. We cannot win, we know this, but we can find reward in heroism."

For the third time in as many minutes, I was shocked into silence. I tried to remember the words of the prophecy, but my mind had stopped working.

"Your role, girl," said Odin slowly, "was never to bring us victory, but to throw a stick in our enemy's spokes."

"You read the prophecy . . . ?"

"Of *course* I read the prophecy."

"I thought it was for my eyes only."

"I am the Allfather. Nothing has been written in the universe that I cannot view."

"So, what does it mean?"

"It doesn't matter now."

I felt my eyes well with tears. "It matters to *me*."

"You are a mortal from Midgard. You would either dismiss my explanation or forget it by tomorrow. Do not ask again."

"Everyone here . . . everyone training, building their skills . . . it's all for nothing?"

"Nothing is for nothing," said Odin cryptically. "Each of them prepares for a battle that may or may not be tied to our eventual doom, but each of them strives for something more important than victory." I waited for the answer, but I already knew it. He had already said it. "They strive to be heroes," said Odin. "Or die trying. There is nothing in life greater than this."

"I don't understand. The last time we talked, you told me the Twelve had written my quest orders. What about that?"

Odin's broad shoulders slumped, but he quickly straight-ened up as if he didn't wish me to see him despair. "Too many things have happened since then, things that forced me to realize my decision to include you was . . . not a good one."

Ouch. That one hurt.

"And taking the seer from his cottage, exposing him to any number of hazards, then breaking the law of the—"

"No one even told me about that stupid lake!" I blurted. "Has anyone around here heard of a *no trespassing* sign?"

Odin smiled, but it was a sad one. "Would that have stopped you, Cinder?"

"Probably not, but if the fine print warned me that I would be dragged down to the bottom of the lake, I might've thought twice."

"What should have been done," said Odin, "is behind us now. No one in Asgard thought you would kidnap the oracle of the Nine Realms and take him out onto a lake infested with water nymphs in the middle of the night."

"So, I made a mistake. Big deal!"

"A mistake? What about interrupting the feast of the fallen? In two thousand years, such a thing has never happened."

"Well, it was time to change things up a little, then."

"And that embarrassing brawl at the dance the other night? I understand you instigated that. And shattered an ice sculpture of me that took me hours to get just right."

"I was trying to get those two bullheaded groups to talk to each other!" I growled. "I didn't think they'd throw down."

"Throw what down?"

"Never mind. Alright, *two or three* mistakes."

Odin stared at me for a while, then said, "And your new sword . . . ?"

Oh no, I thought. *Time to play dumb.* "My new sword?"

"Do not be coy, Cinder. You removed the sword from Fenrir's mouth. Do not make yourself look foolish by denying it."

Now *my* shoulders slumped. There was no use justifying my actions. Before I could ask how he knew, Odin pointed to the two ravens who were perched on either side of the High Throne. "Hugin and Munin made me aware this evening. Now, thanks to you, I have another issue to deal with during a season when I have little time and even less patience."

"Fenrir won't trouble you."

With a great show of restraint, Odin said, "Do you know who the wolf's father is?"

"Loki."

Odin nodded. "Much misery will come from your . . . *dental* work, you will see."

"The wolf has changed, Allfather. He—"

"Freeing Loki's spawn was like a dagger to my heart, girl," said Odin heavily. "Because of your actions, I name you *Stormbringer*, Daughter of Ill-Fortune."

"I've always wanted a nickname," I snapped angrily. I really wanted to punch something. "Anything else?"

Odin's expression suddenly looked pained. "I do not usually say this, especially to a mortal, but I am sorry for everything. I wish you well."

I felt my eyes stinging with tears again. "So that's it?"

Odin nodded firmly, then said, "Farewell, Cinder."

I turned and walked out of the Long Hall. *How fitting,* I thought, stepping into the lashing rain: the storm had only gotten stronger.

ḣAṅṪ iṅ Ṫḣe QUeSṪ jAR

Staring at the ceiling of my tent, I decided I was probably the first recruit to be kicked out of the Proving
Grounds before the first round of cuts.

"Tristan'll be happy," I whispered, and the wind whistled past my doorway as if in agreement.

I fell asleep, but only because it hurt less than being
awake.

Just as the sun was warming the side of my tent, Brunhild
called for me. I'd slept in my clothes, so I was ready to go.
I thought of Carl and Nancy, my foster parents. I had been
gone from home now for over three weeks. Despite what
Freya said, I was sure they had alerted the police. But did
they really miss me? Would they be happy to see me, or
disappointed that I was back? I pulled my hoodie over my
head and stepped out of my tent.

"Ready?" said the Valkyrie. She was sitting on top of her
horse, trying hard not to look at me.

I felt my heart suddenly seize up in my chest. "Will the
Predators travel with us?"

Brunhild shook her head. "They are no longer needed."

I don't need protection anymore, I thought. I found it odd
that I would much rather prefer to have wicked monsters

hunting me so that I could have the Valhuri close. "Can I say goodbye to them?"

"No," said Brunhild. "Allfather feels that it would be best if you leave in secret."

I felt completely empty inside. I would never see Tori and Freya, or Droma and Edda. Never see Brandon . . . And it even hurt to think about Tristan.

The Valkyrie reached out her gloved hand. "You will sit behind me, Stormbringer."

Was Brunhild just rubbing it in with my new title, or was she simply following protocol? I grasped her hand and she easily pulled me up into her saddle. "To the west, Haflestod," she said firmly. The horse snorted in anticipation, but just as it crouched to spring into the air, a Viking rushed up to us, calling for us to stop.

I'm fairly certain Brunhild cursed in ancient Nordic.

The man was out of breath, his face as red as Brunhild's cape. "M'lady," he huffed, "may I speak to you?"

Brunhild steadied her mount, then sighed irritably. "What is it?"

"I have a message from the dwarf that stands guard at the seer's cottage. It was given to him by Saemund himself. He asked that I give it to you."

"I will read it when I return," said the Valkyrie.

"Begging your pardon, m'lady," said the man, "but the seer said you need to read this before you leave." The Viking cringed as if waiting for a blow that would send him flying across the lake.

Snatching the note out of the man's hand, Brunhild

unfolded it and scanned it quickly. When she was finished, she looked across the field towards Saemund's cottage. What was happening?

"Have the dwarf inform the seer that I will not follow this order until my father reads the letter."

"The Allfather already knows," replied the messenger. He looked at me. "The Predators' pledge to protect the mortal has been reinstated by Odin. Though grudgingly."

I didn't care. My heart soared.

Brunhild paused for several moments before saying, "I see. Return to your post."

"Very good," said the man, thumping his chest with his mailed fist. He glanced at me, then turned and jogged away.

My heart did a backflip. "Is everything alright?" I asked. I was trying really hard to contain my excitement.

It was a few moments before Brunhild answered me. "I cannot say for sure, but it appears your departure may be postponed."

My mind was reeling. What could possibly be in that note that would keep me in Iceland? Brunhild certainly wasn't going to give me any answers. She was totally tight-lipped as she delivered me to Saemond's cottage. "Wait here," she said gruffly. She slid from her horse, gestured for Kevin to open the door, then disappeared inside.

I looked out across the grassy plain. Everything seemed normal. Hundreds of recruits were engaged in their various skill-building activities, some canoeing (with permission) across The Mirror, a few braving the Gauntlet, and a large group of traditional Vikings leaving the dining hall. They were laughing and shoving one another playfully. Two of them had broken away from the pack and were playing keep-away with a friend's horned helmet. Another pair was holding hands.

A sharp spike of envy pricked my gut. I wanted to be back in their shoes (or fur-lined boots). I wanted to be leaving the dining hall after eating breakfast, headed towards the combat circle by the lake. I wanted to be crossing swords with Tristan, even if he insulted me after every blow.

I wanted to stay.

If the Predators' pledge to protect me had truly been reinstated, did I dare hope?

I searched the fields for any sign of the Valhuri, or even Brandon. If they were out there somewhere, I couldn't see them. *What's taking Brunhild so long?* I wondered, staring at Saemund's door.

"Hi, Kevin," I said, hoping he hadn't been punished for my stunt the previous night. "So how's . . . sentry duty . . . ?"

"You'll get no information from me, Cindrheim," grumbled the dwarf, "so don't waste yer breath."

"Listen, about last night. I really didn't mean to—"

The dwarf held up his hand and I fell silent. "Everythin' ya do is written in the stars."

I remembered Edda had said something similar when she saw I'd somehow killed the sea serpent. I hadn't known what to say then, and I didn't know what to say now, so I just nodded. I tried to wait as patiently as I could, but

I couldn't bear it. I slid off the Valkyrie's horse and made for the cottage.

"Are ya daft, girl?" growled Kevin. "A Valkyrie ordered ya to stay put. Brunhild, no less!"

"It's written in the stars," I said, but before I could reach the little porch, Brunhild emerged.

"How did I know you couldn't wait until I returned?" said the Valkyrie, looking down at me and frowning.

"Sorry. I really want to know what's going on."

"I am not sure," replied Brunhild tightly. It was painfully obvious that she had been told only what she needed to know, and it was driving her mad with curiosity.

I looked up at Brunhild. "Do I—"

"Yes, go in," said the Valkyrie impatiently.

As I approached, Kevin released the iron bolt in the lock and pushed the door open just enough for me to squeeze through. The dwarf shook his head as I passed him. The door closed behind me, and Saemund was there to greet me, grabbing my hands with both of his. "Cinder, it is good to see you, child," he said, his eyes moist and his tiny voice slightly hoarse.

"Are you okay?" I asked, then I noticed we weren't alone. Sitting on his bed was a cloaked figure, the hood drawn up so that the face was completely lost in shadow. "Oh," I said, abruptly stopping.

A bit awkwardly, Saemund held his hand out towards the stranger and said, "Cinder, I would like you to meet someone."

The person stood up from the bed and threw back the

hood. It was a woman, maybe thirty years old. Long, dark hair tumbled onto her shoulders and framed a very pretty face with dark eyes that looked very familiar. We stared at each other for several seconds, then with trepidation I said, "Hello, I'm—"

"Cinder," said the woman. She smiled, and before I knew it, her arms were wrapped around me. She wasn't much bigger than I was, so I was instantly shocked at how easily she crushed me in her embrace. Just to be polite, I squeezed back. Over her shoulder, I could see the little seer looking up at us. Saemund swiped at a tear that was rolling down his face. I mouthed the words *Who is this?* but he was too busy enjoying the moment.

The woman finally pulled away from me. "It is so good to finally meet you."

"I . . . I'm sorry," I stuttered. "I'm afraid I don't know you."

Saemund blew his nose loudly on a handkerchief, and said, "Well how do you like that? I send for your grand-mother, and you don't even recognize her."

I must've looked ridiculous standing there with my jaw on the floor. "Are you . . . you're . . . ?"

"Yes," said Saemund, pulling out a chair for each of us, "Cindrheim Vustora, meet Cindrheim Vustora."

My eyes had to be bulging in their sockets. I realized she didn't look very grandmotherly. "My grandma? You're too young . . . how is it—"

"You have not caught on to the whole immortal thing yet, have you?" said Saemund. "Come, sit down, both of you."

We sat, each of us never taking our eyes off the other. I shook my head. "There's so much I want to ask you."

"And I you," said my grandma. And now *her* eyes were tearing up just like Saemund's. She dabbed her eyes with her own handkerchief. "It is like I am looking at my daughter when she was your age."

At the thought of my mom, I felt my throat tighten. I pulled my picture of me and Uncle Robert from my pocket and showed it to her. "Do you know my uncle?" I asked eagerly.

My grandma stared at the picture, then hesitated before answering. "Robert," she said softly. "Your dad's brother."

"Yes, do you know anything about him? Where he is?"

She suddenly looked so sad I was almost sorry I'd asked. "I do not, Cinder. He is part of the Midgardian armed forces. His responsibilities—"

"Keep him traveling all over the world," I said, finishing her sentence for her. I tucked the picture away.

"Do you like it here?" said my grandma, her tone instantly brightening. She touched the back of her hand to my cheek. "Are you staying warm? It can get dreadfully cold in this valley."

I smiled. It was such a simple question, and yet I couldn't remember ever hearing such a wonderful set of words in one sentence. "I'm fine, Grandma." And then it hit me. Even though the Predators' pledge to protect me was back in place, I was more than likely leaving. Maybe not today, but soon. Right when I had finally found someone in my family, I was leaving. I looked down. "I won't have to worry about the cold much longer. Odin has released me from his service." When they didn't say anything, I said, "Haven't you heard my new title? They call me—"

"Stormbringer," she replied. "I actually like it. Even a title can strike fear into your enemies."

"I am frightened just looking at you," said Saemund.

I wanted to give him a playful punch in the arm, but it somehow felt wrong hitting the universe's most revered oracle. "I guess I've been called worse."

"Saemund," she said, "tell Cinder why I am here."

The seer was suddenly beaming. "Four days ago I had a vision, which has nothing to do with my intellect, mind you. My stroke of genius came *after* the vision. You see, I was stoking the fire early in the morning and I could see you in the flames, talking to Odin. I saw him tell you that you were going home, and I became very upset."

"Why?"

"For one, it was partly my fault, insisting that we row out to the middle of the lake. I was upset because I could see that there was a part of you that wanted to stay. And I was upset that there was nothing I could do about it. Even if I was able to escape, what could someone my size do against Odin and his surly seven-foot daughters?"

I nodded knowingly, and Saemund continued. "So I stewed and fretted over you leaving, then just this morning, I realized something. The year is almost over and I haven't made my annual request."

"You always ask for books," I said.

"But not this time, Cinder," said Saemund, a triumphant

gleam in his blue eyes. "I requested that before you leave, you be allowed to meet your grandmother."

I looked at her. "Where did you come from, then?"

"Asgard," she said.

Again, my jaw dropped. "You live in Asgard?"

She nodded and smiled. "I will have to tell you about it sometime. A very nice place."

"Saemund said you're a Predator. Are you also a Norse goddess?"

"Goodness no," said my grandma.

"And not just *any* Predator," said Saemund. "Your grandmother happens to be a Huntress of the Nine. She—"

"Speaking of Asgard," said my grandma, cutting the seer off, "there is a very grateful ghost there that wanted me to send his greeting."

"There's a ghost in Asgard that knows me?" I said, wondering if such an acquaintance was good or bad.

"Valhalla, actually. His name is Daas Sturlson, Captain of the Third Flank. He reported that you may have single-handedly destroyed the End of the Battle Festival, but you did it with flair and courage befitting a warrior princess."

"Oh yeah," I murmured. "You heard about that, huh?"

"*Everyone* has heard of it," replied Saemund. "If you haven't noticed already, titles are very important in the Nine Realms. I have heard *Destroyer of Festivals* and *Crusher of Ceremonies*, though I am partial to *Odin's Bane*. It has an ominous ring to it that—"

"Do not be so hard on yourself, Cinder," said my grandma, thankfully cutting the oracle off again. "The festival of the fallen is just an excuse for a bunch of arrogant men to gorge themselves on food, then show off in front of Odin. Besides, Sturlson views your interference quite differently than the rest of the fallen warriors."

I felt a little better. "Well, he did seem like a nice guy." I pictured him floating around the marbled halls of Valhalla . . . "Hey, wait a minute," I said. "If you came all the way from Valhalla, how did you get here so fast?"

Saemund grinned. "Poor Odin wasn't too happy about that part. In order to have your grandmother here before you left, he had to send Sleipnir, his eight-legged steed, to fetch her."

I looked at my grandma. She was grinning. "That strange beast is even faster than the legends claim."

I felt my eyes well with tears. Before Saemund could dodge away, I grabbed him and hugged him. "Thank you, Saemund. You're the sweetest oracle in the Nine Realms."

Gasping for air, Saemund said, "I am the *only* oracle in the Nine Realms."

I released him. "True, but what you did was totally selfless. You could've asked for anything, and instead you requested that I meet my grandma."

Saemund suddenly looked guilty. "Well, do not go gushing over me yet. My motives were not purely selfless."

"What do you mean?"

The seer looked at my grandma. "Do you want to tell her?"

She paused, then nodded. "Cinder, as you know, Odin has released you from your vow. You are no longer in his service . . . but I would ask you to be in mine."

I stared at her, then looked at Saemund. "What are you talking about?"

"I am offering you your quest, Cinder," she said solemnly. "The same one Odin had in mind . . . before he decided against it."

"But how . . . ?"

"Remember, I reside in Asgard," she said. "The home of the gods. Odin has been here, training you, preparing you, but the remaining eleven gods are stationed in Asgard, with the details of your quest." She pulled an envelope from the folds of her cloak, and I couldn't help but notice that she suddenly looked like a child that had been spotted sampling the candy in a convenience store.

"You stole the plans for the quest, didn't you?" I said. I was unable to decide whether I was thrilled at the idea or appalled that my grandma would stoop so low.

"We prefer to use the term 'borrowing,'" said Saemund.

"We? Are the three of us plotting against Odin and the eleven other gods?"

"We are plotting to *help* them," she said quickly. "You see, gods are fickle beings. They change moods with the shifting of the wind. At one time, Odin's sole purpose was to see that you were brought safely to the Proving Grounds, where you would learn of your place in the prophecies, then three weeks later . . . "

"I blew it."

"Entirely subjective," said Saemund quickly, patting me on the arm.

"Three weeks later, Odin changes his mind, decides that offering you your quest would hurt our chances in the end. He reinstates the pledge made by the Predators to protect you, which tells me Allfather wants to keep you in the background, safe and sound, should he change his mind. Half of the Twelve agreed with Odin—that releasing you from your pledge was the best option. But there were others who disagreed, and still do. If any of those gods knew that Odin was sending you home today, they might have done the same thing Saemund and I have done."

"Have you read my prophecy, Grandma?" I asked, suddenly feeling extremely doubtful.

"No, I have not. It is not mine to read."

"Then, how could you—"

"Simply knowing the prophecy exists is enough for me, Cinder. We trust in you, now you need to trust in yourself."

I nodded, my thoughts crashing into each other big-time.

"Plus, I have seen the Cinder merch," said my grandma, grinning.

"Please don't remind me," I groaned.

"I am still very upset with Bragi for letting Borghild get his hands on those sketches," said Saemund.

"Okay, enough about the merch. The two of you want me to go on this quest, behind the backs of Odin and at least five other gods?"

"I would not worry about those on *our* side," said Saemund. "If you choose to complete your quest, focus your fears on the creature that would see us all destroyed."

Pro tip: when a seer tells you a monster wants to bring about the end of all life as we know it, act like you saw it coming.

ΠΟΤ ΥΟUR ΕVΕRΥΟΑΥ ROAO
ΤRiP

I guess all along I'd hoped that my quest would involve
a package that needed to be delivered by a certain
time—kind of a mail-courier job. Get in, get out, collect my
pay. But we all know nothing's ever easy in life, especially
when you're attempting to slow down the destruction of
the Nine Realms.

"A creature?" I asked. "What creature?"

My grandma leaned close, as if Saemund's bed and bookshelf had ears. "Cinder, the information I am going to give
you cannot be shared with just anyone. Technically, no
one but you should hear it, though you may wish to invite
others to help you complete your quest."

I grasped her hands. "Like you?"

Her features tightened. "No, Cinder."

"But I'll need you," I said, my heart dropping.

She sighed. "I cannot. My questing days are over. At
least for now."

"Who says? It's your life, you can do what you want."

"You are right. It *is* my life, but there is another life I am
protecting, and if I leave, even for a day, this person could
. . . " My grandma's eyes filled with tears again. No sense in

pushing *that* angle.

"Fine. I understand. Well, I don't actually understand, but I trust you. So who is this creature, and what is his problem with us?"

She lowered her voice till she was almost whispering. "His name is Bergelmir the Cruel. He is a giant."

"When you say giant, do you mean good for the NBA type of giant, or are we talking Japanese horror movie type of giant?"

"I am not sure exactly what you mean," she said, "but he is roughly twenty feet tall, weighing in around fifteen thousand pounds."

I whistled and leaned back in my chair. "Wow. What'd he do?"

"Bergelmir has started something he cannot be allowed to finish," she answered. "And Asgard has received information that if he is not stopped, he will accomplish his designs very soon."

"How soon?" I asked.

"Two days. Three at the most," she said grimly.

"Two days!" I blurted. "What is Odin *thinking!*"

"His pride blinds him," said Saemund. He frowned. "Do not tell him I said that."

My grandma squeezed my hands. "This is where you come in, Cinder. Saemund has shown you the prophecy. It speaks of *you.*"

"What do I do?"

"Your destination lies on the West Coast of the United States. California, to be exact."

All I could do was stare at her. I guess I thought all along my quest would be somewhere in Iceland. "How do I get there?" I finally said.

"You will need to reach the north side of the island before midnight tonight. There you will find transportation."

"What type of transportation?" I asked.

She shook her head. "Sometimes it is better *not* to know the details beforehand."

I nodded. I was getting used to the grim and dire responses. "What do I do once I'm in California?"

"You will need to go to the city of Seaside as quickly as possible. Once you reach this location, find the Twin Palms mall. Skuld, the norn who sealed your vow, will meet you inside the south doors near a store called the Happy Hot Dog. The norn will give you further direction once you arrive. Now," she said grinning, "the next thing you need is a proper sword."

I looked at Saemund. His grin was even bigger than my grandma's. "Wait till you see the hardware."

She walked over to the seer's bed and returned with an object wrapped in dark cloth and bound with a leather cord. She untied the package and gently laid the object on the small table. The sword was roughly three feet long, the blade and grip a glimmering silver that easily outshone the light from Saemund's lamp. From the tip of the pommel to the needle-sharp point, the sword curved gracefully like an S that had been stretched by powerful hands. Words in ancient Nordic had been etched into the blade, but there was not a single nick or scratch anywhere else. The end of the pommel was carved to resemble the head of a falcon, its beak open in a silent scream and its neck feathers flaring to form the crosspiece.

"It's beautiful," I breathed, reaching out to touch it.

"It is named Talon," said my grandma. She lifted the sword out of the cloth and handed it to me. "It was made by Tyr, the God of War. It is specifically designed to fit my hand."

I held the sword in awe. It was light, yet felt incredibly strong. "Is this steel?"

"No, it is made of Asgardian silver. It cannot rust or break or even nick, no matter what you do to it. The blade is curved, like the talon of the falcon. The bite is deadly."

I pointed to the ancient Nordic. "What does this say?"

"'The hunter will do what the blade cannot.'"

"What does it mean?"

"It means something different to every Valhuri," she replied.

"And what does it—"

"And before you ask, I cannot share what it means for me."

Seemed a little dramatic to me, but what did I know of ancient Nordic super hunters? I shook my head. "I can't accept this, Grandma." I tried to hand it back, but she only held her hand up, her palm out.

"Hold your hand up to mine, Cinder," she said.

Tentatively, I placed my hand against hers. "You see?" she said smiling. "Our hands are identical. No one could tell them apart, without inspecting the prints. This sword was made for me, but it was also made for you. Talon is yours now, Cinder."

I took my hand away slowly. I stared at the sword for nearly a minute, then I said, "So does this thing pierce giant flesh?"

⚭

I spent the remainder of the afternoon with my grandma and Saemund. If it wasn't for our discussion of Bergelmir the Cruel and the end of the Nine Realms, I would've really enjoyed our time together. We talked a little about my mother, though only what she was like when my grandma was raising her. For some strange reason, she grew very tight-lipped when I prodded her for recent information. "Your mother is still alive," was all she would say.

Just before she left, she kissed me and hugged me, then had me look at the scar on the back of my hand. "You made a vow, Cinder," she said. "Though I wish you did not have to be involved in the tangled business of the gods, I cannot change what is written. Do not turn back on your promise. See this through to the end. Be wary of those who would help you, but be open to the offer as well, for you may find valuable assistance in very unexpected places. Whether you journey alone or with trusted friends, however, you will have to take charge, for this is your quest, and should it fail, the responsibility of that failure will be yours to bear."

"So no pressure," I said.

"Such is your fate, Cinder," said Saemund quietly. "Literally."

I grabbed my grandma's hands. "Will I see you again?"

Her smile was sad. "I truly hope so, Cinder." I hugged the little seer and when I turned back around, my grandmother was gone.

&

It didn't take me long to find Tristan. He was in the combat circle near the lake, slashing a rusty sword through the air. He stopped when he saw me approach.

"Stormbringer," he said. "I thought you were leaving us."

I was just happy he didn't call me Crusher of Ceremonies. "I am, but there's been a change of plans."

Tristan raised his dark eyebrows in curiosity, but then he turned away and began twirling the sword again. If he was trying to make it look like he didn't care, he was doing a pretty good job of it.

"Those plans involve you, Tristan," I said.

Tristan stopped and stared at me. "What do you mean?"

"My quest. I'm going to fulfill it."

"Your quest," said Tristan, laughing. "You no longer *have* a quest. Odin dismissed you."

How did I know he was going to make this difficult? "He did, but . . . I'm still going to fulfill it."

"You don't even know what the quest *is*. You—"

"I do now. I talked with Cindrheim Vustora. She had the quest papers from Asgard."

Tristan was looking at me like I had just sprouted a second head. "Cindrheim Vustora . . . as in Huntress of the Nine and the keeper of Talon . . . *That* Cindrheim Vustora?"

I nodded, touching my hand to the leather scabbard at my hip.

"She was here? At the Proving Grounds?"

I could see that my grandma was someone Tristan would have loved to meet. He quickly tried to disguise his wonderment. "Fine. She was here. You say she had the quest papers. What you mean to say is she *took* the quest papers."

I didn't like to think of my grandma as a thief, but well, she was. "She said that half of the Twelve feel that I should still do this, so she took the papers, knowing it would be too late if they sat around and waited to make a decision."

"But how did she know . . . ?"

"It was the seer," I said. "When Saemund found out Brunhild was taking me home today, he used his yearly request to have my grandma brought here on Odin's horse. We met in Saemund's cottage, and she explained the quest to me."

A tiny smile touched Tristan's lips. "Very clever," he said.

I knew I didn't have much time. "Look, Tristan. My grandma said that this was my quest, but that I could invite a few others to go with me. I know you and I are not the best of friends, but Odin asked you to train me, and I can't deny your skills."

Tristan remained silent. Before he could say anything, I added, "And I trust you."

After a long pause, Tristan held up his sword. "You expect me to go questing with a weapon like this?"

I couldn't help it. I grinned. "I may have just the sword for you."

☖

Selling Tori on the idea was not so easy. I even showed her the quest papers, outlining the details. She shook her head and said, "No. I'm not going, and neither are you." When she could see that I wasn't going to back down, she said, "Are you out of your mind, Cinder? You are going to go against the Allfather and at least five other gods. Deceiving them is worse than *not* stopping this creature."

"Really? Because if we don't stop this Bergelmiester the Cunning—"

"Bergelmir the Cruel," corrected Tori.

"Yes, whatever. If we don't stop him, Odin and the rest of the gods won't matter. This is one of those times when the wisdom of others overrides the ignorance of a few."

"*Your* wisdom?" said Tori skeptically.

"No. The wisdom of my grandma and Saemund."

It's always good to have heavy names to throw around. Tori couldn't deny the weight that the Valhuri and the seer carried. "Well . . ."

"Tristan's going," I said on impulse.

Tori's eyes lit up, but she tried hard to suppress her emotions. "You know, this *does* seem like an important thing to do, now that I think about it. Who else is going?"

I hugged her. "Just the three of us. If I can help it."

ॐ

Once I had wrapped the sword I had pulled from Fenrir's mouth in my jacket, Tori and I grabbed Tristan and hightailed it to the Night Forest. Just as we passed under the first ring of trees, Brunhild swept overhead on her gleaming white horse. "She's hunting us," said Tristan, looking up through the swaying branches. Fortunately, night had fallen. "She's a Valkyrie," he said. "Eventually, she'll find us."

"We'll be gone before *eventually* ever gets here." I hoped that I sounded convincing, but even *I* was doubting what I'd just said.

"What is our destination?" said Tori.

I braced myself. "California."

Both Tristan and Tori stared at me, then began pelting me with questions.

"The California in America?"

"The California across the ocean?"

"The California with Disneyland?"

"Yes, yes, and yes," I replied.

"You plan on asking Brunhild if we can borrow her flying horse?" said Tristan. He grunted and turned away. "I knew this was a waste of time."

"Well, Cinder?" said Tori. "How do you plan to get to California?"

"My grandma promised me that if I can make it to the north side of the island, there would be transportation."

"The north side," said Tori, her eyes narrowing in suspicion. "That's the same side we made landfall last month, Cinder. You're not considering taking—"

I shook my head. "No, we're not taking Freya's ship. I would sooner take Odin's spear than do something so stupid."

"Good," said Tori, sighing in relief. "This quest would be over before it began."

"So you don't know what will be waiting for us," said Tristan slowly.

"No, but I trust my grandma."

It was quiet for a moment, then Tori said, "Do we tell the other Predators?"

"No," I said, my heart lurching in my chest. "I don't want to involve them."

"But if it's some type of ship, we'll need Edda's seafaring skills to—"

"No," I said, cutting her off quickly. "Freya's too loyal, or too afraid of Odin to go behind his back, and Droma is not fully healed. I love Edda, but she'll always follow Freya, no matter what. Besides you, Tori, the Predators have to sit this one out. Okay?"

Tori chewed on her lip, then shrugged her shoulders. "You're the boss."

The boss. My grandma had told me I was to take charge, and it was already happening, whether I wanted it to or not. I didn't like the feeling at all.

"So, *boss*," drawled Tristan. "I know the Predator here has decent weapons, but my sword is nowhere *near* good enough for a quest."

"Oh yeah!" I said excitedly. "I almost forgot." I handed him my cloth-covered bundle. "Try this on for size."

"You're giving me your coat?" he asked, fingering my hoodie.

"Open it up, Einstein."

Tristan pulled my jacket away from the object. He started shaking his head. He looked at Tori. "Is this a joke?"

"Who better to wield such an epic sword?" I asked, smiling. I pointed at the battered sword strapped to his hip. "And I agree with you—it's time for an upgrade."

Tristan tossed me my hoodie, then stepped back so that he could swipe the golden sword back and forth as he had done outside the Night Forest, though this time he did it with much more enthusiasm. "The blade that was placed in Fenrir's mouth by Odin himself . . . " He gripped the sword tightly and fell smoothly into his fighter's stance. "This makes it official: Allfather's going to kill me." His swiveled his head from side to side, scanning the dark trees. "I still think that wolf is going to hunt us down and eat us."

"You'll just have to trust me on this," I said.

The three of us heard several loud shouts from far across the lake. We raced to the outer ring of trees and peered through the leafy branches. Even from far away, we could see groups of people moving from tent to tent, their movements marked by the bobbing of torches.

High up in the sky, I spotted Brunhild, and now Trigga was with her on her own horse.

"Everyone in the Proving Grounds is now looking for us, Cinder," whispered Tristan. "It won't be long before they decide to check the forest."

"Then we leave now," I said firmly.

the height of wyrm fashion

I was thrilled with my decision to include Tristan the moment we left the forest. He was familiar with every route that led up and over the shiny black spires that encircled the valley, so he knew paths that were seldom used. We reduced our communication to hand signals and quickly followed him out of the towering trees and up a steep slope that wound in between a series of large boulders. When we made it to the top, I was happy to discover that I was less exhausted climbing now than I was a month ago.

Without looking back, the three of us plunged down the slippery slope, sliding on our backsides more often than not (though Tristan never stumbled once).

The moment we reached level ground, we sprinted across the grassy plains, my heart seizing up every time I mistook a grasping stalk of grass for a sleeping snake. No one asked for a breather, though my lungs were burning as we reached the outer edge of the plains.

Tristan pointed. "The ocean is on the other side of that rise. To be on the north side, we will need to turn left at the shore and travel for some time."

"Lead on," I said, panting.

We left the plains, crested the rise, and heard the crashing of the waves before we could see them in the dark. I suddenly realized how foolish I would look if we arrived on the north side of the island and there was nothing waiting for us. But my grandmother had promised me. I had to trust her. At this point, what choice did I have?

We raced down the last slope, then veered left the moment our shoes struck the gravelly shale rock that lined the beach.

We traveled for over an hour, then I stopped to catch my breath and massage the stitch in my side. I looked up and to the south. I thought I saw a tiny pinpoint of silver winging fast in our direction. "Do you guys see anything over there?" I said, pointing.

Tristan and Tori stared, then the Predator said, "I don't see anything."

"Good, let's keep going."

I was positive I had seen something, and now my heart was counting out a rapid pattern against my ribs. We continued on, and soon Tristan slowed his pace and said, "Well, this is the north side." He scanned the shore in both directions. "Unless our ride's invisible, it's not here."

I, too, searched the shore in both directions. Tristan was right. Besides ourselves and a few bright red sand crabs, we were the only living things on the beach. Some leader I had turned out to be. "Tori, where did we dock when we arrived a month ago?" I asked.

Tori pointed west. "Around that bend over there."

"Let's check it out."

Shaking his head, Tristan took the lead, and we followed.

I smelled the smoke long before we saw it.

"Something's burning," said Tori as she increased her speed.

We raced around the rocky tip and stopped. About a quarter mile down the shore, Freya's ship, *Analisel*, was burning. Half of it had already broken away and sunk into the choppy gray water, and the other half looked ready to follow. A large column of white smoke was spiraling lazily up into the blanket of mist over the ship.

"Odin's beard," whispered Tori.

"Is that *Analisel*?" said Tristan. It was the first time I had ever heard his voice not thick with arrogance.

"It is," said Tori. "Look at the prow."

It was true. The beautiful hand-carved replica of the falcon in hunt was now just a blackened hunk of smoldering wood. Just then, the smaller stern mast exploded in a brilliant shower of sparks and toppled over into the water.

"Who would do this?" growled Tristan, pulling his new sword from the scabbard at his hip.

"Freya . . ." said Tori softly. "She'll never recover from this."

"I will find who did this . . ." growled Tristan through clenched teeth.

I grabbed their arms. "We can't stay here. Whoever did this does not want us to leave. We have to go."

"Where?" said Tristan, spinning around and pulling his arm from my grasp. "Back to the Proving Grounds where we can face Odin and the Valkyries? Or should we continue searching these empty beaches till Brunhild pins us to the sand with her spear?"

I nodded. "Okay, I admit. Our options are limited, but—"

"Hey, guys!"

The three of us spun around, Tori and I whipping out our weapons.

"Who is that?" I demanded, peering into the darkness.

"Cinder, it's me, Brandon!"

Rolling my eyes, I lowered my sword. "Brandon, what in the Nine Realms are you doing here?" (My Norse lingo was really picking up.)

"Brunhild found me today," said Brandon. He looked really afraid. "She wanted to know where you were."

"What did you tell her?" I demanded through gritted teeth.

"That I had no idea."

"Well, you weren't lying, right?"

"Actually . . . " said Brandon, his face turning as red as his hair, "I *did* know."

I stared at him incredulously. "How could you?"

Tori raised her hand. "Guilty."

I turned and looked at her. "Why would you tell him where we were going?"

"He looked so sad to see you go," said Tori. Tristan threw his arms up and spun away. "I'm sorry, Cinder. I didn't think he'd follow."

"How did you follow us without us seeing you?" I asked, turning my angry glare back on Brandon.

Brandon shrugged and grinned. "Half-elf, remember? Light on our feet."

"Great," I huffed. "Anyone else coming?"

"Everyone be quiet!" hissed Tori, pulling my sleeve so that I was forced into a crouch. We all flattened ourselves behind a large sand dune. Tori pointed towards the burning ship. "Look, someone's down there . . . "

Tristan rose up. "That's Freya."

He was right. Freya was walking slowly towards the burning wreckage, her hands clasped against her chest.

I grabbed Tristan by the arm. "Freya can't know what we're doing. She may try and stop us."

"She won't," said Tristan, his eyes fixed on his sister.

He walked away from us. We had no choice but to follow. *This is not turning out the way I'd expected it to*, I thought angrily.

We approached Freya, but she never once turned to look at us. Either she knew we were there all along, or she was grieving too much to care. Or maybe she was still so upset with me for freeing Fenrir, she didn't want anything to do with me. Probably a little of all three.

Tristan reached out and touched her shoulder. "Freya. I promise you, I will find who did this."

Freya remained silent. The five of us stared at the burning ship for a while, then Freya turned to me. Her face was streaked with tears. "I know now why I was sent to retrieve and protect you, Cindrheim. You have been chosen to save us."

I tried to object, but she held her hand up. "I also understand why Odin asked my brother to train you. Aside from your grandmother, only his skills can prepare you for what is to come. For this reason, he should go with you. As prideful as he is, I love him and do not wish to see him hurt, but I cannot stand in the way of fate."

I suddenly remembered Kevin the dwarf telling me everything is written in the stars. "So you know we're leaving on the quest?" I asked.

Freya nodded. "I did not until I saw the three of you. It is obvious now."

"But what about Fenrir . . . ?"

"I believe the great wolf was *meant* to be released. The universe just needed someone as thickheaded as you to make it happen." She gently squeezed my arm.

I was so happy Freya didn't hate me that I lunged forward and hugged her.

"Easy, Cindrheim. I might be immortal, but I can still be crushed to death."

I let go of her, swiping at the tears in my eyes. "I promise you I will help Tristan find who burned *Analisel*."

"Thank you, but I will avenge her myself."

The look in Freya's eyes frightened me. Heaven help the one that torched her closest friend. I grabbed Freya's arm. "I could use your skills, too, Freya. Please come with us."

"No," said Freya. A fresh tear slid down her cheek. "I will remain here with Droma and Edda and I will seek out *Analisel*. The boat was destroyed, but her essence is still whole."

I knew there was no arguing with the Predator. "Is it alright if Tori comes with me?"

"Of course," said Freya. Through her tears, she smiled. "I want at least one Predator to follow your reckless steps." She turned to face Tori. Gripping each other's arms, they leaned forward so that their foreheads were touching. "The hunter will do what the blade cannot," said Freya, her eyes closed.

"The hunter will do what the blade cannot," repeated Tori.

"I don't know what that means," said Brandon, "but it sounds *awesome*."

I looked at Brandon. "What about our party-crasher here?"

"He will return with me," said Freya.

Brandon immediately began to protest. "But Brunhild knew I was lying about Cinder. She said that I've forfeited my right to train and that I'm to return to California this week."

Freya turned to me. "Then it is your decision, Cindrheim. Only you have the right to say who will go and who will not."

Brandon *did* look pathetic. I could see why Tori had given in to him. And our destination would be relatively close to his home in Pismo . . . "Fine, but the tux stays here."

"Deal," said Brandon excitedly.

Tristan sighed. "The quest is doomed."

"Then Cindrheim will face her doom with this," said Freya. From the folds of her traveling cloak, she pulled out a cloth-covered bundle. She pulled away the cloth and held the object out to me. "I think you will remember this," said Freya.

I could only stare. In her hands was a vest of bluish-green scales.

I reached out and touched the gleaming armor. "Are those from . . . ?"

"The offspring of Iormungand," said Freya. "From the scales you saved in the bucket, I fashioned a vest that is extremely light but able to withstand the most brutal attack. It was your hand that slew the creature, and so its hide will now protect you."

"Thank you, Freya," I said, taking the vest. Once my jacket was off, I slid the armor over my head, fastened the straps and buckles, then put my hoodie back on. I patted the sword at my hip. "Besides Talon, this is the best gift anyone's ever given me."

"You are now ready, Stormbringer," said Freya. We hugged, then pulled away when Tristan said, "Mush overload."

"Really," echoed Brandon.

"Can I see the sword before I leave?" said Freya.

"Of course," I said, pulling Talon from its scabbard.

Freya took the weapon in her hands, ran her fingers down the blade. "It is more beautiful than the rumors boasted." She handed the sword back to me. "You have inherited the right to carry Talon, now earn the right to keep it."

Before I could say anything, Brandon nudged me hard and said, "Look! Something's coming!"

All of us turned as one, searching the sky to the south.

"It is Brunhild," said Freya. "She is approaching fast!"

It was my last chance to depend on someone like Freya. "What do we do?"

"I will draw her away," said the Predator. "And may the light of Valhalla shine down on all of you." Before I could stop her, she kissed Tristan on the cheek and darted up the rocky slope. A moment later, she was gone.

"We need to find shelter," said Tori. "If Freya's plan doesn't work, Brunhild will easily spot us."

The four of us quickly scanned the area, but we could find nothing that would adequately hide us. If Freya failed to draw Brunhild away . . .

"The Valkyrie's ignoring Freya," said Tristan. "She's still approaching!"

I wanted to believe the white horse arrowing through the darkness was something else. Something besides the grim and deadly Brunhild, but there was no mistaking her now.

"Do we surrender?" asked Tori, her voice cracking.

"We resist," I said, testing Talon's weight. "For the good of the quest."

"If you come with me, you will not have to."

Turning, we saw a dark-haired man dressed in animal furs. He was crouching in the mouth of a dark crevice in the rocks, his bare feet filthy.

Tori, Tristan, and Brandon looked at me. "Do we trust him?" said Tori.

"Absolutely not," said Tristan.

"It does not matter if you trust me or not," growled the man. "The four of you cannot resist a Valkyrie on the hunt; neither can you defeat her in open combat."

We ducked inside the crevice.

Brunhild swept overhead, her red cape billowing like fire and her spear glowing like a bolt of lightning.

CHAPTER 30

GHOSTS ALWAYS PAY THEIR DEBTS

The five of us huddled in the cave. A flickering torch had been wedged into a crevice in the wall, but the man quickly snuffed it out by throwing it to the ground and stamping it out with his bare feet. The cave went completely black.

Outside I could hear the water lapping against the shore, but the peaceful sound was ruined by the *fwup, fwup, fwup* of the horse's wing feathers.

"Quiet," whispered the man. "Do not move a single muscle."

We waited in silence for what felt like an hour, then Brandon said, "She's gone. Brunhild's flying away."

"How can you tell?" I whispered.

"The gangly boy is right," confirmed the man. "We can go out, but do not raise your voices above a whisper."

Brandon frowned at the man.

We climbed out of the crevice. I scanned the shore in both directions, but there was still no sign of any transportation. I knew it was my responsibility to keep everyone's spirits up, but how was I supposed to do that when nothing was going according to plan?

"My name is Sebus," said the man. I turned to look at him. He was not very tall, but he was corded with muscle. His black hair was long and matted with bits of dried grass and twigs and a few other things that had me wondering. He reminded me of a caveman with his thick hairy arms, large dirty feet, and his over-the-shoulder fur outfit that thankfully concealed at least half of his body. Even from where I stood, I could smell his pungent odor.

"Thank you for helping us," I said, hoping he wasn't about to conk me over the head and drag me by the hair into his cave. Just in case, I kept my hand on Talon's pommel.

"Why are the four of you running from the Valkyrie?" Sebus asked.

Tristan looked at me and shook his head ever so slightly.

"That was a Valkyrie?" I said in mock surprise. "Wow. I don't know why she'd be chasing us. We were just out here exploring and saw her coming."

"Yes, we live over in Reykjavik," said Tori. "Our parents are going to kill us."

"Yeah, we don't know *anything* about the Proving Grounds," said Brandon.

Before I could whack the half-elf with the back of my hand, Sebus said, "I do not care where you are from, but I know you wish to leave the island. I saved you, now you save me."

"How can we save you?" I asked.

"By taking me with you."

Tristan was standing behind Sebus, so he began to vigorously shake his head.

Tori said, "Um . . . "

"The more the merrier," chirped Brandon, clapping the man on the shoulder.

"What makes you think we want to leave the island?" I asked, shooting Brandon a dark look.

"Even your whispers can be heard up and down the shore."

Who is this guy? I wondered. "Are you half-elf too?" I said irritably. I scowled at Brandon again. "Because if you are, I definitely can't handle two of you."

"No," said Sebus, smiling. "I just know when to listen."

"Well, we'd love to have you," Tori said, "but as you can see there's nothing here to take us off the island."

"What about that?" said Sebus. He was pointing towards the water. We turned and watched as a Viking warship erupted (and I do mean erupted) from the curling waves. The ship had a main mast, but the material was shredded beyond repair. I thought that was bad enough, but then I saw the hull. Even from where we stood, I could see that the wood paneling was practically useless, especially since the starboard side had a gaping hole capable of admitting a good-sized shark. Most of the railing had been torn off and the prow was completely missing.

"I'm not an expert on ships," I said, "but that thing looks like it's been sitting on the bottom of the ocean since the end of the eighteenth century."

"Closer to the *eighth* century," said Tori. "If you look at the curving hull and the sloping deck design, you can plainly see that—"

"That's beside the point, Tori," I said pointing. "That waterlogged heap of driftwood couldn't carry us across The Mirror, much less the Atlantic Ocean."

"I would not be too sure," said Sebus.

I gasped. The ship was resting on the backs of at least two hundred men.

Two hundred *dead* men.

"Are those ghosts?" I asked tentatively.

"Or mermen . . . " said Brandon. Everyone turned and stared at the half-elf. Before anyone could respond, a barrel-chested apparition detached itself from the milling crew and drifted towards us. I heard a metallic *zing* as Tristan slid his sword from his scabbard.

"Wait," I whispered, staring hard at the approaching ghost. I almost found it funny that I was more surprised at who it was than at the fact that a troop of spirits had raised a ship off the ocean floor. "It's you," I said. "The one from the feast . . . "

"Good evening, Stormbringer," said the ghost. "I failed to introduce myself upon our first meeting. I am Captain Daas Sturlson." The captain gestured behind him. "I have taken command of this crew so that we may be at your service."

I was speechless.

"Why would you do that?" said Tristan. He was still fingering the hilt of his sword.

The captain smiled through his ghostly beard. "I wish to repay a few friends. One in Asgard, and the one who stands before me."

"Thank you," I mumbled, totally embarrassed and totally grateful.

"Welcome to the *Lady Emrick*, Cindrheim and company," said the captain. He reached out a gloved hand, and though I was more than a little hesitant, I grasped it in a firm and freezing handshake. "We set sail the moment you are all aboard."

⚭

I agreed to let Sebus join us, at least for the journey to America, seeing as how he promised to go his own way once we reached California. Tristan reminded me every five minutes, though, that I was making an Asgard-sized mistake.

"He's a hermit, Cinder," he whispered angrily as we were lifted up onto the ship's deck by a dozen or so icy hands. "You don't know what you're agreeing to."

"It's too late now," I replied. "I've made my decision, and I have to stick with it."

"It's *never* too late," hissed Tristan.

I stepped close. "I trusted *you*."

"The first smart thing you've done since getting to Iceland."

"Just keep your eyes open," I said, shaking my head. "If he turns on us, I would say he's outnumbered."

"It's painfully obvious you don't fully understand our world, Cinder. One person against a hundred can some-times be considered a fair fight." Tristan looked across the pitching deck of the *Lady Emrick* and gestured with his head. "And look. I'm not the only one who's suspicious."

I looked over at Sebus and saw the man was surrounded by a host of apparitions, each of them swirling in for a closer look, then darting away. Sebus, however, seemed completely unaware of them.

"Maybe they like the smell," I said. "Very earthy."

Tristan huffed and walked away.

"See you at five for shuffleboard!" I called out, but if he heard my joke, he ignored it.

I turned and studied the shore, then stared into the night sky. Where was the Valkyrie? My heart suddenly lurched in my chest. Something was winging towards us. My hand drifted to Talon's hilt, then I realized whatever was approaching was much too small to be Brunhild on her horse. I watched as a dove settled on the ship's rail. It studied me with its beady black eyes.

"Hope you're a good omen," I said.

"I would suggest everyone sit down," said Captain Sturlson, "preferably on a section of deck that is not close to collapsing. Once you are seated, grab hold, because our rate of speed will be extremely fast, and we would not want to lose you to the sea."

I quickly did as I was told, sinking to my seat and grabbing an iron ring that was protruding from the deck. I felt the *Lady Emrick* slowly being rotated so that we were facing out to sea. Our ghostly captain brought his arm down. Instantly, our ship rocketed forward so fast that I slid backward. I felt the socket in my shoulder pop as my arm was extended too rapidly.

Captain Sturlson drifted over to me, totally unaffected by the blistering speed. The last tattered pieces of the mast were torn away by the wind, and several hunks of wood splintered off and whipped backwards into the dark water.

"I wish I had had this form of travel back when I was alive," said Sturlson conversationally.

The ghost's voice carried easily over the rushing wind, but I had to shout. "These men who carry us . . . who are they?"

"These are the souls of men who have perished over the centuries while at sea."

"How did you get them to help us?"

"They are restless spirits, unhappy shades who died with unfinished earthly business. This deed will not release them, but it passes the time."

I stared in disbelief. "They're doing this out of boredom?"

The captain nodded. "You would be surprised at the things you would be willing to do after four hundred years of moping about at the bottom of the sea."

Brandon slid past me, screaming the entire way. Sebus reached out a large hand and snagged Brandon by the back of his shirt. A moment later, the half-elf had a rope around his waist and was sliding around on the deck, frantic but safe.

The fur-clad man glanced in my direction. I mouthed the words "Thank you." He nodded once and turned his face into the wind.

I held on to the iron ring till my fingers lost all sensation and then, without realizing it, I let go. Sebus didn't grab me as he had Brandon, but he did toss me a length of rope, which

I caught, then used to pull myself across the deck. I wrapped one end around my waist, then secured the other end to the main mast. Soon, Tristan and Tori were fitted with ropes as well so that all four of us were dangling like pill bugs at the end of a spiderweb. Sebus was the only one still living who continued to hang on with just his hand.

Hours passed. With the mist and clouds flying overhead and the dove watching me from the ship's rail, I fell into an uneasy sleep.

☖

Someone woke me by dousing me with a bucket of cold water. I rubbed my eyes, sat up and found that it wasn't cold water at all. Captain Sturlson had passed through me.

"Daylight will break in under an hour," he said, smiling grimly through his beard. "You and your friends must disembark under cover of night, or you shall find a whole host of new problems."

"You mean we're here?" I said, scrambling to my feet. My leg muscles screamed and I staggered to the side. Luckily, there was a ghost there to prop me up. "Thanks," I said, shivering from his cold embrace. I squinted into the darkness. "Where are we?"

"I believe you refer to it as California," said the captain, "though when I stormed these shores, California had not yet been discovered."

I shook my head in disbelief. "I don't know how to thank you, Captain."

"Call me Daas," said the Viking. "My closest friends do."

"I will." I untied the rope from around my waist. "Daas, back in Iceland, you said that you agreed to this because of two friends. Was the other my grandmother?"

The captain nodded. "An amazing woman. If you knew half the stories, you would wonder why she does not rule the cosmos."

"I plan on hearing those stories someday." I heard a loud splintery crash and turned to see Brandon disappear through the deck.

Tristan was standing suspiciously close to the new hole. He shrugged. "I swear I had nothing to do with that."

CHAPTER 31

PART-TIME EMPLOYEE, FULL-TIME PAIN IN THE NECK

holding my breath, I leaped. We're talking California here, but the water was still frigid. Christmas was right around the corner, and even seaside towns in the Golden State can be cold.

As soon as I broke the surface, I immediately began paddling for shore. It wasn't easy with jeans and a sword slapping against my hip. I made sure Tori, Tristan, Brandon, and even Sebus were swimming beside me. After what felt like an eternity, we slogged up onto the shore dripping wet. I collapsed and rolled onto my back.

I closed my eyes, hoping I could rest for a while, but a large face framed by dripping hair was suddenly looming over me. "Thank you for allowing me to travel with you," said Sebus, extending his hand to help me up. "As I promised, I will take my leave now."

I accepted his hand. "You're welcome. Thanks for saving us. More than once."

Sebus smiled. The seawater had washed away most of the dirt and grime from his face, and I could see that he was a handsome man. "You never know when you will be offered a helping hand, right?" he said.

I thought of the advice my grandma had given me. "I admit I had my doubts, but I'm grateful you showed up when you did," I said.

Sebus turned and trotted down the beach, his long strides quickly carrying him out of sight.

"Good riddance," said Tristan.

I sighed.

"Look," said Tori. "They're leaving."

I turned my attention to the ocean. Captain Sturlson and his crew of undead were sinking into the choppy water, followed by the battered *Lady Emrick*.

"I hope no one saw that," said Tristan.

"Well, the first item of business is to make sure we blend in," said Brandon. "You guys definitely don't look like you're from California."

Brandon, Tristan, and I were in jeans and T-shirts, not too far from the proper look, but Tori was rocking the traditional Proving Ground attire. Unless our destination was lunch at Medieval Times, she was going to stick out like a sore thumb.

"I refuse to wear anything made out of straw," said Tori defiantly. "Or with flower print."

"That would make you a tourist," said Brandon. "I'll help you look as if you've lived here all your life."

"Brilliant," said Tori dismally. "I think I'd rather face Brunhild."

I was about to ask about our weapons, then remembered no one would see them but us.

"Let's go," said Brandon. "We still have a few hours before any clothing stores open, but we can call a taxi and use the heater to dry off." The half-elf headed for the parking lot that sat at the top of the sandy rise.

Maybe he can be useful, I thought. I instantly reconsidered when he whooped and chased a seagull halfway down the beach.

♸

We spent the morning riding around the small town of Big Sur in a taxi painted a sketchy shade of mint green. The grumpy driver almost drove away when he saw the four of us thumbing a ride, but suddenly became very polite when Tori was able to produce wads of American cash. The heater was turned on full force, and soon our sopping wet clothes were dry.

At around nine o'clock, we paid the driver and entered a beachfront store called the Broken Sand Dollar, where everything was half off in honor of the holiday season. Brandon fell into a zone, picking out the clothes that would make Tori fit in with the locals. Ten minutes later she was wearing khaki capris, a navy blue peacoat, and shades that covered nearly her entire face.

"Lookin' good," said Brandon as we walked from the store.

Tori looked down at her coat and capris. "I hope the next time Odin sees me, I'm not wearing this."

I frowned. "I would be more worried about what *Freya* would do."

We hailed a cab, flashed more cash, and gave the driver directions to the Twin Palms mall in the city of Seaside.

He frowned suspiciously but took the bills anyway. Within the hour, we entered the breezy town of Seaside and the driver dropped us off at the mall. We devoured two large pizzas and at least three quarts of cola. I tried hard to ignore Brandon when he stared lovingly at his slice of pizza and said, "This could be my last time ever eating you."

I watched Tristan place his gleaming sword on the table in front of him. With loving care, he began to wipe down the blade with a wad of tissue.

"I shall call you Tyr," said Tristan reverently, touching his lips gently against the blade.

I was about to tell Tristan that my sword had more right to bear the name—since the God of War had actually *made* Talon—but I figured hours before we were to try and save the Nine Realms wasn't the best time to get into an argument.

When we had cleaned up our mess, we asked for directions to the Happy Hot Dog. It wasn't long before we were approaching the little restaurant. I noticed my hands were sweating.

We were close. I could feel it.

I looked around. There were a few customers in line and two teenage girls working the cash registers.

"So where's Skuld?" Tristan asked.

"I don't know," I replied.

"He could be anywhere," answered Tori. "He's a norn."

I nodded and tried to get a better look at the customers in line. I was about to talk to one of them when I heard a watery plunging sound. I turned and saw that a teenage boy with acne and braces had stepped up onto a platform and was mixing fresh lemonade in a huge glass container. He was pushing and lifting a huge plunger, like the kind used to ignite large quantities of dynamite. His motions sent whole lemons and large chunks of ice tumbling over one another. He wore a shirt with red, white, and yellow stripes, and a tall yellow hat sat on a mop of unruly blond hair. He glanced at me in between plunges.

"Come on," I said. "I found him."

I strode up to the glass partition and motioned for the boy to come out.

The girl at the cash register gave me a strange look, then whispered something to her friend.

The boy kept plunging.

"Skuld!" I hissed, holding the back of my hand up to the glass so that he could see my pledge scar. "It's me!"

"His name is *Christian*," said one of the girls at the register. "And he's working right now, so he can't talk to anyone till his break."

I ignored her, and said, "Fine, Skuld. We're leaving."

I turned and found the boy in front of me, his braces gleaming, only inches from my face. "Hello, Stormbringer. Come to play with Bergelmir the Cruel?" he said.

"Hello, *Christian*," I said. "I need the quest details."

Skuld grinned. "Like the disguise?"

"Ingenious." I frowned. "I thought no one could see you but me."

The norn shook his head as if I were the dumbest person in Midgard. "That is when I am on a pledge mission. For

Odin's sake, child, would it kill you to do a little Norse history research?"

"Should I do that *before* or *after* I try and save the Nine Realms?" I asked.

"Mind if I get some lemonade?" asked Brandon, but he quickly said, "Never mind," when Tori socked him.

"Please hurry, Skuld," I said. I glanced up and down the mall, expecting Brunhild or a hoard of drooling grints to come crashing through the kiosks.

"Would-be heroes never have time to chat," said Skuld. He tried to appear sad, but I could tell he was faking it.

I held out my hand. "Give me the quest papers, Skuld."

"What do you think this is, a slumber party scavenger hunt?" Skuld chuckled. "You should know me better than that, Cindrheim. The information I bear is freshly stolen from Asgard. I would not risk writing it down." He tapped the side of his head. "It is all up here."

"Then spill it," I whispered.

"Very well," said Skuld, his voice much too loud for my liking. "I will show you to the entrance of Bergelmir's lair, which unbelievably, lies here in this . . . *mall*. Once through the barrier—"

"Shh!" I hissed.

The norn stopped, apparently offended I had cut him off. "Do you seriously think these silly mortals know what I am talking about?"

"Well, no, but I—"

"Watch," said Skuld, stepping over to a woman holding a squirming child in her arms. "Hello, female human. My

name is Skuld. I am a norn, a bringer of fate. I reside in
Asgard, but I have come to this dismal rock you call Earth
to share sensitive information with the hero of the moment.
You see, Bergelmir the giant has been—"

"I get the point, Skuld," I said, scooting over so that I
was between the norn and the woman.

Skuld's grin widened. It seemed he was happy only when
he was causing problems. "Let's walk," he said, tucking his
tall yellow hat under his arm.

"Hey, Christian!" shouted the girl at the cash register.
"Your shift's not over!"

"So dock my pay!" said Skuld over his shoulder. "And go
soak your head in the lemonade barrel."

I gestured for Tori, Tristan, and Brandon to follow. Off
to my right, a door leading outside swung open as a family
of four pushed their way in. Just before the door closed,
a bird swooped in, narrowly missing getting squished as
the heavy door swung closed. It was a dove. *Coincidence?* I
wondered. I watched it dart about, searching for a suitable
place to land. Several small children (including Brandon)
squealed and pointed in delight. Skuld, Tori, and Tristan
ignored the bird, so I tried to do the same.

"So this is your hand-picked team," said the norn,
glancing back at my friends as he walked. "Not liking your
odds."

It wasn't easy to ignore his insults. "Have you talked to
Odin lately?"

"You mean am I aware that you are carrying out this
quest without the Allfather's authorization?"

I swallowed. "Uh . . . yes."

Skuld nodded. "I am, and I do not care."

"You don't care that I'm doing this behind his back?"

"Not one bit."

"Then why are you involved?"

"It is in my job description. Your grandmother, one of the few people in this silly universe I respect, hand-delivered my instructions to me. I comply or I melt on the spot."

"I see. So what do we have to do?"

Tristan, Tori, and Brandon picked up their pace so that they could hear the norn's words. "In a nutshell," said Skuld, his teenage blue eyes glittering, "you have to stop Bergelmir the Cruel from severing one of the three roots of Yggdrasil, the World Tree."

I stared at the norn. "What happens if he succeeds?"

Skuld shrugged his thin shoulders. "When Yggdrasil finally falls, which it will someday, the gods and goddesses of light will fall as well. If Bergelmir succeeds, the tree will still stand, but it will be greatly weakened. The day of Ragnarök will be that much closer. With only two remaining roots . . . "

I suddenly remembered Odin telling me that my quest was not to necessarily save the Nine Realms, but to put the brakes on, slowing down the end as much as possible. It all made sense. "So are you going to send us into the mountains or something?"

"Why in the name of Odin's leather boxers would I do that?" asked Skuld.

"This World Tree thing," I said, "Clearasil, or whatever."

"You are attempting to stop Ragnarök, not fight acne. It's *Yggdrasil*," corrected the norn indignantly. "No, the giant ash tree sits above the Nine Realms, far from here. One of its roots enters your earth through the Well of Knowledge. That well is here."

I stopped walking and looked around.

"Do not bother, Cinder. Even with your eyes opened, you will not spot it. Go belowground, and you will see that the root is about a hundred feet in diameter."

"*A hundred feet?*" I said incredulously. My mind couldn't wrap around something of that size. And that was just *one* of the roots! "How is Bergelmiester cutting through something so big?"

"*Bergelmir*," said Skuld, "is using a machine to do his dirty work—a wicked contraption with many working parts and a magically enhanced blade. The entire machine is made out of Asgardian silver, the same material that was used to construct your sword. Back in the old days, when I was a younger, handsomer norn, the machine had multiple blades, but they buckled frequently and caused a tremor to pass through this part of Midgard nearly every time. One of the baddies modified the machine so that there was a single large blade instead. Cuts down on the possibility of malfunctioning. You may have heard that California has its fair share of earthquakes."

My eyes bulged. "The buckling blades were the cause of those earthquakes?"

Skuld nodded. "You should hear what causes the nasty twisters of the Midwest and the tidal waves on the East Coast."

"Wow," I said, wondering what a scientist would have to say about this. "Anything else we should know about?" I asked.

"Well, the place *is* infested with dark elves . . ."

I stopped again. "Dark elves?"

Tristan suddenly spit on the ground. "Vile, night-sucking creatures."

I glanced at Brandon.

"Distant cousins," he clarified quickly. "*Very* distant."

"Yes," said Skuld. "Did I forget to tell you about the heartless elves that guard the machine and lurk in the shadows, waiting for unprepared and untrained heroes? Kind of like you, Cinder."

"Wonderful," I mumbled.

I looked from Tori, to Tristan, then on to Brandon. They were staring at me with the same question in their eyes: *What now, O fearless leader?*

I was totally at a loss. "Dynamite?"

Tristan was shaking his head. "No good. We blow the machine up, it could cause another tremor through Midgard, maybe even a giant sinkhole."

"This whole mall would go bye-bye," added Brandon.

"Asgardian silver, remember?" Skuld said. "That machine would laugh at your dynamite."

I turned back reluctantly to the norn. "What do we do, Skuld?"

Skuld fell into a fit of laughter. He used his floppy yellow hat to wipe away the tears from his eyes. "Oh, child. You *do* entertain me. I will give you that!"

I could feel myself getting angry. "Why are you laughing?"

"I am a bringer of fate, Cinder, not a bringer of solutions. How you accomplish your task is *your* business." Skuld thought for a bit, then said, "Although I can tell you the dark elves from Svartalfheim fancy cave mole slowly roasted over an open fire."

"Priceless information," I said.

I heard a fluttering sound whiz past my ear. I looked up and saw the dove execute a figure eight over my head, then soar up towards the painted steel girders above us. For a moment I wished I were the bird, able to flit about through the mall without worrying about giants and dark elves and ticked-off Valkyries.

"What about Mimir?" asked Tristan. "It's *his* fountain. What does he have to say about all this?"

"Is this the same Mimir that traded some of his wisdom for Odin's eye?" I asked.

Brandon nodded eagerly. "Mimir was one of the smartest of all the gods, but he wasn't the world's greatest warrior. His enemies had his head chopped off." I flinched. Droma hadn't told me about the decapitation. "That's not even the coolest part, Cinder," said Brandon. His excitement was really building. "Odin didn't want to lose Mimir because he couldn't bear to see all that wisdom go to waste, so he goes and preserves his noggin with magical herbs, placed a spell over it to protect it from enemies, and gave it the power of speech so that Mimir could continue to pass on wisdom and knowledge till the end of time."

"That's disgusting," I said. "But resourceful."

Brandon nodded like a six-year-old boy who had just found a can oozing with worms. "If we're lucky, we may get to see it. Legend says Odin placed it by the Well of Knowledge!"

"So we have a horde of dark elves, a giant, and the severed head of a god, all waiting for us by a well that leads to a massive underground root that's about to be sliced in half. Did I miss anything?"

"That about sums it up," said Skuld. The norn had brought us to a flight of stairs that led down into a gloomy basement. The only light came from a naked bulb in the ceiling. Its glow was weak and flickering on and off. "Good luck, break a leg, blah, blah, blah," said the norn, grinning. "Let me know how it all turns out."

the god of uber confidence

Skuld was kind enough to give us instructions on how to enter the underground realm that would lead us to the Well of Knowledge. At first I thought he was pulling my leg, but Tristan said, "It's not a joke, Cinder. Magical barriers are often removed through song and dance."

I tried to plead my case, but he shook his head and said, "Sorry, Cinder. This is your quest; you take the stage."

"I don't know," said Brandon. "I've seen Cinder dance and she—"

"Watch it, Brandon," I said. "You're no Michael Jackson, either."

Brandon nodded but Tori and Tristan looked at me in confusion. "Never mind," I mumbled.

We were still in the mall, standing in front of a battered steel door that was squeezed between the entrances to a pawnshop and a video store long out of business. On the door was a sign in glowing Nordic runes. I suspected untrained mortals couldn't see the runes—maybe even the door. Tristan translated. "Only those wishing to die horrible deaths beyond this point," he said. The runes dissolved and a new set of runes appeared. Tristan translated again:

"Seriously, you will die." The runes faded for a second time and a one-word rune appeared. "Painfully," read Tristan. He turned to me. "Well, you can't say you weren't warned."

I sighed, feeling for Talon, and quickly executed the dance steps shown to me by Skuld and sang:

> *"Shown to me by one who knows,*
> *I dance the dance to foil my foes!*
> *Should I forget the steps and words,*
> *my eyes'll be pecked by a flock of birds!"*

As soon as the last word of the lame song left my lips, the door dissolved. The four of us hustled forward. Once over the threshold, I turned and watched the door solidify, though not before the pesky bird swooped through the opening. I was sure now the dove was following us. Was it a friend? An enemy? But my new surroundings made it difficult to worry much more about a stalking bird.

We were in a large, rough-hewn tunnel that stretched deep into the gloom. Fortunately (or unfortunately), torches of purple fire burned at regular intervals, casting the tunnel in a strange, violet glow. By the light of the flames, I could see that the walls were slick with water that appeared to be seeping from an unknown source above.

I was about to yank one of the torches from the wall to use as a makeshift flashlight, when Tristan grabbed my arm and whispered, "Leave it. Let's not announce our arrival just yet."

"Right," I said.

We proceeded through the tunnel, which was beginning to slant downwards. Soon, the ground leveled off and the walls of the tunnel fell away so that we moved into a wide-open area. The torches were gone, but the cavern was partially illuminated by a glittery substance that winked on and off like billions of miniscule stars.

Brandon had stopped moving. He tilted his head, sniffed the air, then turned to me. He looked nervous. "Uh, guys," he said, "I should probably tell you . . . we're being watched."

"Mall employees?" I whispered, falling easily into a half-crouch.

Brandon shook his head. "My very distant cousins."

I stared at Brandon. "Dark elves. You can smell them?"

"And see them."

"How many?" Tristan asked.

"At least three," replied Brandon. "Could be more."

From the side of his mouth, Tristan said, "Give me the time."

Brandon looked at his wristwatch. "It's almost noon."

"No, you idiot," hissed Tristan. "Where are their positions on the clockface?"

"Oh, sorry. A dark elf at . . . one o'clock, and two at nine. They're hiding behind the rocks. Waiting for us by the looks of it."

By squinting, I could just make out a large opening on the other side of the cavern. I pointed and whispered, "We need to make it to that doorway. Brandon, do the dark elves know that we know they're watching us?"

"I don't think so," said Brandon.

"Does anyone know anything about dark elves?" I asked.

"Very good fighters," said Tristan. "They use two curved short swords, like Tori, and they're experts with their small crossbows."

"So it'll be a walk in the park," I said, groaning. The tingling sensation that I always feel before a fight started in my toes and zipped up my legs. Part of me was eager to try out my new skills with a sword, but I was also slightly concerned, seeing as how this wasn't going to be a cafeteria brawl or a training session with Tristan with padded blades.

"I'll take the one on the right," said Tristan. "Cinder, you and Tori take the two on the left. Their strength is their speed. Once engaged, do not hang back and fight defen-sively. They'll slice you to ribbons in seconds. Confront them fast and hard, try to overpower them, as they're not very strong."

Brandon held up his hands. "Do I use my knuckles, or should I just stand back and admire the three of you?"

"That's right," I said. "Brandon needs a weapon."

"He can use one of mine," said Tori heavily. She flipped one of her swords so that she caught it by the blade, then handed it reluctantly over to Brandon hilt-first. "Do not lose it, and if you get any blood on it, clean it off."

"You're giving me *blade-care* instructions?" said Brandon incredulously. He took the sword and tested it for balance.

"They're like a good friend," she said.

I tightened my grip on Talon's hilt, already under-standing how she felt. "Let's go. Brandon, you hang back and pick off any survivors."

Brandon suddenly looked pale in the semi-darkness, as if the realization of what he was about to do was sinking in. He mumbled something unintelligible.

"Don't worry, half-elf," said Tristan, the muscles in his jaw rolling. "There won't *be* any survivors."

We advanced casually, purposely talking out loud so that the dark elves would think we were totally oblivious to their presence. If Brandon was correct, there were two enemies waiting just past the large boulder to our left, and one lurking behind a smaller boulder to Tristan's right.

The moment we passed the line of rocks, Tori slipped silently around the back and I darted around the front. I was so focused on my task, there was no way I could watch Tristan, but one moment he was beside me and the next he was gone.

Just as I rounded the boulder, the dark elf was attacked by something small and gray. It was the dove that had flown in with us. The elf batted it away angrily, but it gave me the time I needed. For a split second, the dark elf's pale white face turned in my direction and his purplish eyes glowed a frightening maroon color. Fortunately for me, they were wide with surprise. I swiped Talon through the air, cringing as the dark elf crumpled to the ground. The dove fluttered up into the darkness. *Guess you're a friend,* I thought.

Then I looked down and saw what I had done. I staggered backward, stumbling over the uneven ground. The blade of my sword was wet with blood. It was strangely dark, but it was still blood. I had killed a grint before, but that was like killing a big bug. This was different. I felt sick. I clutched my stomach, but Tristan grabbed my arm roughly.

"Don't lament his death, Cinder!" he growled. "He would have taken your life with pleasure if you hadn't killed him first. Their hearts are black." He had obviously dispatched his own dark elf because he was wiping his blade on the sleeve of his jacket. Tori came around the boulder, her features grim.

"Let's move quickly," she said. "There could be more coming that we don't know about."

"Any survivors?" said Brandon weakly. He was staring at the boots of a dark elf that were protruding from behind the rock. The enemy I had killed.

"You'll get your chance," promised Tristan. He pointed at the bodies. "Gather up their crossbows and bolts. They may come in handy later."

I hurried to the body of the dark elf and tried not to look at his face while I wrenched his crossbow from off his back. But I couldn't help it. His maroon eyes were still staring, though they were dull and lifeless. His lips were thin and blue, as if he were freezing, and his skin was chalky white.

"Why are they called dark elves?" I asked. "They're not dark at all."

"Named after their environment," answered Tristan, gesturing to the heavy gloom that pressed down on us from all sides. "Grab the pouch at his waist. It's filled with bolts but watch the tips. They're dipped in poison."

Holding my hand over my mouth, I pulled the leather pouch from the dead elf's waist and hurried away. *I'll never get used to this*, I thought.

I was still feeling sick as we slipped through the opening in the far wall of the cavern, but I was determined not to let my discomfort with death distract me from my goal. I had promised my grandma I would fulfill this quest, or die trying.

Tori fell back a pace or two and requested her sword back from Brandon. When he said, "How can you leave me weaponless?" she gave him both the long daggers from the dark elf she had killed, as well as his crossbow and pouch of poison-coated bolts.

"I have my own bow and arrows," Tori said. "Those toothpick shooters are useless to me."

Brandon pried the pouch open carefully and peered inside. "I have a feeling these *toothpicks* can bring down an elephant." He slid the daggers awkwardly through the belt loops of his jeans, but he appeared comfortable with the crossbow, drawing back the thin cable and hooking it behind the little iron pin.

Fully equipped, we hurried down a twisting, uneven corridor. We had to watch our step, though, because the purple-flamed torches were gone. The only illumination came from the glittering silver pinpricks that dotted the tunnel walls.

We ran on, and suddenly the walls to either side of us went totally black. "The bits of silver are gone," I said, reaching out to touch the wall to my left.

"That's because the *walls* are gone," said Tristan, reaching out a hand and grabbing the back of my hoodie before I could topple into the black void.

"Thanks," I breathed, stepping away from the edge. "I need to be more careful."

"Please do," said Tristan. "I don't want to lead this ragtag group."

"Who's to say *I* wouldn't become the leader if Cinder plunged to her death?" said Brandon haughtily. "If Cinder dies, I say we take a vote. It's only fair."

Tristan shook his head. "The lack of oxygen down here has gotten to your brain, half-elf. If anything, the decision would be between me and Tori."

"But—"

"Hello," I said, waving. "I'm not dead yet. Can we decide leadership roles *after* I die?"

As my eyes became more adjusted to the darkness, I began to see that both sides of our path now dropped away into what appeared to be a bottomless abyss. I suddenly felt dizzy.

"Do not stray to either side," warned Tori. "If you fall, your part in this quest is over."

I paused for just a moment to take in my bearings. On either side of me was an endless sea of darkness. Here and there were spires of rock, several of them connected by strands of silvery rope.

"What's the rope for?" I whispered, hustling to catch up.

"That's not rope," replied Tristan.

I stared in disbelief. "You knew there were giant spiders down here, and you didn't tell us?"

"Sometimes it's better *not* to know about something until it's too late to turn back," said Tristan, turning briefly to smile over his shoulder.

Brandon whipped his curved daggers out as he ran. "What I wouldn't give for a big can of Raid right now."

I tried to ignore the fact that the number of silky strands that looped from spire to spire was rapidly growing in number. I said, "I think these spiders would laugh at your can of Raid."

We increased our speed over the narrow stone path, our weapons out and our eyes peeled for any eight-legged enemies.

"Hopefully they're not hunting right now," said Tristan.

"I know *some* of them are done hunting," Brandon said, pointing with his crossbow.

I slowed my pace. "How do you know—?" I stopped mid-sentence. To our left, dangling over the abyss, was a large, human-sized figure wrapped from head to toe in a glistening web cocoon.

"Odin's leather boxers," I whispered, stealing Skuld's words.

All of us gathered at the edge of the drop-off. "That's one big dark elf," said Brandon.

"That's no dark elf," Tristan replied. "Too tall, way too thick."

"Kobold?" offered Tori. "Cave troll?"

Tristan shrugged. "Could be. Either way, he's in for a long night."

I turned to stare at Tristan. "You mean he's still *alive*?"

"Do they not have spiders in Virginia?" asked Tristan with a smirk. When I refused to play his game, he said, "Most spiders, no matter how big or small, encase their victims in webbing, keeping them alive till they can return at a later time and eat them fresh."

"Mother Nature's Tupperware," whispered Brandon.

The large cocoon suddenly began to shake. Then a man's voice cried out.

"It's human!" I exclaimed. "We have to cut it down."

Tristan was shaking his head. "We're jeopardizing the quest, Cinder, and all for what? To save one human? Sorry, no offense."

"Offense taken," I replied.

Tristan didn't miss a beat. "Our quest is meant to save *millions* of humans. Do you want to risk failure because of one unfortunate victim that was too stupid to know you don't come down here without backup?"

"I guarantee my IQ is higher than yours," came the voice from the cocoon. "And my backup betrayed me. Blasted long beards and their greedy hearts."

"I'm sorry if you don't agree with my decision," I said, looking for a way across the void. "I'm cutting him down."

"He could be an enemy!" warned Tristan.

"If you side with the eight-legged beasts," came the muffled voice, "or those good-for-nothing gem diggers, then yes, I am your enemy."

"See?" I said, leaping off our narrow path and landing on a section of slanted rock that formed the pinnacle of one of the spires. "He's on our side."

As I jumped from pinnacle to pinnacle, I whispered my gratitude to those who had forced me to master the Gauntlet; without its training, I would have plunged to my death on the very first leap. A moment later, I was standing on a stony platform beneath the struggling cocoon. "Hold still," I said, surveying my options. "I'm going to cut you down."

The cocoon stopped moving. "If your sword is not enchanted, it will take hours to saw through these webs."

I was fairly confident Talon could sever the webbing quickly, but the most enchanted blade in the Nine Realms would do me no good if I couldn't reach the cocoon. I looked around. The platform offered me nothing to climb. I held Talon up, stretching my arm as far as it would go. On my tiptoes, I could almost touch the cocoon with the tip of my sword. Just as I was considering another option, I heard Tori shout, "Cinder, to your right!"

I looked to my right, just in time to see a giant spider skittering smoothly across one of the silvery ropes, headed in my direction.

"I am about to be supper, aren't I?" said the man. He laughed. "She will have a time of it, though, trying to penetrate my finely crafted armor, not to mention my massive muscles."

"Shut up!" I hissed, trying to think. The spider was at least as big as a small car, with snapping pinchers the size of my arms, and covered in spiky black hair. All eight of its glossy green eyes were locked on me.

Feeling stupid for not noticing it before, I ran to the edge of the rock and used Talon to slash through the silver webbing that was attached to the edge of the platform. The spider shrieked horribly as it fell, shooting out strands of web in an attempt to save itself. But all of them fell short, and the spider was lost in the darkness.

"More are coming!" yelled Tori. "Get back here!"

"You could use my help," said the man in the cocoon. "As I mentioned before, I am very intelligent, corded with muscle, and certified lethal with over five hundred different kinds of weapons."

I spotted four other spiders advancing on my rocky platform from all directions, and one descending from above.

"Come back, Cinder!" bellowed Tristan.

I ran to the edge of the rock, prepared to leap back to the narrow path on which my friends stood, when I suddenly stopped and turned. Gathering all my strength, I ran towards the cocoon and shouted, "Here goes nothing!"

"Well, that is not encouraging," said the man in the cocoon.

I leaped into the air, Talon held over my head. Just as I reached the apex of my jump, I brought my blade swishing downwards, cutting a deep gouge in the cocoon. Talon passed through the webbing as if it were made of butter. With a shout of exultation, the man tumbled out and twisted in the air so that he landed on the platform in a smooth half-crouch.

342 ✵ STORMBRINGER

The spider that had been lowering itself from above dropped the last ten feet and plopped down on top of the large man, wrapping its legs around his shoulders. Before I could thrust Talon at the horrible creature, the man grunted and heaved the thing off of his back and into the abyss.

"You see?" said the man smiling through a set of brilliant white teeth. "My strength is too much for these creatures."

"You better stop bragging and start running," I advised, turning to leap to the first pinnacle.

The man followed me. "I am not boasting; I am simply stating a truth."

The remaining spiders reached an empty platform and began to shriek in rage. Their dinner was getting away.

We soon made our last jump and landed on the narrow pathway. Brandon and Tori were at the edge of the preci-pice, firing arrows and poisonous bolts at the spiders. One by one, the monsters were pierced and sent flying into the abyss.

"Brandon, Tori," I said, my breathing ragged. "Nice work."

Tori's expression was grim, but the half-elf was grinning from ear to ear and looking for another hairy target. "Better than a can of Raid," he said.

Tristan had his sword pointed at our newest arrival, but the man was totally ignoring him. He was too busy pulling strands of sticky webbing from his lustrous brown hair.

"State your name," growled Tristan, "or I will run you through with Tyr."

The man stopped grooming himself long enough to regard Tristan with a curious stare. "You named your sword *Tyr*," he said. "Funny. That is *my* name."

ᴄᴇᴀᴍ ᴄyʀ!

Tyr was at least seven feet tall with chocolate brown hair (highlighted with cobwebs), rosy cheeks, and sparkling blue eyes. His spiky bronze armor made him look even bigger.

Tristan lowered the point of his sword. "Your name is Tyr? As in . . . the God of War?"

"Is there any other?" he said gallantly.

Tristan's astonished grin turned to a suspicious frown. "Prove it."

"If the bloody long beards had not stolen my sword," said Tyr, "I would show you how it resembles one of the rays of the sun, and that would be proof enough. But since I no longer have my cherished weapon, this will have to suffice." The huge warrior held up his left hand, except he *had* no left hand. The iron bracer on his left arm ended at the wrist.

Tristan's jaw dropped. He looked at me, then Tori, then Brandon, then pointed at Tyr and silently mouthed the words, "It's him!"

"What?" I asked, totally confused. "What's the deal with the hand?" I looked to Tristan for an explanation, but he was still gazing in awe at Tyr. I turned to Tori. "Fill me in."

Tori looked at the towering man. "Do you mind?"

Tyr shook his head and promptly began to finger comb his brown tresses. "Be my guest, but leave anything important out, and I shall be forced to toss you over the cliff."

The Predator sighed. "Tyr is the God of War. One of the twelve principal gods, and a son to Odin."

"Oh, then Brunhild is your sister!" I said, pleased that I wasn't completely clueless when it came to Norse history.

"Yes," said Tyr, his expression falling. "Good ol' Brunni. You know, to this day that spoiled little brat claims that her teeth are straighter than mine."

"Let's see," said Brandon.

Tyr leaned down and flashed his blinding white teeth.

"That *is* a good set," Brandon confirmed.

"Anyway," said Tori. "Tyr's full name is Tyr Tiu, which became *Tuesday* in the English language."

"That is right," said Tyr, checking his reflection in the shiny surface of his bracer. "Not many people in the Nine Realms can say that one of the seven days of the week is named after them."

I couldn't believe it. I had actually found someone with an ego larger than Tristan's. "Alright," I said impatiently. "Get to the missing hand part."

"This is good," assured Tyr.

"So when Fenrir was first captured and imprisoned with the enchanted rope," continued the Predator, "Tyr was the only being brave enough to stick his hand into the wolf's mouth as a sign of good faith. But Fenrir, so enraged at the thought of being held captive, bit down on Tyr's arm and severed the hand at the wrist."

"Fowl creature," said Tyr, staring morosely at his maimed arm. "If ever I should meet up with that wicked beast, I shall not hesitate to do more than take off its paw." He stared into the gloom. "To think I played with Fenrir when he was only a pup . . ."

"So it's true," said Tristan. "You were the only god willing to pay attention to the wolf."

Tyr nodded. "We were as close as two living beings could be."

I wanted to say that Fenrir had changed, but now didn't seem like the time or place to vouch for the wolf's rehabilitation. "That's quite a story," I said, eyeing his extraordinary armor. My eyes paused on his footwear. "Are those *Timberland* boots?"

Tyr stopped admiring his reflection long enough to look down at his feet. "They are! Do you like them? I picked them up in a shoe store right next to The Gap." He pointed to the ceiling with the arm that still had a hand. "Right above us, in fact."

Brandon's eyes lit up. "Did you see the sale they were having on crew neck sweaters?"

"Way ahead of you," said Tyr. "I put three on layaway."

Brandon frowned at me. "Cinder wouldn't let us stop."

Tyr looked at my choice of attire and nodded. "Appearance is not your thing, huh?"

"Look," I said, "we're down here to stop Bergelmir the Cruel from severing one of the roots of the great tree, and—"

"You cannot be serious," said Tyr, cutting me off. "Are you Stormbringer, Daughter of Dark-Fortune, Mistress of Mayhem, Lady of—?"

"Okay, we get the point," I said, cutting him off. "Actually, it's ill-fortune. How'd you know?"

"You are the latest thing in Asgard. Everyone is talking about you. There are even shirts with your face—"

"I know," I said, cutting him off.

"Stormbringer," said Tyr thoughtfully. "I love it! Very next-generation. Anyway, I'm here for the same reason you are."

"What? Who sent you?"

"My father."

I bit my lip. Things were about to get messy. "Did Odin happen to say why?"

"Dad arrived in Asgard early this morning," said Tyr, "and found me being smothered by a group of naiads who were shamelessly uncontrollable. He said I was to report at once to the Well of Knowledge, where I would defeat the giant Bergelmir. Then, plans could be made to sabotage the wicked machine that cuts away at Yggdrasil's root."

It appeared that Odin hadn't shared with his son exactly why he was doing this on such short notice. And something else bugged me. "Okay, so he sends you to defeat the giant. But why can't you just chop the machine to pieces too?"

Tyr shook his head, which made his brown locks fan out impressively across his wide shoulders. "Oh no, child. That machine cannot be broken with brute strength, of which I have plenty. It wasn't just the blades that were

made from Asgardian silver, didn't you know? Our only
hope is to dismantle it. But it is built with such cunning,
such intricacy—false pistons, dummy levers, engines, and
entire contraptions to deceive the onlooker—that we doubt
anyone but its maker himself can do so. It is a fool's errand,
but a gallant one!"

"Its maker . . . you mean Bergelmir?"

Tyr smirked. "Bergelmir is the brawn of the outfit, not
the brains."

"Then who?" I said with some exasperation. My quest
was looking more and more hopeless by the minute.

"Kvasir, of course, the God of Inspiration," said Tyr.

Tori gasped.

"That's impossible," blurted Tristan. We all turned to
look at him. "Kvasir is one of the Aesir, a god of light," he
said. "He would *never* agree to harm the World Tree."

Tyr suddenly looked sad again. "The situation is under
investigation, but Kvasir has either betrayed us, or was
captured and . . . *forced* to create and operate this machine.
We've had no news of him for months."

Tristan looked visibly shaken. The olive complexion of
his skin looked a shade lighter.

"So you were sent to stop the giant until someone else
could figure out how to stop the machine?" I said. "And the
only one smart enough is missing. *And* it's only a couple of
days until the root is cut. *What* in the name of Asgard are
you gods thinking?!"

Tyr ignored the accusation. "Kvasir is missing, yes . . ."
he said, "but not Kvasir's son. Although, last I heard, the

Valkyries lost track of the boy Tristan some hours ago."

I gaped, too stunned for words. *Tristan?* My heart leapt when I thought the quest might not be doomed after all. But that would mean . . .

Tristan turned away, and I drew a sharp breath. "Kvasir is your dad?"

"Father of the Year," said Tristan glumly. He kicked a stone on the ground. "I've spent more time with these giant spiders here than I ever did with him."

Tyr was digging something out of his sparkling white teeth, when he suddenly stopped. "Oh, I get it," he said, pointing at Tristan. "*You* are the machine expert! Fabulous! I mean, I do wish it were *me*, but then that would mean Kvasir was my . . . oh, I am sorry."

"Can we just go?" growled Tristan.

I was still in shock. Tristan had just found out that his dad was either a traitor or a prisoner, and even though the two of them had probably never entered a three-legged race together at a family picnic, it was still painful. Especially not knowing the truth. And then it hit me: the God of Inspiration was Freya's father too. *Did she know what happened?* I wondered. I shook myself. Now wasn't the time.

"Tristan's right," I said. "We should get going." I glanced up at the huge warrior, determined to change the subject. "Tyr, do you know the way to the Well of Knowledge?"

"I am afraid I never had the chance to find out," Tyr said, his features souring. "Thanks to those long beards."

"Who are these long beards you keep mentioning?"

"Dwarves," stated Tyr derisively. "Of all the beings my father could have sent with me, he had to choose the one race that will do anything for a shiny rock."

"Odin sent a group of dwarves with you?" I asked. "What for?"

"Oh, he had his list of reasons. Their apparent knowledge of sub-surface terrain and mechanical devices, their extraordinary endurance, and their high tolerance for spider venom. There were other things, but I do not care to repeat them."

"I see," I said, thinking of Kevin, Saemund's dwarven guard. "Since he couldn't find Tristan, he sent the dwarves."

The God of War shrugged, suddenly more concerned with smoothing his bushy brown eyebrows with saliva-damp fingers. "But the thieving whisker-heads sabotaged my drinking water with a sleeping agent. When I awakened, my weapons were gone, and I was hanging upside down with my arms pinned at my sides."

"Someone offered them . . . shiny rocks, to betray you?" I inquired.

Tyr shrugged his massive shoulders. "I cannot say for sure, but why else would a dwarf risk angering one of Asgard's premier gods?"

"Good point," I said, the wheels in my mind spinning. "Well, it looks like we're all here for the same purpose. Will you go with us? We could sure use your . . . fabled strength."

Tyr looked at me suspiciously, then gave in to the compliment. "It is true. No one here can deny that my extraordinary strength would help you immensely. For the Allfather, I will accompany you!"

"Then it's set," I said. "Tristan, lead on."

Tristan dashed forward across the narrow span of rock. He seemed relieved to be leaving the conversation behind. We quickly followed, Tyr's heavy bronze armor clanking and the stalking dove swooping high overhead.

☖

With Tristan leading and the God of War rattling along behind us, we made excellent time. We traveled beneath what must have been the entire Twin Palms mall and burrowed deep into the earth. Fortunately, our path was lit by the strange glittery substance that coated the walls, and we hadn't seen or heard from a single dark elf or spider for hours. I was proud of the fact that I never once had to ask for a breather, though I was sweating profusely and Tori and Tristan were not. The tunnels were beginning to make me feel claustrophobic too. Just as I was about to ask how much longer (as if anyone really knew), Tristan halted and said, "The tunnel splits off in three different directions. I'm not sure which one leads to the Well of Knowledge."

We all turned to look at the God of War. "Do not look at me," he said. "I am here to provide some much-needed muscle and a little style. Orienteering is not my forte."

Brandon stepped forward, his head tilted to the side. "I can hear something far away. It sounds like a . . . *thunking* noise."

"I bet it's the blades of that machine hitting the giant root," I said excitedly. "We must be getting close."

"Can you tell which direction we should go?" said Tristan, eyeing Brandon skeptically.

Brandon strained for a moment or two, then sadly shook his head. "I'm sorry, guys. It could be any one of these tunnels."

"We could split up," offered Tyr. "Those who want to survive this ordeal should definitely accompany me."

Tori rolled her eyes. Tristan nodded.

"No," I said, "let's stick together. We'll just have to try each path till we find the well."

"Or you could just try the left one and be done with it," came a deep voice from behind us.

We all spun around, whipping our weapons out in one fluid motion.

"Sebus!" I cried, wondering if I was happy to see the caveman or deeply concerned by the fact that he kept appearing out of nowhere. "What are you doing here?"

Sebus threw the God of War a strange look as he strode forward. Tyr, however, was too busy brushing the dust off his Timberland boots to notice.

"I must apologize, Stormbringer," said Sebus, bowing slightly. "I confess that after I left you, I decided to double back and follow you."

"Awkward," whispered Brandon out of the side of his mouth.

"You may be grateful in the end, half-elf," said Sebus, glancing over at Brandon.

Brandon flushed bright red. "His hearing's better than mine!"

Sebus shrugged. It was obvious he had visited a few of the outlets in the mall before his descent into the underworld; he was now outfitted in a pair of olive-green cargo pants, a khaki safari shirt, and hiking boots. I didn't want to know where he got the money.

"But how did you . . . ?" I began.

"I suspected you would need my help again."

"Okay," I said, hoping with all my heart he wasn't as creepy as Brandon thought he was. "You mentioned the left tunnel. Do you know something we don't?"

Sebus tapped the side of his nose. "I have an extraordinary sense of smell. Bergelmir is not far off."

I nodded and elbowed Brandon in the ribs when he mumbled, "Getting creepier."

I gestured down the left-hand passage. "Then left it is."

"I can tell you are all highly suspicious of this man," stated Tyr with flair, "as am I. And so I will take it upon myself to watch over him so that he does not harm any of you. I would give the charge to one of you, but frankly I do not believe anyone here is capable of the duty."

This time all of us rolled our eyes.

Tyr looked hard at Sebus, as if noticing him for the first time. "Say, do I know you?"

"Have you ever been to Kruselle, the small dwarven mining village in Nioavellir?" Sebus asked.

Tyr thought for a moment. "Do they worship me in that village?"

"I do not think so," said Sebus.

"Then no, I have not." Tyr stared at Sebus a while longer, then shrugged his massive shoulders. "Lead on, odd-smelling stranger."

We entered the left passage with Sebus leading the way. He paused briefly every time we happened upon a split in the tunnel, but after sniffing the air and placing his ear to the ground, he would rise up and move on with full confidence. After an hour of this, he brought us to an enormous wooden door that was bound with thick bands of corroded steel and secured with a large rusty padlock. The thunking noise that Brandon had mentioned was now unmistakable. The machine was very close, and it was hard at work.

"The Well of Knowledge and the giant are behind this door," announced Sebus, his deep voice low. "And there is something else . . ."

"What?" Tristan asked eagerly.

Sebus shook his head. "I do not know exactly. A vibration in the air, like electricity . . ."

"Lightning?" offered Brandon.

"Belowground?" said Tristan, rounding on the half-elf. "It appears Pismo turns out academic all-stars."

Brandon bristled. "Hey, put that sword down and *then* say that."

I stepped between the two boys just as Tristan was balling up his fists. Did Brandon not know that Tristan could pulverize him with his arms tied behind his back? "Stop it, both of you," I said. "Do you really think now is the time for this?"

"It is always a good time to prove one's courage and strength," said Tyr. "There was this one time when my mother was about to bear her twenty-first child and I—"

"Tyr," I said, "can you hold that story till after we stop Bergelmir?"

The God of War looked slightly put-out, but nodded.

"Okay," I said, my nerves tingling with anticipation, "what's the plan?"

"Let us begin by opening the door," said Sebus.

CHAPTER 34

ΠEVER ШAKE SLEEPIΠG GIAΠCS

I have to admit, the machine reminded me a little of Tristan's Gauntlet. Only bigger. And much shinier. I could see now why Odin had wanted Tristan to tag along. This thing was right up his alley.

It sat in front of us like an enormous silver insect, and Tyr was right: it looked impossible to figure out. Steam burst from twisting Asgardian silver pipes. Gleaming silver machinery thrummed. Silver pistons hammered. Silver engines roared. Silver gears groaned. You couldn't tell where one piece ended and another began. And silver cabling wound in and out of everything, twanging like the strings on an instrument badly out of tune.

But all of it paled in comparison to the gigantic blade that was even now slicing horizontally through the air as it chipped away at the magical tree. It moved in a flat arc, spun through the air by a central hissing piston as large as a wheat silo. The blade, a giant slice of deadly Asgardian silver, seemed to have a life of its own, gobbling hungrily at Yggdrasil's flesh.

And the noise. The grinding of gears, the whistling of hoses, and the sudden scream followed by a sickening *thunk* of the great blade, caused me to instinctively clap my hands over my ears. *Tristan's dad built this*, I thought. Couldn't he just make ships in a bottle like other dads? And how did he acquire so much Asgardian silver?

The moment I recovered from the earsplitting cacophony, I took in the root. It was massive. Heavy-duty mountain climbing equipment would be required to scale it. I decided the root would have to be mind-bendingly large if it helped to support the World Tree.

The root rose up out of a glimmering pool of water, though from where I stood it looked more like a good-sized lake. Glittering waterfalls spilled down the root in large, cascading rivulets, sending up billowing sprays of mist wherever they crashed into the lake. The pool was surrounded by a stone wall adorned with millions of sparkling gems inlaid in the stone in intricate patterns. I knew at once I was looking at the Well of Knowledge, and unless there were multiple gods named Mimir, this fountain belonged to Odin's uncle, the same man who traded a truckload of knowledge and wisdom for Allfather's eye.

Again, ew.

But despite the beauty of the well and the immensity of the root, my eyes continually roamed back to the ever-widening wound in its side.

"It's nearly severed," Tori whispered sadly at my side.

We stared in horror as huge chunks of wood burst from the fissure every time the cruel blade bit into Yggdrasil's enchanted flesh, some of the pieces spinning off into the darkness and the heavier sections falling down to land in the choppy waters of the well.

It made me sick, and for the good of the quest, it made me angry.

"Let's shut this thing down," I said through gritted teeth.

"Hope you have a well-formed plan, love."

The voice had come from the low wall of the well. It was a very distinguished-sounding voice, like a wealthy British aristocrat. Hoping it wasn't a dark elf from London, I approached the wall slowly, my hand going to the hilt of my sword. "Excuse me? Who said that?" I demanded.

"I know that voice," said Tyr. "First, because I never forget a voice. Second, Mimir and I go *way* back. Like fifteen hundred years back."

"Mimir!" gushed Brandon, blowing past me as he raced to the well. "I can't *wait* to tell Mom!"

"It's okay," Tristan called out. "It's not like we're trying to save the Nine Realms or anything."

Knowing it would be easier to stop Bergelmir the Cruel from killing the World Tree than stopping Brandon from fanning over Mimir, I sighed and followed him. The God of Wisdom, reduced to a severed head, was chilling on the wall like a grinning jack-o'-lantern. He had sparkling gray eyes, a long narrow nose, and a white beard that flowed down over the wall and sat in a fluffy pile on the ground.

Oh, and he was wearing a headband with Nordic runes stitched into the fabric. He smiled and the runes lit up and transformed into English. "*Team Cinder!*" flashed across his forehead. Did Borghild's line of merch know no bounds?

"Ah, the Stormbringer!" said Mimir, winking one gray eye. "Well met, love, well met."

"Hello . . . sir," I said, unsure what to call him. He was a god *and* an adult, after all.

"Call me Mimir, love." His eyes shifted upwards. "Like the Cinder gear?"

"It's . . . nice . . . " I mumbled. My face was heating up.

"Headbands?" said Tristan. "Really?"

Mimir sighed. "I would've sprung for the T-shirt but, you know . . . "

"I'm not accustomed to *not* being the most adored in the room," said Tyr, frowning at me, "so let's get on with our quest."

Mimir smiled at the God of War. "Tyr, good to see you, old boy. Looking robust and well groomed as usual."

"Hello, Mimir," said Tyr. "I would pat you on the shoulder as a friendly gesture, but you have no torso."

"Ah, and still just as tactful," replied Mimir with a frown. His eyes swiveled to take in the rest of us. "I don't know the rest of you but I'm sure you're a delightful bunch. Should I assume not all of you know my story?"

"I do," said Brandon excitedly, "but there's nothing like hearing it from the source."

Tristan groaned again.

"If you insist," said Mimir. "You see, two millennia ago, the Allfather comes to me and says, 'Mimir, I am really smart but I need to be much smarter. What if—"

"Like Tyr says," cutting off the God of Wisdom as gently as I could, "we really need to continue with our quest."

Mimir looked a little deflated, but he quickly recovered. "Is this about inspecting the wall? If I'm being honest, very shoddy work. I could tell the dwarves were just phoning it in that day."

"No, we're not here for that," I said. "We're here about the machine that's cutting into the World Tree."

"Ah, *that* quest," said Mimir. "Yes, sorely needed, love. Fate of the Nine Realms and all that. Well, on with it then. Yggdrasil won't save itself."

I turned my back on Mimir and had everyone huddle around me. "This is it," I said. "Tristan, we all know you're here to dismantle that machine." Tristan nodded, his eyes grim with determination, and something else that I figured had to do with the news about his dad. I looked at everyone else in turn. "I say we follow Tristan, let him get to work and watch his back. When the machine is shut down, we'll deal with Bergelmir as a group, because once he hears that the blade has stopped cutting, he won't be happy. If we can escape without a fight, I say we leave as quickly as possible. My quest instructions were to stop the mechanism. It didn't say I had to defeat the giant."

Everyone seemed to agree except Tyr. He was shaking his head. "I never run from a fight."

"You don't even have any weapons," said Brandon in a rare moment of foolish bravery.

The God of War scrutinized Brandon as if seeing him for the first time, then picked him up, flipped him over, and shook him till his two long daggers fell to the ground. He set Brandon back down and snatched up the daggers.

"I seem to have found some," he said, smiling.

Brandon was trembling. "I hope those work out for you."

"Just as I suspected," said Tyr, frowning. "My well-formed hands are too large for these pathetic weapons. Here, take them back."

Brandon took the daggers, but I could tell he was quite content with his crossbow.

Just as I was about to issue further instructions, I heard a metallic *ping*, followed by a whistling noise very close to my ear. I thought it was a stray bolt that had nearly pierced my ear, but I saw that it was the dove, perhaps trying to warn me to find shelter.

"I was just struck by a dark elf's poisonous bolt," Tyr casually stated. He rubbed the tiny indentation in his bronze armor with his thumb and frowned again. "They will pay dearly for that."

I yelped and staggered backwards. It felt like someone had thrown a fastball right at my chest. I looked down. An iron bolt with a wicked tip was lying at my feet.

"That would be your clue to find cover!" shouted Tori.

I dove to my left, rolled a few times, and popped up behind a multi-colored stalagmite. I silently thanked Freya. If not for her sea-serpent vest, I would've been out of the game. Benched for eternity.

I looked around. Everyone else had found cover. A fresh torrent of bolts zipped past us like angry insects. One buried itself near my sneaker. Another stung my hand when it bounced off my exposed blade.

"Stay hidden till they charge!" I hissed.

Everyone obeyed my order, except Tyr and Brandon. The God of War, his face creased with a deep scowl, strode directly into the barrage of oncoming bolts, letting his body armor deflect the missiles and shielding his face with the bracers on his forearms. By the time he reached the first line of dark elves, it was difficult to distinguish his armor spikes from the multitude of iron darts protruding from his bronze chest plate and shoulder guards. I cringed as I watched Tyr hoist a dark elf into the air and fling him into the darkness, then another and another.

"Good throw, old boy!" shouted Mimir from the wall. "Never cared for those red-eyed demons!"

Brandon was popping up from behind his stalagmite to release his own poisonous darts, and even though I angrily swore at him to stop and take cover, I was happy to hear that nearly every bolt he fired met its mark.

"Cinder!" yelled Tristan. "I cannot wait any longer!"

"Wait for her word!" shouted Tori. "She commands us now."

Tristan nodded, though I could tell it was killing him inside. *Let the God of War thin our enemies' ranks*, I thought. *Why risk our lives just for the sake of killing?*

I peeked around the stalagmite and saw that Tyr was far away, searching for any dark elf foolish enough to raise their crossbow at him. But at least half a dozen of the creatures were advancing towards us, their crossbows replaced with gleaming curved daggers.

"Now!" I hissed, jumping up and bringing Talon around in front of me. "Brandon, stay back and pick off as many as you can! And don't hit *us!*" Tristan and Tori leaped out, swords in hand, their faces grim.

The three of us moved against the six dark elves.

Remember everything you've learned, Cinder, I told myself.

"Fast and hard," said Tristan, stepping forward and in front of me. "Do not give them the chance to take the offensive. They're too fast."

Tori, too, slid over so that she was blocking me from the elves' view. "Cinder," said the Predator over her shoulder, "stay back and—"

Before they could talk me into watching from the side-lines, I sprinted forward, shouldered my way past Tori and Tristan, and engaged the first dark elf. The elf was caught off guard by my mad dash and threw his dagger up a moment too late. Talon cut the air between us with a silver arc, and I moved on, not wasting any time to watch my enemy fall.

"Careful, love!" shouted Mimir. "If you die, there will be no reason for the headband!"

"Odin has us all!" shouted Tristan, issuing the famous battle cry of Allfather's warriors. With his blade held high, he rushed forward, and before I could register his move-ments, the dark elves' numbers were down by two more. Not to be outdone, Tori fell into a mesmerizing dance with her twin blades and a moment later, all six of the dark elves were lying still and silent on the ground.

"Tristan," I said, glancing back to see if Brandon was hurt. "Go to the machine. We'll cover you."

Nodding, Tristan sprinted nimbly through the stalag-mites and entered the tangled mess of silver beams, armatures, and tubing. Like a jungle cat leaping from branch to branch in a giant tree, Tristan maneuvered his way up and into the machine's belly.

Off in the distance, I could still see Tyr flinging dark elves like Frisbees. "Lucky we ran into Tyr, huh?" I said.

"If he runs out of strength," said Tori, "he can always crush them with his ego."

I stole a glance up at the machine and saw that Tristan had made it to a tiny platform that jutted out from a panel that separated him from the giant blade. I whispered a tiny prayer for him and looked away.

"I guess there's no hoping to escape without confronting Bergelmir," said Tori.

"Yeah, but where is he? He must know we're here."

Tori squinted into the gloom. "Not sure. I know giants sleep during the day, and when they sleep it takes an earth-quake to wake them."

Just then, the dove flitted past my ear again, and I instinctively spun around. Standing behind me was a dark elf, his dagger raised. I leaned backwards, felt the blade graze my nose, and brought Talon across at the same time. The elf slumped to the ground.

"Cinder! Tori! Look out!" It was Tristan calling down to us from above.

"Keep working!" I shouted, ducking another dark elf's vicious attempt to give me a haircut. Tori rushed forward, slid beneath one of the machine's thick silver beams, and popped up in time to halt the advance of two enemies at once. I moved between two elves myself, thrusting, parrying, spinning, feinting, then slashing with Talon till I could see nothing around me but the images of my white-skinned, red-eyed targets.

"You cannot turn your back on them until they're down, Cinder!" shouted Tristan. "My lessons on that were *very* thorough!"

"Are you kidding me?" I yelled back. "Focus on the machine!"

Tristan shook his head and turned back to his work. I watched him study a bird's nest of twisting wires, which he picked through with the tip of a tiny dagger that he had pulled from his back pocket. Sparks flew, some of the wires whipped around like angry snakes, then fell limp. He then moved to a set of complex gears. After scrutinizing them for several seconds, he began to reverse the rotation on some of them, ignoring others. Next, he moved to a small silver box and used his dagger to pop the lid. He peered inside the box, dug around with the tip of the dagger, jerked his hand out, cursed, sucked his finger for a moment, then returned to his work. Finished, he pocketed his dagger, then dropped to a metal beam below the platform he had been working from. He skittered across, ducked beneath the swiping blade by falling in one fluid movement and hanging from the beam like a spider monkey. The blade was so big and moved so fast that the wind from its passage nearly ripped him from the beam. When it was safe to move, he swung back up onto the beam and ran lightly across it before the blade could catch him again. Once on the new platform, he pried open a second box and repeated the tedious process.

All at once, I heard a loud whistling sound coming from the huge central piston that powered the blade. The giant steel shaft that was pumping up and down suddenly began to slow. My heartbeat quickened. *Are we really going to do it?*

A moment later, the shaft went still, stuck halfway in, halfway out of the piston casing. The blade stopped inches from biting into the magical tree.

"It's shut down," stated Tristan. He sounded like he had just finished a minor adjustment on the Gauntlet.

"Now can someone look into mending the wall!" shouted Mimir. "It's not Nine Realms important, but it *is* where I sit all day!"

My heart leaped in my chest. It seemed too good to be true. As if right on cue, an enraged roar echoed through the cavern. Tristan nearly fell from the machine.

"Nothing is ever easy when you're trying to save the realms," lamented Tori, spinning around to search the gloom with both her swords held out in front of her. "We woke up Bergelmir."

Quick as lighting, Tristan dropped the last twelve feet to the ground. He tucked his dagger away and whipped out his sword in one fluid motion. He looked at me. "It's your call, Cinder," he said, "but I don't believe we have the option of running. The giant is coming. I recommend we stand and fight."

"I agree," I said. I could feel Talon's handle slipping in my sweaty hand, but my combat senses were tingling. "The machine is shut down. According to Tyr, the giant won't be able to start it back up without your dad . . . or you. So part of the quest is over. Good work, Tristan." I smiled at him. The corners of his mouth raised a tiny fraction, and he nodded.

"Now we just have to survive."

I turned around to see who was talking. It was Sebus. He had no weapons, but I could tell just from the savage gleam in his green eyes and his disheveled appearance that he had been engaged in combat with more than a few dark elves.

"Sebus," I said, grateful he was there. "Thank you for helping us—again."

The man bowed and said, "You are welcome, Cinder, but it is not over yet. For now, the World Tree is safe, but if the giant captures us, he may learn of Tristan's skills and force him to return the machine to full functioning status."

"Then we fight," I said resolutely, hoping they couldn't hear the trembling in my voice. I looked around. "Where's Brandon and Tyr?"

Sebus pointed into the heavy gloom, the area of the cavern we had not yet explored. "The God of War is still on a rampage, quite upset over his dented armor. He has defeated at least sixty dark elves and frightened a hundred more into running from the cavern. Even weaponless, he will come in handy if we are to face Bergelmir."

Brandon! I thought, my heart clenching in my chest. "And Brandon? Have you seen him?" *Please be alright!*

"The half-elf ran off into the darkness, gathering bolts and firing them as he ran. I had always pegged the boy as somewhat of a coward, but he has proven me wrong. It would seem he has a personal vendetta against his dark cousins—and a deadly aim to go along with it."

I smiled, though my smile faded quickly when Bergelmir split the silence with another deafening roar, and this one much closer.

"Bergelmir approaches," announced Sebus. "Please allow me to tell you what I know of giants."

"*I* can tell you!" shouted Mimir. "Been here a while, you know!"

We ignored him and gathered around Sebus. "Bergelmir comes from a long line of powerful giants," he said. "His kind will usually carry a giant war hammer, but many of them choose to use their heavy fists to smash their smaller victims. His greatest weakness is his lack of speed. The three of you have quickness on your side, and so you should not have a difficult time dodging his attacks. But if you make a single mistake, it will be your last. My suggestion is to dart in for quick strikes one at a time so that it keeps him guessing. Capitalize on his lack of speed. When he figures out your strategy, which he will if we do not defeat him quickly, rush him at the same time." Sebus looked directly at me. "Cinder, your weapon, I believe, will determine the outcome of this battle. Do not loosen your grip for one moment and take courage. You have friends at your side."

I swallowed. Sebus was right. I *did* have friends at my side. The best friends I had ever known, in fact. But where were Brandon and Tyr?

The ground suddenly shuddered. I was forced to reach out a steadying hand on one of the machine's beams. A moment later, Bergelmir burst from the shadows like an angry bull that had broken through his fence.

"In this corner" shouted Mimir, "from somewhere in Midgard, standing a bit too tall for her age, the Lanky Lass of the Long Hall, Ciiiiiiiiiidrheiiiiiiiim Mooooooooss!"

"Mimir!" I shouted back, "please, not—"

"And in the far corner, from the Pits of Torment and Despair, weighing in at an uncomfortable six thousand pounds—"

"Not now, Mimir! We need to focus!"

"Fine, I'll remove all class and style," said Mimir.

"As our leader, Cinder," said Tori, "you should say something to inspire us. It's the Viking way."

"Keep it short, though," warned Tristan, glancing over his shoulder into the gloom.

I reached out and gripped Tristan's and Tori's shoulders and said the first thing that came to mind. "Stay frosty!"

Tori and Tristan gave each other a puzzled look.

"How about *go team Cinder!*" shouted Mimir.

"We'll definitely circle back later to your speech, Cinder," said Tristan. He winked at me and darted off, screaming: "Odin has us all!"

I watched him slant to his right, sprint up an incline of stone so that he could take the higher ground. "I'll draw him away from you!" he shouted. "When he's distracted, attack him from behind!"

As if we had practiced this a thousand times, Tori sprinted to her left, all the while shouting something in ancient Nordic.

Bergelmir ignored Tristan and the Predator and came straight for me.

So much for the distraction ploy, I thought, tightening my grip on Talon.

The giant was something out of my darkest nightmares. He stood at least two stories tall, his shoulders and torso bulging with misshapen muscle. He had only one arm, but it looked capable of crushing a minivan. His skin was thick and grayish, with a tint of green, like a really sick elephant. His head was small compared to his enormous body, and it sat on his rounded shoulders like a mottled gray coconut. Two horns sprouted from each side, but one of them was busted off at the base. His eyes were piggish and yellow, and two walrus-like tusks jutted from his lower jaw and sat on either side of his bulbous nose. Bergelmir wore only a loincloth of dirty leather, which I hoped would not lose its drawstring.

And I thought my foster dad looked bad in a swimsuit.

"He has a hammer!" shouted Sebus, falling in beside me. "He will use overhead chops, so roll to the side to avoid them!"

If what the giant had was a hammer, I was a dark elf. The haft was at least ten feet long and the head was formed from a tree trunk. I didn't have time to marvel at the weapon for too long because the giant took aim, bellowed, and swung the hammer just as Sebus had predicted. I leaped to my right and felt the ground tremble as the hammer's head buried itself in the hard-packed earth.

"Stand behind me, Cinder!" urged Sebus.

"No!" I shouted back. "You don't even have weapons!"

Sebus turned, grinned, and said, "Hopefully I will not need any."

Totally confused, I watched as he arched his back, threw his arms wide, and screamed in what sounded like overwhelming agony.

"Sebus!" I cried, approaching him in alarm. "What's happening!"

Sebus motioned for me to stay back. He was moaning now, sinking to his knees and clawing at the ground. "Keep your distance, Cinder! I do not want to trample you before you have a chance to prick that devil's hide!"

Trample me? I wondered. What was he doing, transforming into a giant?

I looked on in fascinated horror as Sebus doubled over, clutching at his chest and neck as if he were being attacked by a swarm of killer ants.

He did transform, but it wasn't into a giant.

"Did *not* see that coming," said Mimir.

CHAPTER 35

ATTACK OF THE KILLER HUMMINGBIRD

The enormous black wolf growled and charged the giant. Bergelmir was so shocked at the transformation that he failed to use his hammer in any useful way. The wolf barreled into Bergelmir, knocking the giant back.

"Fenrir!" I gasped. I felt my spirits soar. Sebus was Fenrir. Or was Fenrir Sebus? It wasn't important, really. All that mattered was that our odds, which seemed very bleak twenty seconds ago, had dramatically improved.

All of us watched as the wolf and Bergelmir rolled back and forth across the ground, Fenrir snapping his huge fangs at the giant's neck and Bergelmir trying to pry open Fenrir's jaws to the breaking point. I considered darting in with Talon, but Tristan seemed to read my mind.

"Wait, Cinder!" he shouted. "They'll crush you!"

I hesitated, realizing he was right. I felt a tiny twinge of joy. *Tristan actually cared that I was in danger!* Now was probably not the best time to consider his motives, though. At that moment, Brandon circled around behind me. I gave him a quick hug. "Do you always come late to parties?" I asked breathlessly.

Brandon smiled through a dozen cuts and scrapes on his freckled face. "I've been known to be fashionably late." He fitted his crossbow with a fresh bolt and took aim.

"Careful," I warned. "That wolf is on our side."

"Where'd *he* come from?"

"That's Sebus. Sebus is Fenrir."

Brandon nodded. "How lucky are we?" Before I could answer, he released a bolt, and a split second later, the giant bellowed and slapped at his neck as if stung by a hornet. Rolling out from under the wolf, he staggered to his feet, dropped his hammer, and clutched angrily at his new wound. Fenrir took the opportunity to swipe his paw across the giant's head. Bergelmir skidded backward, obviously dazed because he flung his one arm out in order to keep from toppling over. Fenrir rushed forward, grasped the hammer in his jaws, and flung the weapon as hard as he could. I shouted excitedly as the huge hammer flew end over end and disappeared into a dark cleft in the ground.

If Bergelmir wanted to make jelly out of us, he would have to use his fist. Or his feet. His feet would *definitely* do the job.

"Good shot," I said to Brandon. "Take cover and pepper him with darts to keep him off balance. We'll do the rest."

"Thought you'd never ask," said Brandon. He quickly positioned himself behind a large rock, and within seconds, Bergelmir was sporting three more darts in his elephant-like skin.

A flash of white against the black roof of the cavern caught my eye. It was the dove, circling close to Bergelmir's head, just out of reach. The giant, already furious over the loss of his hammer and the constant stinging of Brandon's crossbow, swiped his huge hand madly at the dove. The bird just narrowly escaped, which for some reason had me sighing with relief. *What was* with *this bird?* The stupid dove darted back in, striking the giant in the face with its beak. *Aren't doves supposed to be symbols of love?*

Bergelmir roared so loudly, small sections of the cavern roof rained down on us. Again, the dove darted back in, and before Fenrir could circle in for another attack, Tristan leaped from his perch atop the ridge and landed on the giant's back. Wrapping his legs around Bergelmir's thick neck, he raised his sword and brought it down hard. It might've been a killing blow if his blade hadn't struck the thick iron collar that Bergelmir was wearing as a necklace.

His sword made a really loud clanging sound and bounced harmlessly to the side. Tristan cursed. Before he could adjust his aim, the giant reached up, grasped Tristan, and threw him as hard as he could. Anyone else would've hit the ground and broken every bone in their body. Tristan simply twisted in the air so that he landed on his feet like a cat. He did cry out, though, grabbing at his ankle.

Tori streaked forward, waving her two swords in front of her so quickly they blurred together to form an arc of silver. She fell into a smooth roll, narrowly missing Bergelmir's first awkward attempt to squish her with his club-like fist. Once she was beneath the monster, she began to weave in and out of the giant's legs, slashing and cutting as she moved. Bergelmir stomped his huge feet. He even tried plopping his enormous backside down in an attempt to pin the Predator to the ground. But Tori was too fast. She swiped one last time at Bergelmir's calf, then slipped around to face him as he stumbled backwards.

"Do not ever touch—"

Tori never got to finish her threat. Bergelmir, whether by accident or design, kicked his grubby foot out as he toppled over, catching Tori under the chin. The Predator flew up into the air, but unlike Tristan, she was unable to twist into a position that would ease her landing.

It was hard to twist in the air after being knocked unconscious.

Tori hit the ground with a sickening *thud*. I winced and actually tasted anger like bile in my throat. I watched the giant climb unsteadily to his feet.

"Very uncalled for, Bergelmir!" shouted Mimir.

Brandon was about to make a pincushion out of the giant with his poisonous darts, but I held my hand out and shouted, "Hold your fire, Brandon!" I sprinted forward, bringing Talon back. With all my strength, I slashed at the giant's knee.

Hoping I wasn't already crushed and on my way to Valhalla, I raced to my left and gave Brandon the signal to continue firing his crossbow.

I looked back desperately to see what my blade had done to Bergelmir. There was no blood, but if my eyes weren't playing tricks on me, it looked like the giant's leg below his knee was . . . disappearing. Bergelmir staggered to his right, bellowing in frustration.

A moment later, his left leg was completely gone.

I stared at the blade of my sword in shock.

Bergelmir grunted something in a language that actually hurt my ears.

"He is calling for reinforcements!" growled Fenrir.

I searched the darkness behind the monster but could see nothing. I felt something tickle my ear. I looked up and saw the dove had returned. It fluttered away from me, but somehow I knew that it was trying to get my attention. The bird hovered in the air, flapping its wings so vigorously it lost more than a handful of feathers.

That's when I saw her. Or *him*. Or *it*. Whatever the creature was, it was flying near the roof of the cavern, flitting in and out of the dark stalactites. I pointed, and said, "Everyone, look! Something's up there!"

The wolf's voice was a deep rumble. "Shoot her down, boy! Now, before she can cast her magic!"

So it was a *she*. The creature flitted closer, even though Brandon was firing a constant stream of poisoned darts. She continued to descend, easily dodging each missile, then stopped and hovered like a giant wasp, teasing Brandon, who was quickly going red in the face with frustration. She had the body of a woman with skin so black it was nearly purple, but where her head should have been, there was only a skull with empty eye sockets and a gaping mouth. A pair of shiny black wings, beating as fast as a hummingbird, kept her aloft.

"*That* is the source of energy I sensed," snarled Fenrir. He leaped off the ground and tried to grab the ugly thing, but his jaws snapped on empty air. She was too fast and nimble. He landed with an earsplitting thud. "Bergelmir has himself a gulblix," he barked. "Very rare. They are the gate guardians to the realm of the dead."

"*I* could've told you that," said Mimir. "No one asks the head on the wall . . . "

Trying to keep one eye on the giant and the other on the gulblix, I said, "How do you know this, Fenrir?"

"The Queen of the Dead in Niflheim is my sister," growled Fenrir.

I shook my head. Talk about a dysfunctional family.

The wolf jumped again, this time swiping his massive paw through the air, but the gulblix tittered gleefully and darted away. When Fenrir landed, he said, "Her magic can transform a living creature from one form into another. It's almost impossible to revert the enchantment."

I wanted to go to Tori, but I knew that it would take only a moment for the fluttering creature to see that I had taken my eyes off of her, and my part in the quest would be over.

Brandon cursed beside me. "I'm out of bolts!"

Bergelmir grunted again in his horrible language. The gulblix fell into a steep dive, her black arms outstretched, and her wings folded flat against her back.

"Do not let her magic hit you!" Fenrir barked. "Quick, boy! Your crossbow is our only chance. Find more bolts and kill her!"

Brandon didn't have to be told twice. He scurried around, snatching up darts from the ground and stashing them away in his leather hip bag.

Of course the gulblix ignored everyone else and came for me. When she got to within twenty feet, she screamed and extended her fingers in my direction. Bolts of dark electricity left each of her fingertips. I barely rolled out of the way in time. The magic pounded the ground where I was standing and left the air smelling like rotten eggs. Before I had even jumped to my feet, she wheeled in the air and took a shot at me again. I leaped the other way, this time feeling the heat of her magic on my arm.

"That was close, love!" shouted Mimir. "*Too* close!"

Mimir was beginning to grate on my nerves, but he was right. I rolled to my feet and immediately began to panic. I couldn't see her. "Where'd she go!" I screamed, hoping someone had a visual on her. Tori was still out cold, and Tristan was hobbling over to where we were.

"She's up there somewhere!" yelled Tristan. "Find cover!"

The gulblix popped out from behind a stalactite, aimed, and released her magic. I had no time to roll away this time so I threw my arms up, hoping foolishly the sleeves of my hoodie would minimize the effect.

Just before the black tendrils hit, something gray and white swooped in front of me. It was the dove! Forget symbol of love, this bird was the symbol of insanity. It chirped once when the magic smashed into it, then fell to the ground. I looked back up, glad to see how angry it had made the gulblix, but sad that the dove had given its life.

The gulblix screamed in fury and brought her hand back to fling another dose of magic. As if in slow motion,

I watched as Brandon hurriedly loaded another bolt into his crossbow. He took aim, but it was too late. A stream of sizzling black tendrils hit Brandon square in the chest. I cried out as I watched him topple over backwards. The gulblix tossed her head back, cackling hysterically. For the first time ever, I didn't care what might happen to my sword. With all my strength I flung Talon at the laughing gulblix, still hovering above us. A moment later I heard a piercing shriek, then watched as the monster plummeted to the cavern floor, her dark, filmy wings folded around her body.

I scrambled over to Brandon, who was now lying on his back. Falling to my knees at his side, I gripped his shoulders. His *Yggdrasil or Bust* T-shirt had a hole the size of a tennis ball, the edges singed and smoking. There was a goofy smile pasted on his face as his eyes searched for mine.

"You got her," he croaked. "What a throw . . . "

"Don't talk, Brandon," I said, trying hard not to let him see me cry.

From somewhere behind me, Tristan shouted, "Don't watch, Cinder!"

I shook my head, but Tristan had grabbed me by my arm and was pulling me away. "Cinder," he urged, "there's nothing you can do for him now."

I jerked away from Tristan. I ran back to Brandon, but found only a large, red-coated dog. It was sniffing the crossbow, when it looked up at me with sad brown eyes.

"Brandon . . . ?" I said softly. "Is that you?" The dog whimpered and touched my leg with his nose. "What have I done?"

"One down, one to go," said Fenrir, coming up behind me and turning me around with his huge wet nose. Bergelmir released a roof-trembling roar. "Now is not the time to lose your focus, Cinder."

Tristan handed me my sword, though I was reluctant to touch it now. "Tristan," I said, my voice breaking. "Brandon . . ."

"You saved the rest of us, Cinder," said Tristan.

I nodded. The wolf was right. I had to forget about Brandon. At least for now. Gripping Talon, I moved forward. Bergelmir was still growling over the loss of his most lethal companion, as well as the loss of a second limb. I almost felt sorry for the giant, watching him hop around on one leg, his gray face now red with frustration.

"Bergelmir!" I shouted, not knowing or caring if he understood English. I held my sword up. "You know that I carry Talon, the blade of the Huntress of the Nine! You see what it can do, and you've lost your gulblix! Leave now and we will allow you to live!"

"Now *that's* a speech!" shouted Mimir.

The giant steadied himself. He glared at me, his piggish yellow eyes gleaming like two live coals. "I am going to send you back to Odin in two pieces," he panted in perfect English, though it came out sounding like an avalanche. "And then I will let the Queen of the Underworld know it was *you* who destroyed her gate guardian. She will trap your soul and torment you till the end of time."

"I've had detention that lasted longer than that!" I shot back.

Lowering his head like a charging bull, Bergelmir hobbled towards me.

Brandon tried to bark a warning, but I ignored him. Gritting my teeth, I waited for the giant. *So this is how it all ends, huh? Squished flat beneath a mall with Old Yeller.*

Fenrir seemed to have other ideas. He jumped in front of me and bared his huge fangs. But Bergelmir just swatted him away, then reached for me. I heard a sickening *thunk*, then watched in confusion as the giant bellowed in pain and fell to his one remaining knee. Lying on the ground was Bergelmir's huge hammer. Someone had thrown it and hit him squarely in the back.

Was there another giant in the house? Who was strong enough to even lift that thing off the ground?

Then I heard Tyr's wonderfully arrogant voice. "Right between the shoulder blades!" he gloated, trotting out of the darkness. "Of course only *I* could have pulled off such a feat."

Bergelmir grunted and reached out, intent on squeezing me into Cinder Moss jam. I leaned back and brought Talon around in a downward stroke, which connected solidly with his arm just above his wrist.

The giant bellowed again and reared back, a look of pure dismay spreading across his ugly features. He muttered a few ancient curses and staggered backwards like a pogo stick on his one remaining leg. I had to hand it to him—he was smart enough to know when it was time to cut his losses and run.

I held my breath as the giant shook his head in disbelief. He turned around and retreated into the darkness.

"In your face!" shouted Mimir.

I raced over to Tori and dropped to my knees. I knew enough not to try and move her, but luckily, I didn't have to. She suddenly coughed and rolled over.

"Tori!" I cried. "You're not dead!"

"Are you sure?" she muttered. I didn't have to be a doctor to see that her nose had been broken, as well as several teeth. "That bad, huh?"

"You look better than ever."

Amazingly, Tori climbed to her feet, shaking her limbs to check for serious injury.

Fenrir padded up to us and said, "It takes more than a wicked uppercut to put down one of the Valhuri." Tori nodded her thanks. The wolf stepped closer to me. "Cinder, just like your sword, Bergelmir was created from magic. When his flesh made contact with your weapon, Talon was able to neutralize the elements from which the giant was formed. I had heard rumors of the sword's power, but I had no idea . . ."

I let Talon droop. I suddenly had no strength left. Or maybe it was that I had no more heart left to raise it. I looked down and found Brandon's furry head pressed close against my leg. It felt very strange, but I reached down and rubbed his head between his floppy ears. "I'm so sorry, Brandon," I whispered. "I promise you I'll find a way to reverse this."

I yelped in surprise as a sleek brown rat skittered over my sneaker. Brandon barked and chased the rat around my legs a few times, then grew bored.

"That rat used to be the dove!" said Tori.

I nodded, realizing with even more guilt that the brave, stupid bird had taken the full impact of the gulblix's magic. For me.

Che Fenrir Express

Tyr walked over to us. He had somehow found the giant's hammer. It was still too big, even for the God of War, but he carried it in one hand as easily as I would carry a loaf of bread. He looked angry enough to use the weapon on all of us. He jabbed the hammer at Fenrir. "What is *he* doing here?" he said through gritted teeth.

"Sebus is Fenrir," I said, inching back a few feet.

"I am aware of that," said Tyr. "I am asking what the hand-eating devil spawn is doing *here*."

"This is a whole new level of awkward," said Mimir. "And *I* know awkward."

"I never ate your hand, Tyr," said Fenrir. "I bit it off and spit it out. I see your knack for drama has not changed at all."

"*My* knack for drama!" exclaimed Tyr. "Where did you get the name Sebus? Is that your *stage* name?"

"I am not ready to reveal my true identity yet," replied Fenrir. "Too many gods want me dead."

"And the drama continues," said Tyr.

"I think it is time we put this behind us," said Fenrir, his voice suddenly gruff.

"Talk to the back of my exquisite armor," Tyr called out as he spun around.

The wolf moved closer to Tyr. "We were friends once. We can be friends again."

Tyr took a deep, steadying breath. "It *has* been really difficult styling my hair with only one hand . . . "

"When I was just a pup, you helped me look presentable to the gods. The glittery ribbons were a bit much, but I turned heads because of you." Fenrir padded a few feet closer to Tyr. "I can help *you* now."

Tyr turned around. His chin quivered, then his eyes filled with tears. "Get over here, you oversized flea magnet."

Fenrir grunted happily and trotted over to the God of War. After lowering his massive head to the ground, Tyr buried his arms and face in the wolf's neck fur. When he finally backed away, Fenrir swiped at Tyr's long brown hair with a tongue the size of a beach towel.

"Not right now, Fenny," said Tyr under his breath. Patting down the huge cowlick in his hair, Tyr turned and smiled at me. "Who would have thought a mortal girl could lead such a charge, eh? Certainly not me."

I looked up at the giant root. Even with the enormous gash at its base, it seemed to me that it was standing a little taller, and the light that surrounded it seemed a little stronger. I should've felt happy, but terrible things had happened, and I just couldn't help but wonder why I had chosen to come. "Let's go," I said softly. "I want to leave this place."

As we trudged along the gem-encrusted wall that encircled the Well of Knowledge, Brandon trotted over to Mimir and began licking his face.

"Now stop that," said Mimir, then yelped as he tipped backwards into the well.

I raced over, nudged Brandon out of the way with my leg, and peered over the wall. There was Mimir's head, bobbing in the water, spluttering and cursing in ancient Nordic.

Without thinking, I reached in and scooped Mimir's head out and placed it on the wall. The glowing runes sparked and fizzled out, leaving a jumbled combination of Nordic runes and a few English letters.

"I do thank you, love," said Mimir, blinking the water from his eyes. He spat and out came a shiny gemstone.

"You're welcome," I said. I frowned at Brandon. "Sorry, Brandon's just really happy to finally meet you."

"Seven hundred years I sit on this wall, perfectly safe, and then an overeager fan knocks me into the well."

"So much for Odin's protection spell," said Tristan.

"Everything has an expiration date," Tyr said.

Mimir sniffed. "Hey, no harm done, really. Just water, right?"

"You have at least a thousand years to dry off," added Tyr.

Mimir frowned at the God of War, then turned and smiled at me. "Job well done, love, job well done indeed!"

"Thank you," I said. "We need to be going . . . is there anything we can do for you?"

"You could remove my headband . . . "

My heart sank. "You don't want it anymore?"

"Great Valhalla, love, I just want you to squeeze the water out of it and put it back on!"

Smiling, I pulled the sopping wet headband off Mimir's head, squished the water out, then replaced it. "It was so nice to meet you, Mimir," I said. "I hope someday—"

"Quiet," growled Fenrir, stooping to put his furry ear to the ground.

"Fenrir, what is it?" I asked.

"The floor of the cavern trembles."

"Please tell me the machine's not starting back up," I said, spinning around.

"Impossible," grunted Tristan.

Fenrir gazed back into the gloom. "No, it is not the machine. It is something else. Something moving this way."

I frowned. "Is Bergelmir that stupid?"

"We should get moving," growled Fenrir. "I fear the trembling is from many feet, not a single, hopping foot."

Before I could even question the wolf, I saw them. It had to be at least four hundred dark elves, flowing around the Well of Knowledge like spilled ink.

"Into the tunnel!" I shouted.

"Good counsel!" barked Fenrir. "I cannot keep a tide that size from harming you."

Tyr was shaking his head. "Perhaps good counsel for those who know fear, but not for one such as I!" And with that, the God of War sped towards the oncoming dark elves, Bergelmir's giant hammer raised above his head.

"At least we parted as friends," grunted Fenrir sadly. "To the entrance!"

"Goodbye, Mimir!" I called out, wondering suddenly if I should scoop him up and take him with us. Odin was already furious with me, right? But Tristan had grabbed my arm and was dragging me away.

"Farewell, love!" shouted Mimir. "If you return, bring back something to eat! Preferably something loaded with carbs!"

We turned and struggled up the incline, slipping on loose slabs of black rock. I looked back and saw Tristan wincing with every step he took but gritting his teeth against the pain.

"Tristan can't run!" I called out.

"Don't worry about me!" shouted Tristan. "Keep moving!"

I ran to Tristan and ducked under his arm. Tori must've been thinking the same thing because she threw his other arm around her neck and hoisted him up. Tristan started to object, but I said, "Don't even *think* about pushing us away."

"Please don't tell Odin about this," begged Tristan. "Or Tyr. Or Freya. Or—"

"Tristan, shut up!" we said together.

"They are gaining on us!" growled Fenrir. "They are too fast!"

I turned and saw that Tyr was cutting a good-sized path through the dark elves with Berglelmir's massive hammer, but hundreds were flowing around the God of War, totally ignoring him. They obviously had a single goal in mind, and it had nothing to do with Tyr. I pulled hard on Tristan's arm. "We have to hurry!" I yelled.

"I'm strong enough to carry him, Cinder," said Tori.

Tristan shook his head vigorously. "Do *not* pick me up."

"I wish we could use your pride as a weapon," the Predator shot back. "We could've ended this fight a long time ago."

"Just keep going!" I barked.

I risked another look over my shoulder. A group of about twenty dark elves was closing in fast. We weren't going to make it. If we stopped to fight, the other three hundred would eventually reach us and—

"Cinder!" barked Fenrir. "I have an idea, but it could prove more dangerous than facing our enemy."

"I'll try anything!" I shouted, panting under Tristan's weight. We had nearly made it to the huge wooden door that led to the tunnels. "What is it!"

Fenrir plunged forward, bursting through the door so hard he knocked it right off the hinges. Once through, he fell onto his belly. "Everyone climb onto my back!" he ordered, then waited while we clambered on, each of us using his spiky fur to pull ourselves up. "Everyone aboard?" he growled.

I made sure, then shouted, "Yes, go!"

"Hold on!" Fenrir shouted, exploding forward. All of us managed to hold on, except for Brandon, whose paws weren't made for gripping fur. He slid past me, howling the entire way, but Tristan grabbed him by the scruff of his furry neck. Brandon let out a series of barks. "That had better mean 'thank you,' half-elf!" Tristan shouted.

The dark elves screamed in fury as they flowed through the wide opening. Several iron bolts whizzed overhead, one of them embedding itself in the fur near my hand. Fenrir yelped, then yelped again as more darts pierced his shaggy coat. He roared and turned on the speed.

"Are you okay, Fenrir?" I yelled over the din.

"Nothing more painful than a bee sting to you, child," he growled, "but with enough hits, the poison will eventually bring me down."

I looked back at Brandon. He didn't look very pleased to have Tristan's arm wrapped around his furry midsection. Tristan wasn't any happier. "If I find a *single* flea on me," he shouted, but his threat was cut off by Brandon's angry barks.

The terrifying journey continued, each of us barely holding on as the wolf bounded over narrow rock spans, skidded around corners, and zigzagged through caverns filled with stalagmites.

The dark elves were always just a step behind, their poisonous darts and angry shouts filling the air. Fenrir's backside was beginning to look like a furry pincushion. His huge pink tongue was dangling out of the side of his mouth, and his breathtaking speed was starting to falter.

"I am sorry, Cinder," Fenrir said over his shoulder. "The poison from the darts . . . "

"Then we'll turn and make our final stand," I said. I couldn't help wondering what it would feel like to actually die.

"A little farther," Fenrir mumbled, panting heavily.

I was about to insist the wolf stop when his front legs suddenly collapsed. All of us flew forward, tumbling over

Fenrir's head as he slid across the ground. Tristan's training had never covered how to scramble clear of a giant wolf collapsing from too many poisonous darts, but I managed to hit the ground in a roll, then kept on rolling till I was sure I was out of the way. I came to my feet, and immediately started searching for the others. Had they been crushed by Fenrir? The wolf, lying on his side, his eyes closed, wasn't moving at all.

No, I thought. *No no no no!*

I heard Brandon barking and Tristan and Tori yelling my name, but I barely registered it because I was frantically calling out their names at the same time. Something red and furry suddenly slammed into me, nearly knocking me down. "Brandon!" I cried, staggering backwards beneath his weight. I gave the half-elf a quick hug, then pushed him away before he could lick my face. Then I saw Tori round the fallen wolf, propping up a limping Tristan. Both had their weapons out, but what could they do against the approaching dark elves? There were too many of them and Fenrir was—

"Run, Cinder!"

The order had come from Fenrir. My heart flipped over, then shot up into my throat. His eyes had opened, but just barely. "Run . . . " he panted. "All of you . . . get out . . . "

"I'm not leaving you!" I cried.

"Do not make my last effort be for nothing."

"The wolf's right," said Tristan. "All of us will die if we don't leave."

"Then go!" I snapped, rounding on Tristan. I looked at the Predator. "Tori, get Tristan and Brandon out of here." I moved close to Fenrir and reached out to lay my hand on his muzzle.

"Little Mouse," said the wolf.

"Just rest," I said, pulling Talon out.

"Your quest is over, but there will be more."

More? I didn't want more. Not if it meant that my best friends were injured and cursed by dark magic and poisoned by dark elves.

I flinched as several bolts struck the rock beside me.

"Stubborn till the end," murmured Fenrir, then his eyes closed.

I felt someone grab my arm and yank me backwards. "We're leaving now, Cinder," said Tori. "Brandon, bite her if she refuses."

Brandon bit me anyway—or at least I thought he did. It actually felt like someone had jabbed my hip with a sharp pencil. Then I felt it again, on my leg just above my knee. I tried to remain standing, but it was no use. I fell over, realizing I had been hit with dark-elf bolts. *Wow,* I thought. *That's fast-acting poison.*

The last thing I saw before I died was Tori's face, hovering over mine. She was speaking rapidly, her words ancient and filled with light.

CHAPTER 37

ALLFATHER'S MAIN SQUEEZE

O kay, so I didn't die. Instead of waking up in Valhalla (or wherever they send wannabe heroes), I woke up in a bedroom whose walls were covered with pictures of grunge bands and NBA players. There seemed to be a good-sized storm going on right outside my window. Through the curtains, I could see wind and rain lashing against the windowpane.

I had had the worst nightmare of my life. There were huge spiders and dark elves with gleaming red eyes and a giant with one arm and a hummingbird lady that could shoot dark magic from her fingertips. Worst of all, Fenrir had died, and Brandon had been turned into a dog.

It had to be a dream, because a severed head with a British accent had tried to tell me his life story.

I attempted to sit up, but there was a pain in my hip and leg that had me thinking twice about moving. The pain caused me to realize it *hadn't* been a nightmare. This was real.

"Welcome to Pismo."

I turned and found Tristan sitting in an old chair by a dusty bookshelf. Several impressive cuts on his face tried to make him ugly, but it was no use. He was wearing a pair of flowered yellow and blue board shorts, probably because his left leg was now encased in a neon-green cast. A pair of crutches leaned against the wall beside him.

"Hey," I said. I felt really groggy, like I'd been drugged. "Did you say Pismo?"

"We're at Brandon's house."

I nodded, taking in the room's décor.

"If this is how Midgardian boys decorate," said Tristan, frowning, "I'm glad I'm not mortal."

I grinned, and it hurt a little. "Don't like music or sports, huh?"

"Neither offers a challenge."

"Still humble, I see," I said.

Tristan hesitated. Something passed over his face. He was about to say something, when the door opened and in padded an Irish setter, followed by a black-bearded man in a khaki vest and badly scuffed hiking boots.

It took me a moment, but then I realized who it was.

"Brandon! Fenrir!" I said. At first, I felt totally happy, but then a wave of guilt washed over me. Fenrir had apparently recovered from the dark elf poison, but Brandon was a dog now. *Why had I allowed him to go on the quest?*

Brandon barked happily, though, as if he'd do it again without question. His tail swished back and forth, and he put his paws up on the bed. I patted him between the ears.

"Little Mouse," said Fenrir. "It is good to see you awake and well."

I tried to sit up again, but when the room suddenly began to spin, I flopped back down. "I'm awake at least," I said. "Where's Tori?"

"The Valhuri is currently . . . indisposed," said Fenrir carefully.

"Indisposed?"

"She's talking to Brunhild," said Tristan.

This time I sat up, ignoring the intense pain in my leg and hip. "What!"

"Everything is fine," said Fenrir, patting the air.

Tristan looked away. "Everything's *not* fine."

"Tristan," said Fenrir, "it is sometimes difficult for the young to understand the ways of the old."

I held my hands up in the shape of a T. "Time out. Can someone please tell me what's going on? Why is Tori talking to the Valkyrie? How did she find us?"

Tristan opened his mouth to speak, but Fenrir cut him off. "You may not remember your last moments in the caverns beneath the mall, Cinder, but you were struck with several poisonous darts, and you would have died in seconds if Tori had not gotten to you in time."

My head still felt fuzzy. "What . . . what did she do?"

"She used her life gift," said Fenrir solemnly.

I was stunned into silence. I had totally forgotten about the Predators' ability to use their life gift to keep someone alive. And now that she had used it, it was gone forever . . .

I could only shake my head.

"Let me guess," said Tristan, "you want to say something like, 'Why didn't she use it on someone who matters?'"

"Well, yeah," I said lamely.

"You're so predictable," said Tristan.

Brandon growled and Tristan said, "Easy, mutt."

Brandon exposed his sharp teeth, his ears laid back.

"I don't care if this is your house," said Tristan easily, wagging his finger at the Irish setter. "I'll put you out in the backyard if you don't behave."

I didn't like when Tristan and Brandon bickered, especially when Tristan was making dog jokes, but I had to admit, hearing them fight meant that we were all alive and back to normal. If you could call any of us normal. "So what happened after Tori . . . ?" I couldn't finish my sentence.

"You blacked out," explained Fenrir. "We thought the Valhuri's gift had failed somehow, but of course we carried you out anyway."

"But the dark elves . . . " I said.

Fenrir smiled through his scruffy black beard. "I wish you could have seen it, Cinder. The moment Tori ignited her life gift, a brilliant halo of white light erupted from where she knelt. It was like a silent explosion, but it only harmed our enemies. The dark elves who were not caught up in the light fled in terror."

For a long while, I was speechless. Finally, I said, "Did Tori know this would happen?"

Fenrir shook his head. "It was her first and only time. She did not know."

I wished Fenrir didn't have to remind me that she would never be able to use her gift again.

"There is something else regarding the gift's magic that we did not foresee," said Fenrir.

"You think now is the best time to tell her?" Tristan said. He sounded nervous, and a nervous Tristan is reason to freak out.

"What's wrong?" I said, throwing back the covers. "Did I grow a third leg?"

"Relax, Mouse," said Fenrir, patting my arm. "Nothing so drastic as that. Tristan, hand her the mirror."

Reluctantly, Tristan passed me a small mirror from Brandon's dresser. I stared at my reflection. "I don't see anything different . . . wait . . . my eyes . . . " I said, suddenly breathless. "They're kind of . . . *gold* . . . "

"I like it," said Tristan, smiling. I started to blush, then he said, "Reminds me of Asgardian money."

Fenrir frowned at Tristan.

"What . . . happened?" I said, unable to take my eyes off my eyes.

"A side effect of the magic, it would seem," said Fenrir. "As far as I know, very few life gifts have been used on mortals from Midgard . . . "

"Is it temporary?"

"I cannot say," said Fenrir. "A small price to pay for your life, though, wouldn't you agree?"

I nodded. He was right, of course. I would take gold-tinted eyes before death-by-dark-elf-poison any day.

"I wouldn't worry too much," said Tristan. "Anyone who hasn't been taught to see will see your old boring eyes."

"Ouch," I said, tossing him the mirror.

"You know what I mean," said Tristan.

"I guess it's better than sprouting a third leg," I said.

Before Tristan could dig a deeper hole, Fenrir cleared his throat and said, "I think the look suits you, Mouse. We are just pleased to see you safe and sound."

"And what about you, Fenrir? I thought you had died."

"No, just needed a nap," replied Fenrir. "I was out for several hours but when I awoke, we were free to continue to the surface. We met up with Tyr, who was still searching for stray elves to smash or throw, and we left the caverns. All of us made it out in one piece—even the rat that once was a dove survived."

"Really? How do you know?"

"Apparently the thing jumped on the Wolfie Express when we did," said Tristan. He made a face. "Between the wolf, the dog, and the rat, I'd be really surprised if I didn't pick up at least a tick or two."

Brandon tried to nip Tristan's leg, but Tristan danced out of reach. Fenrir didn't seem to mind the accusation. "That *thing* saved me from the gulblix," I said, eyeing Tristan dangerously.

"Which is why we haven't called pest control," said Tristan.

"The rat's . . . here?"

Tristan nodded. "Let's just say Tyr has a new best friend."

This time Fenrir growled. "Sorry," said Tristan, "I meant besides ol' Wolfie."

I breathed a sigh of relief. I had grown to like the God of War. And he *had* helped us. "Where is he?"

Fenrir looked unsure of himself. "He is in another room, watching a game of . . . football . . . with the rat."

"I gotta see *that*," I said, grinning.

"Oh, yes," said Fenrir, "that reminds me. Before we left the caverns, we came across a group of dwarves who were very sorry to see Tyr."

I gasped. "Was it the dwarves who betrayed him?"

Fenrir nodded. "We convinced him not to kill them, so he took their treasure, their weapons and their food, and threw them into the spiders' webs."

I winced. "That's the same as killing them."

"Tyr gave them a fighting chance," countered Fenrir.

"Even though they didn't deserve it," grumbled Tristan.

I didn't know if I liked that Tristan wished Tyr had smashed the dwarves with his giant hammer, but then again, when it came to the God of War, Tristan was totally biased.

Tristan seemed to be reading my mind. "Hey, those traitorous long beards threw his sword down into the deepest, darkest hole they could find." Tristan patted his own sword that was lying across his lap. "I don't know if I would've been so merciful if I had lost *my* weapon."

Fenrir looked at me intently. "Tyr pressed the dwarves for a name. They couldn't be convinced to confess."

My shoulders slumped. *Who was against us?* "There's nothing we can do about that right now. What about Brunhild?"

Fenrir seemed eager to leave our suspicions behind. "We entered the mall and found Skuld the norn and Brunhild waiting for us."

"But how?" I said. I suddenly frowned. "Did Skuld rat us out? That's *exactly* the kind of thing he would do, just for kicks. Maybe *he's* the one that betrayed Tyr to the dwarves!"

"No on both accounts," said Fenrir. "Norns are mischievous, but they would not interfere with one of the Twelve. And secondly, the gods were alerted to your location the moment Tori expended her life gift." Fenrir sighed. "Another side effect none of us saw coming."

"So was she angry?"

"The Valkyrie did not look amused," admitted Fenrir, "but she did not try and kill any of us, as Tristan feared she would. In my weakened state, I could not have stopped her."

"I didn't *fear* she would kill us," muttered Tristan, shooting Fenrir a dark look. "I *thought* she would kill us. Big difference."

Brandon's bark sounded amazingly like laughter.

"Okay," I said, "so Tori's outside talking to her. About what?"

"I think we will allow the Valhuri to fill you in on her conversation with the Valkyrie," said Fenrir.

As if on cue, Tori burst into the room. "Cinder! You're awake!" I fell back as she leaped onto the bed, tackling me like a free safety would hit a running back. She pulled away and I saw that her face was covered with cuts and scrapes and bruises and tears. "You rock, Cinder!" she exclaimed.

I untangled a lock of my hair from the cord on her earbuds and said, "I don't know how to thank you for what you did."

"I would do it again in a heartbeat, Cinder," she said.

My face fell. "If you could."

Tori reached out and gripped my upper arm. "You better not beat yourself up over this. Every Predator dreams of the day they can use their life gift, and I wouldn't want to give it to anyone more than you."

I was going to start crying, but then I looked at Tristan and Fenrir. Both of them looked very uncomfortable. Even Brandon was trying to cover his ears with his paws.

"Alright," I said, brushing at my eyes. "Tori and I will just high five each other next time she saves my life. Geez."

Everyone left and I was able to talk to Tori alone. I asked her about Brandon's chances of living a life without a shaggy fur coat. I could tell by her expression that his chances weren't good.

"But that doesn't mean that either of us stops looking for a cure, Cinder," she said, hopefully. We talked about our time at the Proving Grounds, though it wasn't long before I felt a heavy wave of exhaustion wash over me. The last thing I remembered was the Predator tucking my blanket up under my chin and dimming the lights before she left.

⚮

When I stumbled out of Brandon's room, the storm had lost most of its fury and night had fallen. From the noise I could hear coming from the kitchen, it sounded like everyone from the Proving Grounds had come for dinner.

Except for Tyr.

The God of War was reclining in a large leather lounger with a bag of barbecue chips perched on his massive chest.

He was way too big for the poor chair. His arms and legs were hanging over the edge, but he didn't seem to care. I tried really hard not to laugh. He was dressed like a gangster out of a rap video. Apparently he hadn't escaped the mall unscathed. He actually looked pretty menacing, though the potato chip crumbs in his perfectly combed beard and the big foam finger he had fitted over his arm stump, took some of the edge off. Los Angeles was battling Oakland on a small television set in the corner of the room. Seeing the Chargers reminded me of Odin and his football jersey. I cringed. What did Allfather have to say about the quest? My thoughts were interrupted when the rat crawled out from beneath his beard. It was nibbling on a potato chip. It watched me while it ate, its black eyes glittering. All I could do was shake my head.

Tyr pumped his fist and looked away from the TV. "Our mortal hero wakes from the dead!"

"Hi, Tyr," I replied. "I see you like football."

"I do, but I find the commercials even *more* enjoyable. Who knew skin cream could bring a family together?"

I laughed, even though it hurt my hip and leg. "Who's winning?"

"I have no idea," said the God of War, "though you can imagine how the tide would turn if *I* were on the court."

"The field," I said, grinning.

"Field, court, corpse-littered mountaintop," said Tyr with a flourish. "Who cares! I would reign supreme."

"I have no doubt you would," I said, eyeing the massive war hammer he had taken from Bergelmir the Cruel, lying on the grass outside the window. I shuddered just thinking about how narrowly we had escaped being made into jelly. "So everyone else is in the kitchen?"

Tyr turned his attention back to the game, groaning as someone from the Raiders fumbled the ball. "Yes, they're halfway through their evening meal."

"No dinner for you?"

Tyr held up the bag of chips. "This will do. I found that once I started, I could not stop."

CHAPTER 38

DADDY ISSUES

Brandon's dad, Mr. Turnbull, was a normal-looking man in his early forties, with neatly combed red hair that was graying at the temples and a potbelly that hung over his belt. His mom, though, was stunning. She whisked into the kitchen carrying a glass pan loaded with a roast the size of a holiday turkey. She was so light on her tiny feet it was almost like she was floating rather than walking. Her hair was long and full, which I expected, but it was sable black—something I didn't see coming. Her flawless porcelain skin, her narrow pixie-like features and almond-shaped eyes, however, left no doubt in my mind.

Brandon's mom was an elf.

The pointed ears poking from her hair made it pretty obvious as well.

Seeing her and Mr. Turnbull together was proof that love is blind. Maybe I had hope.

Mrs. Turnbull smiled at me and said, "You must be Cinder."

"Hi," I replied. "And you must be Brandon's mom. I'm sorry we have to meet under these . . . circumstances."

At the mention of her son, her smile faded. She glanced down at the dog that was curled up on the tile floor near the table. She looked back at me. "We'll get through this. Welcome to Pismo."

"Thank you," I said, silently berating myself for being so stupid. I smiled at Mr. Turnbull. "And thank you for letting me stay in your home."

"No problem," said Brandon's dad, dipping his reading glasses. "It's not every day we get a real live hero over for dinner."

Tristan, who was sitting at the table, stopped eating his green salad for a moment and said, "Wait, allow me." He put on a high, annoying voice. "I'm no hero. Everyone around me is a hero. I just happened to be in the right place at the right time."

I punched him. "Good to have you back, Tristan. Back there in the caverns, I was beginning to think you'd gone all soft on us."

Tristan pointed his fork at me. "Never." He looked deadly serious, as only Tristan can look, but there was the hint of a smile.

"Pull up a chair," said Mr. Turnbull. "We're having Eberline's pot roast. It's truly magical."

"Thank you," I said, wondering if Mr. Turnbull's description was literal. I took a seat between Tori and Fenrir.

Whether or not the pot roast had been prepared with magic, it was delicious, and the conversation was even better. No one said a word about the quest, which I appreciated. Even Tristan left me alone. After dinner we had German chocolate cake that *had* to be enchanted, because I felt a warmth flood my body and I couldn't stop grinning.

Mrs. Turnbull wouldn't allow me to get up from the table until I'd finished off two helpings.

We all helped with the dishes, except for Brandon. He was too busy chasing Tyr's rat.

The God of War tried to help, but his hands were so large he kept dropping the dishes. "Is nothing in Midgard built to withstand my phenomenal strength?"

Everyone regrouped in the living room. Mr. Turnbull launched a game of charades with highlights of Tyr as a professional bowler. When the game was over, Tori and I slipped out the back door and took a seat in the rusty porch swing. There was still a misty drizzle falling from the dark clouds, but the moon was glowing silver and bright.

"Loving the new shade of eye color," Tori said, smiling. Then her smile faded. "And I hope you like it, too, because it kind of happened because of me . . . "

And just like that, my feelings about my golden eyes changed. "Pretty cool, right?"

"Super jealous," said Tori. After a few moments of silence, she said, "Are you ready to talk about the quest?" said Tori, turning down the volume on her earbuds.

I nodded. "I can't avoid it forever, right?"

She shook her head.

"So what's Brunhild's story?"

"Fenrir told you about the gods knowing of our location the moment I transferred my gift, right?"

"Yes," I said.

"Well, the Valkyrie was waiting for us as soon as we emerged into the mall," replied Tori. "There was no escaping her. Or Borghild."

"Borghild?"

"Odin's grandson, president of your fan club . . . "

I buried my face in my hands. "Please tell me he wasn't there."

"He was. With a dozen CVM members. They had a banner and everything, congratulating you on your victory."

"Why would Brunhild let him come?"

"Well, he *is* the God of Obstinance. Sort of hard to tell him no."

"If you bought one of his Cinder merch shirts, I will never speak to you again."

Tori pulled her jacket closed and quickly changed the subject. "You were out cold, though I thought you were dead at the time. I had no more will to run. Tristan was badly injured and Fenrir was so drugged with that dark elf poison, he could barely climb the steps."

"I still can't believe he recovered from that. So what did Brunhild say?"

"Not a whole lot," said the Predator. "She was angry, but there was something else behind her words . . . some-thing that I'm just now understanding."

"What?"

"She was pleased, Cinder. Pleased about the outcome of the quest. I don't know how, but she knew what had happened. But at the same time, it was obvious she had been sent by her father, who wished his anger to be conveyed in her message."

I sighed. "So Odin's ticked off, huh? There's no pleasing that guy."

"Who knows what the Allfather's really feeling right now," said Tori. She stared up at the moon. "He lost face with some of the gods because you completed your quest successfully after he tried to send you home. He must be afraid that anyone who knows about this truly believes that he made the wrong decision. That's not easy for any leader to stomach, especially a god."

"Wow," I murmured.

Tori turned to look at me. Her grin was contagious. "I can just imagine the uproar in Asgard right now. A mortal twelve-year-old girl putting the brakes on Loki's plans." Tori clapped. "I love it!"

I laughed with her, then stopped abruptly. "Wait. What did you say?"

"A mortal twelve-year-old—"

"No, about Loki," I said, eyeing the Predator closely.

"Oh. Well, if you haven't guessed by now, Bergelmir the Cruel was never really the brains behind the whole cutting-down-the-World-Tree thing. Loki is the true mastermind."

"Loki, as in Fenrir's father?"

"That's right," said Tori. "That's probably how the giant was able to get one of the gulblixes to help him. And we're thinking his influence reaches into Asgard more than we realized—how else would he have gotten enough Asgardian silver to make that machine?"

"How do you know this?"

"My thoughts on the gulblix are just theories, but Brunhild said Odin is fairly certain Loki is behind this. Fenrir said he's known this for about three hundred years, but up until now, he never cared. Now it's killing him."

"What does Loki want?"

"He wants to see the gods of light and everything good in the Nine Realms destroyed, of course. What else is there for an evil god to aspire to?"

I frowned. "I don't understand. If Loki wants this, why doesn't he do it himself?"

"Surely by now you know how the Norse gods work. They have others do the work for them."

I nodded. "Bergelmir was just a puppet, then."

"Aren't we all?"

I sighed. "Freya said she wasn't sure which god sent the norn to pledge me. Do we know now?"

"We do," replied Tori, "but it was actually a goddess—not a god."

"Really?" I said, my curiosity fully piqued. "Which one?"

"Strangely enough, it was Fjorgyn."

I stared at the Predator for several seconds. "I'm sorry. I got nothin'."

Tori shook her head. "Fjorgyn is Odin's wife. Also Thor's mother. Brunhild said that she probably fears the Allfather's fate more than anyone—possibly even more than Odin himself. She sent Skuld out from Asgard, knowing he would find and persuade you better than any norn alive."

"So I guess all of this is not over," I said heavily. "Just like Fenrir said."

"Not as long as Loki is alive."

"So what do we do now?"

"Well, Loki's plans are halted for the time being. He will have to find another way to cause mischief and mayhem. Until then, we lay low and hope you don't get called on to conquer anymore giants."

I couldn't help but smile. Two months ago, my biggest challenge had been making it through the lunch line at school without getting in a fight. Part of me wanted to go back to Copperpenny just to see if anyone wanted to start something. They would get a big surprise.

I looked over at the Predator. "Did you know Tristan's dad was the God of Inspiration?"

"Yes," replied Tori, looking away again. "But Freya didn't like to talk about it."

"Speaking of Freya, how's she doing?"

"Not good. Brunhild said Odin's furious with Tristan's and Freya's father for agreeing to build that machine for Loki. He told Freya her success with you will determine Kvasir's fate, once they find him."

I struck my palm with my fist. "*That's* why she was so nervous around Odin! I *knew* something was up." I suddenly felt angry enough to storm Odin's Long Hall. "That guy's a piece of work, you know? Give me a break! Kvasir probably has a very good reason for helping Loki."

"We may never know," said Tori sadly. "And mercy has never been one of Odin's strongest qualities."

"Does Tristan know about this?" I demanded.

"No, Odin purposely kept it from him because he feared

Tristan wouldn't help him shut down the machine."

"Well, the machine's been shut down. Tristan should be filled in."

The Predator vigorously shook her head. "No, Cinder. We cannot be the ones to tell him."

I looked away, scowling. "I can't believe Freya kept this from him."

"She was afraid of what her brother would do. Tristan's temper is legendary."

I fumed in silence.

"On the bright side," said Tori, beaming, "Brunhild no longer wants your head on a pole."

I sighed. "And she doesn't want to take me back to her father for a court hearing with twelve angry gods as my jury?"

"That's just the thing," said Tori. "Half of the Twelve are thrilled with you, so Odin cannot punish you just yet. Brunhild came to get the details of our time in the caverns. An official statement of the World Tree's condition, if you will. She wanted me to tell you your fate will be determined at a later date."

"Oh great," I said. "Nothing like having something to look forward to." I turned to look at Tori. "That was sarcasm, by the way. I'm really not looking forward to that day."

"And neither would I. But I'll be with you."

We sat shoulder to shoulder watching the moon till it disappeared behind a bank of tattered clouds.

CHAPTER 39

GRANDPARENT FIRST, PREDATOR SECOND

We all stayed at Brandon's house for three more days. The majority of our time was spent down at the beach, skipping rocks into the waves and buying enough hot dogs and ice cream to feed a stadium full of people.

We never talked about the quest, or any quests that might be coming in the near future. For the time being, everything was how it should be, if you were on vacation with a good friend who was now a dog, a god who could transform into a giant wolf, and two immortal teenagers who could take down a SWAT team with their bare hands.

On the afternoon of the third day, I took a long walk by myself along the beach. The sun was out, so I rolled my pant legs up, took off my sneakers, and carried them as I strolled. When I had walked nearly a mile down shore, I rounded a spur of jagged lava rock and found myself in a little sandy bay. Perfect for thinking things through. Before I could sink down into the soft sand, I heard a sound behind me that had my heart seizing up in my chest.

Feathers. Lots of them.

Brunhild had returned to skewer me with her glowing spear for embarrassing her father.

I turned and found that it wasn't the Valkyrie. It was my grandma, sitting on top of a huge reddish-gold falcon. I went from totally freaked out to totally stoked. "Grandma!" I shouted, running towards the bird.

The falcon jumped back and screeched a warning that had me clapping my hands over my ears.

"Stay back, Cinder," my grandma warned. "She does not know you yet." I quickly did as she asked, subconsciously patting my hip for Talon. But of course, it wasn't there. I had hid it in Brandon's messy closet, knowing it wouldn't be found for at least a thousand years.

My grandma slid off the falcon's back, fed the bird something out of her cupped hand, then turned to me. "Cinder, it is so good to see you!" She gave me a crushing hug, then held me at arm's length to look at me. "You look the same . . . and different, all at once."

"Is it the gold tint in my eyes?" I asked.

"Well, yes, there is that."

"Fenrir said it's a result of Tori's life gift magic."

"Perhaps it was written in the stars," she said, smiling.

"You sound like a dwarf I know." And then I paused.

Windows of gold.

The words from the prophecy flitted through my mind. Was it a reference to my post-death eye upgrade? I was about to ask, then hesitated. Saemund had told me to keep the words of the prophecy to myself. Stupid end-of-the-universe-rules.

"You are the same height," she continued, "roughly the same weight, give or take a few pounds of new muscle. Aside from your eyes, your beautiful features are still the same."

I blushed. No one had ever called me beautiful. "So what's different?"

"The quest has aged you in ways most people would never notice." She shook her head. Was she sad or pleased?

"Is that a good thing?" I pressed.

"In a way. You seem wiser, more mature, but it also wears on you like a heavy burden."

I nodded. "I feel it, Grandma. The heaviness, I mean. Will it ever go away?"

"Some of it will. Part of it will not. That is part of life, Cinder. Keeping some of that burden, some of the regrets and worries and fears. These things will help you survive future trials."

My heart fell. "So there will be more trials?"

My grandma smiled warmly. "Trials could mean anything. It could be a sick son or daughter, an unem-ployed spouse, or heartbreak. Or it could mean a future quest."

I knew it. There would always be more quests.

"Grandma," I said, "can you tell me anything about Mom?"

She pursed her lips, then sighed. It looked like she was going to cry. "Cinder, there are some things you should know. Things I would not have told you when first we met. After all that you have seen, all that you have been through in the last two months, I think you are better able to understand . . . and handle the reality of your life. I know you may feel bitter towards your parents, especially your mother. You were left at such a young age."

"I never really felt bitter towards my dad," I said. "He left before I was born. He never saw me—never held me. Mom, though . . . she was with me for a few days."

My grandma's expression tightened. "Cinder, your father didn't actually leave. He was killed."

I sort of saw this coming. Like she said, two months ago, this news would've floored me. But now, knowing my father had been killed didn't exactly shock me. I had never known him, so it wasn't very painful, but it still hurt. I felt sorry for him mostly. Sorry that his life had to end so early and so violently. "How'd it happen?" I asked.

"First I should explain why your mother left you at the hospital. Her sudden departure will better explain your father's death. You see, your mother knew of the prophecies."

"But I thought only I could read them?"

"Well, she didn't read the words, but she knew that you were the one mentioned in the ancient text even before you were born. She dreaded the danger that awaited you, and while you were in the womb, she grew so attached to you that she couldn't bear the thought of losing you some day. So she petitioned the gods and applied as an alternate hero." When I frowned in confusion, she said, "She tried to go in your place, Cinder."

"She . . . offered to go for me?"

My grandma wiped at a tear that was leaking from the corner of her eye. "Yes."

"Can she do that?"

"Quest code states that only a parent may voluntarily take the place of their child. She made the request nearly a month before you were born. Skuld carried the message to the Twelve in Asgard. Her request was accepted. The moment she was accepted, our enemies were alerted. Emissaries were sent to your home. They found your parents. Your father . . . he kept the creatures at bay while your mother escaped."

Now I was floored. "Were they grints?" I asked.

She nodded. "Your mother stayed with a friend after your father was killed. That friend took her to the hospital when it was time for you to be delivered. There were complications . . . "

This, too, was news to me. "Complications?"

"Immediately after you were born, your mother started hurting herself so that she could stay in the hospital."

I gaped. "But why?"

"The hospital was the safest place for the two of you. She could not go to the police—they would never believe that creatures such as grints were after her. They would have thought she was insane. The hospital did not require her to tell the unbelievable truth."

"The truth *is* unbelievable," I whispered. Then I remembered something that had been bothering me. "Is my mother immortal?"

"No."

"But Saemund said *you* are immortal—so wouldn't that

make Mom . . . ?"

"I did not start out immortal. I was born perfectly mortal—just like you. The day I became a full-fledged Valhuri, I was blessed—or cursed, as some would say— with everlasting life."

"So why'd my mother leave?"

"The hospital was not as safe as she had hoped. A grint nearly got to her. She decided that to keep you safe, she would have to leave you in Husavik."

"Husa-what now?"

My grandma seemed to brace herself. She gently touched my arm. "It is time you hear the truth, Cinder. You were raised in Richmond, Virginia, but you were not born there."

"What . . . ?"

"You were born in Husavik, a small fishing town in Iceland."

"But . . . " It felt like the wind had been knocked out of me. Several seconds passed before I could speak. "Are you sure . . . ?"

"I was there," she said, smiling.

"Then how . . . how did I . . . ?"

"I was instructed to take you to America, where Carl and Nancy took you in as a foster child. Odin thought it would be safer. And it *was* safe until the grint found you."

I barely heard my grandma. What little room I had left in my brain was suddenly filled with more words from the prophecy.

Born at the crux of the world's spine . . .

"Is Iceland important to Norse history?" I asked.

"Iceland is the heart of Midgard," replied my grandma. "All of your world's magic stems from there. Why do you ask?"

"No reason," I said, my mind spinning. Saemund had said I would find clarity at unexpected times and in unexpected places . . .

"This must be hard for you, Cinder," said my grandma. "But I wanted to be the one to tell you."

Despite the bombshell she had just dropped, I could feel the bitterness seeping away. A moment later, I felt nothing but love and a deep respect for my mom. "After I was taken to America, did Mom go to the Proving Grounds?"

"Yes," replied my grandma. "She began her training, as your replacement. Things were going well. I was there to oversee her, which made things much easier for her. Though I was terrified of her future, I was very proud of her progress. But then she began to change. Her progress slowed, then came to a halt. She began to get sick often, she never smiled or hardly talked."

"What happened?"

"She was heartbroken, Cinder. She missed you so much, it broke her heart to be away from you." I felt my own eyes welling up. My grandma said, "I tried to talk to her, but it was no use. She requested a meeting with Odin, which he was all too eager to provide, since she was the one who would determine his fate, and she told him she was finished. That she wanted to go back to Richmond. To be with you."

So this was why Freya had told me that only one person had turned down a request to be a hero. It was my mother she was talking about. I was afraid of the answer, but I said, "So what did Odin say?"

"He was furious. You know how he is. In his anger, he turned her into a dove."

I stared at my grandma, then I felt a gut-punch as the pieces of the puzzle fell into place. "It was her all along," I mumbled softly.

My grandmother suddenly reached out and gripped my arms, her expression startling me. "What did you say?"

"There was a dove . . . it traveled across the ocean on Captain Sturlson's ship . . . it followed us down into the caverns . . ."

Her fingers bit into my shoulders. "Are you sure about this?"

I nodded, still too stunned to really form any coherent thoughts. My mom had been turned into a dove and now a rat? Poor lady couldn't catch a break.

My grandma's eyes welled with tears, but she looked happy. "Cinder, I have been taking care of your mother in Asgard ever since she was transformed. You remember when we met in the seer's cottage and I told you I could not come with you on your journey?" I nodded. "It was your mother that I had to get back to. But when I arrived, she was gone. None of the Twelve or the wandering spirits knew of her whereabouts. Now I know. She left to find you!"

I smiled. "And she found me."

She grabbed my shoulders again, this time careful not to hurt me. "Where is she?"

My smile faded. "There was a gulblix in the caverns, Grandma. She flew in between me and the monster's magic and . . . she was transformed into a rat."

My grandma stared at me. After a while, she nodded, wiped her face, and said, "Sounds just like her. Putting her life in danger to protect you."

I sighed. "I'm just glad she's with me."

"So where is she now?"

"She's back at the house," I said. "Tyr has adopted her."

"Well, good. Nothing like the God of War as your bodyguard. Now we just have to find a way to reverse the magic."

My heart leaped. "Is there a way?"

"There is always a way. We just need to find it."

"Do you want to see her?"

She thought for a moment and then said, "I have spent over thirty years with her. I think it is your turn. Someone will be coming soon to take you back to Richmond. After you leave, I will have her brought back to Asgard with me—where she will be safe."

"Okay," I said, unsure if I liked the idea of my grandma and mom leaving again. "I'll tell her you said hello."

"And tell her how proud of her I am, as well as angry that she did not have the common sense to leave me a note."

We both laughed, and her falcon looked over at us, curiosity gleaming in its golden eyes. "Your mother must be so proud of her little Stormbringer," she said, grinning.

We laughed again, then I said, "Speaking of titles, why do they call you Huntress of the Nine?"

Her grin faded. "Are you sure you want to talk of such things right now?"

"I don't know when I'll see you next."

"Fair enough. Under the direction of Odin, the Valhuri are led at all times by a Predator from each of the Nine Realms. That Predator is named Huntress. They hold the title till death, then a new one is chosen."

"You are one of the Nine?"

My grandma nodded. "I represent Midgard."

"Saemund told me to ask about the ring," I said, glancing at her right hand. "Anything to do with your title?"

She frowned. "The seer needs to stop being so meddlesome." She held out her hand, allowing me to look closely at the ring. Mounted on a band of tarnished silver was a gleaming green gemstone. "Worn by the Nine. Each was fashioned by Ullr, God of the Hunt. A constant reminder of our commitment. I assume Saemund encouraged you to ask about it because then I would be prompted to tell you of my station. Sly fox, that one."

I better understood now why so many that knew her spoke her name with such reverence. Even Odin. "I can't believe my grandma is a Huntress of the Nine . . . "

She arched an eyebrow. "You do not have to act so surprised."

"It's not that—just really cool knowing my grandma is *famous*."

"It is not all fancy clothes and lavish dinner parties.

There are times I would give the title back for a different life." At this her expression softened. "Perhaps the title of *grandma* and nothing more." Before I could respond, her features instantly lost their softness. Like that, she was the Huntress.

"If we are to talk of such things, I want to show you something." I watched her reach into her coat and pull out a flat oval-shaped rock the size of her palm. "Besides your weapon, this is the Valhuri's most valued tool."

"A rock?" I said, wondering if my grandma had spent too much time on her flying falcon.

"It is called the *Valhuri Stein*, or Predator's Stone. It contains the ancient history of the Aesir and Vanir, secrets from the Underworld, Asgard's dealings with the frost giants, and many other things. Each Huntress holds one, making it nearly impossible for our enemies to steal all nine stones."

I leaned in for a closer look. "All of that is written on the stone?"

"It is written *in* the stone."

"What? How?"

She handed me the stone. "Rub your thumb across the surface."

I did as she instructed, and instantly tiny lines of bluish-white rune symbols appeared as if etched into the stone's surface. I nearly dropped it. I looked at my grandma and found a strange look in her eyes.

"Just as I had hoped," she said, almost to herself. "And feared."

"What just happened?"

"You are able to activate it."

By swiping my thumb across the stone like I would with my phone, hundreds of new symbols materialized. "This is incredible," I breathed, scrolling through line after line of super-secret Nordic intel.

"Now hold the stone away from you," she said.

I moved the stone away and instantly the symbols sprang into the air like a hologram. My breath caught in my throat.

"Now rub your thumb across the stone's surface as you did before."

Once I did, the symbols swirled around me in a circular pattern, depending on how fast I moved my thumb. "How can I get one of these?" I asked, twirling in place to see the glowing symbols revolve around me.

"It is not a toy, Cinder," she said, reaching out her hand.

Frowning, I handed the stone back. She quickly tucked it into her coat pocket. "There will come a time when you will learn from the Valhuri Stein."

"Learn from it? But I don't read ancient Nordic."

"You will."

"Me? Learn ancient Nordic?" I sighed. "I guess you haven't seen my grades."

"I *have* seen your grades. Those marks are a choice."

I nodded. "You sound like my school counselor."

"Listen to your counselor and listen to me: contained in the stone are the secrets of the Valhuri—secrets you will need to learn if you are to succeed."

"But . . . I'm not a Predator."

She smiled. "It is time for me to go, Cinder." Before I could question her further, she hugged me tightly, kissed my cheek, then whistled. Her falcon pranced over obediently. She leaped up onto its feathered back, gripped the leather reins, and said, "By the way, Brandon's closet is not a sufficient place to hide Talon. If you choose not to wear it, find a better place."

"How did you know—"

"Goodbye, Cinder," she said, cutting me off. "I love you."

"I love you too," I said. Her falcon launched into the air, kicking up a spray of sand. A moment later, my grandmaslashHuntress was gone, leaving me with a kajillion new questions.

CHAPTER 40

VALHURI DOWN

Of course the first thing I did when I got back to Brandon's house was look for Tyr, because he would be hanging out with the rat, which was actually my mom.

I found the God of War in the Turnbulls' backyard, my mom perched on his shoulder as he attempted to master a hula-hoop. Tori and Tristan were watching from a nearby picnic table, cheering Tyr on and doing a terrible job at hiding their amusement. Brandon was asleep under the table.

Tori patted the bench beside her. "Have a seat, Cinder. Tyr just threw his hip out, but he's fighting through the pain."

"Only one of the Twelve would succumb to this torture in order to prove a point," said Tyr, suddenly swiveling his hips so hard the rat flew off his shoulder. "Are you hurt, Blom?" he cried out, dropping the hula-hoop and stooping to pick the rat up.

"Blom?" I said, glancing over at the picnic table.

"That would be Norse for *flower*," said Tristan.

Oh no, I thought. *My mom was officially Tyr's pet.*

Petting my mom's head, Tyr walked over to me. "Cinder, can you hold Blom while I continue my training? She is so incredibly adorable, I find myself distracted."

"Sure," I said, taking the rat into my hands. "Don't worry, Mom," I whispered as I walked to the picnic table. "I've got you."

&

Tyr seemed more worried than surprised when I told him about Blom's true identity, which didn't make it any easier knowing my mom would return to Asgard without me. But Tyr assured me Ragnarök would come and go before he would allow any harm to befall her.

"I will see you shortly, Blom," he said, touching his cheek to my mom's nose before handing her over. She twitched her whiskers, which I assumed meant: Goodbye and safe travels!

Tyr's spoils of war included his new weapon (sorry, Bergelmir, your hammer *does* look much better in Tyr's hand than yours) and a month's supply of barbecue chips. "All Nine Realms must know about this salty-sweet nectar from the gods!" he declared. When I let him know how grateful I was for his help, he flashed his thousand-watt smile and said, "I think we all know you could not have completed your quest successfully without my help, but I want you to know I am deeply impressed with you. You remind me of myself at your age. Just not as handsome, nor as strong, nor—"

"I get it, Tyr," I said, cutting him off. "Are you sure you can't stay?"

"Important Twelve business," he said, carefully gathering his hair into his bronze helmet. "They cannot do *anything* without me."

"I wouldn't think so," I said, smiling and patting his huge arm. I gestured at the hula-hoop, leaning against the porch wall. "Want to take it with you?"

"The ring of death will remain here in Midgard," said Tyr, gingerly touching his hip and grimacing. "It is my fervent prayer Asgard never learns of its existence."

⚭

Trigga and two of her Shield Maiden sisters, Plyvis and Hildr, turned up that night at the Turnbulls' house. I was disappointed to see that Brunhild hadn't come. The Valkyries dropped out of the sky on their white-winged stallions, crushing Brandon's volleyball net and laying waste to Mr. Turnbull's meticulously manicured lawn. I was happy to see each of the Valkyries' magical steeds also bore a Predator.

Freya, Droma, and Edda dismounted and rushed to wrap me up in a four-way hug. Edda demanded I recount my story beneath the mall, but Freya said there would be time for that later. We all turned as one when Mrs. Turnbull stepped out onto the back porch and warned us we wouldn't get dinner if we didn't come at once.

After a delicious meal, we sat around the large farm-style table and traded stories over a magically enhanced peach cobbler pie (the dessert replenished itself three times before I ordered it to stop). At one point, Droma took my spoon away and said, "No more dessert for you, Cinder, till you tell us in detail what went down in the Night Forest between you and the great wolf."

"I am slightly offended you do not want *my* account," said Fenrir. The Valkyries eyed the man/wolf with narrowed eyes, still not comfortable with the fact they were sharing food with the son of the Nine Realms's most wanted criminal. I'm sure if Fenrir hadn't turned out to be such an MVP during my quest, he would've long been skewered on all three of the Shield Maidens' golden spears.

"Your version would be the more accurate one, Fenrir," Droma conceded, "so we will hear what *really* happened after Cinder's finished."

"Only a Predator would be so painfully honest," I said, grinning at Droma. With Freya's blessing, I launched excitedly into my story, pausing for dramatic effect at all the appropriate places. I even did a really awesome impression (in my opinion) of Fenrir's gravelly, growly voice.

"That *totally* sounds like Fenrir!" Tori hooted, rocking back in her chair.

"Had I known I would be exposed to such painful torture," said Fenrir, "I might have passed on dessert." He winked at me. "I believe I go next, Mouse. Be prepared for a less-than-flattering rendition of *your* voice."

"Anyway," I said, turning back to my audience, "I used some modern slang and Fenrir had *no* idea what I was talking about." I looked at Fenrir. "Remember? You were totally confused. What was the word?"

"A solid," said Edda.

"That's right!" I said, pointing at Edda. I paused.

"Cinder, what's wrong?" said Tori. "Finish your story."

I laughed and continued, but something felt off. I finished and turned the floor over to Fenrir, my eyes on Edda the entire time.

Fenrir cleared his throat. "Now for what *really* happened . . ."

I stood up, grabbed my now-empty dessert bowl, and said, "Edda, can we talk?"

"But I want to hear the *truth*, Cinder," she said, pointing at Fenrir. Several people laughed.

"It'll just take a minute," I said. I walked to the door that led to the backyard and held it open.

Edda stood up. "I'll meet you out there; just let me use the bathroom."

Nodding, I stepped outside, hoping against all hope I was wrong. Night had fully fallen, though a bright moon had bathed the grass and bushes in silvery light. A moment later, Edda joined me, her traveling pack slung over her shoulder.

"Is everything alright, Cinder?" she said.

"Going somewhere?" I asked, gesturing at her pack.

Edda shook her head. "No, why?"

"Never mind."

"You're acting strange, Cinder. Even for you."

Please be wrong, Cinder, I thought. *Please, please, please be wrong.* I took a few paces in her direction and stopped directly in front of her. "When I mentioned the slang word I couldn't remember, you said it." Edda hesitated a moment too long. "You had left the Night Forest . . . and I've never shared that with anyone. How would you have known that unless—"

The tip of Edda's gleaming sword was beneath my chin before I could finish my sentence. "Only someone as imbecilic as you, Cinder, would come outside alone with an armed Predator and accuse them of treachery."

I swallowed, felt the tip of her sword press up into my throat. "Only someone as imbecilic as *you* would mention something out loud you *aren't* supposed to know."

"It was bound to come out anyway. Maybe I did it on purpose."

"Maybe. Very risky, though. Three Valkyries, three Predators, Tristan and Fenrir. Not a group I would want on my bad side . . . "

"You should see who *I* have on my side, Cinder." She jerked her head towards the Turnbulls' kitchen. "It makes your little group of friends look like Clora and her healers."

Pieces of the puzzle began to fall into place, but much faster than I could process. "Meeting Fenrir in the Night Forest was your plan all along, wasn't it? You were hoping he would kill me. Then you stayed and listened to my conversation with Fenrir before going to get Freya and the others . . . "

"You're not as dumb as you pretend to be," she said, grinning. It was not the kind of grin I had ever seen her use before. It was unsettling, more like a grint smile than anything human.

I felt my eyes suddenly sting with tears. Not because I was afraid to die—I was just heartbroken. The pain was so severe it was all I could do to keep my knees from buckling. "Why, Edda?"

"Brunhild was right, you silly mortal," Edda snapped. "You can never understand our ways. You look for kindness in a world that cannot afford to show it."

"*You* showed me kindness, Edda."

"Then I did a masterful job of deceiving you, Cinder."

A thousand images from the last month flitted through my mind, causing me to feel sick to my stomach. Was it possible Edda had been involved from the very beginning?

"The grint at my school that day . . . " I said, searching Edda's face in the gloom of the Turnbulls' backyard for any sign of humanity. "Did you have anything to do with that?"

"I let it get through our perimeter, but it failed to kill you."

"And the sea serpent?"

Another wicked smile. "My doing. Who could've guessed a mortal—especially one as pathetic as you—could survive such an encounter?"

Okay, now she's just ticking me off, I thought. "Droma almost *died* that night! Her death would've been on *your* hands!" I slowly moved my hand towards my hip, where I knew Talon was sheathed. But I needed to keep her talking till the time was right.

Edda shrugged. I could see she was incapable of remorse. "And I'm guessing it was you that betrayed Tyr to the dwarves . . . "

"That self-loving oaf doesn't deserve to be one of the Twelve."

"That *self-loving oaf* is another one I wouldn't want angry with me."

Another shrug. The blade bit deeper into my skin.

"Tori, Freya, and Droma . . . *they* showed me kindness," I said, almost to myself.

Edda laughed, a coarse, ugly sound. "You mistake kindness for calculating patience. Have you fooled yourself into thinking—even for a moment—that those three *care* about you?"

I stared at Edda, unable to fully comprehend what was happening. I could feel the tip of her sword dig a little deeper up under my chin. "You're wrong, Edda. They—"

"They would've turned on you when the time came!" she whispered harshly. Her eyes flitted to the Turnbulls' house, then back to me. Her face, once pretty and soft, had contorted, and even in the heavy gloom, I could see the veins bulging on her neck and forehead. "That is the way of the immortals, Cinder! We bide our time, waiting for the moment when we can turn a situation to our advantage. Things will never change. Not in our world."

"You're sick, Edda."

"Do you think that Freya protects you out of love? Or friendship? It is her *duty*, Cinder, nothing more. She wishes to advance just like the rest of us, and this is her ticket. Same with Tori and Droma and Tristan and Trigga and all the rest. That mangy half-elf mutt you think is your friend is using you to climb the ladder. Wake up, Cinder. Even Odin has all but said he is using you. And *still* you push blindly on, just like the foolish, pathetic mortal that you are."

My hand inched closer to Talon, my fingers twitching. "You could've killed me yourself. Why get others to do your dirty business?"

"My oath to protect you wouldn't allow me to touch a hair on your head. I had to find another way."

I smiled. My fingertips touched my sword's pommel. "So you can't harm me . . . "

Edda's smile eclipsed my own. "The magic that bound me before is no more. I asked Odin to release me from my pledge when I returned from the Night Forest, and he was all too ready to grant me my wish." Her eyes flicked down to my hand and back to my face. "I see you're about to draw your sword. Tristan may have taught you a trick or two, but I would strike you down before you could get a single swing in. Do not be so foolish to think you can cross blades with a Valhuri and survive."

"You don't deserve to carry the title of Valhuri," I growled.

"I am the *only* Valhuri!" snapped Edda. "The only one that truly *deserves* to carry the title!"

I could see Edda was losing her grip on reality. The malicious glint in her eyes was quickly turning manic.

"You're not just sick, you're insane."

"You *have* to be to get anywhere in the Nine Realms."

"What will be your reward? What will you gain from betraying me and everyone who loved you?"

"It's simple, really. A life much better than the one I have now."

"Are you working for someone, or are you totally evil on your own?"

"You mortals always put such an ugly spin on adjectives. I don't see myself as evil, so much as ambitious."

I would have laughed if I didn't have the tip of a sword pressing up into my jaw. "Ambitious? You're about to *murder* me!"

"In the end, the steps I took to reach my goal will not be viewed in such a harsh light."

"Who sent you, Edda?" I pressed. Before I died, I needed to confirm everyone's suspicions.

"That's none of your business. Just know that this simple act will ensure his imminent victory."

"So it's a *him*. It's Loki, isn't it?"

"Shut up, Cinder! I wouldn't even let you taste his name on your unworthy lips."

I knew my time was growing short. "Where will you go after killing me? You'll be on the run for the rest of your life. Always looking over your shoulder, always—"

"I have friends in high places, Cinder. Don't worry about me."

I paused and stared at her for a moment. "You haven't killed me, Edda. You can't because down deep you care about me. Otherwise you would've done it already. You wouldn't kill me out of greed."

Edda shook her head. "It is not just greed, Cinder. The blood on your hands is what drives me."

"What blood?" I asked. "What are you talking about?"

"Your—" Edda stopped when a scratching sound came from somewhere to her left. Both of us instinctively looked at her pack. I knew I would never get a better chance. In a flash, I had Talon out. I batted Edda's sword wide to the right, then jumped back, falling smoothly into a combat stance.

Edda recovered quickly. Flinging her pack to the grass, she waded towards me, grinning her grint-like grin. "Just when I think you can't be any more stupid, you go and do something like this . . . "

"I was going to die anyway, right? Better to die fighting than watching you shove your sword up into my brain."

Edda slapped her blade with the flat of her hand. "My sword's going there anyway." She lunged forward, the point of her sword aimed at my head. I sidestepped to the left, spun, and brought Talon down in a chopping motion that cut deep into Edda's wrist. She cried out, dropped her sword, and fell to her knees.

"One of Tristan's tricks," I said.

Edda tried to lunge for her sword, but I hooked the blade with the toe of my shoe and kicked it out of reach. "It's over, Edda," I said. "Come inside, confess what you've done, and we'll see to your wound."

"It's *never* over!" she hissed, her hair now hanging in front of her face in clumped, sweaty strands. Her expres-sion was savage, like a rabid dog. She crawled to her pack, ripped it open, and pulled out what had been scratching from inside.

Edda had never gone to the bathroom; she had grabbed my mom and shoved her in her pack as collateral if things went sideways. Boy, had things gone sideways.

"Put her down," I said evenly, my eyes narrowing.

Edda whipped a gleaming knife from her boot and held it to my mom's furry throat. "Fall on your sword, Cinder, or your mother dies."

I hesitated. My mom's gleaming black eyes stared at me. I knew what she was thinking: *Don't do it, Cinder. Let her take my life and save your own.*

"Edda . . ."

"Do it!"

I knew I couldn't watch her kill my mom. I just couldn't. I slowly brought Talon around so that the blade was pointed at my stomach. I positioned the tip so that it could slip under my wrym mail vest. It would be pure agony, but it would be quick. Or at least I hoped it would be. I had never died before.

That's when my mom acted like a true rat. She bit down hard on Edda's hand. Edda screamed out in pain and released her. My mom didn't waste any time scurrying into the bushes that lined the backyard. I sighed with relief.

Edda, still on her knees, cradled her bleeding arm. Through her sweat-slicked hair she said, "I would rather you kill me than turn me over to the Valkyries."

"You know what makes me sadder than anything else, Edda?" I said, turning Talon away from me. "Burning Freya's boat. She was like a sister to you. You knew how she felt about *Analisel*. Whatever it is you're feeling, it has turned your heart to stone."

Edda glared at me, her eyes glinting with madness.

"I want to kill you for what you've done, Edda, but I know killing you will make me more like you than I care to be. Now tell me what you meant about blood on my hands."

Edda turned away.

"You recognized my uncle Robert in the picture, didn't you? Do you know him?"

She turned back to me and spit in my direction.

"Then leave now before I change my mind about killing you," I said.

Edda stared at me. Something passed across her eyes. I wasn't sure what it was, but it was gone in an instant. Without a word, she climbed to her feet, staggered to the gate still cradling her arm, and disappeared into the night.

the hunt begins

I stumbled zombie-like into the Turnbulls' kitchen, my mom tucked into the crook of my arm. Tristan was the first to notice that something was wrong.

"Cinder, is that blood on your neck?" he asked, leaping to his feet so abruptly he knocked his chair to the floor.

I reached up, wincing as my fingers made contact with the cut under my chin. "It's nothing."

"Where is Edda?" he demanded, his eyes suddenly smoldering.

"She's gone," I said, my voice breaking.

Everyone jumped up and started talking at once. Trigga whistled for her steed as she flew past me and burst through the door that led to the backyard. Everyone crowded around me, pelting me with questions.

"Stop!" shouted Freya, taking control of the situation. The room fell silent. She gripped my forearms. I almost felt sorry for Edda; Freya looked furious enough to chew nails. "Cinder, tell us what happened."

I paused, wondering if I should divulge such sensitive information in front of everyone. "Are you sure you don't want to talk in private?"

Freya nodded. "I am confident this affects us all."

I related what happened in the backyard as calmly as I could. As I talked, Freya's eyes filled with tears. Tori turned away, her hand over her mouth. Tristan sank into the nearest chair, his gaze distant. Brandon slumped to the floor and covered his face with his paws. Everyone else stood rooted in place, staring at me in obvious shock.

It wasn't until I finished that I noticed Fenrir was missing.

All of us went out into the backyard to wait for Trigga. I assumed Fenrir had gone to look for Edda as well, though you can never be sure why the son of Loki might leave a dinner party early. It wasn't long before Trigga returned, looking both furious and clearly frustrated. Fenrir returned a few seconds later in full wolf-mode, stepping as carefully as he could over the fence. He transitioned back into a human male as he walked across the yard to join us.

Trigga slid from the back of her steed. "She's gone," she said, ripping her aviator shades from her face.

Fenrir nodded. "Edda had help in her escape. Only someone very powerful—possibly with the use of magic—could have eluded a hunting Valkyrie and myself."

I knew neither one of them would have hesitated to use torture to get the information they needed. Part of me was grateful Edda had escaped. Trigga walked up to me and I almost shrank back in fear. She looked like she wanted to kill something. Or some*one*.

"Tell me what happened, Cinder, and leave *nothing* out."

☖

It made me seriously depressed that our time at the Turnbulls' was soured by Edda's betrayal. It felt as if everything we had accomplished, everything we believed in, was for nothing. I was grateful Tori was there, though, as she did a wonderful job convincing me things could be worse. Later that night, we sat side by side on the back porch, my sword laid across my lap.

We huddled closely as the shadows deepened and tried to take comfort in each other's presence. The deepest, darkest shadow, however, was the one cast by Edda's deception. It was a shadow I wasn't sure I would ever be free of. I stared at the Nordic inscription etched in Talon's gleaming blade. The mantra of the Valhuri.

The hunter will do what the blade cannot.

I couldn't help but wonder what the words meant to Edda.

&

It was harder than I thought it would be to say goodbye to everyone. Tori hugged me so hard I thought I heard one of my ribs snap, but it was just Trigga's horse accidentally stepping on the Turnbulls' barbecue. Tristan hobbled forward on his crutches like he was about to hug me as well, but then he stopped and stuck out his hand. I took it awkwardly, my heart suddenly hammering in my chest.

Stop it, Cinder, I told myself, glancing quickly over at Tori.

Tristan pulled away, his skin a suspicious shade of red. "Well, don't go ruining any more ancient Viking traditions," he said. With the Valkyrie's help, he clambered up behind Plyvis where he was joined by Freya. He handed me a black felt-tip pen. "Apparently it's Midgardian tradition to sign someone's cast," he said.

I took the pen, removed the cap, and scribbled a short note on his neon-green cast. At the end, I wrote: *Stay frosty.* Tristan read my note, nodded, then said, "You never told me what it means to stay frosty."

I smiled, thinking of a man that had held me as a child, who loved me because my father had loved me—my father who was killed protecting my mother. "It means to remain cool in the face of danger." And I wondered again for the millionth time where my uncle really was.

"I like that," said Tristan. "Very fitting for Iceland."

"And very inspiring," added Tori, kissing the top of my head. "I've been released from my duty of protecting you, Cinder," she whispered. "Be careful. Stay alert."

"I will," I said back. I already missed her, and she hadn't even left. She vaulted easily up onto Hildr's horse.

Droma pulled me into a tight embrace. "The wolf is growing on me," she said, "but please talk to us before freeing any more imprisoned gods." I nodded, laughing. She leaped up behind Tori, and the two Predators started arguing over the loud music blaring from Tori's earbuds.

"Not everyone enjoys industrial rock, Tori," Droma complained.

"*Someone* needs their own pair of earbuds," Tori replied airily.

"*Someone* needs a better *pair* of earbuds," Droma shot back.

Their bickering was music to my ears.

Freya stepped up to me, placing her hands on my shoulders. "I have a strong suspicion Edda tried to convince you that I do not care for you. It is true there are times I want to throttle you . . . or at the very least blacken your eye. But do not doubt, Cindrheim, that you are dear to me." Like Tori, she kissed the top of my head. "I, too, have been released from my pledge to protect you. Now I protect you because you are my friend." She smiled at me, and in one fluid movement, she spun away from me and vaulted up behind Trigga.

It broke my heart to part with my mom, but I knew she would be far safer in Asgard than Richmond. Kissing the top of her furry head, I handed her up to Freya. "Take her to my grandma," I said. "Or Tyr. Not sure which of the two I'd rather have angry at me."

Freya nodded, cradling my mom in the crook of her arm. "A grandmother or the God of War—it will not be an easy choice."

With a wild snort, the creatures exploded off the ground, and a moment later, they were lost in the dark clouds.

I felt a heavy hand on my shoulder. I turned and saw that it was Fenrir. "I, too, must go, Mouse."

"I guess you won't be going back to the Night Forest," I said.

"No," he replied. "I hope not to see that place for many years." With a wink, he added, "Besides, can you imagine Odin's reaction if I returned? He is the one who put me there in the first place."

"Where will you go?"

Fenrir shrugged. "I do not know at the moment, and that is the most exciting part of all. I can go anywhere, really. Even board a boat and sail around the world."

"In human form, I hope," I said, smiling sadly. "Will I see you again?"

"I am sure you will," said Fenrir, his face suddenly growing serious. "Like the others, I suspect Loki had a hand in all this." I nodded, and he continued. "And if I know my father, he will have a backup plan, a second try at defeating the gods. Rest assured, Cinder, the God of Mischief is not finished."

I was surprised when Fenrir suddenly pulled me in and gave me a bone-crushing hug. As if he was suddenly embarrassed, he backed away. "Look what you have done to me, Mouse," he sputtered. "A month ago, I would have eaten a young mortal like you."

I was too choked up to laugh. Before I could respond, he turned and raced into the shadows that lined the Turnbulls' yard. A few seconds later, I caught the steady rise and fall of a great black shape as it loped through the silent neighborhood.

⚬

Before saying goodbye to the Turnbulls, I promised them that I would not stop searching for a cure that would transform Brandon back into the happy, goofy, redheaded half-elf that he was before I allowed him to go on my quest with me. Mr. Turnbull gave me his business card, and Brandon barked excitedly when I told him I would use the address to write to him as soon as I got home.

With Talon strapped to my back, I hopped up onto Trigga's horse. I waved to the Turnbulls as we ascended into the night, hoping they didn't hate me for letting their son get turned into an Irish setter, and hoping that seeing them in the future wouldn't necessarily mean I was out to slow down the end of the Nine Realms again.

Soon, their neighborhood was just a tiny collection of houses, winding streets, and twinkling lights. I forced myself to turn my attention to what was in front of me. Shadowy mountains and rivers, buildings and fields and parking lots.

And home.

I couldn't help but think of the prophecy. Talking with my grandma had brought me a bit of clarity, but there were still so many questions. Daughter of Nine? Darkness falling before its climb? What did it all mean? I was tempted to ask Trigga, but she would never say, and knowing that made it all the more frustrating.

Saemund had been right, though. I was beginning to believe.

I pulled my picture from my back pocket, taking courage in my uncle's smile, the way he held me. My eyes went to his right hand, to the ring he wore on his first finger. A ring I had seen every time I looked at the picture. But this time it was different. Holding the picture closer to my face, I squinted. Silver, with a green stone. Unless I was mistaken, it was the same ring my grandma wore.

The ring created by Ullr, God of the Hunt, and worn only by a Huntress of the Nine.

"Trigga, can I ask you—"

"Buckle your seat belt, Cinder, we're about to enter some heavy turbulence."

You're telling me, I thought, tucking the picture away.

I tightened my grip on the Valkyrie and glanced down through the clouds that were whipping past me. And was Edda down there somewhere, plotting her next move? Why would Loki choose her of all people to further his schemes? Had she been a kind person before he had gotten to her, or had she always been filled with hate and greed?

More than anything, I wanted to know why Edda said I had blood on my hands.

It would be a long time before thinking of her didn't feel like a blade being twisted in my gut. I blinked away a few tears. I thought for a moment that I saw Fenrir in wolf form, bounding through a grove of spindly trees. *But no,* I thought, squinting so that I could see better. *Fenrir would be just one huge shadow against the ground. Not many, and not nearly so small.* Something else was flying through the trees at an unbelievable rate of speed. I peered up at Trigga, but the Valkyrie was staring straight ahead, her blue eyes hidden behind her aviator shades.

When I looked back, the shadows were gone.